LOST CHILD

by

Marrianne White

PUBLISH AMERICA

PublishAmerica
Baltimore

First printing

ISBN: 1-59286-106-7
PUBLISHED BY PUBLISHAMERICA BOOK PUBLISHERS
www.publishamerica.com
Baltimore

Printed in the United States of America

To the one man
who has been my rock.
Without him,
I wouldn't be who I am
or have had the confidence to do
the many outrageous
things I've done.

I love you, Ori.

Thanks also, mom and dad,
for reading so many
diverse books to me and
for making me look up
all those words
by myself.

I thank you, Joshua, as well,
for ripping my first manuscript apart
and showing me a much better way.

I would also like to thank
Marion Gibbs
for making me break up
all those run-on sentences, and
Nancee Clark
for making history my favorite.

ONE

The man sat uncomfortably in the vinyl booth as he looked his son squarely in the face. Eighteen years old – the time had flown.

Visibly measuring the weight of his words, Joe tried to decide how to explain this incomprehensible mess.

Adam, a young man comfortably dressed in blue jeans and a Nike t-shirt, sat studying his father. The boy's piercing blue eyes had an old look about them, undoubtedly the result of losing his mother at such a young age. They had known very few moments like this. Perhaps the only one that had quite measured up to this one was when Joe had taken Adam out for his thirteenth birthday and they discussed the birds and the bees, being a man, and the consequences of stupidity in any and all fields of life.

Clearing his throat, Joe began. "Adam, I came by some information the year after your mother died. I was sent a letter from England – Buckingham Palace, no less. Remember when we took that trip – and while we were there I had an appointment with some very interesting people. They gave me some information, proof really, that said some things....

"The information implied that your mother was still alive, but–" he paused, studying his son's face and seeing the excitement there, the boy had always maintained that Katharine was alive. "I didn't know whether I could believe it or not, the story they were telling me was really out there. Something about some Scot paying for some parchments to be vaulted in the Tower of London until a certain time. The stuff had our name, address, and phone number on it, for goodness sake, from a time when those things didn't even exist, but, well, it certainly wasn't something I could share with you at the time. Your life had been through enough upheaval.

"I kept thinking that at some point in time I would know you were ready to hear it, but I kept putting it off. I can't put it off anymore. This information belongs to you and it's high time I gave it to you so that you can decide for yourself what it means. I really could never quite believe it. Maybe you'll be able to.

"Happy Birthday, son. I feel kind of lame telling you that after laying such

5

a load on you."

He handed Adam a brown cardboard box, not even sealed with tape or anything, just with all the corners tucked into each other, the way Joe always closed boxes.

Adam almost leapt at the thing, greedily pulling the flaps open to look. Inside, looking ordinary and unimportant, were several pieces of parchment written in what looked like his mother's hand, a blotch of red-colored sealing wax still intact, though no longer sealing the letter closed. Along with the papers was an ancient ring. It had obviously had a gemstone of some sort set in the top of it at one time, but now the setting was empty. Strange carvings and pictographs were engraved into the band.

Adam gingerly put his finger out and touched it. He yanked his hand back, as though he had expected some bolt of lightning or something to leap at him from the piece, then touched it again.

Nothing.

His mind ached with disappointment, at the same time that he was chiding himself on the silliness of his expectation. He looked at the newer papers that accompanied the artifacts, reports and documentation of time and historical accuracy, even appraisals of the items' values.

Joe squirmed uncomfortably in his seat. The kid looked like he used to on Christmas morning. It almost made him angry, but he checked himself. He would feel the same way if he had been told for almost twenty years that his mother was dead and then been offered verifiable hope that she might be alive.

Still, he couldn't help himself, "Be very careful with that stuff, I'm assured it's over six hundred years old."

Adam reached for the parchment.

Hainault, 1330

The quiet young girl of ten and three years stood straight and tall in the great hall, shoulders square, hands tucked discreetly into one another, almost invisible under the cuffs of her sleeves. Tears rolled down her pale cheeks, her soft brown eyes clouded with fear and uncertainty. A credit to her training, Philippa did not fall to her knees and beg her father to change his mind, but stood upright and stately, the only sign of her distress the tears on her cheeks and her toes curling silently into the rushes beneath her feet. Desperately she wanted to twirl her hair around her fingers and alleviate this horrid nervousness she always felt when she had to stand before her hard-as-iron father.

Her voice strained, she tried to keep it from cracking. "No, papa, please don't send me away. England is so far from here, and they hate Normans. I shall never be happy in such a horrid place, and you have told me I'll not be allowed to return home once I have been wed! My heart will surely break. And momma...."

The father cleared his throat impatiently to silence her protests and began to pace in front of the fire, reining in the frustration he always felt when trying to explain logic to the weaker sex. When he had curbed his anger, he spoke slowly, distinctly. "You shall become queen of that benighted realm. You shall have all you need, Pippa, all you desire. And I shall receive a great deal of gold and title to more lands than I had ever dreamt of, both in England and Normandy. For a man to be rich in title but poor in coin is difficult. This marriage will alter the state of our house considerably. 'Tis an excellent bargain, daughter. For you, young one, and for your family's honor and future. The treasury of our household will not suffer either, I assure you. You well know how difficult these long years of war have been on our coffers." Pausing in front of the fire, he took a moment to readjust the logs before renewing his lecture.

"Of course, as an honorable daughter, you must surely want to bring wealth and property to your father – that is to say your household. It is the only way a daughter can be of benefit to her kindred.

"I am not a man blessed with sons to earn honor and riches for me in the eyes of the king. Nay, I have none but girls – prancing little playthings of no real use but to bear children to enrich another man's house." He paused a moment and nodded his head in frustration. "Therefore, Philippa," she winced inwardly, he never called her Philippa unless she was being difficult, " it is your duty – nay, the duty of any obedient child – to bring honor, wealth and respect to their father's household. I am certain that you will consider no course but obedience, and that you understand the kindness I have done you in giving you explanation."

He doesn't love me.

She bowed her head submissively, not wanting him to see the pain he had caused her. He had always felt that way, she knew, but had never said it so openly before. Wanting overly much to please her father and prove her value, but desperate to escape the wedding plans he had made for her, she was torn. She would have been most happy to marry for her household's benefit, but did she have to marry *him?* The thought was repulsive.

Even the children in the noble households had heard the rumors that circulated about the English king. Although he was still young, he was a rogue and a philanderer, given over to ... *excessive* appetites. Of course, kings were forgiven all, and queens were expected to smile prettily, say nothing, and open their beds whenever it was asked of them. With war being waged officially between the two countries every few years and the occasional peace never being true or lasting, England and France wanted this alliance badly enough for both countries to offer her papa much in return for her hand.

And father had what he liked to call ambition, but she knew the truth. Papa was greedy. Nothing meant more to him than wealth, not even his flesh and blood. The other truth that seemed to be the only truth the nobles and royal families staunchly served was that it was impossible to accumulate enough wealth or power. Why, England's last king had been murdered horribly by his own mother and uncle, if the rumors could be believed, and from what she knew of the Saxon dogs that peopled that foul island ... well, it was certainly true.

Tis untrue. Papa's flesh and blood means more to him than his treasury. Doesn't he call us his little pets?

Yet the little voice that would not allow her to lie to herself held its ground. *Then why is he selling you? Allowing you to marry before your sisters? And in a country he will not set foot upon? Yes, you mean a little more to him than the beasts in his field, but only because you fetch a higher price.*

"Pay attention, Phillippa. It does not befit a queen to daydream!"

Keeping her true feelings silent, she answered, "Yes, papa ... but please – pray you consider once more! My sisters are so much better befitted to this match than I. They are older, wiser, and more comfortable with the toilsome ways of court. By the stars, they have a true fondness for fashion and jewels and having gifts showered upon them by men. I am young, and know nothing of the English ways!" *Please, please, my Heavenly father. Please allow him to listen to reason.*

"True, Pippa. But you, little one, are the most comely among my daughters. It is you who will wed England's king. And you will do so gratefully, with all the decorum of the queen you will become. I will brook no more argument from you. The servants are packing your belongings as we speak. Go instruct them as to which of your things you will be taking with you."

Philippa's chin came up just a bit, and her teeth ground together so that her jaws ached. *I shall not miss you, and I shall never again be your Pippa. The money you are paid for me shall bring you ruin.*

Yet in her heart, she ached – for the future she desired but would never see, for the greed that sealed her doom. There would be no reprieve. The stable master's son, the young and irretrievably common man she had secretly loved since she was but seven harvests, would wed another – a farmer's daughter. And she would wed an immoral king who bedded any and all who would have him, and even some who wouldn't.

Not knowing whether to sob or scream like a shrew, both of which would dishonor her, the unfortunately beautiful Philippa chose retreat. She left her father mentally counting the coins he would gain from his beautiful daughter as he studied the blazing fire and dreamed of his newfound wealth.

London 1342

"The babe is a girl, Your Majesty. Would you like to see her?" The young priest looked worried.

The king nodded. Leaning over in the dim light to see the face of the newborn infant, the little wrapped bundle being held out for his perusal, he grimaced and waved it away.

"She has the look of her mother. I can already see it stamped upon her tiny face. Conceal her from my sight, and when all is attended to here, I will send someone for her."

"For her, Sire?" the priest inquired.

"To take her where she can be cared for. Tend to her needs quickly, for my man will be here within the hour. And watch her mother carefully. If her condition becomes any worse, I wish to be called immediately. Do I make myself understood?"

Hastily adjusting his brown cassock, the recently-ordained priest bobbed his head in agreement. "As you wish, Highness." He reached down and gently put his hand on the forehead of the unconscious woman lying among the tangled sheets of the bed. Her fever was growing worse; he feared she wouldn't last the night. Had her eyes been open, they would have danced with the bright fire of dementia.

"You shall call me if she worsens, or face hot oil."

"I shall call you, Majesty. Lay your fears to rest – I am faithful to your wishes."

The king nodded and took his leave of the small servant's cottage, muttering to himself in a most distressing way. The young priest's eyes followed him until he was gone from sight, then turned back to the newborn child he was clinging to. Such a beautiful child, so precious, so trusting. To send her away – had Edward no heart? If the unconscious woman had any likeliness at living, the king would dash it by this unfeeling edict.

Pulling a small stool to the head of the bed, he began to whisper gentle comforts to the dying woman. "You have a precious daughter. She is your very likeness in appearance, and you will love her very much."

9

He laid the child in her mother's arms, and the woman instinctively closed her grasp over the babe. His voice shook as he made the empty promise – "You shall both be very happy here in the years to come...."

A knock sounded on the door of His Majesty's private apartments.
"Enter!"

Randall sauntered through the door. "You had need of me, Sire?"

The king downed a goblet of spirits and belched rudely. He found a half-hearted smile for his old friend. "Ah, Randall. Tis good to see you again. You have been away from court far too long."

"It has been too long. You had need of me, Sire?" he reminded his old friend gently. He had no patience for pleasantries, or reeling drunk monarchs, today.

"Yes. A very delicate business, not at all like the assignments you are accustomed to being given from me, old friend. This is of particular importance, and I can think of no more trusted vassal to care for this matter."

Randall remained silent, impatiently waiting for the king to get through his usual bluster and attend to business.

"I have been given a daughter by Isabella–" he began, his voice breaking with emotion. Silently he poured himself another healthy drought of the amber spirits and, lifting the goblet to his lips, downed the contents in one gulp.

"I had been informed," Randall prodded.

The king laughed, "Then your spies are more efficient even than my own. Under the circumstances, I wish for this child to be installed in a home – somewhere far from the palace, you understand – where she can be brought up with the proper education and background to make a good marriage to someone of means. I do not wish to know the details, mind you, but I do wish to see to her future. Tis the least duty I owe her. The babe is awaiting you, along with a few small things for her immediate care, in Isabella's cottage. The attending priest will see to her handling until you arrive, although I would prefer it be a hasty departure for the babe. To draw out the leave-taking would be a good deal too cruel for her mother. See to it immediately, man." His bleary eyes began to mist.

Randall bowed before his king, careful to keep his eyes averted. Surely the contempt he felt for a grown man's tears would show in them. "As you wish, Sire. It shall be done."

The king slapped his friend's shoulder in forced enthusiasm. "I knew I could depend upon your loyalty. Send word when all is accomplished."

Nodding his assent, Randall backed from the chamber, careful to keep his expression contained. In the back of his mind, he was already planning the bastard child's demise. She could not, of course, live to upset or even inconvenience the monarchy at some later time. The babe would have to be disposed of, although not in a way which would seem intentional. He would have to find a way to rid himself of his charge without seeming to have done the evil deed upon his own resolve. But there was a woman of his acquaintance who would do very nicely....

The queen's man, who had been stationed outside the king's door, was quick to appraise Queen Philippa of her husband's cruel plans. She nodded, her tender heart breaking over the abject cruelty of her husband's decision to steal the babe away from her mother.

Always having wanted a babe of her own, yet being without that blessing, her heart was overwhelmed at the disloyalty being shown by the king to his own blood. A man should know better. Her father should have known better. Few men in this world dedicated to the pursuit of money and power did. God help the babe, it was better to be a farmer's daughter than a king's.

Thanks to her place as queen, she was at least in the position to right a few of the many ghastly wrongs of her husband. With God as her aid, she would do all in her power to save another young soul from being lost to England's greed.

"Fetch me my Father confessor," she ordered her friend and faithful lady's maid, Guinevere, beginning to hatch a plan to save the poor babe from that bloodthirsty assassin Randall. He was a murderer with no redeeming qualities whatsoever. He even took pleasure in his foul pursuits, and this time was no different. She had seen murder in his eyes – this child would be no different than his other assignments. If this cruelty was indeed carried out, there would be no blood on her head. But God help him if he touched one hair on that tiny babe's head.

"Your Majesty, you are needed immediately on a matter of particular importance," the little man in the gold brocade uniform knelt on the steps of the dais.

"In a moment, George." The king turned to address Philippa, "I'm certain, my dear, that you'll forgive me for excusing myself to take care of this little matter. Of course, I will count the moments until I may again have the pleasure of your company."

She looked into his face, willing him – no, silently begging him – for once, to tell her the truth about where he was going and what he was doing. Truth, although oftentimes unsavory, was the way Philippa preferred to deal with her world – although she rarely was given the opportunity by her husband. The man was constantly excusing himself from various duties with the advent of some outlandish tale to give his attentions to some lovely in his apartments.

"Your Majesty, my love, stay. If you might," she amended, not wanting to appear the shrew.

He bent and kissed her hand. With a lighthearted and practiced smile, he apologized. "I'm sorry, my lovely. As much as it would give me pleasure to keep you company throughout our evening meal, I am needed elsewhere on important," he hesitated, usually preferring his man to be the one to break the commandments on his behalf, "state business. You understand, my beauteous Philippa, I'm certain." His warm brown eyes embraced her, caressing her, his unfeigned affection reaching out and wooing her. It was obvious the man loved her. If only he didn't love so many others.

She sighed. "Very well, my lord. Have a very pleasant evening."

"As always, my love. Sleep well, and may heaven give a care to your dreams."

He always said that before he betrayed her. Her heart sunk as she realized she never wished to dream again. Phillippa extended her hand to him and he grasped it lovingly in both of his. She smiled resignedly, "I shall miss you, husband. I will see you in my apartments this night?" Her eyes were full of hope.

"If time permits, my sweet. Good evening."

Bowing her head to her husband, she returned the civility. "Good evening, my lord."

Stepping smartly off the dais, he followed George's retreating back. His private guard fell into step behind their king. As soon as they were out of earshot of Her Majesty, George turned, bowed, and stepped close enough to be heard at a whisper.

"Your Majesty, tis the servant, Isabella. The priest has summoned you – the court physician informed him that her condition has worsened muchly. The fever has caught hold much more severely than he had before thought. He does not expect her to survive the night. She has been calling for you, Your Majesty, and since you had asked to be kept apprised of her condition, I assumed...."

"Good heavens, man, why did you not tell me the issue was so pressing? Take me to her!" the king interrupted the servant before he could defend himself. "She cannot depart this world as of yet. Tell the physician and the priest to do all they are able, but she must not die! Do you hear me? Isabella must not die!" He had grabbed hold of George's shoulders and was shaking the little man roughly.

"Yes, Your Majesty! I'll see to it, Your Majesty!"

The king let go. "You do that. NOW, George! GO if you wish to keep your head attached to that doublet you are prancing about in! I will follow after shortly."

George bowed low, then turned and ran from the king's presence. The monarch signaled to his guard to follow him. He led the way to his apartments. Once inside, he stopped for a moment in the middle of the large sitting area and took a deep breath, attempting to control the frantic beating of his heart.

While the guard waited patiently outside, the king crossed his sitting room to the small carved ivory chest on the table. With violently shaking hands he opened the lid. He dug through it for a moment, until he found what he was searching for.

Withdrawing a small, spare chain, he fumbled with his trembling fingers to open the tiny clasp and put it about his neck. From the chain hung a small amulet, a pewter likeness of a mother and child, worth little to anyone except to the man who wore it. A trinket really, of the meanest quality, it had been fashioned by a smith at the marketplace and sold for a penny. Sweet Isabella had given it to him right before the bairn was born to her.

Better than anyone else save the king, she understood that her child could never be raised in the palace, and told him that the amulet would remind him of both of his dearest loves. She never told him that she had paid the smith a very dear price for the talisman, but no one ever noticed the feet of a servant in any course. Had Edward bothered to look, he would have seen her bare and torn soles – her leather shoes a small price to pay for the man she had always loved more than life.

Since three days ago, when the babe had been spirited away, Isabella had cried inconsolably, and never in all of his wretched life had Edward felt more destitute than when he had seen her and she had wiped her eyes and smiled up so bravely at him.

Until now. Before he had felt the vast weight of his cruelty. He had loved her, yet had given her such pain. *God save any piteous woman to whom my heart turns.*

He had heard the servants whispering among themselves that she was dying. It was her very heartbreak, they would suggest, that made her unable to recover from the birthing. The exhaustion and fever were as nothing compared to her sorrow....

Edward shook himself. His cruelty, *no, his sage judgment,* had been a necessary evil, hadn't it? Of course. Everything he did was essential. He was the ruler of a great nation, not a silly thoughtless man. Isabella was his life's blood. Thoughts whirling through his head, his chest became tight with disquiet as emotion threatened to consume him.

To save himself from complete emotional bedlam and to give himself a moment to compose himself, he took a deep breath, dusted his hands upon his hose, and busied himself searching about his apartments for one final gift to give his love.

His mind would not cease its hateful accusations. Edward denounced himself for his cowardice. There had been no great need to hide the child. Kings' bastards abounded in and out of many castles across many a countryside. He did not find himself in a novel situation from other noblemen. In truth, he could not stand to look upon the babe, let alone love the child. The pain of looking daily at a face so much the likeness of her mother's would have been his undoing – or at least that's what he told himself. It was a passable rationalization – an excuse to send the child away.

But Isabella – now she was a different parchment altogether. He had loved the pitiable little maid with all of his heart and for as long as he could remember, and had she but been nobility…. It was shameful of him to think, although every now and again he would allow his heart to wander into the fanciful nation of "if I weren't king." It was the fabled land where his country's well-being didn't depend upon who he married. A land where his heart ruled his life – not the dictates of the wants of thousands of people whom he had never met. The needs of the people and all that rot – or so he allowed himself to privately believe every once in a very long while.

Squaring his shoulders, he released the breath he hadn't realized he was holding. Brittany was his duty, his responsibility – although no one had asked him if it was a duty he wanted. It had been thrust upon him with his father's death and he had accepted it.

That was yet another reason the child had to go.

Except in all truth he was the king, and Isabella was but a servant, and never would the two cross in any type of society. In his chambers, however, it was a totally different matter. So many nights they had lain together, taking the only allowance afforded them, talking and dreaming about the lives they might have had. He had even felt a twinge of sorrow for his queen. She was a good woman, her being Norman notwithstanding, and Philippa had proven her character many times over. He cared for her, perhaps even loved her, but she could never be his Isabella.

Eventually it had become too painful to not be able to have the serving girl to himself completely. For a time, the king had selfishly banished her away from him. That pain had been even worse than the pain of wanting what he could not have. It had been only a matter of days before he had changed his mind, ordering Isabella to return to the palace.

Only now, after all this time, was she truly leaving him. And for all the power he wielded, there was nothing he could do about it. God took orders from no man. Edward and Isabella had loved each other for almost twenty years, since he was a child, before he had even thought about taking the throne. At that time his training had been simply an entertainment, a diversion from what he really loved – plucking out tunes upon his forbidden lute. He constantly found himself hiding and rehiding his beloved instrument to keep it from being banished to the woodpile. How Isabella had loved to hear him play. To lose her now – it was more than he could bear.

Looking about him in desperation, he spotted the lavish bouquet of roses in the large porcelain pitcher beside his bed. They were violet, her favorite color, and grown especially for him by a very talented gardener. On impulse, he grabbed them up into his arms. His full, ruffled sleeves became wet, and he even pricked his thumb and little finger on the sharp thorns, but the king was far beyond caring. Isabella needed him. But never like he needed her.

Without further hesitation, he threw open his chamber doors and strode hurriedly toward the small private quarters in which she lived. The servants all knew of the arrangement, although none minded or confessed to others. Isabella was such a dear woman and they found it tragic that she had the bad fortune to devote herself to a man she could never have. They lived their lives and she lived hers. As she lay on her deathbed, her friends looked on from afar in sympathy.

The king hurried out of the palace and toward the tiny, quaint cottage where his love lay dying. Every step punctuated the words of a prayer, mumbled petitions for the Lord's good will and forgiveness for his sweet Isabella. He was so preoccupied with his frenzied requests he hardly noticed the enormous rose bushes that had grown up on either side of the low door to the cottage. They were the same tiny twigs he had given her for the harvest festival just five short years ago.

Fragrantly framing the narrow stone front walk, a thorn from an errant branch caught his billowing sleeve as he hurried past. Not giving it a thought, he tore the sleeve free and kept his stride quick.

The moment his hand touched the rough wood of the door he could smell it – death was here. The truth pierced him as the blade of his enemy, her life was ending. *Isabella!*

It was too much to ask for more time – it would have been cruel. The grief that had been masquerading as consumption was so painful in itself, and during the birthing Edward had seen her coughing blood. He knew it was her melancholy that ate at her life, for the symptoms had begun as soon as she had known she was with child. Isabella would talk about the life they could never have with the babe. Her voice would grow quiet and her eyes would become wet, and then she would begin coughing. Only the selfish part of him wanted her to stay on this earth for him. Although he didn't want her to suffer any longer, he didn't want to live without her, either. *God help me. Sweet Isabella.*

Bracing himself and taking a deep breath, Edward threw open the door and stepped through.

"Isa? Sweet one, can you hear me?" His voice was loud in the quiet, still room. It took a moment for his eyes to adjust to the dim candlelight, but in a moment he could see her – lying listlessly on her small, soft bed. The carved headboard had been a gift from him, as had the small carved chest at the foot of the bed. Edward's eyes took in the table that sat at the bed's head, also a gift from him, and the lovely damask draperies on the small windows.

True glass – cut and painted with colored stains of rose and violet. None can say I neglected my Isa.

The windows had been made of real glass – an extravagance even the wealthiest of nobles were only beginning to afford. He had seen to it. But there was nothing too precious for his Isabella.

The covers were tangled around her feet. Her face was so pale. Her tousled head was moving from side to side deliriously, the sheets drenched with sweat. Moaning, she murmured a mixture of words – most incomprehensible, but her lover's name could be picked out clearly from the soft tones. His name, over and over, and that of her stolen babe. The sobs that racked her frail body when she whispered the name of the child invoked excruciating torment to the anguished king.

My fault. My fault. MY fault. MY FAULT.

Edward rushed to her side, laying the cluster of roses gently on the small engraved table at the head of the bed, since she was in no condition to receive them herself. He was careful to keep them away from the candle flame, as they would smoke. He would not be responsible for making his love even more uncomfortable than she already was.

"Your Majesty," Dancourt, the court physician's voice was low, "she recognizes no face. Her mind is gone. Her body will soon follow. There is very little time." The priest nodded his agreement, keeping a choke hold on the ebony rosary that hung from his belt.

"Then leave us," he ordered hoarsely. Before the physician or the priest could object, the king promised to call him when the last rites were required.

Dancourt and the priest backed out of the small cottage, heads bowed, as the king knelt down at Isabella's side. He gently took hold of her hands, cold

16

already – he noticed, and brought them to his lips.

"Sweet one, listen to me. I brought our promise with me. I'm placing it in your hands now," he paused as he pulled the chain over his head and placed it in her palm. Gently, he closed her fingers over the amulet. "Remember our babe? Our little girl? I do. She's going to be splendid, Isabella. My man Randall has found a home for her. She will be raised by wealthy landowners as their own child. Her life shall be a good one, full of privilege and grace," he lied. There hadn't even been time to receive word. "She is set to be married to a fine man, a man of property, and will be very happy. She shall not even be a servant. She will be a lady, educated and able to sit at the finest table without bias. I thought you would like that. Let it ease you, sweet one. Your babe, our babe, shall be cared for."

Whatever he could say to give her ease, he would say it. In truth, right now he would have renounced his crown for her, if she had but asked.

Her head stopped thrashing, and her eyes flew wide open. She sat bolt upright, staring deep into her lover's eyes. He could do nothing save stare back. "Promise me, my love."

"I promise."

She grasped his hands and squeezed them hard. "NO! Promise me that you shall take care of my child – no matter what!"

"I promise, Isabella."

"On your crown?" she asked desperately.

He nodded vehemently. "On my crown. On my very life!"

For a moment she gazed into his eyes. Then she nodded slowly and sank back down. As her head gently settled into the pillow, her breathing slowed. It became labored, then, a moment later, stopped altogether.

The king grasped her by the shoulders and hauled her up against his chest. "You may not die! I command it, Isabella! You may not die!" Her chest remained still. He shook her. "NO! You can't leave me!" Pulling her lifeless form tightly to his chest he whispered her name into her ear. "Isabella? Isa? *Isa?*"

Her head fell backward, mouth slack, hair limp with sweat. He stroked her lifeless face, whispering endearments and loving words into the ears that would never again hear his promises of love, kissing the mouth that would never again kiss him, speak to him, shout at him.

Gently he laid her back upon her pillow, then dropped his head onto the damp sheet beside her and wept for the first time since he was a child.

She was gone. His whole life, his every breath, was gone. The stolen happy nights that made up for in pleasure what the crown took away through responsibilities and duties – they were over. The sadness, the utter desolation

– it was overwhelming. The tears seemed like they were endless, as if springing up from an ocean, not from the brokenhearted cries of a king.

After a time, the man straightened up. Using all the discipline instilled in him since he was a child, he gained control of his tortured emotions – wiping his face and straightening his appearance. He stood, dusting off his knees, and leaned over to give her one last kiss.

His lips brushed hers, he heard himself groan softly when finally he pulled away from her. With the dangling edge of his ruffled cuff he wiped his eyes, then walked across the polished wooden floor of the cottage to the door. The sheen of the wood caught his eye, and he gazed at it for a moment. *None of the other servants had a wooden floor. I was good to her. I was good to her.* This time his lie began to ring true, and he breathed deeply in relief. *I have done nothing for which to feel guilt.*

Opening the door slowly, the king of England stepped out, stoic and imperturbable, although anyone who had bothered to look would have seen the redness of his eyes. No one did.

He cleared his throat, found his voice, and addressed Dancort. Not even a tremor of voice betrayed what had gone on before in private. "Dancort, she has passed from this world. By royal command, she will be entombed in the shrine on my cousin's family's holding in Coventry. I wish her to be dressed in gold and ivory brocade with pearls laced through her hair. She is to meet her Maker fit for a throne. Have I made myself clear, man?"

"Perfectly, Your Majesty. On my life, it shall be done."

"Thank you, Dancourt. This means much to me. You will be recompensed for your loyalty and your discretion. Send word when all is accomplished."

Edward turned to the young priest. "Father? You may deliver the last rites."

"Many thanks, Your Majesty." The priest scuttled into the small cottage and prayed forgiveness over the woman's soul, and over his king's as well, as he had killed this lovely lady with his cruelty and selfishness. It was a sin, that, and the young priest recognized that his own thoughts would require several novenas as penance.

The king absently nodded in response. He straightened his brocade doublet and strolled from the small residence, seemingly tranquil. Guards in tow, he reached his royal apartments, entered, and closed the door – leaving them in the hallway.

Leaning back against the cool, carved wood of the door, Edward closed his eyes. Of all the difficult times of his sovereignty, this was the worst he had ever endured. He would rather be in the midst of a war, on a sinking ship, in front of a sharp-sighted arrow, or underneath an executioner's axe than feel the agony that seemed to twist his very soul. Even as a child, when his mother had died, he hadn't felt the pain this deeply.

Of one thing he was certain, his life would not be the same again. Why had God taken her? Didn't he have enough saints to pleasure him with their praise?

Slowly Edward opened his eyes. The world still existed. He was still breathing. There was nothing else save to go on. Rising to his full height, he straightened his shoulders and breathed in deeply. He would mourn no more. The king of Brittany must do his duty.

Finally ready to face his men, he opened his chamber door and stepped out into the corridor. Perhaps he would call for his evening meal or read one of the works in his library. Indecisive for the moment, he stood staring at the wall.

On a last-minute impulse, his majesty went in search of Phillippa. He would make love to her, and then, maybe- just maybe, he would feel a little better.

Ellshope 1350

No sound came from behind the locked door. Outside, in the small sitting room, Gray paced the floor, waiting for some news – any news – from the midwife or his mother. Both were attending the birth of his first child, and he was terrified, no matter that it was beneath a warrior to feel such things. He was learning much more than he ever wanted to know of his frailties through this extremely difficult ordeal. The fear he had felt when he heard the agonized screams ripping their way out of his young wife was nothing compared to the terror he felt at the silence crushing down on him right now.

The door opened and Katharine exited, a drawn look on her mature, pretty face. He looked helplessly at his mother as she stood silently across the room from him. As grown up as he was, and as accomplished his feats, she found herself looking at her son at the age of five, when his favorite dog had been killed in a fight with wild dogs. So lost, so alone, so vulnerable – looking at her with the hope that she could do something, *anything* to fix it. And she had thought she couldn't feel any worse.

I'm so sorry, baby. I tried, I tried so hard to help – there's nothing more I can do.

Her face betrayed her, and Gray's face crumpled. Tears filling her eyes, Katharine took several steps toward him and opened her arms. He backed away from her, begging God to stop up his ears that he could not hear what she was there to tell him. The wall arrested his retreat, but still he could not bring himself to look at his mother.

19

Oh Lord, oh God, please no! Not my wife, my bairn!

Taking a deep, steadying breath, she spoke, "It doesn't look good, Gray. The cord became wrapped around the baby's neck. And Gray – um.... Abigail is bleeding overly much, and neither Eloise nor I can seem to stop it. I don't know what to tell you, except to pray."

His head came up in a swift, wolflike movement. "The *babe*? Is it...? What of Abigail? I wish to see her."

"In only a moment more. Eloise will call you when she is ready."

Please don't let him see the lie. She didn't want to lie to him exactly, just let him handle it in increments, absorbing one devastating blow at a time instead of an entire barrage. Maybe that way he could–

There is no possible way I can make this better.

Katharine's hope was in vain, for he no sooner looked into her eyes than he knew the full truth. His eyes filled, overwhelming grief and emotion stealing his usual steely discipline and composure.

He's so young, God, isn't there any way–

The tears that had been brimming finally overflowed her lids as her huge, strong son collapsed weakly into her arms, truly defeated for the first time in his life. The weight of his enormous body knocked her off her feet. They fell as a unit to the settee, where the man who rarely, if ever during his life, had shown his feelings began to weep, his huge shoulders quaking as his tears soaked his mother's skirts.

Huge, racking sobs convulsed his massive chest and in turn, his mother's body, as he poured out the oceans of grief he carried within him for the wife and child he had lost in this cruel twist of fate. Katharine rocked him as she had when he had been a toddler. There could be no greater sorrow than to watch a child in this torment.

The door to the bedroom opened quietly and Eloise, the midwife and his wife's own mother, stood silently in the opening. Katharine looked up over Gray's shuddering back and into her best friend's face.

Eloise, her eyes stained red and full of sorrow, shook her head sadly, telegraphing her message through the air to her friend. Katharine dropped her eyes. She understood. Abigail would be laid out with the babe. Wordlessly, Eloise retreated into the room and shut the door.

Shoulders sagging, her head dropped to rest on the soft dark hair of the son she held encircled in her arms. Weeping shamefully, she whispered words of comfort to her boy, willing all the pain to flow from him into herself. Still he sobbed.

When he had spent all of the emotion within him, he sat back upon his knees and looked into his mother's eyes, his tear-streaked face heartbreakingly tender. His striking gray eyes held an emotion Katharine could not read.

His voice shook. "I never understood, until now, how it must have felt for ye, mother, to be torn away from yer son. I am so sorry. I'm sorry for ye, I'm sorry for yer boy, and I'm sorry for me. But most of all, I'm sorry for my sweet Abigail. She was so young, so excited about our babe." Gray wiped his eyes with the backs of his hands, his eyes having aged twenty years in an equal number of minutes.

"As was I." he paused, using his hand linen to wipe his nose. His soft Scottish brogue made even his anguished words sound musical to her ears. "Now I'll never know the joy of what my child would have been. Her pretty smile. Or the sound of his boistrous laugh." He breathed in with a little hiccup, a leftover of his subdued tears.

Katharine reached out and stroked her young son's face. "Sweet boy, my sorrow cannot even compare to yours. My child is still living. I did not grieve his death, I grieved for my own loss," she said gently.

He stood to his feet and dusted off the knees of his breeches. An image of him as a very young boy, playing in the dirt with his brother, came unbidden to Katharine's mind. The motion was the same for both a six-year-old boy and a man of three and twenty. The poignancy of it tore at her heart. Without her permission, a picture of Adam, as she had imagined him a thousand times, danced in front of her eyes, taunting her, enticing her.

Find me, Mommy. I need you, Mommy. Amazed that she could contain any more pain, the memory of Adam's birth tore through her, threatening to steal her from this son who needed her now.

She shook her head to chase the familiar thoughts away and concentrated on Gray. He had just lost his own child, for heaven's sake. How selfish could she be?

"Do you want me to accompany you inside?"

He shook his head almost imperceptibly. "Nay, Mother. This is a door I must pass through alone."

Gray crossed the room to the closed door and knocked tentatively. Unlike his normal ramrod-straight posture, his shoulders sagged under the weight of his agony, his head bowed. He looked beaten – his unbending, unconquerable spirit dashed.

Eloise answered his knock and allowed him to enter. She had carefully arranged his wife and child – her own daughter and grandchild, but she could not think of that now – on the huge bed for him to look at one last time, to say his words of farewell.

The two innocents were quite beautiful really, even in death. Not a mark spoiled them, they looked as though they merely slept. For Gray, that made it worse. He sank to his knees beside the bed, dropping his head into his hands, his unmanly tears falling on the coverlet. He reached out and touched his dead wife's cheek. Still warm. *God, help me.*

Oh, Mother, if only ye could have saved her. God, would ye not have taken me instead?

He uncovered the babe in her arms. Ten fingers, ten toes, and a–

My son.

That knowledge brought a new flood of tears. Gray was unable to stem the flow, so he let them come, let the grief tear at him, rip at him, until his soul felt shredded – only a hollow resting place of the love that had once lived there. The decision was made.

I shall never love again.

Katharine stood outside in the sitting room, watching her child – heart breaking for the son she had loved so dearly, for the daughter-in-law she had loved dearly since the girl was a child. Eloise's daughter. Poor Eloise. Having to watch her own child die in such a tragic, useless manner. There wasn't even a grandchild to comfort her that at the very least her daughter had not died in vain.

Alec, Eloise's husband, Abigail's father, would be crushed. Katharine would have Garrett tell him, Eloise was in no condition to do so. The two men had been friends for almost thirty years.

Garrett! How had she forgotten? She would have to not only tell him, but be ready to comfort him as well. It was so hard to remember that the man who handled war and death so easily would need her comfort. He had loved little Abigail since she was a wee lass – and the babe? Oh, how he loved babies! There was no way to deal with that. It would just have to be said, then endured. Their hearts would still beat, their chests would yet breathe. The sun would continue to rise and to set, the seasons would yet change. *Pity.*

Katharine stood at the doorway a little longer, watching, waiting, making sure that young Gray would survive this horrible blow. When she saw his head come up and the hardness slowly etch itself across his face – the hardness that had just as surely stolen the warmth from his eyes – she wasn't sure which was worse, the tragedy they were all enduring, or the decision Gray had made to harden himself to life.

Although certainly a decision she had personally faced, it was not a path she would have taken. It was, however, a decision that would allow him to go on, to breathe in and out, to eventually go back to his life – if not one that would allow him to find happiness. So many times in this world Katharine had seen it – when a man hardened his heart, nothing short of a miracle could soften it again.

Dear God, please grant him a miracle.

Katharine pulled herself from the scene in front of her and left in search of Garrett, to tell him of the death of his grandchild and daughter-in-law. She prayed silently for grace. Could there even be enough? She asked that grief would make way for acceptance, and that acceptance would lead to a new road for all of them.

Passing a window, she noticed it had begun to rain.

TWO

London, England – Present Day

Adam stood in front of the low glass counter, waiting expectantly for the man to finish contemplating the archaic ring. The man's rheumy eyes possessed an intelligence that his outward appearance belied. He was tall and thin, shabbily dressed in a moth-eaten cardigan over a shirt that was missing buttons. Long fingers misshapen by arthritis, the man's wispy gray hair stood at attention atop his head, reminding Adam a little of Albert Einstein, only with far less hair.

Since the moment Adam had stepped off the plane so many weeks ago until now, he had spent all of his time going from shop to shop, asking questions of people who either wanted to take him for a ride or throw him in an asylum. Finally he had learned to keep his mouth shut about his real intent and pretend he was merely a collector. The little back alley shop he stood in right now looked like a combination dusty book store, antiques dealer, and taxidermist's shop. The large stuffed boar staring at him from behind the counter was unnerving.

The old man pulled the jeweler's loop out of his eye and sighed, "I'm sorry, son. I don't 'ave anythin' like this 'ere. Interstin' piece though, where'd you say you came across it? I'm sure I 'aven't ever seen anything like it before...." He scratched his chin and contemplated the ceiling. "But I 'ave a friend with a curiosity shop up in a little town in Wales who 'as a bigger collection of antiques than most museums and 'andles all manner of oddities, and maybe 'e can 'elp you in your search."

Adam's face fell. "Are you certain? I had been told you were the man to see." After so many false leads, he was afraid to even *think* about hope. The boar just continued to stare at him with his glassy eyes.

John Coleman bobbed his head up and down as he spoke to the young American in front of him. Truly sincere in his desire to help the handsome young man, John's heart went out to him. The boy seemed so lost and alone. Maybe it was because he was too young to be traveling throughout England, searching for something no one had cared about in hundreds of years – but to Coleman, it seemed much deeper than that. "I wish I could tell you more, son, but I just can't."

Adam sighed heavily and turned to leave, "Well, thank you for your time anyway, sir."

"Wait, now, young man. I'll ring old Colin for you. Ask 'im if maybe it's worth your trip over to show him your little trinket. 'E's ear deep in the 'istory books day and night, but I know 'e'd be real interested in that little beauty there. Give us a moment, please, boy." Coleman turned to his telephone with a great deal of effort, perhaps even pain, Adam thought, and dialed some numbers with his long, bent fingers.

As the call went through and connected, the shopkeeper's accent grew much thicker for the short moments he spoke to his friend. "Colin? Johnny-boy 'ere. 'Ow goes it? Splendid, splendid. Did ye find the piece ye was lookin' for last month? Just so. By the by, I got me an American boy 'ere what wants to have a li'l visit wif someone what has a good knowledge of your favorite fing – antiquities. Eh? A ring. Looks to be druidic to me, p'raps even older. Aye. Splendid. The festival? Good show. Aye. Just a moment then, Col."

Holding the receiver to his filthy sweater, John's accent cleared a bit as he slowly turned once again to address the American. "'E says 'e might be able to 'elp you. Said 'e couldn't be sure wivout givin' it a look, but agreed that your little piece there just might be something druidic, maybe once 'ad a bit of magic about it. Ain't no place like Wales for that kind of wicked information. All kinds of strange and sinful goings on up there for centuries now. And nobody knows strange goings on and old witchery like my friend, Colin. 'E'd be 'appy to 'elp you – no charge even, young man, for a good look at that ring. It'll just cost you a train ride up there, it will. Shall I tell 'im you're coming?"

Adam shifted from one foot to the other, quickly deciding. "Yes. It's the best lead I've had in a month. I might as well go to Wales as keep lurking through all these antique stores around here. There must be a thousand in London, alone."

The man laughed, nodding his head in agreement. "Aye, son. There's a fair number. You'd be better served to call on my friend as spin your wheels 'round 'ere."

He spoke a few short words into the telephone. "'E says 'e'll take the sleeper. Aye, then. Until next time then, Col. Aye." John replaced the hand piece into its cradle.

"I guess you'll be needing this." Leaning down under the dirty glass counter, the old man retrieved an ancient shoe box from some hidden recess and began digging around in it. When he found what he was looking for, he popped back up and with a gap-toothed grin handed his prize to the young American in front of him.

"'Ere it is!" He handed Adam a filthy, tattered business card, evidently the address to his friend's curiosity shop. "Don't make 'im wait, the perfessor's a busy man."

Adam's heart leaped. Finally someone who had a clue of what they were talking about, or at least that was what he hoped. He couldn't find better than a professor of antiquities.

The dirty rectangle was printed on cheap cardstock, obviously several years old and well-used. It read:

> *ODDS AND ENDS*
> *(and advice on how to use them)*
> *A Curiosity Shoppe*
> *Colin Merrill, Ph.D.– proprietor*

The address was printed on the back of the card.

Adam read it twice, committing the address to memory. He started to hand the card back to the peculiar old man in front of him, but the gnarled hand waved the card away.

"No, son. You keep it," the shopkeeper told him. "I've got another one 'round 'ere someplace. Don't let the address fool ye. It's a small village, for certain, but some things is mighty difficult to find."

"Thanks so much. I really appreciate it. You have no idea what this means to me," the young man said, and he left the store with a grateful smile and a wave. *Wish me luck, Mom.*

As though he had heard the silent plea, the shopkeeper's words floated out the door before it closed. "Good luck, boy."

Moray Firth, Scotland, 1359

Garrett lifted his eyes to the narrow juncture the small group of men would have to climb to reach the pass. They would have to go one by one.

Perfect place for an ambush. Tis a good thing we're at peace with our neighbors.

Something made him uneasy, and Garrett made it a personal law to obey his gut. He lifted his leather-gloved hand above his hand and silently fisted it. All the men in his company, including his two sons, Alane and Gray, saw the signal for caution and immediately heightened their vigilance. All men rode with their reins in one hand, the other resting on the hilt of their weapon.

The laird nodded his approval and moved on, his eyes relentlessly searching the trees and the ridge for enemies.

One can never be too prudent. ...

Continuing up the cramped and rocky path, he felt the eyes upon him before he heard the roaring shout from the ridge above them....

Blast it!

"RETREAT!!" There wasn't even a question of action, their provisions were too low, the men too tired from their long journey to fight the numbers he saw pouring through the pass.

As a unit, the men turned their mounts, only to see that two hundred men were filling up their only fallback position. Garrett quickly scanned the crowded pathway for any way out of this fight, six contingents below them, another six above – and he with only fifty men–

Nothing.

At that moment, he spotted the face of the man leading this charge of men – his allies, friends.

Cumming. I should have known you had no honor. Garrett drew his sword. "Gray, Alane, look ye to our Judas, and remember him well. If we survive, ye shall see his face again." The oath had been made. Gray and Alane committed the scene, and its originator, to memory. They, along with most of the company with them, said low prayers under their breath for heavenly assistance.

Cumming gazed blandly down upon his prey, his reptilian smile making even his own men uneasy. No good could come of this deed, there would be retaliation for this betrayal and it would be ruthless. Many of them would die against this small squadron of men, all knew this.

Garrett's voice was heard loud and clear in the crisp morning air. "Here's to us!"

The soldiers on the hill drew their swords.

"Who's like us?" again Garrett's booming voice was heard and answered by the ring of swords leaving their scabbards at the base of the hill.

The answering shout from his men resounded throughout the hillside. "Damn few, and they're all dead!"

The ram's horn sounded from above them, and Garrett's men charged with a feral bellow of rage.

Sitting on the bench waiting for the tube that would take him back to the small flat where he was staying, Adam reread all of the documents that had accompanied the antique ring in the simple cardboard box his father had given him. For the hundredth – or maybe the thousandth – time he took out the ancient ring and stared at it forcefully, willing it to give him an answer. The ring remained stubbornly silent.

His father, Joe, hadn't known what to do with any of the incomprehensible mess, so he had given it all – lock, stock, and barrel – to Adam on his eighteenth birthday.

To Joe, it had been a puzzle, offering only a headache and frustration.

The words of the letter were indelibly etched on Adam's mind. He could not only quote it, he could see every word written to him by his mother.

My dearest son,

I don't know how to tell you this so that you can believe it. I will give you as many verifiable clues as possible.

Adam, I was stolen away from you and the year 1992 and taken through time to the early 1300's. I was brought here by a bishop in the Catholic church by the name of Cooke to England. I was to be a part of a plan to breed out some undesirable traits of the English king. The broken ring that is enclosed made the time travel possible. I don't know how it was accomplished, except that the ring works only during the solstices. Without the crystal intact, however, the ring doesn't work at all. I tried it. I was brought from the summer solstice in Phoenix to the winter solstice in England, although I'm not sure that the ring always works that way.

Before I could be married to the king, I was saved from that fate by a Scotsman named Garrett Duncan, a wealthy and powerful merchant of the time. I fell in love with him and married him, and at the time I write this letter to you, I am bearing his child. I have asked him to find a way for this letter to be placed in your father's hands, and can only hope that at some point in time, when he has recovered from the shock, he will give it to you.

My dearest Adam, had the ring not been broken, I assure you, I would have returned to you. I crossed part of England by myself and went into some pretty dangerous situations trying to get the ring back. The bishop I mentioned previously broke it intentionally. Before he broke it, he told me that the ring only worked on the solstices and something about being able to look into another time for a few days before. Bishop Cooke was a vastly evil man – in our time he would have been a Ted Bundy. I'm sure you understand the reference.

I now live on an island off of the coast of Scotland in the German Sea, Ellshope it's called. Very few people know of its whereabouts, so I am safe from harm. I am happy and loved. I can only hope and pray

*that Joe made you feel the same way. But Adam, he always loved you
dearly, so I took comfort from that fact when I would begin to worry
about you. I know he helped you grow up to be a good man.*

*I love you, Adam, with all my heart. And no matter how difficult
this is to believe, the story I have told you is true. By the time this
letter gets to you, over 600 years will have gone by. Test the paper
and the ink, son – test it all, then make an educated decision based on
facts and evidence – not emotion.*

I love you and would never have left you. You were my life.

I am and always will be your mom.

Katharine

To Adam, the letter was the jumping off point for a plan – a crazy, fantastic
plan. The letter was a treasure map to his mother. Like any good treasure
map, it had no place markings and no directions for where to start – a
complete mystery. Only those who were willing to really work at the hunt
and had a passion for the treasure had a chance of figuring it out. There was
only one person that really fit that description – Adam.

Finding a beginning point had been a real trial. After working full time for
four years and saving every cent possible, he had finally been able to start
looking for the solution to his puzzle. He had finished his undergraduate
education at the same time, studying all he could on related subjects –
history, fencing, sailing, antiquities, and the like. He had even taken a
survival course so that if he had to live off the land during his treasure hunt,
he would be somewhat competent to do so. He committed every word, every
suggestion, every nuance of all he learned to his very competent memory.

Once out of college, Adam had decided to travel to England to begin his
search. If the ring had originated there, it was a whole lot more likely he
could find someone to fix it there. He began his systematic search in London.
There he exhausted himself and his possibilities on a daily basis by
painstakingly looking through shop after shop – antiques, curios, oddities.

And now, a month after his arrival in London, he found himself standing
and waiting for his train. And after that, his flat, and after his flat, Wales.

In this last month of wandering down dark alleyways and coughing over
centuries-old dust, he had encountered the most bizarre people. The denizens
of eccentricity who ran the little shops he had perused had been as odd as
their merchandise. Adam had enjoyed them thoroughly. Although he had, at
first, felt like he was on the right track, after a month of no clues, Adam
started to think about devising a new strategy. Until now.

"What time is it, chum?"

He looked up into the nondescript face of a businessman carrying a briefcase and a cell phone, jarring him back to the reality of now. When the lines between the history Adam was searching for and the reality of present day became blurred, coming face-to-face with today always seemed to shock him.

"What?" Adam looked as confused as he sounded.

"Oh, yer a Yank, eh? I thought as much." A friendly smile crossed the man's tired features.

"Oh, yes. I'm American. We kind of stick out like sore thumbs over here. What was your question?" Adam realized he was still holding the ring and precious documents and quickly shoved them back into his knapsack.

"Do you have the time? My clock seems to have stopped." He shook his wristwatch as if that might help.

"Um, yes. It's 4:30, um, half past four. The train should be by anytime." Adam put what he hoped was a friendly smile on his face as he fastened the clasps on his pack.

"Very good. Can I sit?"

He was already in the process of settling himself on the bench when Adam smiled and nodded.

"Big country isn't it? America, I mean. From where do you come?"

"Me? I live in Arizona."

"Grand Canyon and all that? Splendid. No grass, desert, big giant prickly trees, too, if I remember correctly. John Wayne and all that. I saw pictures in a book once. Arizona the place?" The man nodded as he spoke, as though he was answering his own questions.

Adam nodded, for just a moment transported back to the mesas and desert he knew so well. "Cacti. Jericho trees. Painted Desert. That's the place. It's hot and dry and beautiful, in a rugged sort of way. John Wayne fits in perfectly." The thought of that dazzling sun and the immense heat put a half-smile on Adam's lips. He hadn't seen the sun for more than a half hour since he'd gotten to London. "Very different from here. Makes me glad I brought my jacket. It's hot like parts of Africa, but the countryside looks very different." For another moment he was transported to the bazaar in Tangier, Morocco, that he visited. Earthy scents of live animals and hot food invaded his memory as though he was still there. He could still taste the rich brown bread he bought for twelve cents a loaf and the couscous he had devoured like a starving man. Adam had liked that dish even better than the paella and sangria he had feasted on and loved in Spain.

He shook himself back to the present, still feeling the gnawing hunger the memory had evoked.

The businessman nodded, as though privy to Adam's memories, but turned away towards the heavy, throbbing noise coming from their left. "The tube," he announced.

Both men stood. The train came to a halt in front of them and the sliding glass doors opened.

The businessman turned, and bowed slightly. "After you, chum. And enjoy your stay here in London."

"Thanks, I am – immensely. Have a nice day." Adam moved right after stepping through the sliding doors, his new acquaintance moved left. Both found a seat and the train pulled away from the station.

Gray's bleary eyes opened on amazing carnage. Blood was everywhere, soldiers coated in their own death. Bodies littered the small clearing, but nothing registered in his bleary mind except one bloodied face.

Father. Oh God, please no ... Father....

The enormous man lay in a pool of his own blood. Even though it was evident he was mortally wounded, his eyes were bright and he called wordlessly to his eldest son.

Gray.

Heedless to his own serious wounds, the son, a baron in his own right, crawled over the gory, trampled grass to his fallen father.

"Are ye well, Father?" It was a foolish question, yet their traditional greeting popped from Gray's mouth before he could stop it.

With enormous control, the older man kept his wince contained. "The wound is fair deep. I have only a paltry few breaths left in me. I will no see yer mother's fair face again."

"Hush, father. Ye will. Tis the pain speakin', not the wound. I've seen worse on a wee babe." It was meant to encourage Garrett, yet the jest fell flat between the two men.

"Nay. See with yer own eyes. The blade struck near to me own heart. Tell yer mother, my beloved Katharine, I love her. I will wait for her in eternity."

Gray's jaw clenched as his eyes burned with bitter fury. *Too much!* His voice was fierce. "I will not. You'll tell her yerself. Let me get ye to yer feet."

As he slipped his arm beneath his father's back, the older man groaned in agony. The threat was more than true. *NO!*

Through the older man's haze of pain he watched his younger son, Alane, crawling over the slain bodies of their enemies toward him. He quickly ascertained that a leg wound, and not a mortal one at that, was the boy's difficulty. *He shall live.*

31

Relief washed over Garrett, giving way to bitterness. He should have known. He should have been better prepared. He should have known his allies had betrayed the clan. He should have triumphed. He had promised Katharine he would come back to her.

The Cumming clan was full of foolish, poorly trained soldiers – nothing more than senseless children garbed in leather studs. That's why they had sought Garrett's help in the first place. They wanted him to train them so they could become a force like his own – to be reckoned with, feared.

Yet in a second of ambush, and with the help of Garrett's own allies against him, it had all been over. He had lost so many faithful warriors – and over nothing more than cattle-reaving. After so many years of deviling England's king and countryside, he had refused to take part in Laird Cumming's plans. Why should they steal from each other, when they could pay? England – maybe, but steal from other Scots? There was no honor in it. The two lairds had waged a war of words, Garrett had won his point, and that should have finished it. This carnage should never have occurred. They were men of honor.

Just as Garret felt the beat of his own heart slow, he also felt his own tunic soaked with new warmth. Another, slower, quieter heartbeat, more warmth.

Blood. My blood. Please God, no, don't let me die. I promised.

Alane was now at his side. "I have bandages to wrap you with, Father. Be still. No Father, don't move." The dark blood soaked his father's clothing even around to his backplate, and the sleeve of his shirt had soaked through red all the way down to his elbow. The son could not ignore the abysmal stains steeping through the iron-studded leather that had failed to protect his father's chest. Gray watched as the blood slowly seeped farther down his father's arm.

It's deep. So deep. Please God.

The rattle in his father's throat kept Gray from speaking his concern. He must not wound Father's pride, to acknowledge grief or worry would dishonor the older man.

"Avenge me." Never before had those two words escaped Garrett's lips. *Avenge me. Avenge the promise I could not keep.*

The whisper echoed through Gray's mind as he watched his brother cradling his father. Alane could not be the one. It was not even his duty. He was the youngest.

Mine, I am the oldest. I will avenge you, Father.

Bending down to look his father straight in the eye, Gray pulled his father's dirk from the older man's closed fist and used it to slice open his own palm. Letting the blood drop onto his father's chest, he gave the required oath. "I swear it by the mingling of my blood with yours. I will avenge you, Father, and on my soul I forge my oath. May the racks and trees witness the oath I swear with my own blood to my father. As you ask, so it shall be done."

Betrayal. Murder. Death. Father.

Too much, too much.

Gray and Alane watched helplessly as their father wheezed small amounts of air into his failing lungs. Blood trickled out of the corner of his mouth and the ear that was tipped toward the ground. Inexplicably, a smile settled over the old man's face. As the last breath rattled out from Garret's lungs, peace – the kind he had only known when with the woman he loved, his dearest Katharine – swept over him. Body and mind were at peace. All would be done. His sons would make all set to rights.

Once settled, Adam pulled the tattered business card from his pack. *Wales. Haven't been there yet, I'm getting more adventure than I bargained for.*

It really couldn't hurt to give this a try. He still had plenty of money, which translated to time, and no other clues whatsoever. The funny thing was, now that he was actually facing a possible lead on this very old, very mysterious ring, he actually felt a little apprehensive. It was great to anticipate going on a huge adventure, but actually doing it could be a bit overwhelming. After all, he was from the nation that watched adventure on a little square box, not lived it. Spectating was a vast bit different than participating.

As the train came to his station, Adam stood and moved to the doors, his mind consumed with the details of leaving for Wales. If, by some huge coincidence, this little oddities dealer could fix his ring and tell him how to use it, he could be off on his treasure hunt in no time at all. The "X" that marked the spot, however, was the real problem. *When? Where? How can I possibly know?*

If Adam was to believe Scotland Yard and the British Monarchy's court historians – and he did – he had in his possession a ring of at least a thousand years of age, possibly even much older. Several times enterprising dealers had tried to pry it out of his young hands with inordinate sums of money, but he wasn't selling. They couldn't possibly understand. It would be like selling them the air he breathed.

Adam also had in his possession an official report from laboratories in the employ of the queen of England herself that stated the parchment on which his mother had written her first and last letter to him was over six hundred years old. The sealing wax and ink dated the same way. Difficult to believe, to be sure, as his mother had disappeared eighteen years ago. He had been six years old. But, ever the one to love a good mystery, Katharine had made sure that she left her six-hundred-year-old thumbprint in the sealing wax of the letter so there would be no doubt that she had written it.

I always loved your sense of humor, Mom.

Joe, who had endured a horrible year of upheaval after his ex-wife's disappearance, had closed his mind to the possibility that the letter might contain the truth. It did contain one whopper of a tale, though – being kidnapped from her own time to be married to an idiot king and then kidnapped again from that situation. Like Patty Hearst, she fell for her captor, but unlike Patty Hearst, he had been good to her and for her. Okay, his mind could somewhat get around that. The really annoying part was that, just like in a fairy tale, she had been transported by a magic ring. The one he now held in his hands, broken of course, so there could be no proof of this insane story. Why not kidnapped by a troll or held for ransom by an elf who turned straw into gold? Please!

Too weird to be true – yet that was why this particular twenty-four-year-old man stayed on his wild goose chase to see if he could find someone, anyone who could repair this ring. Repair? No, he would be happy to find someone who could simply give him the smallest hint, the tiniest fragment of information, regarding this cheap piece of metal.

His mother's letter had made mention of the summer and winter solstices, but the references weren't clear enough for him to understand for sure what she had been talking about. Nothing seemed clear to him just now, except this compulsion that drove him on. June twenty-first was nearing quickly, though, and Adam felt an undeniable sense of urgency in his search. He was almost certain that, if he didn't get the information he needed by that date, he would be stuck for another six months without answers. And after waiting all this time, he did *not* want to wait until December twenty-first, the winter solstice.

He sighed quietly as he again fingered the modern documents from the strong box. Six years he had carried them with him, hoping for some clue, some burst of inspiration, that would lay bare the secrets of his mother's disappearance. Scotland Yard and Her Majesty the Queen didn't think Adam was crazy – they had used all available resources to verify the dates, and the proof, their reports, were in his hands. They were, in a very British way, quite proud of the mystery they had handed over to him, and because of the tabloid papers that had carried the story when it had first broken, some of the people Adam questioned even recognized the ring and remembered the story.

The FBI didn't think he was crazy, they thought it was some elaborate hoax – one they couldn't figure out though. They were the ones who had matched the print in the sealing wax with his mother's prints left at her abandoned house. Their report verifying the thumbprint was in the box as well. The letter, written on authentic six-hundred-year-old parchment, was in his mother's own handwriting. Adam had given it over to be analyzed at least ten different times by as many different experts.

Then there were the dreams. Still clear as crystal in his mind, Adam could recall every frightening detail. Since childhood, he had dreamed the dreams – visions, more like; wishful fantasies, Joe had insisted. Adam had dreamed of his mother often since her disappearance – almost always in conjunction with wolves. In some of the earlier visions he had looked on helplessly as Katharine was chased by wolves and hurt by them. In his later dreams, she seemed to become more successful, instead of being caught by the vicious beasts, she eluded them.

The last dream he had ever had of his mother with wolves was again of her racing them for her very life. They were gaining and he could see the ravenous hunger in their glinting eyes and snarling jaws. At the last minute, Katharine had turned, jeweled dagger in hand, and plunged the sharp knife into the leader – causing the pack to disperse and leave her unharmed. At the moment she had turned, Adam had also seen that his mother was fat. As a child, he had thought that particular element of his dream strange, since he had never seen Katharine fat before. That detail had always bothered him – made the dreams seem less authentic, until as an adult he had realized that in that particular vision Katharine had been pregnant. Now that particular detail seemed to confirm some link he must have maintained with his mother, as no six-year-old would dream up a pregnancy.

As Adam grew older, he had often dreamed of her in the company of an enormous man who he couldn't quite see and babies that made her happy. He always thought one of them looked like him. The boy in his dream could have been himself or his twin, but he knew the dream-boy was neither. Sometimes in his visions Katharine would look sorrowful and he had *known* at those times she was thinking about him.

After the first couple of dreams, and the consequent first couple of visits to the psychologist, Adam had learned to keep his dreams to himself.

Joe kept telling him he was insane to believe in fairy tales, but supported his eccentric belief that he would find his mother anyway. At least, Adam reflected with a smile, he paid for all the bizarre courses his son had insisted on taking in college – fencing, survival, medieval culture and dress (Adam's favorite), and enough history courses to sink a ship. He kept hoping that his son would get this nonsense out of his system once and for all by this idiotic trip. He had even given him a year's leave from his job at the construction company, with the expressed terms that if Adam had no success after a year, he would come to his senses and come run the small corporation Joe had agreed to wait to retire from until then.

In his mind Adam replayed the conversation they had hobbled through before he boarded his plane. Joe had been visibly upset, yet he accepted his son's departure.

"Do what you have to do, Adam. I understand how hard all of this has been on you. Don't come back until you've either figured it out or are ready to give this quest of yours up. You owe that to yourself. I'm always going to love you, kiddo, but you're driving me crazy with this obsession of yours.

"Frankly, I just hope you come back in one piece. I think you're walking around in lots of pieces, and you think this is the glue that will fix that. I honestly hope you're right." Joe embraced his son, praying silently that if there were answers to this riddle, Adam would find them.

He stepped back and stared Adam squarely in the eye. "She did love you, you know. If you're trying to make it seem like you weren't abandoned, I can tell you right now that nothing short of death would have made your mother leave you. I know she and I weren't on the best of terms, but I do know that."

Adam nodded. "I know, Dad. That's why I really need to do this. I just need to be sure."

Joe sighed and hugged his son one last time. "If you need anything, kiddo – call. I still think you're crazy, but I'm always there."

"I know, ready to love me with straightjacket in hand. Be sure to pad my room while I'm gone." They both laughed.

"You know it. Really, sport, if you get into trouble...." Joe couldn't finish. His throat constricted around the lump that had installed itself there. He did his best to keep the tears that were threatening to overwhelm him at bay. It wasn't that Adam was leaving, exactly – kids left home all the time. There was just some sort of permanence to this departure, like even if the boy returned, he would never be the same. Joe shook himself free of that thought.

"I know. Don't worry, I'll be all right. I love you, Pops." Adam attempted valiantly to keep his own emotions in check, but leaving his father combined with his anxiety over the unknown threatened to break the dam.

"I love you too, Adam." Joe's voice was husky. He hoped that everything would turn out all right. Experience told him he couldn't really be sure. The only thing he could count on was that he and Adam loved and respected each other, and that would have to be enough. So much better than what most families had – it was really quite something.

Over the loudspeaker came the last boarding call. With a jerky little smile and a wave, Adam shouldered his backpack and boarded his plane. To Joe he looked painfully like that small, vulnerable child he had been so long ago. He sighed and nodded. Everything was always so final.

Adam hurried down the jetway to the open door of the plane. After installing his backpack and luggage in the overhead compartment, he sat down and thought about his extraordinary quest while he buckled his seat belt and waited for the aircraft to roll away from the gate.

As the plane swallowed up his only son, Joe slowly made his way out of the terminal and back to his pickup. For the first time in his life, no matter how strong his work-hardened body was, Joe felt old. He fumbled for the proper key and, finding it, revved his engine slightly and backed from his parking place. Time to go back to work. The Caliche Building was waiting for his expertise.

Within minutes of his boarding, the door was shut tight by a crew member, and Adam heard the whine of the engines as they started. Smashing his paper pillow into a comfortable wad, he tucked it between his head and the window and settled down into his seat.

He was asleep before the beverages were served.

By the time Adam had finished ruminating on the past, his decision had been made without qualm – no shots fired between the often warring factions of his will. Without a conscious thought, he had packed every last one of his things and tidied up his rented room for the nice lady who owned the place. He was even on the way down the stairs to tell her he would be vacating his room, what she grandiosely called his flat, when he realized what he was planning to do.

He didn't even have a train ticket yet, but Adam had trusted his instincts so far, and was not about to stop now. After he broke the news to the kind, elderly lady – she had cried loudly and made him feel frightfully guilty – he walked the many blocks to the train station in a daze.

Adam's mind never quit, and his body seemed to obey unspoken commands without ever seeming to make the connection in his conscious mind. It used to make his dad crazy. He couldn't even count the times Joe had told him he was just like his mother for that very reason. Why couldn't he just relax and let it all go? Why did he constantly have to be doing something? It most certainly hadn't helped his father that Adam looked so much like her, either.

Like Katharine, Adam possessed thick, wavy hair, but instead of her auburn color, his hair was so dark it looked black – until he was in the proper light, when it could be seen for the very deep red color it was – like oxygen-rich blood. He had been fortunate enough to get her eyes from the gene pool as well, grey that changed to green and blue depending on his mood and what he was wearing. Girls loved them, or at least always commented on what they called 'his beautiful eyes.' He had inherited his dad's size, fortunately, as Katharine had been rather small for a woman – five three or four when she stretched. She had the personality of an Amazon, though, and that was not always a good thing. Adam was more easygoing than his mother had been, but he was just as stubborn when he had his mind set.

Not what would exactly be considered a big man, Adam stood six feet one inch. But he made up with muscle for what he didn't possess in height. His six years of construction work, after classes let out every day and in the two years since he had graduated college, had given him an enviable physique.

Lily, Adam's adopted mother, was always telling him how handsome he was, and he didn't miss it when the girls' heads turned as he walked by. More of a planner than a player, Adam just never thought much of it. He was so busy thinking about his plans that he had never had much time for girls. He even took his cousin Katie to prom because he didn't particularly want a girlfriend until he had his ducks in a row.

Adam had even been asked by some of his less familiar friends if he was gay. He would laugh good-naturedly and tell them he really just had a head for more important things right now. They would smirk and walk off with mocking falsetto voices and limp wrists – and Adam would ignore them just like he had before. One thing Adam was not insecure about was his manhood. He had just decided that he would know who he was and have things figured out before he looked in the direction of any of the pretty young things that flocked around him.

"You're too serious," his dad would tell him.

"Get a date," Lily would say.

"A guy's gotta play," his friend Aaron would tell him.

They didn't understand. They knew their mothers. They could even hug them. For some reason, he simply could not let this drop. Adam was on a mission.

Standing on line to purchase his ticket, Adam dug his wallet out of his pocket and counted out the appropriate number of pounds for his ride to Cornwall. He had decided to start there, see a little of the countryside, then go meet the professor.

He had spent all of his free time in the last two years of college studying the fourteenth century. To say he was a little concerned about what he learned would've been an understatement. It was the century of the Black Death, The Hundred Years War, and William Wallace. Men lived and died by their swords. Cruelty reigned, and the only thing that mattered was money and position.

This was one of the reasons he spent many hours on the piste with his fencing instructor, practicing with everything he could get his hands on – foil, epee, saber, even a dirk. He insisted that his teacher, Sir Rene, help him master the art of fighting with a saber in his right hand and a dagger in the left. His instructor had always laughed when Adam would tell him you could never tell when it would come in handy. The two would practice for hours, Rene commenting loudly at the end of each session that the boy was impossible to fatigue, and he never gave up.

Sometimes Sir Rene would confront him about what he called Adam's 'obsession.' Adam would shrug it off with a laugh and a "A guy's gotta have a hobby," ignoring the older man's concern. Then Adam would challenge him to another bout.

Adam bought a ticket from a nondescript man behind the little window. Taking his pack off and laying it on the bench beside his duffel, he sat down and waited to board the train for a very long ride.

Like a sponge, Adam soaked up anything anyone would teach him, and when the professor wouldn't teach him to fight with a broadsword and lance, Adam found someone who would. Under the tutelage of his friend, Willy – who insisted on being called Wills because it sounded British, he learned a vast amount. Wills was so obsessed with the same historical period he had dropped out of school to work as a knight at the Dallas Medieval Times. Working with him, Adam had even learned to joust. Wills introduced him to a quintain, a padded square target set on one arm of a T-shaped bar with a weighted leather bag on the other. The objective wasn't merely to hit the square target, but to be able to maintain your balance in the saddle and not get hit by the weighted leather bag. Adam spent a month tending some rather nasty bruises before he got the hang of it. Wills would laugh every time he hit the ground, then tell him he was doing amazingly well.

Curious, Adam had worked at the dinner theater himself for a short time as a waiter to see if he could learn more. The fighting that went on in the dinner theatre was an amazing combination of stuntwork, choreography, athletics, and equestrianism. The only difference between the shows and real life was that almost all fights during the medieval period involved various levels of bloodshed or death. The other thing he learned was that if he had to make his living being a waiter, he would definitely starve. Serving soup and roast chicken didn't seem to be his forte.

Beyond Adam's training with Wills, the two would drive for hours to go to renaissance fairs and listen to historians give lectures. Adam even learned to sew and work leather, and kept a bevy of period costumes which, he also maintained, might come in handy someday.

The train whistle made him jump, and Adam realized he had almost fallen asleep. Shouldering his bags, he stood and joined the congregation of people milling about on the platform. With an ear-splitting hiss of air brakes the train slowed to a stop, doors opening to allow its passengers to trickle out and make room for the next ensemble.

Walking down the thinly carpeted aisle, Adam found a couple of empty seats and stowed his bags. He sat in the aisle seat, hoping to discourage anyone from sitting beside him, and settled himself comfortably. It wasn't long before the train was moving again and he could sink toward sleep. The ride would be an all-nighter. The conductor came by a few minutes after they pulled out of the station, punched his ticket, and handed him a paper pillow. Adam tucked it between his neck and his shoulder, thanked the man, and closed his eyes.

The two years since Adam had graduated college had been spent working various jobs in his father's construction company, being groomed to take over after Joe's retirement

Concerning his mother's whereabouts, Adam had done enough research to make some educated guesses. The king that his mother was stolen to marry, the one supposed to be an idiot, was probably Edward II. He had been gay, not stupid or impaired, and those around him had made many attempts to change that. He wondered if his mother had not been an attempt to breed Edward's homosexuality out of him that failed. Adam had discovered that there was some speculation that his advisors might have drugged him on a regular basis in order to accomplish their own designs. Unwilling to comply with their wishes, the poor man had died horribly – he had been taken to an isolated church where a red hot poker was inserted in his rectum and he was burned to death from the inside out. Of course, it was of the utmost importance that there were no visible marks on his body, what good was treason if the perpetrators forfeited their lives for it? It was said the screams could be heard for miles. *And my mother's stuck in that place. God help her.*

He considered that his mother might have been an unwitting part of one of the many ill-destined plots prior to the king's death. Katharine hadn't mentioned the name of the king specifically in her letter. He wondered if she had ever bothered to learn it. Being so much like her, he knew that had it not been important to her life at the moment, she wouldn't have bothered to learn the poor king's name. She would have been busy making plans to change her situation. She was not one to sit idly by and let fate tell her what to do, no sir, she would have *done something*. It was that very thing, Joe had always told him, that got her into constant trouble and was the biggest reason she worked for herself. The whole having-a-boss-thing chafed too much.

The train lurched for a moment, throwing Adam almost a foot and scaring the daylights out of him. Looking around, he noticed that no one else seemed concerned, so he resituated his pillow and resettled his mind.

Adam wished that Katharine had put down on paper the rest of the history surrounding her adventure so that he could pinpoint exactly where and when she had disappeared. In her defense, it had probably never occurred to her that he would attempt to find her or even that he might be able to – not that he could. All he had to go on was the lab report, and lab results could be inaccurate.

On a fairly regular basis, he prayed that someone somewhere would have a direction for him to start in. Just a hint, a clue, some little tidbit would be nice. He hoped the little oddities dealer in Wales would be his compass.

Here goes nothing.

THREE

The woman knelt in front of the chiseled headstone marking her husband's grave. Back straight, head bowed – the movement of her lips was barely discernable. When she crossed herself and raised her head, her long hair fell back over her shoulders and the face of a stunning beauty revealed itself. Her beautiful hair, once auburn, cascaded down her back in thick waves – now streaked with gray. In defiance of the convention adhered to by older women, she still wore it down, but her youthful face belied her age. She had few wrinkles around her eyes and mouth, looking to be in her early thirties instead of her late forties. Her figure was youthful as well, not having spread through the middle as so many older women in the village were prone to do. Tears rolled down her face as she kissed her fingers, then pressed them to the grave marker.

"I miss you, love." Her voice was strained. "I would never trade the twenty-five years I had with you, but I miss you desperately. Especially at night. There's no one to hold me anymore. The children are gone. I miss them, too, but I miss you the most. You would be so proud of your sons, they are so like you. Strong, handsome, courageous. Gray has made a name for himself in trade, as you did, though his heart has not yet healed from the death of his wife and child so long ago. The burden of your death is worse than even that, I think. Alane spends his time driving the king of England to distraction, carrying on in your footsteps as well. Gray helps him at every turn, but he's a bit more subtle in his business. They've both been given the title of baron by Edward III, believe it or not. The king must want their money desperately for his war with France in order to give such a title to men with no noble blood – notwithstanding that they're your sons, and Scots besides. I know you were proud of the hatred he bore you They pay a baron's taxes as well, but it's a small price to pay for the information they get while they're at court. Annabella is happy, married to a highlander. He's a rough one, coarse and stuck in the old ways of the clan, but good to her all the same. You'd like him. He's the laird of his clan, he reminds me a lot of you when you were younger. She'll be having our third grandbaby sometime in the spring." She took a deep breath to maintain her control, wiping her tears away with her fingertips.

Her voice shook slightly as she sighed out her breath and continued, "Every time I look at them – the children I mean – I see you. It hurts – but it's wonderful at the same time. Don't ask me to explain. If I did, you would just roll your eyes at me during my explanation and say, 'Rabbit trail, love.' I miss that, too. I would give anything for you to roll your eyes at me in exasperation and bite your cheek to rein in your temper." Her voice dropped to a sorrowful whisper, "Some say this ache will go away after a time, but it's a lie. I'm sure of it. At least now I can come talk to myself by your grave and our vassals won't whisper that I'm daft." She laughed at that, a sad chuckle that caused her to tears to start rolling again.

"I'm sorry. I'll try not to cry too much. But I've been trying for the last year and it's not getting any easier, love." Her jaw tightened as her eyes lit with fire. Just a hint of a Scottish burr wove its way through her words. "And I'll try not to kill that son of a boar MakLaughlin that felled you when I see him next. Gray says, as your oldest son, it's his right – not mine. But blast, fifty-nine is too young to die!" Her anger drained out of her. She grew soft again, wistful. "And you were still so strong, so handsome, such a wonderful man."

Brightening a little, her voice took on a lilt. "The boys will be home in a fortnight's time. That's why I've come to speak with you. I have to apologize to you again. I must go on another adventure. I know you'll be angry, and since you're not here to yell at me, I thought I would come down here and give you another chance. Maybe the men were right, maybe I am daft. Alec had the audacity to tell me I was getting too old for this sort of thing. As if he has the right to talk about being old – his hair is completely white and he's older than me by at least ten harvests. It doesn't matter anyway, though, I have to go. I'll be careful, love, I promise." The woman paused, sighed heavily, then slowly, sadly got to her feet. Again she kissed the tips of her fingers and pressed them this time to the grass in front of the stone. She stared at the ocean surrounding the sheer, rock cliff she stood on. "Thank you for living to be an older man so I only had to miss you for a short time. And thank you for bringing me to this beautiful place and loving me." She sighed again and delicately wiped her fingers across her cheeks once more. "Goodbye for now, love."

She turned away from the stone with one last shuddering breath and straightened her shoulders. As she strode back up the hill, with each step she became a different woman. Each step gave her just a little more power, a little more control. By the time she reached the walls surrounding the beautiful castle where she lived, she was again the mistress of the manor.

In the courtyard, Katharine watched for a moment the mothers who had brought their babies out for some fresh air, and the women who had decided to complete their mending in the warmth of the sun. They were chatting together and enjoying the beautiful morning Ellshope had gifted them with. When they spied their mistress, they waved. Smiling warmly, she returned the gesture and continued toward her home to make preparations for the coming of the boys.

The castle was a legacy for her and her family. Her husband and his warriors had built it together with their own hands. It was where they had raised their children and she had been happier than any other time in her whole life. Where now she was mistress of all she surveyed, and the warriors that had taken the place of their fathers in service were loyal to her with their very lives.

The woman moved like a queen – back straight, head high – wearing her dignity like a second skin. She never flinched, never looked back. She had a job to do. Excitement tingled within her. As she stepped onto the drawbridge that had been lowered for the day, she paused and took a deep breath – dear God, she missed Garrett.

Adam passed the inconspicuous little street the shop was on three times before he finally located it. It was a back alley in the pretty little village of Cowbridge. The village had long ago been a thriving market center in Norman times, and even now was bustling with small-scale commerce. The streets were, in fact, surprisingly and outrageously packed, and Adam wondered what could possibly be going on to turn such a picturesque little town into a wall-to-wall circus.

The village was basically one long main street, with a few little side roads, if you could call them that, intersecting it here and there. South of the main street, Adam walked past the ruins of the walls that had surrounded the town in its medieval period, just to try to get a feel for them. He stared at them in fascination, wondering if his mother had ever walked through those ancient gates. They weren't ancient as far as the Welsh were concerned, however, just a little old.

Of course, being from America, where even the oldest structure was brand spanking new relative to Britain and Europe, the place looked ancient to Adam.

Outside the ruined walls were tents of every shape and description, all set up for some type of fair or festival. Innumerable people in medieval-period dress wandered in and out of the cluttered grounds. For a moment, Adam entertained the fleeting thought he had been transported backward through time without his ring, then laughed at his own flight of fancy. Of course, it was just a festival, but for such a small village, it was huge. Cars and people were everywhere. The entire population of Wales could turn out for this fair, and it would not be more packed.

Although he wanted to stay and explore the festival, Adam wandered back through the town, looking for the little shop. On his third pass down the main street, he finally spotted a small sign that indicated he should turn to get to his desired street. Not a street really, but an alleyway. Of course, in comparison to American roadways, none of the narrow roads qualified as anything else. They were narrow, hardly wide enough for two cars – one car in many places – but charming. And the countryside they wound through was amazing to look at.

In front of the tiny shop itself, there was only a small rectangular sign – maybe a foot long – above the door. Because of the grime that had accumulated on the wood, it was largely unreadable. When Adam finally realized the door was the entrance to the shop he was looking for, he took a deep breath and grabbed the knob. It wouldn't turn. He tried pushing the door, it wouldn't budge. He knocked – no answer. He knocked louder. Nothing. He reached up with his fist to pound on the door when a barely understandable voice hollered down at him from above.

Adam looked up. A bald, round man of about fifty was shouting something to him about being closed. "Are you," Adam consulted the business card, "Colin Merrill?"

"Aye, son. But we're closed for the festival. You'll 'ave to come back later." The man's accent was extremely thick and his burr made him hard to understand.

"Please sir, I've come a long way. Your friend called you about me from London," Adam explained.

"You're the American boy John called about?" Colin called down to him.

"That's me. What festival are you closed for?" Adam called back up, feeling very foolish standing here in the middle of an alley and carrying on a shouting match with a man he didn't know.

"The Royal National Eisteddfod, of course! Gracious! The things they don't know these days...." he said to himself. "Tell you what – I'll open for long enough to look at your piece. Be down in just a minute, lad." His head disappeared from the window and the sash dropped back down to the sill with a bang.

It seemed like only seconds later Adam heard the scrape of the lock being turned and the door flew inward. Standing in front of him, wearing a huge grin, was a man no taller than five feet with an enormous belly and a bald head, except for a small fringe of hair around his ears. The man looked more like a troll than a human. Adam could not help but grin at the man. He hoped it looked like a friendly grin and not an I'm-laughing-at-you grin. Being so much like his mother, it was sometimes difficult to rein in the thoughts that crossed his face. Joe was always telling him that every thought he had was either tattooed across his face or came rushing out of his mouth. Adam had been working on the latter, but had no idea how to take care of his facial expressions. He prayed that 'comical troll' wasn't written on his forehead. It wasn't a good way to begin a relationship.

Thankfully, the man saw his smile as simply friendly and grasped the boy's hand and enthusiastically pumped it up and down. "The name's Colin, and you are...."

"Adam Talbot."

"Well, come in, Adam Talbot, and show me your treasure. After we've decided what it is, you can accompany me to the festival and learn more about Wales in one day than most people, even the Welsh, ever know." The little man turned and led the way down a very dark hallway and then up some narrow stairs. One bare lightbulb hung from the sloped ceiling and illuminated the stairway. At the top, the man turned left and opened a low door which opened on a very small room with a few spotless glass jewelry cases filled with what appeared to be very old junk. The friendly troll scooted behind one of the sparkling cases and leaned down to get something. When he stood back up, he was holding a piece of black velvet and a jeweler's loupe. He put the loupe on his eye and held out his hand for the object.

"Well? Let's see it, boy, time's slippin' away." The man was wearing the most ludicrous smile. Adam had never met anyone quite like him before, but he liked him immensely. He dug into his backpack and brought out the small strongbox in which he kept the few treasures from the safety deposit box. He opened it and, carefully moving aside the official papers and the pieces of parchment, fished out the ring.

"This is it," Adam said simply, placing it into the man's outstretched palm. "I need to find a way to fix it. There used to be some kind of crystal set into it which has been broken for a very long time. Mr. Matthews said that if anyone would know about this ring, you would."

"Matthews said that, did 'e? 'E's a funny old bird, but I love 'im like me own da. Plays a mean game of chess, 'e does." The little man chuckled to himself, and Adam noticed that his belly shook. He couldn't help making a comparison to Santa's belly shaking like a bowl full of jelly and smiling to himself. Colin looked up at Adam, smiled happily, then turned his attention back to the ring as he examined it out loud, "Oooh, Matthews was right. This is a beauty. It definitely is the right time period to be druidic. Looks to be eighteen 'undred or so years old. Possibly even a hair older."

"That old?" Adam was incredulous. He had never touched, let alone been in possession of, something anywhere near that old.

Merrill chucked, expressing the boy's thought aloud, "There's not much in your whole country that old, is there, boy? You'll find some pretty amazin' things in ancient 'istory. Druids were the practitioners of a pretty odd pagan religion from about the second century B.C. to the second century A.D. They had priests, prophets, sorcerers – everythin' a good religion needs to scare the devil out of everybody. They worshiped oak trees and mistletoe. Liked 'uman sacrifice, too, but who 'asn't thought about sacrificing one or two of the people they know now and then?" He kept talking while Adam just listened, committing everything the man said to memory. "Lots of ignorant people think that the druids built old Stonehenge, but it's been around a lot longer than they were. Not that they didn't use that creepy old place to their full advantage. 'Ave you seen it, son?"

"Yes, I did go look at it. I've always liked that kind of thing. It was amazing, but the feeling I got there.... It's hard to describe. Spooky sounds silly, but it was."

"I know what you're talkin' about, boy. The feeling of history there is tangible – and you can tell it wasn't a nice piece of history. It was something … maybe mysterious would be more like it," the man answered, shaking his head in agreement.

"History was always one of my favorite subjects, but it's taken on a really important role in my life lately." He paused, watching the old man carefully.

"History 'as an important role in everyone's lives, son, only most people aren't bright enough to know it," he lectured. "It's good to meet someone under the age of fifty who does."

Adam's impatience got the better of him. "Can you fix it, or point me toward someone who can?"

"Fix it? Now, that I don't know about. I could put somethin' where the stone was, but who knows if I'd put in the right kind of crystal? Was there any of it left that we might be able to identify?"

"No, sir. I'm afraid not. That was exactly how it was found." Adam shook his head sadly as he answered, thinking he had once again hit a dead end.

"Well now, lad – might you know the story be'ind this ring?" the smiling troll-man asked.

"How much can you stretch your imagination? The story I can tell you sounds a lot more like a fairy tale or science fiction than the truth. I believe it, but sometimes I think it might be because I want to so badly."

"I'm not an old man, but I've seen things that would make me old if I didn't 'ave a rather large mental ware'ouse where I can put things that are unbelievable. A dear old friend of mine calls it my 'vast cesspool of worthless knowledge.'" Adam and Colin chuckled at the same time. "You just 'ave to suspend a bit of disbelief to see the world through a whole new pair of eyes." Adam was nodding. "I can see from your face you understand what I mean, boy. Though, in truth, most people who live today 'ave been trained out of believin' in the fantastic. Cynics, and all that. Livin' 'ere, in an ancient place, you know of things that 'ave 'appened that no one would ever believe if they stuck to a traditional belief system. You 'ave to believe in the 'boogey man', I think you Americans call it, to believe much of what 'istory teaches us." Colin took the loupe out of his eye, placed the ring on the glass counter, and folded his hands on the velvet square in front of him. "Now, son … what story do you 'ave to tell me?" He leaned forward on his elbows and looked the boy square in the eye, prepared to listen. Not a hint of skepticism showed on the man's face.

So Adam told the kind old man about his mother disappearing when he was six years old and his father's search for her and the police investigation. He told the man about receiving a letter from Buckingham Palace a year after the disappearance and about the information they gave his father when he came to England at their request. He told Colin about the report from Scotland Yard's lab that authenticated the six-hundred-year-old letter they had found and the fingerprint that had been embedded in the sealing wax that the FBI had identified as belonging to his mother, Katharine. Producing the documentation that he pulled from his strongbox, Adam told about having the handwriting analyzed over and over, and the historians' opinion of the ring. Lastly, throwing his last thread of caution to the wind, he handed the curious little man the parchments that he had retrieved from the safety deposit box.

Colin read the letter. Then he reread it.

He looked up at Adam and smiled warmly at him. "So you're wantin' to go find your mum, is that it?"

"That's it exactly. I know it sounds crazy, but I think that if I can find a way to fix this ring, I might be able to use it to find my mother." He knew he sounded foolish, but this was the first time he had found someone who might be able to believe him.

"Yer cracked, boy. I don't think I've ever heard such a tale as this, and I've heard them all."

Colin chewed on his lower lip, deep in thought. He didn't speak for several moments, and when he finally did, there was a note of authority in his voice that told Adam he might just believe the farfetched story. "Say, boy, let's go to the festival and walk for a bit. I'll show you the world I grew up in and do a bit o' thinkin'. I do my best thinkin' when I'm walkin'. The bard contest is today and tomorrow. You'll find it very interestin' and a lot of fun. Many of the contestants come in costume. There'll be lots for you to learn. It's been a while since I've 'ad a young friend about, and I'd be eager to see 'ow you like my country. 'Ave we got a plan then, lad?"

"I'm game if you are," Adam answered, nodding and grinning. He could think of nothing he would rather do than attend the Welsh festival, and he couldn't find a better tour guide.

Adam was astounded at the amazing number of people who attended. They had come from all over the world. The assortment of folk art, poetry, music, dancing, ancient weaponry, and food was amazing. Adam would have been overwhelmed by it all had not Colin been explaining everything they saw each step of the way. They spent two hours listening to various poets and readers of ancient poetry and texts, then another three hours listening to the contest of the bards. The costumes were fascinating as were the music and the instruments. The food was terrible, but Colin seemed to enjoy it immensely, so the young man kept his mouth shut. Adam was on sensory overload by the time the two headed back to Colin's shop.

"'Ave you settled into a 'otel yet, son?" Colin asked as they walked down a street close to Merrill's shop.

"Not yet. I came straight to your shop. I don't carry much, so it's just a matter of finding a place close," he answered.

"Well now, lad. I think you should stay with me. I 'ave a friend you might want to talk to about your little treasure there. He's 'ard to catch, busy and all, but I could ring 'im for you. What do you think?"

"I don't know. I don't want to cause you too much of an imposition—"

"I'll 'ave none of that, boy." Colin waved his hand impatiently. "Now, my friend might just be able to tell you 'ow your ring worked. 'E can't repair it, but I figure the information on 'ow to use it is just as important as the fixin' of it. Now, would that kind of information be worth keepin' an old man company for a day or two?"

Adam laughed and shrugged his shoulders. "You've got me there. I haven't really had anybody to talk to the entire month I've been over here. I'd be happy for the company as well. But you have to let me take you to dinner as a thank you." Adam stuck out his hand.

Colin shook it. "So we've struck a bargain, then." So the two men set off for Colin's favorite pub to get a bite to eat. They had a wonderful time. The old man was a font of information concerning the fourteenth century, and Adam listened raptly. He was grateful for the ale, it dulled his tastebuds enough to make the food edible. After several hours, they paid the check and headed back to Colin's flat.

"Of course, your Royal Majesties are acquainted with the Baron Gray Duncan, who has been so kind as to gift His Majesty's treasuries most generously." The courtier bowed solicitously as he presented the enormous young man to the king and queen. The handsome man bowed low on one knee, grinning roguishly, green eyes twinkling. The monarchs studied him thoroughly.

In his early twenties, the man was extremely tall and broad, well-muscled, with thick hair that looked almost black – until the sun shone on it, when it gleamed the deepest red. Gray wore his hair a little longer than fashion allowed, not that he had ever paid attention to the dictates of fashion – he was too much like his mother for that – and a bit shaggy around the edges. There were enough scars on his face and forearms to evidence that he was seasoned in battle – even though they didn't take away from his rugged good looks. The huge man had a wild look about him, but control and discipline registered in every move he made, making him seem like a walking controversy. Fascinating to look at, Gray drew the eyes of all the young ladies at court.

The queen was the first to speak. "Ah yes, you must be that handsome young fellow our niece has her heart set on. She talks of you incessantly – Baron Gray this, Baron Gray that. And poor little Chelsea has it for your brother as well. It is amazing you are not already firmly ensconced in the family." She smiled benevolently at the giant of a man on one knee in front of her and held her hand out to him. "I understand you are quite a boon to our war effort."

With her permission, he rose to his feet, looking Phillippa square in the eye. Gray bent and kissed her extended hand. "Well, I don't know if I would say that...." he began. He spoke with just the hint of a Scottish burr ringing warmly through his words.

"Now baron, your false modesty does not suit the warrior I have heard tales of and that I now see before me," King Edward interjected. "Your gold, and that of your brother, has bought many arms for our men. Though I daresay that would anger your dear departed father, God rest his soul. He did, after all, spend the better part of his life stealing that gold from these very coffers." Everyone within earshot found this statement very amusing, and the twitter of polite laughter filled the air.

"Yes, Your Majesty, he did take great joy in pestering your father. But the gold I give to your efforts is my own, earned by my own efforts and with my own hands." Gray smiled warmly at the monarchs, "Now, Your Majesty, if you would allow me to take my leave, there is a man I must speak with regarding your next shipment to France. I understand that you are getting ready to make another push at Poitiers. And of course, I would be more than pleased to be of assistance to the crown."

"Well, of course, dear boy," the king assented, waving his hand benevolently and sniffing delicately into his embroidered linen. "We can only thank you for your generosity to England and the crown. Take your leave if you must, baron, but for the love of God and king, don't stay away from court for too long. My niece might miss you and take to her bed." Gray forced himself not to squirm at the thought. The king's niece was ugly, no matter what amount of paint they applied to her hideous features. Even the vast amount of money and land that was her dowry had difficulty making her attractive enough for a man to court – and there were many willing to marry for money alone. Gray mentally shuddered and returned his attention to the king.

Edward was staring at him critically, as if he could read the young baron's mind concerning his niece. "By the by, young Gray, how is your mother faring? I have heard tell that your father's untimely death was a great blow for her."

Startled by the question, it took a moment for him to change subjects mentally. "My mother? Lady Duncan is well. She mourns my father's passing deeply, of course, but she has always been a strong woman. She finds many diversions with which to occupy her time." Gray smiled at that, amused at the thought of his mother's 'diversions.'

"You will have to bring Lady Katharine to court so that we might meet the dear lady at long last," the king smiled solicitously at his baron.

"You're most gracious to extend your hospitality, Your Majesty, but my mother suffers from a shameful lack of decorum. She's a wonderful woman, do not mistake me, but set upon defying the rules convention would attempt to put upon her."

"Attempt, ay? So the woman is successful in her defiance, then?" The king gave an amused grin and lowered his voice conspiratorially while wiggling his eyebrows in a way Gray found comical. "I find those kind of women the most interesting," he said, winking at his wife.

The wink was not lost on Gray. "I, personally, must agree with you, Your Majesty. A spirited woman would certainly make life more interesting. At least my father found such to be true. And being raised by such a woman, my

51

childhood was truly an adventure."

"I have heard, from more than one source here at court, that your mother is quite a beautiful woman." A flicker of something Gray could not define flashed across the monarch's face.

"It is so, Your Majesty." Gray was becoming most uncomfortable. Forcing his defenses to remain hidden, he watched the king from under his lids.

"I would like to meet her." It was not a suggestion, but a command.

Why, Gray wondered. He decided to feign ignorance concerning the king's demand. "As I am sure she would enjoy meeting you as well, my king." Gray tried not to choke on the words. "I thank you for the invitation and will be certain to convey it to my mother when next I see her. Though I have no doubt she will regretfully decline Your Majesty's kindness." He bowed politely and again attempted to leave.

"And when might that be, Baron Duncan?" King Edward called after him. Calling him formally had the desired effect on the reticent baron – Gray felt as though his mother had just called him using his complete name. That always meant he was in trouble.

The man was not going to let this go, Gray thought in frustration. He turned back to give his answer, a strained smile on his handsome face. "I will be visiting my family home after I leave London, Your Majesty. It will take me a fortnight to reach it, barring any unforeseen circumstance." Gray bowed, hoping this foolishness would go no further. His mother would be hanged before she would kneel and kiss Edward's ring. She might even draw her dagger and plunge it through the man's heart, or her own – just to be dramatic in her defiance. He smiled inwardly at the thought. A shameful lack of decorum, indeed! If the man only knew!

The king bent down to his subject's ear and said, quietly and forcefully, "You will bring her when you return."

He had no idea what to say. Gray stared at the king quizzically, then nodded his assent. With that, he bowed crisply and turned and left the throne room, going over in his mind the strange conversation he had just had with Edward. How on earth could meeting Gray's mother serve the king?

Once in the hallway, he met up with an impeccably dressed nobleman who was moving back and forth by the wide windows, pacing in frustration. Gray's frown deepened at the sight of Alistair, he was a simpering fool who enjoyed inflicting pain on anyone he considered inferior. He stared the prissy man up and down before venturing further down the hallway. The man's high heeled riding boots, although not disguising his shortness a whit, made loud clicking sounds on the tile floor.

When Alistair spotted Gray, he stopped pacing, waiting for the baron to reach the end of the corridor so that he could speak to the wealthy giant without being overheard. Alistair, smiling maliciously, was obviously eager to see him, shifting from foot to foot in his impatience.

He tried to sound authoritative rather than nervous. "It's about time, Duncan! Where have you been? I've been waiting more than a quarter of an hour for you!" He straightened his ruffled tunic anxiously while he spoke.

"Ye'd better stuff yer impatience, man. Remember, it's ye that needs my gold, and not t' other way around." His Scottish brogue was unleashed in full along with his temper, as he no longer attempted to hide either one.

Alistair smoothed his perfectly groomed hair back from his forehead. His eyes narrowed angrily at the set-down. "Yes, yes, of course. Forgive me, Gray. I'm in a lather to attend to some preparations I must make." He excused his rude behavior with a shrug. "In any event, I have news. The king's ship, a beauty called the *Laney*, will be sailing in four weeks time. It sails from Hythe, bound for Normandy of course, carrying arms and gold. On it will be a large enough supply of longbows and enough arrows to make a pincushion of every man, woman, and child in the Norman kingdom." Alistair grinned maliciously at this. "Our longbow was quite devastating to the Norman forces at Crecy."

Gray thought the foul man might actually be picturing Norman women and children as pincushions and locking it away in his memory for pleasure at another time. It would probably be his present to himself at Michaelmas. He shook his head to clear his anger.

"As I told His Majesty, I'll be more than happy to donate to the king's effort. I shall have a fair amount of gold sent to the treasurer within the week." Gray dismissed the man with a wave of his hand.

Alistair ignored the dismissal. "And I, that is to say the king, will be most grateful for it. Have I told you? As a gift to reward my unwavering loyalty, the king is allowing me to have the pleasure of accompanying the *Laney* on her journey. She will also be accompanied by a warship to protect her. She'll sail from Hythe to Dunwich, where she'll pick up her escort. As you well know, the king's ships have been plagued by that roguish Gentleman Pirate of late. Can you imagine – the man calls himself a Gentleman Pirate! As if a man could be both a gentleman and a pirate!" He huffed dramatically, indignant.

He continued, placing his hand on his hip in a gesture that was supposed to appear fierce, but came off as feminine. "In the last year, three of our treasure and arms ships have been ransacked and all the men aboard them have been disappeared to another place. The ships were found, anchored and empty, at sea – never too far off the coast. There is never anything of value left on board, and the villain always leaves a parchment of apology secured to the door of the captain's quarters with his dirk, giving his word – his word, mind you! – that the men are unharmed. It is frustrating that we cannot discover where the men are being hidden away." He stamped his foot in frustration and pointed to Gray.

"Much of your gold was lost as well. It makes a man's blood boil! The warship hopes for attack, as all aboard will be ready. I am personally looking forward to watching the Gentleman Pirate meet his maker. I did tell you I would be aboard, did I not? If fortune is with me, I may even be allowed to watch the battle of Poitiers once we reach Normandy – from a safe distance, of course." He was like a child who had just been given a treat.

"Of course." Gray glared at him. "Ye may take yer leave now," he said forcefully.

Alistair ignored him with a sniff and a wave. "Are you going to call on the Lady Sara? She has been eagerly awaiting your arrival at court, she told me so herself." He arched his eyebrow knowingly.

"I do not court married women." His temper was growing, begging to unleash violence and mayhem on this disgusting beast of a man.

"You're a fool. She's a beauty, everyone says so. And her husband has made no secret that he would share her – for a price."

"Neither do I repeat myself, Alistair. Ye told me ye were in a lather to leave." He bit the words off in his mouth, knowing he was only a hairsbreadth from using this creature as target practice for his dirk.

Alistair shrugged and grinned wickedly, ignorant of his peril. "She wants you, you know. You don't even have to marry her. That's done. What man isn't interested in having a bit of enjoyment for himself? Although, you have been so loath to share yourself with the women at court, there have been rumors circulating bringing your choice of – shall we say – dancing partners into question." His grin broadened, provoking Gray past his willingness to control himself. He was on the small, prissy man in a flash, holding him suspended in the air by his throat, Alistair's feet flailing for purchase.

"There is no question. I am mourning a wife. Now be gone from me." Gray put him down.

Rubbing his reddening neck, Alistair contemplated what nasty thing he could say to regain his dignity and put this uppity Scot in his place. He smirked and began to speak. His huge adversary took a threatening step toward the prim little man. The small man's eyes grew huge with fear.

"Be gone Alistair, before I lose my temper entirely and make ye incapable of leaving this castle on yer own two feet, not to mention your precious journey." Gray's voice was soft, but his face was terrifying. Alistair – finally understanding the leashed menace in front of him – blanched, bowed curtly, and left the hall like he was on fire.

Gray shook his head, "Vile creature."

Not wanting to spend any more time than was absolutely necessary in this place, he left the castle, bound for the stables and then home. London was pretentious and stuffy – the people frivolous and immoral. But for Gray, the palace itself was absolutely suffocating.

In the stable, he found both his horse and his second in command, Percy. Percy was a tall and very handsome man, women would stop and stare as he passed. Fair-haired and thin, with patrician features, Percy was the antithesis of his liege lord, but in looks only. They were of like mind and purpose in every other way. The handsome blonde man was deep in conversation with a sweet little servant girl. They were closeting themselves away in a back stall, and the poor girl looked smitten. Gray tried not to grin – he couldn't remember how many times he had seen Percy's arms around women who looked thunderstruck. The man was a master. He had stolen more hearts that Gray had stolen chests of gold.

"Percy, we must away. Make your apologies to the woman." He didn't wait for an answer. He didn't have to. Immediately upon his pronouncement, the girl began to wail. Gray couldn't get the stable master to back out of the stall with his horse fast enough. Women were such a nuisance. He'd never met one who didn't caterwaul at the slightest little thing and cling like a wet tunic. Except his sweet Abigail. Just thinking about her made his eyes mist. He shook himself mentally, and the cold, hard look crept back into his eyes. There was no room for that kind of thinking in his life. He had the contents of one of his merchant ships to inventory and attend to and many things to tell his mother.

He thanked the stable master for the excellent care given to his horse, and in one fluid motion gained his saddle. He turned to see Percy right behind him, mounted and ready. The girl stood in the center of the stable, wringing her apron in her hands and weeping enough tears to fill a river. She raised a hand in farewell. Percy blew her a kiss in return. She smiled warmly, looking as though he had given her a treasure chest.

Intending to turn his attention from his most recent conquest, Percy slapped the flank of his lord's horse. It worked, making his surprised friend take several minutes to get the spirited stallion under control, and when Gray turned to glare at his second, Percy was laughing hysterically. The baron glared him into silence, and they were on their way.

Gray finally smiled when he was out of the city. Percy was happy to talk with his lord of their upcoming journey. After they were finished with the contents of Gray's ship at Hythe, they were riding for home, and Gray's mother would be waiting.

Eager to see her, Gray smiled at the thought of his homecoming. It had been several months since he had seen her, far too long. Katharine would be overjoyed to see him, and he loved to see his mother happy, especially after his father's death. A change had come over her since then. Instead of the happy, laughing woman she had always been, she was quiet and withdrawn, spending an inordinate amount of time talking to Garrett's grave.

Once upon a time not so long ago, his mother had been a true adventure. It was impossible to tell what she would do or think of for the family to do next. He still remembered when she had, with the help of several of his father's men, made something she had called a hang-glider and jumped off the top of the waterfall over the lake– "...just in case it didn't work," she had told them. The woman had flown! And the entire village had watched. His father had tried it next, but no one else had possessed the courage. The games she had dreamed up for the people to play had been enormously enjoyable as well.

A remarkable woman, Gray enjoyed her company almost as much as he enjoyed pricking her temper, which was fairly simple to do. He had taught her, in secret, to handle a sword when he had been a young man training under his father. She had taken to it immediately, and now, knowing her inclinations, he regretted doing her that service. She could best almost any of the men he knew with her sword and her bow, and if she had not loved him as she did, he might have been a wee bit afraid of her when she was in a rage at him. Of course, he would never be afraid of his mother. No matter what kind of state she had worked herself into, he knew she loved him and would never hurt him. Percy would remind him that it never hurt to err on the side of caution.

Percy was definitely cautious around Katharine. The woman had bested him at the sword more that once. His father, Rychard, had died when his mother was still carrying him. When Percy's own mother had died in birthing the boy, Katharine had taken on his care. She had felt it was her responsibility. The men had been raised as brothers – had fought like them as well, but when it came time for Gray to choose the man who would watch his back, there had been no other choice. Alane, his younger brother, had been too young, and Gray trusted Percy implicitly.

"The king ordered me to bring Mother to court."

"Surely you jest!"

"I do not. Can you imagine – mother at court?" Gray couldn't resist a chuckle.

Percy joined in. "The man truly has a death wish, doesn't he? She'd make short work of him – and his men." The two laughed harder at that.

Gray knew that when she heard he had promised her at court, she would probably take her dagger to him. He looked forward to telling her. She was so interesting to watch when she was in a rage, as long as you didn't get too close. Percy didn't even like to watch, but he loved to hear the stories afterward.

Alane would be meeting Gray at the ship and going home as well, he knew. It had been every bit as long since Gray had seen him. His brother had been busy with his own life of information gathering – his mother's euphemism for spying – and it had been far too long since the brothers had played chess. When the two men were together, they didn't play by the traditional rules. In their games, the first one to take the queen was the victor. It had been their father's favorite game, and he had passed his love for the strange rules on to his boys. Normal chess games were quiet, sedate. When Alane and Gray played, there was much laughing and, in the end, shouting. More than once the boys had been thrown outside to settle their chess-playing disputes, and more than once, they had both sported black eyes over the game. Gray smiled. It was fun. He had spent the last months forming a new strategy that was sure to humiliate his brother. If he succeeded, his mother was sure to roll her eyes and throw them both out again. Alane would be furious.

He prodded his horse into a gallop, Percy close behind. It would be so good to get home.

FOUR

"Amazing. I didn't ever expect to come across someone who could tell me so much from so little information," Adam told Colin after replacing the receiver of the little man's phone.

"'E is a wonder, ain't 'e?" Colin answered him with a nod and a wink. "So what did old Hugh 'ave to say about your ring?"

"Your friend Hugh was quick to say that anything he would tell me was purely theory, and that he didn't believe in time travel in general or the ring's powers specifically. That disclaimer aside, he explained to me that the markings on the band of the ring were operating instructions. They indicate, just as my mother said, that the ring could only be used on the summer and winter solstice, but that for the four days before the solstice one could look upon a different time. It doesn't tell you how.

"He explained that there had to be someplace in particular that corresponded with markings on the ring and the solstices, probably the only place the ring would function. He said this place would be significant in a non-conventional religious way, as the solstices used to be considered holy, or mystical, in the pagan religions. He told me to try ancient places of druid worship, starting with Stonehenge and looking at other similar altars if Stonehenge didn't pan out. He did laugh when he told me that if he was a magician and making a ring for time travel, he would use the grandest altar for his timepiece. The reason being that magicians usually have healthy egos and like themselves to appear greater than they really are.

"Hugh said the ring's markings didn't specify how one would choose their destination, but that it might be possible for him to research this in some of his ancient texts. He'll call back.

"He also said he'd really like to look at the ring if it was okay with me. Of course I told him it was. He thinks he might have seen one like it before, but that whoever owned it hadn't known what it was capable of. If it's okay with you, he'd like to meet us at the festival tomorrow to check it out. He'll meet us by the bard contest at noon, unless he hears from us otherwise." Adam finished his recitation with a sigh.

The older man slapped him on the shoulder, obviously pleased. "Sounds like a fine idea to me, son. It's been far too long since I've seen my old friend anyway. We went to university together. For a while we even competed for the same girl, Caroline, but she gave us the boot and married a barrister. Neither of us could believe we'd wanted a girl with such unbelievably bad taste. By the way, do you know what you call an honest barrister? Broke." Colin chuckled at his little joke. "Needless to say, Carolyn's barrister 'ad plenty of money. It's 'ard to believe anyone would give up this, isn't it?" He waved his short pudgy hand around his two room flat and grinned again at his own sense of humor. Adam laughed along with his host.

Colin Merrill's flat was directly opposite his one room store. The doors faced each other. Both were low, opening onto tiny dark rooms. The flat, at least, had a couple of windows that faced out onto the narrow alley and let in light. There was a tiny kitchen with a small, two-chair table that comprised the whole of the other room. The bathroom was down the hall from the flat. Colin shared it with the two other tenants of the floor. He slept on a hideaway bed that made back into a couch for daytime use. A dresser sat on the opposite wall. There was one other chair in the room and the only other furniture was several bookshelves, full to overflowing, with stacks of books in every spare corner and on every flat surface. There was no television or stereo in sight.

Adam examined the plethora of books. They were either written about different facets of history, archaeology, and religion, or the books were ancient texts themselves. Adam was sure the ancient texts were worth a fortune, yet this man lived such a Spartan existence.

Colin watched Adam move about, inspecting the room, and commented sheepishly, "I don't need much. Just my books and my insignificant treasures. They could keep my mind busy for years. Would you like to see some of them?"

"I'd love to!" Adam almost shouted, his eagerness evident.

The roly-poly little man practically danced to his closet and removed from it several large boxes. He looked exactly like a small child on Christmas morning. He carefully opened the first box and began gently laying many different sized boxes and bags on the floor in a semicircle around him. Adam had seen the same pattern around the man's easy chair. There had been a semicircle of books lying around the chair when they had first entered the flat. The man had quickly gathered up the books and placed them on top of one of the stacks in the corner, apologizing for his clutter. Now his clutter was a selection of precious trinkets Colin had gathered over the years and carefully saved.

He motioned his young guest over to the floor beside him and began unwrapping one item at a time. The things he was carefully laying out on the floor for Adam's perusal were museum quality pieces. He had never seen such treasures so closely, and he had the supreme pleasure of picking them up and examining them closely. It was completely fascinating.

His mother would have loved this. Joe told his son that his enjoyment of history had come from his missing mother. She had, as his dad had put it, wasted her time in college on all manner of history courses that had nothing to do with her major. They were the only classes she didn't cut on a regular basis. Adam understood the obsession. He loved his dad completely, but their interests had never coincided. The overwhelming total of their mutual interests could be summed up by two things – the basketball court and construction projects. Sometimes they even shared the odd Sunday afternoon football game and the occasional bowling match. But in things that were not physical, they had very little rapport. Adam had inherited far more than his mother's looks.

By the end of the evening, Adam knew exactly where Colin spent his money and why he lived such a Spartan existence. He was probably worth a couple of million pounds, but all the money he had went into his "collection." It was impressive, amazing even. So was his knowledge, the man was a veritable encyclopedia. By the time the two finally went to bed, Adam in his sleeping bag on the floor and Colin on his fold-out couch, Adam had learned more about the history of Great Britain than he knew about all other subjects combined.

His mind was whirling and he was happier than he had been in years. When he got back from his quest, he decided, he would go back to school and immerse himself in the study of history. Maybe, if he applied himself, he would one day know what this man knew and be able to ... well, he didn't know what one could do with that kind of education. What Adam did know, however, was that men who did what they loved were happy – no matter how much money they made.

He fell asleep hoping Hugh could tell him a lot more about his ring and looking forward to the next day.

They met outside a tent containing medieval embroidery samples and tapestries, right across from the ongoing bard competition. Hugh was a surprise. Adam had expected someone who resembled his new friend, but instead was greeted by a tall, handsome man, crisp and formal in his demeanor. The two were as different as rain and sun. How these two men had become friends was beyond Adam's imagination. Time travel he could believe, but these two as friends defied the imagination.

They greeted each other, Colin warmly hugging his old friend, who remained as stiff as an ironing board while waiting for the ritual to end. Adam could tell from the sparkle and warmth in the handsome man's eyes when he spoke to Colin, however, that he cared a great deal for his friend. The gentle way he spoke to his diminutive colleague left no question that the friendship was substantial and longstanding. The two old friends spent the first five minutes catching up on their lives.

Adam watched them, wondering how one woman could like such divergent men. Where Colin was short, bald, and looked like a troll, Hugh had a tennis player's build along with a full head of gray hair and movie-star good looks. His manner was intimidating, he could have been a crowned prince for the way he handled himself. He certainly intimidated Adam. Hugh spoke with the accent of a king, Colin sounded like a fishmonger. These two were their very own paradox.

When the pleasantries had been dispensed with, Hugh got right down to business. "Did you bring the item with you, I hope?" Hugh directed the question at Adam, who immediately pulled out his strong box and, carefully sorting through its contents, presented him with the ring.

As the tall man examined the ring closely, Colin said, "It's a beauty, isn't it, Hugh? I've not seen anythin' like it before, that's why I called you, the druids being your specialty and all."

"Astonishing! Do you know, perchance, if there were any fragments left of the stone that was set in it?" Hugh was still looking at the ring as he spoke.

"No, I'm afraid not. It's as it was found and given to my father. I was hoping you might know what had been set into it so that I could have it repaired." Adam was beginning to feel let down again. If Hugh didn't know what the crystal had been, he doubted anyone would.

"Well, it isn't important, one cannot know how it was cut even if the type of stone was known. However, if I remember correctly...."

"And 'e always does," Colin interjected happily.

"I have seen something much like this in a little shop over in Aberaeron, a small fishing village on the northwest coast. It's only a few hours' drive from here. I am interested in this intriguing puzzle myself, so if you have nothing else to do with the rest of your afternoon, I would be more than happy to lead the way to the little antiquities shop which houses, I believe, a ring identical to this."

Colin jovially slapped his friend on the back and offered to drive them all. Hugh diplomatically declined, stating that he had driven his own auto and it was parked just a block or so away. It would, no doubt, be infinitely simpler to let him drive.

Colin rolled his eyes playfully. "You're not still vexed over that insignificant mis'ap with the bus, are you now, Hugh?"

"No, no," he protested. "It's just that my auto is closer. Now, if there's no other discussion on the matter, let's be off."

They followed the tall man the length of the festival and back onto the main street where his tiny car was parked. Adam would never get used to the size of European cars. There was something to be said for gas guzzlers. At least in a gas guzzler you didn't have to sit with your knees wedged into your nostrils. When all three men had folded themselves into the automobile, they drove north towards Aberaeron.

It wasn't long before Adam was wishing he had taken a healthy dose of dramamine. He hadn't felt this motionsick since he had been driving through the smoky mountains of Tennessee with a bunch of his college friends. He desperately hoped he wouldn't have to ask his new companions to pull of the road so he could throw up.

Colin was in the middle of relating one of many humorous anecdotes from his past with Hugh. He turned to make a comical point to Adam and stopped short. "Hugh, you'd better open your window a mite, or it looks like our young friend there might be sourin' your floorboards. 'E's a bit green, 'e is."

Hugh was quick to respond. He rolled his window all the way down, gesturing to Colin to do the same. "Is it better back there now, young man? I'll slow it down a bit as well."

Adam had leaned back in his seat and was breathing deeply. "Thanks."

The three drove on in silence for a while, until Hugh spoke.

"It won't be long until you've grown used to our twisting roads. They can make a man ill, on occasion." He was obviously trying to comfort the young man, and Adam smiled in response.

"I'm sure I'll be fine in a moment."

The next few hours passed without incident, for which Hugh was extremely grateful. It wasn't long until they were passing into the small coastal town of Aberaeron.

The screaming and bellowing could be heard by the entire village.

"Get out, you little guttersnipe! No money in the world is worth keeping you another second!" an outraged woman's voice was screeching. "You've shown your ignorance for the last time in my home, make no mistake."

The beautiful sixteen-year-old girl sucked in her breath sharply. "Nana Inez, do you mean to say that you're paid to keep me?" the girl asked, astonished.

"Of course I'm paid to keep you! I most certainly didn't keep you because

I loved you! Do you think I would keep a nasty little orphan girl out of my warm heart? Nay, wench. Your mother was a whore, and you'll be nothing better yourself! Get out!" Inez hurled her cruelty like hatchet.

Ysabelle couldn't focus, she kept hearing the hurtful words. "You really never loved me?" she whispered, tears forming in her eyes.

"How could I possibly love something defiled and filthy? You're not fit to walk on the dirt of my floor!"

The words hit her like an armored fist. The girl visibly flinched against the older woman's cruelty. She tried to gather her thoughts, "But my tutors, my lessons...."

"I'll tell them you ran away. They'll believe me, they will. You were always such a stubborn, rebellious, puny little rat. Everyone will believe me. Be off with you, ingrate, and let the roving bands of thieves take you in. You'll pay them as well, but they won't want money. They'll teach you a trade befitting the daughter of a whore, they will." Inez grinned wickedly at the girl.

The girl gasped, unable to catch her breath, as understanding hit her. "I will not prostitute myself to anyone!"she shouted, tears beginning to flow. "And I won't stay where I'm not wanted." Ysabelle lowered her voice, struggling for control. "All I ask of you is that you tell me who my parents are, or at least who's been paying you for your tender care." She almost gagged on her words.

"Fools and trash, all of them. I told you to get out of my cottage, gutter rat!" With that, Inez picked up the water pitcher and threw it at the girl. Her aim was poor and she hit the wall, but Ysabelle was already out the door anyway. It slammed behind her as the wind took it. Pulling at her long, dark hair, the frigid wind bit through to her bones as if to aid the old woman's unkindness. Not enough to just throw the girl out, the nasty woman ran to the door and shouted for the whole village to hear, "You, girl, are the bastard child of someone who could never love you. If they did, they'd be raisin' you in their own home instead of peddlin' you off to the likes of me! You're the child of a whore, and no better than a whore yourself! It's all you're good for, and all you'll ever be!" Satisfied that she had shamed the girl sufficiently, the woman retreated into her cottage and slammed the door shut.

Ysabelle, weeping openly, walked toward the edge of the village. The wind was like a knife, and she had only her thin cotton dress to keep her warm. Inez always told her there was no money for such frivolous things as cloaks or woolen stockings. Although the woman had a fur-lined cloak and two pairs of woolen stockings of her own – a muff made of fur as well. Ysabelle had been hoping for a pair of woolen stockings as a gift for the village celebration of Aphelion – the day when the sun stands still – only four days from now. It was of no consequence, she wouldn't have been given a gift anyway. She squared her shoulders and began walking purposefully, but she could not stop her tears.

She spotted Liza, the dairymaid, coming toward her, pulling her small wagon. Liza was gazing at her with such barefaced sympathy it made Ysabelle cry even more.

Liza rushed forward and patted her friend's shoulder, "There, there, sweet Ysabelle. What 'appened this time?"

She wiped her eyes with the tips of her fingers. "She's thrown me out."

Liza sucked in her breath. "No! What did you do this time?" her friend asked sympathetically.

"I'm not sure. I had snared a rabbit for our evening meal. While I was cooking it, the spit came loose and dropped the poor thing in the fire. By the time I drew it out, it was completely scorched. She struck me on the back with her broom over and over and then she threw me out. She'll never let me back. This time I've done it, there'll be no going back." Ysabelle was hiccuping now. She wiped her eyes with her apron.

"You're better off without the likes of 'er, Ysabelle, and you know it. She was mean and coarse with you always. It's better to be alone and unharmed than 'ave to live with that witch!" Liza's eyes were blazing just thinking about how her friend had been treated for the whole of her life.

"Liza, she shouted to the whole village that I was a bastard child. That she was paid to keep me. I didn't know." She sniffed pitifully. "Everyone in the village knows now. And you know how people are."

"It's not true!"

Ysabelle shook her head. "It's true, Liza. It's true." She paused, "I have nowhere to go. I have no money, no food," she began to weep again, "I don't even have a blanket to lie under tonight, and it's so cold out now."

"Now, now, Ysabelle. It'll be made right in the end. It always is. God takes care of widows and orphans, remember?" Liza held her friend until her shoulders quit heaving.

"That's not what I've seen." Ysabelle's words dripped bitterness.

"Watch yourself, Ysabelle. That old witch in there has nothing to do with God, and you know it. Father Corey has shown you the way of it, hasn't he?" she lectured.

"I suppose he has. He's a good man," she began.

Liza interrupted her, "And God's a good God. And if I 'ear you say anything different, I'll box your ears!" She grinned and Ysabelle grinned and soon enough both girls were laughing. "Now, girl, you wait 'ere, I'll be back in less than a moment's time. 'Ere, eat this while you wait for me. No doubt, there was little enough food for you today, tender girl." Liza grabbed a piece of cheese off of her cart and tossed it to Ysabelle. Then she grabbed the cart by the handles and pulled it toward home at a run.

Ysabelle went to a wide tree that was by the side of the dirt road and sat down to gather her emotions and wait. She gathered her hair up in a bunch behind her head and used it as a pillow against the hard bark of the tree. When her tears finally subsided, she laid her back against the broad trunk and closed her eyes. Nibbling on the cheese absently, Ysabelle carefully considered the horrible things Nana Inez had screamed at her.

You're the child of a whore and you're no better than a whore yourself! It's all you're good for, and all you'll ever be!

If she was a bastard child of someone who had enough money to pay for her raising, then her parents were probably still alive. She was no longer an orphan!

You, girl, are the bastard child of someone who could never love you. If they did, they'd be raisin' you in their own home instead of peddlin' you off to the likes of me!

Her excitement was cut off before it could even register in her mind, for now she was a child born out of wedlock – and unloved at that. Much worse. And frankly, living with Nana Inez had made her think there was nothing worse. Now she knew better. As did the entire village.

Liza showed up on the road a few minutes later, running to meet her with a bundle in her arms. She was smiling broadly and shouting something. Ysabelle stood up, waiting. Threading her fingers through her hair absently, she attempted to neaten it a trifle from the rat's nest she'd turned it into using as a pillow.

When Liza was in earshot, Ysabelle called to her, "What've you got there?"

The girl stopped running just a few paces from her friend. "Come and look! Papa sent it." Liza's eyes took on a devilish twinkle. "He always hated that old Inez."

She joined her friend under the tree and laid the parcel down. When Liza unwrapped the string from around the parcel, Ysabelle almost cried with gratitude. A heavy wool blanket opened before her, loaded with bread, cheese, and two leather pouches.

"Milk?" the now homeless girl asked her friend.

"One skin holds milk, the other one ale. Papa said that even though you're young, it'll 'elp keep you warm now that the nights have turned so cold. When it's empty, fill it with water."

"I'm older than you." Ysabelle's eyes flashed at the opening of their old quarrel.

"Oh, yes, you're absolutely ancient."

Ysabelle huffed and raised her chin defiantly. "Many women are already married at sixteen. Some even have children."

Laughing, Liza agreed. "And what with your dowry and all, the men 'ave been flocking to your door."

Ysabelle joined in the laughter, rocking back on her knees. "Yes, they can't wait to get their hands on my extra pair of shoes!" As the girls screeched and laughed, it occurred to Ysabelle that she hadn't brought her extra shoes with her. It was just as well, she decided, since she would only have to carry them.

"I also put my woolen dress inside the blanket for you, Ysabelle. It's got a bit of weight to it. My other woolen stockings as well. You might need them." Liza was suddenly serious.

"Your papa will beat you for that, sure." Ysabelle knew she needed the warm clothes, but was torn between her own needs and not wanting her dear friend to get in trouble.

The other girl laughed. "'E won't. 'E never does, just threatens to anyway. 'E's all bluster. I've just almost finished a new one, I 'ave. And that one's a trifle too snug for my, well…." Liza said, looking down at her chest, "My assets. You know I'm more – what does my father call it – sweetly rounded than you." Both girls laughed uproariously at that.

"I brought you something else – something special." Liza reached behind her back and pulled something from under her cloak with all the flourish of the puppeteer at the fair.

Ysabelle gasped as she recognized Liza's mother's woolen cloak. Her father had been keeping it in a chest for Liza's wedding trousseau. "But it was your mother's!" she protested.

"Papa said it would be right. Mama always loved you. She wouldn't want you to be cold, not when she could 'elp you." Liza's eyes misted as she stroked the warm cloak lovingly. It had been less than a year since they had put her mother in the ground. Pulling the cloak around Ysabelle's broad but thin shoulders, Liza pulled the hood up and tied the ribbons tight. "And it's so cold now. I don't 'ave anything for your 'ands, but you can keep them wrapped in the blanket while you walk. You know, I never saw it before, but you're just the size of my mother." Her eyes shone wetly – the love and sorrow more than either girl could speak.

"Thank you, Liza. I can never repay you. You've been such a good friend to me." She reached out and stroked her friend's cheek, studying her for the last time. She would commit this moment – and her dear friend Liza's face – to memory.

Liza was a head taller than Ysabelle, and was muscular like an ox. Her blonde hair, cornflower blue eyes, and pretty face made those who met her think of her as feminine, a saving grace for her. She had broad, strong shoulders and a frame that could pull a plow. Ysabelle, on the other hand, was of average height and a bit on the thin side. Of course she was only given one meal a day, and that was little more than would barely sustain life. She was certain that with a week's worth of proper meals she would fatten right up. Her dark brown hair had a hint of red threaded through it, and when the sun shone on it, it gleamed like copper. It was thick, wavy and to her waist – she was told it was beautiful. Her face was beautiful as well, or so Father Corey told her. He told her it was God's compensating gift for the woman she was being raised by. Ysabelle had seen young men stare at her, so she decided the priest must be right, though it meant nothing to her.

She didn't feel pretty though. She felt like the unloved bastard child she was.

You, girl, are the bastard child of someone who could never love you.

She shook herself. All that was going to change right now. Her whole world could now be a new one. No one here knew where she was going, and she wasn't about to be rejected her whole life because of something she'd had nothing to do with. Her mistreatment stopped here. She couldn't help who her parents were, but she could help how she decided to live because of it.

"You'd best be going, Ysabelle," her friend hugged her tight. "If that nasty woman comes looking for you, you know she'll use the whip on you. Your back has enough scars to last you a lifetime."

"I'm sure they will," Ysabelle said bitterly, pulling away and shaking her head. "Last me a lifetime, I mean."

Liza hugged her friend again, tearing up yet again. Ysabelle's eyes clouded over as well, and before the girls were done with their good-byes, both of their gowns were soaked at the shoulder. They were too close and their friendship too unspoiled to require them to hide their feelings for each other. Giving Ysabelle one last squeeze, Liza hurried back in the direction of her cottage. There was still so much work to do before the sun set.

Ysabelle watched her go, wanting to cry until she felt better but knowing she must get on her way before the sun set and it grew icy out. She threw the straps of the leather pouches over her shoulder, retied her parcel, and set out on the road, hands shoved deep inside the blanket for warmth..

She felt at her waistband for the dagger Father Corey had given her, grateful for his lessons on protecting herself from others. The dirk was in place. Strengthened by its cool, smooth, metallic presence, Ysabelle knew she would be just fine. No roving bands of thieves would get the better of her.

Thinking of Father Corey, she thanked him silently for all the lessons he had given her over the years – reading, writing, scriptures, sums, French, Gaelic. Laughing to herself, she could just see the look on Nana Inez's face if she knew precisely how well educated her hated charge had become.

Father Corey made her memorize what he called the 'key to a satisfactory life,' "In a man's world, knowledge is power. Your mind can defeat a man's muscle through cunning and strategy on every day of the week."

The kind and gentle man of God had talked the blacksmith into giving her riding lessons, and being on a horse, saddled or bareback, had been her only beloved freedom. The priest had even taught her the basics of using a sword, but he would never tell her where he had come by that skill. It wasn't the kind of thing every parish priest knew. There was something intriguing in his past, she was certain – if only he had been willing to tell. Ysabelle blessed him out loud.

With a final whispered prayer, she decided to go north. Not stopping to look behind her, Ysabelle left the tiny village of Woodford behind her forever.

Today, my life begins.

FIVE

The three men entered the low door of the little odds and ends shop. A small bell announced their presence. As they allowed their eyes to adjust to the inadequate lighting, they waited for the proprietor to appear. No one came to greet them. Adam, not one to stand still for long, spent the time looking around the small shop.

Souvenirs lined the shelves, although there were no tourists to buy them. There was a small table crowded with clear glass jars full of old-fashioned candy. On the floor was a stack of cheap Oriental rug knock-offs. Everything but the candy jars was covered with a thick layer of dust. Spattering the surface of the jars were scores of fingerprints in the thick dust. There were a few glass cases at the far end of the shop, also under a thick coating of dust, housing different odds and ends of more than souvenir value. The ring rested in this case. It looked to be exactly like his own, right down to the markings he could see on the band, except that the stone in this ring was intact.

He recognized it immediately. Adam was so excited he could have smashed the case to get at the ring. Sensing his agitation, Colin hurried over to where the boy stood.

"Well, blow me down!" He whistled softly through his teeth. "Now boy, if you can keep your 'ead about you, we might just be able to walk out of this little place with this 'ere treasure for a song." Colin gave him a knowing look. "My friend Hugh, 'ere, will 'andle the negotiation, you just keep your American tongue between your teeth. We Welsh love to take a fair chunk out of an American tourist's wallet." The short trollish man grinned .

At just that moment, the shopkeeper bustled through the door. "What's that? Oh, customers!" He seemed surprised to have company. "Sorry, I didn't 'ear the bell. Now," he rubbed his hands together in anticipation of a sale, "What can this old man do for the likes of you gents today?"

Hugh addressed him, "I had heard that you might have some quality pieces of costume jewelry. I promised my wife that I would bring her a bit of something from my visit home, but I don't want to spend more than ten pounds."

The shopkeeper raised his eyebrows behind the half glasses perched on his nose. "Ten pounds, that's not much, you know, but I do have a few nice pieces over in my display cases."

"I've looked at your display cases," Hugh said disdainfully. "There really wasn't much to catch the eye."

The shopkeeper nodded his head jovially, "Oh, I'm sure that it's just the dust that put you off. My girl hasn't been around for a while. It makes for a harder time seeing the pieces clear enough to make a good judgment of their value. Where are you from, gents? If you don't mind my askin'." He bustled over behind the display cases with a rag. While he wiped them off, the three men trailed over to watch.

"We're from Cowbridge," Colin answered the man jovially. "Just doin' a bit of explorin' today."

The spectacled man was pulling out of his case several pieces, each laid casually on the dirty black velvet he set out for their display. "There now. Them's all fine pieces. Look 'em over, friend. I'm sure you'll find something for your sweet pretty at home." He was looking at Hugh steadily, willing him to find something that would enrich his store.

Hugh gave them a peremptory glance. "What about that piece there? What are you asking for that? It's not the usual thing. My wife might like it." Hugh looked as calm as Adam felt excited. As a matter of fact, the man looked flat bored. It was evidently a gift. Had Adam been negotiating for the ring, he would have offered the man all he had and more. Watching this was almost painful.

The shopkeeper was thrilled. "Now this isn't your usual piece. Found it in a cave, I did. It's old, maybe a coupla hundred years. Looked right ugly til I cleaned 'er up a bit. It's not ten pounds though. It's much too nice a piece. Won't take less than fifty." The man grinned, clearly thinking he had the handsome gent on his hook.

Hugh simply said, "No, thank you," and turned to leave the store. Adam feared a heart attack was coming on, but obediently turned to go.

The shopkeeper frowned and then, making some decision, followed him closely. "What would you be willin' to give for it?" he asked.

"Twenty."

The man about swallowed his tongue. "Twenty? For this? You've got to be bonkers, man! Won't take less than forty-five."

"Twenty-five."

"Forty."

"Thirty-five."

"Done!" The shopkeeper could hardly contain his excitement. Adam could hardly believe what he had just witnessed. He behaved himself, though. The only sign he gave of interest was a scant squeeze he gave Colin's arm while Hugh worked his magic. Colin had grinned at him and winked.

Hugh extended his hand to Adam, who dutifully gave him thirty-five pounds from his wallet. In turn the man gave them a small bag containing their priceless, inexpensive treasure. The three called thank you's through their smiles and headed out the door.

As the shopkeeper recognized Adam's accent, he smacked himself in the forehead, muttering, "Bugger, if that wasn't an American!"

Hugh, Colin, and Adam contained their laughter until they reached the safety of Hugh's car. Then they laughed and whooped. Adam scared the life out of both older men by giving a horrific Indian battle cry.

"Sweet heavens, boy! Where on earth did you learn that?" Hugh looked like he'd been slapped. "Is it an American custom?"

"Didn't mean to startle you, Hugh. It's just that way back somewhere in my dad's lineage is a Comanche Indian warrior. It's an old tradition. Whenever anyone in my family does something particularly wonderful or amazing, or has something equally good happen to him, they give the victory cry."

"That could scare the hair off an ape, boy!" Colin was laughing. Hugh started in as well, and it was no time at all before all three men were howling with laughter. Whether it was at their coup or Adam's behavior or both was anybody's guess. When the men had recovered themselves, Hugh handed the ring to Adam and asked him to compare the two.

"You can't imagine what this means to me. I'm so grateful. Thank you, Hugh. Colin."

"That'll do now, son," Colin told him. "We were only too happy to help."

"That we were," Hugh agreed. "The look on your face was priceless, much like the ring you now possess. Now we'll have to study a bit to find out the proper way to use it."

"Aye, we will, Hugh. But knowin' you as I do, I'm sure you'll find us an answer. I'm absolutely certain of it." The little round man was slapping his friend on the shoulder. Hugh seemed entirely too pleased with himself. Adam felt like he'd been given the world.

He pulled the ring from his strong box and compared the two. Identical. Except.... "Colin, what do you make of these?" When he leaned forward to hand them to Colin for inspection, he thanked his new friend again. The man patted his hand and took both rings from him.

"Simply amazing, Hugh. Identical. That fool had no idea what he just parted with. It's completely intact. Astounding." Colin looked the two treasures over thoroughly, making sure there was not even a symbol's difference. He smiled as he whispered praises of the object to himself.

Adam kept his laughter in check. The man was a collector, after all, and this was an amazing thing they had just acquired. "But look here,"Adam said, pointing to the inside of the ring. "These are different from mine."

"By gum, they are." Colin studied the symbols intently as they continued to drive.

As Hugh headed south towards Cowbridge, all three men postulated on how the ring might be used, what time of day, if there were words to say, and so on. Hugh was in the middle of an explanation of druidic religion when Colin inhaled sharply.

"What is it, old friend?"

"It's not possible, it's too simple." The round man was staring at the symbols on the ring, then looking inside the band and turning it slowly.

"What is?" Hugh persisted.

"The symbols on the inside of this ring aren't on the other. If I'm not mistaken...."

"You seldom are, Colin," Hugh said.

"That was what I was trying to tell you," Adam said.

"Well, blast if it's not true! It's Stonehenge! The symbols on the inside of the ring look like Stonehenge!"

Hugh pulled over to the edge of the road and brought the car to an abrupt stop. "Let me have a look."

Colin handed the ring over. Adam hung over the back of their seat, watching the two men in anticipation.

"By gum it is! Old friend, you're precisely right! And if you were to turn the stone in the ring towards the Altar Stone, it tells you exactly where to stand. Look! It does!" Hugh was as excited as Colin now. It didn't matter how hard Adam looked, he simply wasn't knowledgeable enough to understand what the two scholars were talking about. He could make out a vague resemblance, no more.

"I didn't think of that, but you're right! It tells you precisely! Adam, we may 'ave you on your way to your mum yet! And there's only six days til the solstice! Well, well, well, my boy. You just may 'ave a bit of good luck runnin' in your favor. Let's get 'ome and figure this out."

Adam agreed wholeheartedly. "We've got two days."

Hugh pulled back onto the narrow road and pressed his gas pedal to the floor.

The natural dock and, beyond it, the German Sea came into sight. Percy and Gray were atop a high hill where their vantage point was good. Although there were several more miles to travel before they would reach it, the two men could see their destination clearly. The ship had not arrived for them as of yet, so there was plenty of time to reach the shore. Smoke could be seen from a campfire at the site, Gray hoped it was his brother Alane. Explaining his presence at this port to prying eyes was not high on his list of entertainments. The location of Ellshope could only remain quiet if all of its inhabitants traveled with extreme caution.

At that moment Gray's attention was drawn by Percy, who had nudged him and was motioning down into the small valley at the bottom of the hill they were on. He pulled his eyes away from the smoke and focused on the scene unfolding before them. There was quite a commotion stirring down there. From their vantage point, Gray could tell that there was an altercation going on between a handful of the king's soldiers, identified by the colors of their tunics, and the dwellers of four tents. From the colors of the tent materials, Gray could tell they were rovers, or gypsies as they were called in some parts.

It appeared that the soldiers were bullying an old man and a handful of women. The old man had long, snow white hair, and a stringy long beard. The soldiers – young, strong, and heavily armed – were circling the ancient man, pushing him from all angles into each other – making sport of him. It was apparent, from the way the old gypsy moved, that he was having a hard time remaining on his feet. He was so thin it looked like a stiff wind would blow him down. Though not necessarily a short man, he was definitely frail-looking. And if the wrinkles on his face and hands were any indication of his age, it looked as though he should have been buried several years ago – or perhaps had been. Of the three women with him, one was as ancient as he was, one appeared middle-aged, and the last woman looked to be just hitting womanhood. A small child hid behind her skirts and there was a babe in her arms. Percy would no doubt be interested in saving her from the dastardly soldiers.

Gray glanced over at his companion. Anger burned and swelled in his eyes. Now, as far as Gray was concerned, bullying a band of thieves was acceptable, unless of course they were women, or if they were only protected by an extremely old man and the odds were grossly unfair. Five men against a handful of soldiers wouldn't require intervention. Five soldiers against three women, some children, and an old man required someone to even up the odds. He goaded his mount into a gallop, Percy fast on his heels, and rode down the hill at a breakneck pace. He swung off his horse in one fluid motion, the muscles in his chest and arms rolling easily under his skin. Before the soldiers even realized they had company, Gray was standing in the center of them, apparently calm – even a trifle bored, but obviously looking for trouble.

"Gentlemen, it seems ye're sufferin' from a bit of bad judgment. Disband now, leave these innocents as they were, and ye'll be saved a thrashin' from me." His smile was easy, deceptive.

"And who might you be, bloke? Are you really so foolish as to defend a band of thieves from the king's soldiers? They stole something from our camp and we're 'ere to retrieve it." The largest of the soldiers puffed out his chest in a display of his great masculinity, although he only succeeded in impressing himself. He was nearly as tall as Gray, but nowhere near as muscular. "You're quite the fool to blow such smoke at us without so much as a sword to assist you."

Gray looked down at his side in mock surprise. "Well now, it does appear that I've forgotten my sword. Percy," he called over the soldiers heads, "did ye find my errant weapon?"

"Aye," Percy called in return, holding up the weapon with a grin. "It appears to have jumped from yer belt to yer saddle. Would ye like me to bring it to ye, milord?"

"Nay, friend. I'll not have need of it for now."

The small band of gypsies were looking fairly relieved until the soldier made that observation. When they examined their savior, they saw that he indeed did not even possess a dagger to fight these armed soldiers with. They watched as his second reattached the sword to their would-be savior's saddle. The tall handsome man that was his companion didn't even bother to dismount. He leaned on his horse's neck, his arms lazily crossed over the top of his saddle, idly watching his friend talk his way to his death. What could possibly be wrong with him? He was obviously strong of body, but weak of mind.

Now that Gray was close to the old man, he could see that not only was his body frail and weak, but his eyes as well. He was squinting and craning his neck to see up to Gray's face and identify his champion.

"We dint steal nuffin from them what stands there. We's jus tendin' to our li'l ones and tryin' to pull up stakes. They won't let us leave wiv our tents. Ow's we to keep our li'l ones warm in this cold wind?" The old man ended his speech with a loud, hoarse cough, that made it sound as though his ribs were rattling together. Gray looked on him with sympathy. It was deadly cold out here and this ancient patriarch was trying to take care of his women – wife, daughter, granddaughter, babes.

"What did they take from yer camp, soldier? Yer sense? Or simply yer mercy?" He was baiting the group now, angered by the cruelty of their sport.

74

Men of honor didn't tread on weaklings.

"They stole our...." the leader paused, obviously trying to come up with some object to accuse them of pilfering, "our peace of mind."

His companions broke out into rowdy laughter at that, and one shoved the old man again. Gray caught him and, glaring at the circle of the king's men, helped him out of their midst and put him into the thin, strong arms of his middle-aged daughter.

"Now, gentlemen, and I use that term in the broadest of definitions, if ye're so desperate for a fight that ye'd assault a blind old man, then be sure ye may have one."

"Now you're spoutin' your mouth off, fool. We've got more than the likes of you can 'andle, no matter 'ow big you are!" A different man, grinning viciously and showing several gaps where missing teeth once rested, shoved Gray in the chest, and blanched when he felt the solid muscle underneath his mail shirt. He quickly recovered himself, however, and spit on the ground in front of Gray's feet.

"Aye, men! The bigger they is, the harder they hit the ground!" shouted the smallest of the soldiers.

"And the bigger the dent they leave!" bellowed another through a peal of laughter.

The youngest woman glanced up to see Percy's reaction to that insult, expecting him to dismount and help his friend. Percy grinned at her and winked. She decided he was daft. He decided that she was much too pretty to not have any male to protect her. He winked at her again, causing her to blush and turn back to the trouble brewing in front of her.

"I have terms. We'll discuss them before ye beat me senseless. I assume ye are capable of honoring yer word." Gray glared at the one who had spat at him, and the man glared back, waiting impatiently to be given the word by his superior.

"We are, and I'll not ignore the insult. Your mouth 'as earned you an early grave. What be your terms?" The soldier stood, hands on hips, waiting.

"If I win—" He was interrupted by their bellows of laughter. He began again, ignoring their malicious behavior, "If I win, ye'll allow the rovers safe passage through this area without exactin' any vengeance on them."

"And?"

"And nothin'. Those are my terms. Agreed?" Gray's stormy eyes had turned cold and almost black. Raw power radiated out from him like a hot wave, and when one of the soldiers looked up into his face, he took an involuntary step backward. Fear etched itself on his previously arrogant face.

The leader didn't notice. "Agreed. Fetch your sword. I've only the time to dispatch your arrogant corpse before my evening meal. And I don't like to wait for me food."

"I'll fight as I am, but it 'll be most difficult for ye to eat your evenin' meal without a full complement of teeth," was Gray's answer. He flexed his hands, itching to begin. He watched their eyes, waiting for one of them to telegraph his first move.

"I'll be sure to recite those words over your funeral pyre." There was the ring of metal on metal as the five soldiers pulled their swords simultaneously and began circling Gray like wolves moving in for the kill. He started smiling – a vengeful, angry smile. He looked as if he were going to enjoy this immensely, the woman standing and holding her father thought to herself. At that moment, she had no doubt that this giant warrior in front of her would best the cruel soldiers.

The circle tightened around Gray. As soon as the first man was within striking distance, Gray became a blur of powerful motion. He planted his boot in the man's chest and the air rushed out of him in a whoosh even as the sickening sound of splintering bone filled the air. The blow sent him sailing through the air backward, a look of terror blended with agony of his face. The man was in a heap on the ground and his sword had been flung to the feet of the youngest gypsy woman before he even had a chance to strike. She picked up the sword and slid it out of sight behind the fabric of her tent.

As soon as the action registered in their minds, the two soldiers closest to him set upon Gray, lunging in his direction at the same time from both of his sides. He smashed their skulls together, leaving them in a bloody heap on the ground. Neither moved. The last two shouted as they ran at him, one from in front and one from behind, swords swinging, blasphemies coloring the air. Gray turned in a flash, grabbed the soldier on his right by the arm wielding his weapon, and propelled him toward his compatriot – driving the sword through the man's chest completely. The mortally wounded soldier sunk to his knees, eyes glazing over, staring at Gray in astonishment. The last one on his feet, the leader of the small band, had only time to turn slightly before he started howling in pain as his arm snapped and excruciating pain radiated its way instantly up to his neck and invaded his chest. He hit the ground, mewling like a cat – eyes wide and glued on Gray, terrified of his next move.

"Do ye yield?"

"Aye."

"Then leave this place. And be quick about it."

"But my men...." he began.

"Have gone wherever the devil 'll send them. Be gone from here and leave these people in peace." Gray towered over the soldier. The broken man was perspiring freely and holding his arm, agony etched on his face. He stood with great effort and, without a backward glance, took to the trees on the edge of the clearing, leaving the five horses behind.

Gray surveyed the damage, satisfied that there would be no more cruelty to these defenseless people. He wasn't even winded. He turned to the tiny group who had watched the display in amazement, and smiled kindly. The expression he wore when he looked at them was gentle – completely opposite the savage they had witnessed fighting. He was no longer the raging animal who had defeated five men without even breathing heavily.

The patriarch approached him boldly. "I thank you for your assistance. We don't 'ave much, but what we 'ave you're welcome to take wiv you." He bowed slowly and painfully.

Gray waited for him to straighten up. "I thank ye for yer hospitality, sir, but I must continue my journey. A wise man would leave this place quickly. No doubt the men who were traveling with these will seek vengeance. And don't take the horses they left behind, or there will be reason for them to hunt ye down and hang every member of yer band, guilty or no, right down to the babe in arms. If ye wish sanctuary, seek the home of Lady Ullswater, and tell her that Gray Duncan sent ye. Her home is but a short distance from here to the west, across the first hill and to the other side of the lake. Go quickly now." Gray bowed to the band and mounted his horse with the same grace and fluidity he had fought with. He smashed fists with his companion amiably, Percy winked again at the young woman, and the two were gone.

"Father, are you well?" the middle-aged woman asked, approaching the old man.

"Aye, but we'd better do what the fine gent told us to. Pull up stakes, we 'ave a bit of walkin' to do yet before dark."

"Yes, Father," she said with a nod, and motioning to the other two women and the children, the small band of rovers packed their scant belongings and headed to the promised sanctuary.

They were warm and fed and asleep in their tents by nightfall, safe inside the courtyard of Lady Ullswater's castle.

"There's a ship, milady! A ship!" The young watchman came rushing down the steps from the tower, shouting at the top of his lungs. "Lady Katharine," he called again as he ran into the great hall looking for her, "a ship's approaching!"

She dropped the tapestry she was working on to the seat of her chair and followed the sentry, Cedric, back up to the tower lookout at a run. To Hades with dignity, her boys were coming home! When they entered the turret room overlooking the ocean, the lookout pointed, then had her look through his glass.

Katharine could see the pennant flying over the flag of England – donkey facing lion, both on hind legs. It was Gray and Alane! She slapped Cedric on the shoulder and whooped loudly. Lifting up her skirts, she ran swiftly back down the steep stone steps, shouting orders to the servants in preparation for the coming ship.

He stared after her in shock, his mistress had never behaved with so little dignity before in his presence. Cedric had heard stories, of course, but he never believed them. The closest he had gotten to witnessing her behaving in a shocking manner himself was when the soldiers and their wives were playing the game she had taught them, bat and ball. He had still been a child then. Her son Alane had thrown the ball to Lord Garrett and gotten her 'out' on base, and she had let loose with a most unladylike expletive.

Cedric's mother had covered his ears and told him that although their mistress was a wonderful woman and full of kindness and compassion, sometimes her temper got the better of her. She was able to drive their noble leader daft with a simple kiss, and the warriors told stories of both her courage and her foolishness. Often the stories caused the men to bellow with laughter. But whenever a few men were needed to go with Lady Katharine on any routine chore or hunting trip, there was never a shortage of volunteers. She always led them on glorious adventures, and no one ever knew what would happen when she was about.

If she had been dead, they would have called her a legend. She hunted as well as any man, being expert with her bow. On the first of every month she had called for everyone on Ellshope to have a day of games and tournaments as a break from their daily work. In the footraces she could still run several miles without stopping, often beating a good many of the men. She was always in the top scorers at target shooting, her arrows always in a tight grouping at the center of the target. She had taught their children many wonderful games that were enjoyed by all. And she was an old woman, that was the wonder of it. At forty-nine, she should have been sitting by her fire working on her tapestries, not spurring the warriors on to best her.

Until the last year, Lord Garrett had stood by his wife's side, proud as a peacock. Of course, he could afford to be proud, he was the only one who could best her consistently – a fact that chafed her to her very soul. He had been the legend she was married to – legend because of both his size and abilities. An enormous and skilled warrior, he himself had bested the English monarchy more than once on the battlefield. A born leader, his men's loyalty was unswerving. He was a merchant who had amassed a great fortune through his cunning and silver-tongued gift of persuasion. Until the Laird MakLaughlin had killed him in an ambush, Garrett Duncan had been a man only a fool would pit himself against. The retribution the Duncan warriors had meted out upon the MakLaughlin clan had amply demonstrated that. But most of all, Lord Garrett had been an example to all of his vassals and warriors of how a man should love his wife.

Lady Katharine had taught all of the women of the island to read and write, and had insisted that the girls be allowed to sit in on the lessons previously only given to the boys from childhood on. She had showed the women how placing certain foods beneath the frigid waters of the lake for storage would keep them from turning foul quickly. Against the dictates of the church, she had taught the women more about childbirth and health in general than anyone else knew anywhere. And she had made them quit burying women who died in childbirth in unhallowed ground, persuading the priest that a loving God would never condemn a woman for dying doing her duty to her husband and country. These things Cedric had grown up with, so he knew them to be true. His mistress was definitely a woman to be reckoned with.

Other stories circled the village every now and again concerning her – that she had been the one who showed them how to bring water into their houses through pipes and heat it with the sun, that she had been the one to teach them how to make their spyglasses, and taught them how to use the black powder Lord Garrett brought back from the Orient to hurl projectiles at their enemies. But to believe that a woman had been the intellect behind their most effective weapons was beyond his ability to imagine. The rumors were hog swill. It was easy to believe Lord Garrett was brilliant, but Lady Katharine – smarter than even the learned men of their time? That was hard to swallow. Cedric believed that she was a fine lady with no question, even quite unique, but not extraordinary in that way.

Cedric had been at his post for the year since his training was completed, and considered himself very wise in the ways of his world. He shook his head over the mistress. If all women were like her, he would never marry. After all, a man should understand his opponent before he goes into battle. He put the glass back up to his eye to check the progress of the ship. Sails flying, oars in the water – it wouldn't be long before the vessel made it to the mooring. Cedric mulled over the rumor that she had been behind the new design of the ship they were in the process of building – it had no oars and several more sails than the ones they had been using for the so many years he couldn't count. All of the warriors were enthusiastic, it would save them rowing.

The barons, he had to chuckle at that title, would be here soon. It was always good to have them back. Everyone participated in the feasts and dancing. Laughter and music could be heard late into the night when they were home. And since their father had been murdered by that turncoat MakLaughlin, it seemed to be the only thing that brought Lady Katharine's laughter out of hiding. Her laughter used to echo through the stone passageways of the castle. Now they were quiet most of the time. Although Cedric was skeptical of her rumored abilities, he hated seeing her sad. She was such a beautiful woman, it was wrong for her to frown.

From the tower Cedric could see the welcoming party heading toward the mooring. Not satisfied to sit and wait for anything, Lady Katharine was with the warriors, keeping them at a bustling pace. The small-but-well-armed group was trooping through the fields and up to where the path cut through the cliffs sheltering the island from both weather and invaders. A contingent of soldiers with bows at the ready had been posted around the cliffs above the mooring on the off- chance that an enemy was flying the Duncan colors. The ship was getting close.

"Make haste, men, they'll be putting up to the mooring any moment now, and I don't want to miss them!" Katharine was running now.

Garen caught up to her and held her back by the arm. "Milady, for the sake of caution, slow your pace. It would be best to allow us to greet our visitors at your side, and we are not dressed for a race." He was smiling broadly at her. Fair-haired and handsome, Garen had been trained by Garrett to take over as second in command if his close friend and advisor Lance ever stepped down. During the battle where Garrett was killed, Lance lost an arm and, concerned that he could no longer fulfill his position, had turned his duties over to the younger man. Garen had shown his unswerving dedication and ability time and time again since then.

Katharine smiled at him sheepishly. "Of course, Garen. My enthusiasm ran away with my logic. Please forgive me." She held her hand out in front of her to allow him to lead the procession, missing the smiles of the warriors in her company. Her enthusiasm was largely why they liked her, and worried about her, so much.

At the top of the cliff the path became narrow and treacherous. Here they stopped to wait, much to the lady's chagrin. It wasn't long before the party could hear the excited calls of men down below, and the stomping of feet on the hidden path. After a few moments Alane appeared, followed closely by Gray. Percy was the next to come up off the path, closely on his friend's heels. As Katharine ran forward to meet them, her two sons engulfed her in their giant arms and hugged their mother tight. Percy waited for the boys to finish greeting their mother and then stepped up and took his turn.

Gray spoke first, "The men will finish unloading the ship. I'm eager to get home and tell you what I've learned. I believe Alane has some useful information as well. Although I'm sure you won't find what he has to say nearly as useful as the information I have to tell you." He looked meaningfully at his brother, the twinkle in his eye clear.

"I am quite sure you're wrong, big brother. And the secrets I learned in France will be most useful, certainly more so than yours, brother, for our next … well … adventure." He looked around at the men accompanying his mother to gauge their reactions. Their faces gave nothing away.

Katharine decided to interrupt their sniping and ignore them completely. "And Percy, how have you been faring? Still breaking hearts?" she asked the tall, handsome man standing behind her son. "Or have you decided to make some poor, sighing woman very happy indeed?"

"Ah, milady, you know me well. Tis true I've been unable as yet to choose only one. Women are such wondrous creatures. But of course, I never would have known that had you not been kind enough to raise me. I'm afraid I may never find a woman to measure up to you, milady." He bowed deeply and kissed her hand.

Katharine laughed and then smacked him playfully on his chain-mailed chest. "Percy, you devil. I should have had Garrett put you over his knee more often. Now boys, let's get started. Cook will be waiting the evening meal on us, and you know how impatient she is."

"And has been since I was a child. Surely she's getting too old to cuff us anymore." Gray looked hopeful.

Alane laughed. "She'll never be too old to beat a rake like you, brother. An invalid could best your strength. You're so small and frail." He enjoyed his joke immensely, being slightly taller than his older brother. Both brothers' shoulders were as broad as a doorway, well muscled, and strong. They were constantly attempting to best each other, both with wit and strength.

"And none of you gentlemen will ever grow up enough to quit pricking her temper, that's certain," Katharine said, laughing. "And before we reach home, I'll tell you boys – and if you've more than half a mind you'll take my warning to heart – there will be no fist fighting and no playing capture the queen. I've welcomed home men, *gentlemen*, not rough and tumble children."

Alane and Gray eyed each other and grinned mischievously as they fell into step behind their mother. Gray pulled a chess piece from the leather bag dangling over his shoulder and waved it at his brother, eyebrows raised in challenge. Alane nodded vigorously, then pointed to his boot. When his brother looked down, he made a grinding motion with his heel, then kissed his fingers and waved good-bye. Percy broke out laughing and Katharine turned to see what the joke was. The three men did their best to look innocent, but she knew better.

"Garen, perhaps I should consign my sons to your care. It seems they are already plotting against me."

"I'm sure, milady, that your new whip will be quite satisfactory at keeping your ill-behaved children in line." Garen emphasized the word children and smiled at the men. "She has been practicing with it, gentlemen, and I assure you, her aim is quite lethal." He grinned when the huge men blanched at the threat. "Ah, it's always good to see grown men afraid of their mother. It shows they were brought up well."

Everyone in the small procession laughed but Alane and Gray, and after a moment they joined in as well. Alane reached over and gave his brother a playful punch on the arm, and Gray returned it. Both men smiled.

It was good to be home.

Ysabelle pulled the woolen dress over the one she had on. The wind was cutting cold, and bound to grow colder after the sun finished setting. She pulled the heavy woolen socks Liza had stowed in the blanket over the thin, ineffectual ones she was wearing and then pulled the cloak tightly about her. She put the leather bags on the ground, wrapped the blanket about her, and lay down to sleep with her head on the soft bags. She said her prayers as Father Corey taught her, and begged God to keep her warm inside this tiny, inhospitable opening she had stuffed herself into. Father Corey had told her a small space would help her own body keep her warm. She hoped it was true.

Ysabelle hummed to herself a song that had kept her company ever since she had been a small child. And if she ever needed comfort, she needed it now. It was hard to go to sleep when she wasn't sure if she would wake up.

"Please, God, keep me warm enough tonight. And if it's not too much trouble, send me someone to talk to." She crossed herself and resumed her tune.

She had heard the tune somewhere, she was sure, but Nana told her not to be dim-witted. "It simply isn't possible for you to have heard anything so silly from me, I never sang to you. You made it up in your foolish youthful head, just like all those other tunes you annoy me by singing."

In one way, at least, Nana was right. Ysabelle had always loved to sing and was forever making up songs. The old woman would screech at her to shut up her noise whenever she was around, but she could never make the girl quit in her heart. The music was soothing, and it put wings to her dreams. Dreams needed to fly, Father Corey told her that, and there was no sin it. Nana said it was sloth, even as Ysabelle cooked and cleaned and mended and tended the garden and hunted for their suppers. To Ysabelle, it gave her a way to escape her life, even while she was a prisoner of it.

She sang out loud her favorite lullaby. Even though it was melancholy, it had always given her hope, but especially now that she knew of her true origin, it meant even more to her. It was sad and sweet, and something she imagined her mother would have sung to her once upon a time, had life been different. Her father confessor had taught it to her, weaving a beautiful, imaginary story of a loving mother and her much-loved, missing child.

Far away, long ago –
I, my sweet one, loved you
Once upon a better time,
You were my sweet child.

And someday you will find
Someone destined to love you.
Once upon a better time,
You'll be someone's love.

But Ysabelle had changed the words as she grew up. With all the romance blooming in any young girl's heart, she now she sang:

Far away, long ago –
Someone, somewhere loved me.
Once upon a better time,
I was someone's child.

And someday I will find
Someone destined to love me.
Once upon a better time,
I'll be someone's love.

A song for an innocent young woman who wanted more than anything to find a place for herself. She knew it was silly that it should make her feel better, but it was a piece of her childhood she wasn't yet ready to relinquish..

Ysabelle fell asleep humming to herself quietly, savoring the only comfort she had ever known.

SIX

A loud clacking sound woke her from her fitful sleep. It took Ysabelle a moment to identify the source of the sound. It was her teeth. They were chattering in tempo with the shivers that were convulsing her freezing body. She couldn't remember ever being quite this icy before. The sky around her had lightened to a metallic gray, and although it was early, she could see and smell the clouds. They were threatening snow, probably lots of it. Not the weather of choice for traveling on foot.

She sat up, trying to keep the blanket from pulling away from her and letting the icy air into the small pocket of warmth it provided. There was no sense in attempting to sleep anymore, she would be warmer on her feet and moving. Her bread and cheese half gone, she had kept the remainder of the food under the blanket with her so they wouldn't be too frozen for her to eat this morning. When she cut, with a bit of difficulty, a small piece of cheese with her dagger and popped it into her mouth, she was grateful for her foresight. It was very cold, but at least she could chew it. There was such a long way to go today, she would definitely be needing her strength. After polishing off what was left of the piece of cheese, she tore the end of the one loaf of bread she had left and ate it. She polished the meal off with a good drink of her milk, then tucked the leftovers into her apron and tied it up. She cleaned her dirk – a weapon would get dull as quickly if it wasn't kept clean – and put it back in her waistband. Wrapping the blanket around her tightly, she began her day's trek to her new life. Although she wasn't sure where she was going yet, she knew it would be a long way from here.

Father Corey had explained to her that making a new identity wasn't all that difficult, had even told her how to do it. Even though she had no doubts of his sincerity toward his calling, Ysabelle was relatively sure he spoke from experience. So many things about him didn't fit with the life of a man of the cloth. There was the vast amount of knowledge he possessed on subjects a priest should know nothing about, then there was his skill at combat and his ability to handle a sword. He wasn't half bad with a dirk either.

He had been preparing her all this time, she suddenly realized, for this eventuality. Had it been so plain, then? Had everyone known save her that she would end up out here alone? She silently thanked him for his kindness and foresight. So many orphans and widows were left to forge their way alone, without the skills she had been taught. She thanked Liza and her father as well, and said a prayer for her three benefactors, asking God to bless them for their kindness towards her.

She would reach the stone monument that marked the times of the ancients by tomorrow nightfall. Ysabelle hoped to be far enough past it that she could sleep beyond its plain. So many stories were told by firelight about the mysterious, magical place. Ghosts, witches, and other terrors were said to walk the ruins by night. Not being one to believe in such nonsense, Ysabelle didn't feel like testing her resolve by the dark of night in such a frightening place. It was much easier to courageously not believe by the light of day and far away from evil's playgrounds. She shuddered in spite of herself. Pulling her cloak and blanket tighter about her, Ysabelle hurried on.

"Now Adam, If you'll stand at the opening of the 'orseshoe formation and 'old the ring in front of you, stone in ... that 's right ... now it's exactly the same shape as the rock formations. All right now – no, I said the stone should be turned toward you – turn to your left ... look at the ring, boy ... you'll see that the first symbol to the left of the stone in the band is shaped exactly like that formation there. See it?" Colin was speaking, instructing Adam on how they had decided the ring had to work. "Now if you look to your right now, see that there, son? It's the same. The pattern on the ring is the same as the sarsen formation." He paused. "To my way of thinking, you'll start where you are – at the mouth of the horseshoe shape – with the ring on your hand and pointed directly in front of you. But from there, I don't know what to tell you." He stopped, thinking, his face screwed up into a very strange expression. For just a moment, he truly did look more troll than man.

Hugh walked up at that moment, arm extended towards the enormous outer ring of rock formations, counting them. "As long as we're making up such impossible theories, think about this. Perhaps each sarsen formation is a portal. A different time period through each one. It could be that all one has to do is walk between the stones. After all, all things being considered, the simplest theory is usually the right one."

"Amazing. Simply amazing." Adam stared at the identical configurations on the ring and in front of him. "I'm not sure what I would do if I hadn't found you guys. Still, we're almost out of time. Tomorrow is the solstice. We've been fooling around here all day for the last three days."

"Not to worry, not to worry. This is as much excitement as we've had since we were chasing Caroline around the university, isn't it, Hugh?"

"I have to agree with you there, Colin. Even though I must tell you I think this is so much rot. Take heart, young man. If this doesn't work out for you, there are at least nine hundred structures of a similar nature throughout England and Wales." Hugh nodded his head decidedly.

Adam groaned goodnaturedly. "Nine hundred – really?"

"Absolutely. Maybe there's a ring that fits each one. You never can tell. Your ring may not fit this monument. It might be for another one entirely, that would most certainly be more likely than both rings fitting this one, especially since yours didn't have these markings. Maybe this ring was made for a particularly inept magician who had to keep his instructions written down. It would only take the next ten or fifteen years to check them all out. Take heart." Hugh laughed heartily at the distress on the boy's face.

Colin chuckled to himself, "Don't listen to 'im, son. If 'e really thought it was rot, 'e wouldn't be 'ere. Let's just say he wants to keep his skepticism healthy unless there's ample reason to damage it." Both Hugh and Colin laughed at that.

"I suppose you're right, old chum. I like to keep all of my airs intact until I absolutely must make a fool of myself." He chuckled. Stepping towards Adam to take the ring, he stopped dead in his tracks. "Good heavens," he whispered, staring with his mouth open towards the stones they had been discussing.

"You look like you just swallowed a hornet, Hugh. What on earth...." Colin stopped as well.

It took Adam a full minute before he realized that his friends had become totally quiet. When he looked over at them and saw their faces, he looked in the direction that held them paralyzed. Between the upright sarsen stones they were staring at was a landscape that was totally opposite the one surrounding them. All around Stonehenge it was summer – warm June weather, beautiful sunshine. Between the two upright stones, it was gray and bleak and – he rubbed his eyes, unbelieving – snowing, of all things.

"Impossible! It's just...." Hugh stood aghast.

"Impossible, Hugh? I'd say we're lookin' at it, so it must be possible." Colin looked to his left. "And look there! It's another one. Well, old buddy, I would say your theory was correct – no matter what it was born of."

Adam followed Colin's gaze to see a rock and sand landscape. If you were totally quiet, you could even hear the ocean at a distance.

"Astonishing! I'll be darned," Hugh followed his friend's gaze.

Adam said nothing. He turned back to the snow-dusted landscape and just stared. Then he walked over and stepped between the stones.

"NO BOY!" Hugh shouted, but Adam had stepped through and the snow disappeared. He turned around, looking at the sunshine surrounding him, shook his head and returned to his original position. As soon as he no longer occupied the space between the upright stones, the odd picture returned.

"I guess that was what my mother meant when she said we could only look," he said simply.

Colin was leaning over, hands on his knees, trying to keep from hyperventilating. When he straightened up, he shouted at Adam, "Son, that was about the stupidest thing I've ever seen anyone do. You didn't even know what time period you were lookin' at! You could have stepped through and been kissin' a tyrannosaur! Let's at least try to determine which times belong to which doors before we do anything stupid! Do we have a deal?"

Adam looked sheepish. "Deal. I'm sorry, I just couldn't believe we'd actually done it. I guess my enthusiasm ran away with me."

"I don't know if I'd call it enthusiasm or ignorance, but your apology is accepted. Now don't do that again." Hugh answered him, finally recovering from his own scare. "Colin," he was back to business, "it seems that only the ones with their cross stones intact are viable. Look for yourself."

"Seems you're right, old boy. Well, seems our three pound seventy a day to get in 'ere 'as been worth it. We've solved the riddle, at least as much as we will solve this part of it. Now, gents, let us watch our ancient tellies and see what we may learn."

They spent the next three hours before the monument closed watching each of the viable portals, and taking notes. Amazingly, they were fortunate enough to not have to share their discovery. The tourists seemed to have taken the day off. When they were finally thrown out at closing time, the young American man and the history scholars had formed a plan.

At four a.m., the hotel clerk rang Adam's room. A very stiff and formal voice pulled the young man from his sound sleep. "You asked for a wake up call at this horrendous time, sir?"

"I did."

"Well, you have it, sir."

"Don't forget to wake the old gents in the next room as well."

"It's already been done, sir."

"Thank you for your time."

"You're very welcome, sir." The line went dead.

Adam dressed quickly in the clothing Colin and Hugh had helped him choose. He threw the tunic over his head, then added the doublet. Although they had tried, chain mail was too difficult to find on short notice. Next, he put on the leather boots that laced up the side and folded over at the top.

Lastly, he put on his sword belt and slipped the gleaming sword – the one he had spent two months' pay on – into the scabbard. He prayed they had chosen well. Slipping a dagger into another, smaller sheath on his belt, Adam then wrapped the heavy fur-lined cloak they had bought around himself, tying it at the neck. The animal rights activists would have a fit, he thought, if he were caught wearing it in public. It was extremely hot and heavy, and no doubt he would be sweating rivers before the morning was over. With that thought in mind, he slipped the heavy cloak back off, threw it over his arm, and picked up the leather drawstring bag he was going to carry with him if he succeeded.

The bag was about the size of a duffel, but was worn over the shoulders like a cape and held in place with a leather strap. It held a pistol and several boxes of ammunition – just in case. Also in the small bag was a good supply of dried food, an insulated bag full of water, a change of underclothes, a pair of fleece-lined leather gloves and a pair of woolen socks. Against Colin's advice, he also carried a deck of playing cards, arguing that he might be spending quite a bit of time alone and need something to do. With him Adam also carried a survival guide and map of the British Isles in the 1300's, just in case his memory failed him or he came across things that were unfamiliar. A small-but-warm sleeping bag, a lighter, and a huge box of safety matches completed his packing.

Adam placed around his neck a small leather money pouch. It held thirty small gold fingers about the size of bullets. Colin had been kind enough to make them for him and sell them to him at wholesale. Even at wholesale it had cost a fortune, but adventure was never cheap. Adam would be able to trade the small pieces of gold for goods or the currency of the day – gold was money in any time.

As he stepped from his room, Colin and Hugh met him in the hall. When he turned to close his door and his scabbard clanked against the door frame. He gave a short, embarrassed chuckle. "It looks like getting used to this will take no small amount of time. I hope I get the chance."

"Hear, hear," Hugh said quietly. Colin gave the boy's elbow a little squeeze for reassurance and the three men walked together down the hall towards the entrance of the quaint old hotel. They drove the two miles from Amesbury in silence, parking a long way from the stone monument itself so as to not attract any unwanted attention. After unfolding themselves from their auto, they began their hike towards Stonehenge. At the fence, Adam hugged both men and thanked them sincerely.

"Good luck, boy. I hope you find your mother." Hugh hugged him in return. "And don't forget, at exactly sunrise the axis of Stonehenge is perfectly aligned."

Colin hugged him twice. "Give your mum a kiss for me, if you find her. When you come back, look me up. I can't think of anything I'd rather do than 'ear of your adventures. I'll keep your things – forever, if I 'ave to. And Adam," the man's voice dropped and became thick with emotion, "be careful."

"I promise." Adam turned and threw the leather bag over the fence. Then he began to climb. Once on the other side, he didn't look back until he was in position. Standing at the mouth of the horseshoe, he waved once more through the lightening sky at his friends. Then he waited.

It was time. Their mistress cleared her throat loudly. "I said, give me your attention please, gentlemen!" Katharine, Gray, Alane, and the most faithful and proven of the chosen warriors were in the war room. "It is time again for another adventure. There will be a ship departing in a fortnight's time for France, with our enemies' supplies on board bound for another battle. I'm sure you will agree with me that the Normans cannot endure another battle like Crecy. Too many families lost too many husbands and sons. Therefore, to prevent that end, we have only four days to prepare for our journey. Alane has ensured that a French ship will be waiting to take our captives off of our hands and deliver them someplace safe...."

"Wish you'd let us kill the English dogs!" Inan shouted. Several warriors shouted their agreement.

"We've discussed this before, we only kill when absolutely necessary. Tis the cross you bear serving under me. As before, I'll not force anyone to go – knowing it will be your very necks at risk, I only want those of you who will volunteer without reservation. No men with wives or children, of course, I would not rid your families of their husbands in order to simply nettle a king. That is the very thing we fight against. However, before you step forward, it should be known that there will be a warship, complete with a full contingent of soldiers, waiting for us. Evidently the crown has decided to take us seriously now. Know that it will be dangerous, as our adventures always are, but not impossible." She paused and looked carefully at the warriors surrounding her. "Now, men, tell me – who will go with me?"

Every man in the room, starting with her own sons, leapt to his feet with a rousing shout of "Aye!" They finished with their ritual.

Gray began it. "Here's to us!"

"Who's like us?" Alane joined in.

The men answered, "Damn few, and they're all dead!" Amid shouts and cheers and much backslapping, the warriors all pledged themselves to the venture. The rest of the evening was spent forming a strategy. Long after midnight, when the men finally dispersed, plans had been laid. All that was left was to prepare the ship.

The bitter wind cut through her outer garments like a well-sharpened sword, making the layers Ysabelle was wearing of little more protection than her thin sleeping chemise. She huddled her body closer to itself and kept walking, hoping to find some sort of shelter soon. She was near that frightening ancient place – she could feel it. As soon as she crested the hill, she would be able to see it as well, and Ysabelle was more than a little curious. The sun was setting and the air growing more frigid by the minute. The poor girl had never felt more alone.

Be off with you, ingrate, and let the roving bands of thieves take you in. You'll pay them as well, but they won't want money.

NO!

Fear, birthed of terrifying tales used to scare curious children into obedience, goaded her to walk faster. Her legs felt wooden under her, they were so tired and cold. She had covered many miles in the last few days, and her body was impossibly weary. There were dark smudges under her eyes and lines of fatigue and strain were etched around her young mouth. Ysabelle crested the hill and stared.

Could this truly be the resting place of the good king Arthur? Or was it the terrifying dwelling places of witches and ghosts? If it weren't for what she *sensed* about this mystical field, the waves of *something* that she could feel hitting her in an even more substantial way than the wind, Ysabelle would believe that all the stories were simply lies. But now, here, staring at it, she could feel its *presence*. It felt … strange … as if the balance of all men's fate was embedded in, maybe even decided by, those very stones. She couldn't pull her eyes from the sight. It was magnificent. The enormous hand-carved stones, the impotent sun hardly brightening the sky except for the few places it thrust through the heavy snow clouds in daggers – it looked like a looming fairy tale place, the streamers of light framing it like a picture. Beautiful. Frightening. Strange.

Looking at the landscape in front of her, Ysabelle was surprised to see that there were large holes in the ground everywhere, no doubt due to the digging of would-be treasure seekers.

Ysabelle began walking toward the megalith as if drawn. On her way down the hill toward the flat plain the stones rested in the middle of, she found the ideal place to rest – a large hole sheltered from the wind by a huge rock on one side and the hill itself on the other. She debated on whether or not she was willing to sleep here, so close to this eery place. Knowing the tales that circulated about this place, she felt certain that few others would accost her here. Fear or danger – such an appealing range of choices. Finally deciding to face her fear, she put her leather bags down in the hole, and then lowered herself into it. Safe from the wind for the first time in three days, she heaved a sigh of relief. Ysabelle cuddled down into her thin blanket and cloak and fell instantly asleep.

He was standing at the mouth of the horseshoe shape, the symbols of his ring perfectly aligned with the stones. Adam had checked and rechecked the proper sarsen structure for the 'x' they had made the day before with a small rock. He was only dimly aware of his anxiety as he made his preparations and got into the proper position. It would be only moments now before the sun would rise. The sky was lightening to a muted gray, and the horizon was glowing silver.

Turning to give one last glance at his friends, he was surprised to see astonished looks on their faces. Colin shouted, "The ring boy! Look at the ring!"

Adam turned his face back to the ring and was blinded by a flash of light. His hands felt hot. The sun was rising and with each millimeter it raised above the horizon, the light coming from the stone of the ring increased dramatically. Adam felt as though he were caught in the beam of a search light. The amazing beam flared intensely brighter. Then, as though a switch was thrown, the light winked out.

"Now boy!" came a call from over his shoulder. Adam nodded, picked up his bag from the ground beside him, shouldered it, and walked over to the portal they had selected.

He stepped through.

SEVEN

The world lurched wildly to one side and instead of remaining upright, Adam fell – but there was no ground to catch him. A moment later he hit the ground. Soft ground, cold ground, grassy ground. Stomach swirling, threatening revolt, Adam's knees buckled and he fell on his backside. For just a moment he lay there, enjoying the frigid air on his face, letting it revive him and settle his stomach. Then he opened his eyes.

It was snowing. The sky was gray and overcast, and it looked like the sun was setting. Adam sat up and looked around. He was still at Stonehenge, but it looked different somehow. Now he knew why, all but one of the uprights still had their cross stones intact. And there was no fence. No security. No road leading to the megalith. No booth to pay your three plus pounds. It was obviously winter and nighttime was falling. Now all he needed to know was exactly what year – decade, century – he had stumbled into.

Realization hit him – it didn't matter all that much. The ring had worked. It worked! Adam, unable to contain himself any longer, let loose his victory cry. There was no one around to hear anyway. No matter where he was, one thing he knew for certain – he had made it! He had traveled through time! Before he forgot, he picked up a small rock and marked the portal, very distinctly and on all sides of each sarsen stone, so he would be able to find it again and get home. If he could get home.

Adrenaline rush fading, Adam noticed the cold. He put on his gloves and cloak, then looked around for where he might find shelter. Maybe up the hill. Pulling the fur lining of his cloak tightly about him, he began his search for a place to hole up for the night. It was dangerous enough to travel in foreign territory during the day, much less the night. There was no way he would be able to sleep, he was certain, but it was incredibly cold out here, and Adam was sure it would get worse before it got better. Finding a place to stretch out that was somewhat sheltered from the wind by a large rock, he pulled his bedroll out of his bag and laid it out. He pulled off his sword belt and tucked it safely into his makeshift bed. Then he crawled into it, using his traveling bag itself as a pillow and thanking God for thinsulate.

He stared at the clouds for a while, wondering what the sky would look like here – without lights to obscure the stars. Adam had always loved the stars. Too bad his mother hadn't been shanghaied to the moon. Right now, he felt as though he would have been able to find her there as well. Mind whirling, Adam was asleep before he realized he was sleepy.

Ysabelle woke with a start, heart pounding a riveting beat under her skin. The gossips had been right! This must be a place of witches! The most horrible shriek had jolted her out of her sound sleep. It had been terrifying! If that bloodcurdling noise had been a human sound, the person had to have been meeting their Maker in a most horrific way. Wanting to keep her head down and wait for the terror to pass by warred with her infinitely curious nature. Her curious nature won out over her fear – she had to look.

As she slipped her head out of the hole just enough for her eyes to show, she saw the most peculiar sight. A man, of not too many years, was dancing around the stone statues below her like a fool. He spun and danced jerkily in a parody of grace for a minute or two, then picked up a rock and made some evil design on all of the stones in one particular formation. Wild eyes jerking in seemingly all directions at once, the man looked possessed, he truly did. Ysabelle was certain he was practicing some sort of incantation or casting a spell even as she watched.

Perhaps he's Arthur's wizard Merlin! The thought chilled her. She wanted to gather her things and run away as fast as she could, yet still she could not pull her attention away from the daft man by the huge stones.

She watched him turn toward her and, lifting his head, he gazed straight into her eyes! Like a bird trapped in the gaze of a cobra, she froze to the spot. The man gathered his cloak about him, walked a small distance up the hill towards her and, shocking her, laid his blankets out on the ground. Without another look towards her, he laid himself down to sleep. He was toying with her, that had to be it. He knew she could not escape him and he was toying with her. The thought of someone placing her under their power made her blood burn. Ysabelle had lived that life for the last time, no one would press her into servitude of any kind again. She had to make a plan. But what if the man hadn't seen her at all and was merely looking up the hill for a place to lie? Perchance he hadn't seen her and it was her fear playing upon her imaginings. That seemed likely. Still, Father Corey had always told her that discretion was the better part of valor. She most certainly needed a plan.

Sitting perfectly still, Ysabelle watched the man. He was just lying there, as if he thought he were alone. In turn he would look at the brooding clouds in the sky, then look around him, studying everything carefully. While he studied his surroundings, she studied him. He wasn't overly large, though he could best her without effort, although he was somewhat handsome – for a witch, she qualified. He seemed to have no cares, so easily did he lie.

After a while he drifted off, and Ysabelle crawled out of her hole. She wandered over to where he was lying and looked at him, trying to objectively assess his threat to her. He was much too handsome to be a witch, she decided. Everyone knew that witches were old crones like Nana Inez. This was a young man, nicely built and dressed in fine clothes. He had thick, wavy, extremely dark hair – it looked black – and a fine face. He looked like a man with money, yet he traveled with no horse. She reached down and felt his blankets, but they must have been very costly as she had never felt anything like them before. There was a strange closure on the side. Running her fingers along it, she was fascinated by the cold, smooth metal. She had never seen metal fashioned in this way.

The man stirred. Ysabelle instantly stilled her movements and waited for him to settle again. She would have to immobilize him in order to get him to answer the many questions she had in her mind. He was extremely muscular and could do much harm to her if he chose. Before anything else, she must find out who he was and what he was about. Perchance she could even persuade him to be her ally. She didn't want to hope for too much, but traveling alone could be a bit scary. He was no small man, and if he had any honor and was headed in the same direction she was, perhaps he would agree to travel with her. Two was ever so much more safe than one. And he was a strong man, she would wager. She kept herself from hoping.

Immediately Ysabelle set to work. She took her dagger and went in search of a proper tree. A quarter of an hour later she found what she was looking for. The snow falling all around her didn't hinder her on her mission. Ysabelle was concentrating so much on her task, she barely felt the cold. After cutting enough of the smaller, more supple branches, she heaved them onto her shoulders and started back toward where the strange man was sleeping. Upon reaching him, she put her burden down on the ground and began placing the young branches, one by one, over the sleeping man – careful to keep her touch feather-light. The branches cris-crossed over him, covering him head to toe, and not until all was ready did she pull the lashes tight around his sleeping form.

Adam woke instantly when he felt the lashes pulled tight. There was nothing he hated more than being restrained. His eyes opened on the face of a beautiful teenage girl peering at him with emerald green eyes from just beyond his arm's reach. She was holding a dagger ready in her hand and watching him intently. The girl looked ready, tensed to spring – perfectly capable of doing him serious bodily harm. Still, he was relieved. This kind of trouble he thought he could handle.

"Tell me who you are, sir," she commanded him.

"I would be happy to introduce myself to you. It's rather hard from this position, however. You have me at a disadvantage, I'm afraid." He hoped his tension didn't show on his face.

"I'll not untie you until I know you will not harm me. Again, sir, I ask you to tell me your name." Without moving any closer to him, she waved her dirk in his direction for emphasis.

"I'm Adam Talbot. It's my pleasure. And do you also have a name, miss?" Adam grinned at her. She really looked terrified. If she only had an inkling of how anxious he felt, he was sure she would feel a whole lot better.

"Of course I have a name. What a ludicrous question." She stared at him, her gaze narrowed on his face.

"Would you be kind enough to tell me what it is? I prefer to deal with people by name. It's not as if I can do you any harm tied up like this."

"Well," she paused as she considered whether giving him this information could harm her, "I suppose. My name is Ysabelle. Where do you come from? Your accent is strange." She couldn't keep from staring at him, he was really quite a nice-looking fellow. Such interesting green eyes, or were they blue? She really couldn't tell in the relative darkness.

"America. I'm sure you haven't heard of it, few in this country have. Do you always tie people up before you introduce yourself to them?" he asked, an amused grin on his face. No longer nervous, he was enjoying this girl, she was gorgeous. Too bad she wasn't older. She kept staring at him in a peculiar manner, though, and had he been in another situation, he might have thought his fly was open.

"It's necessary," she said simply. "You might be a witch. I have no desire to go through life as a toad or a rock. Or you might be a bandit, or worse." She half-suppressed an involuntary shudder. "There are many roving bands of men who would hurt any they come across. Some hunt their game to steal, some for pleasure alone. A woman traveling alone would be at their mercy," she explained, then cursed herself when she realized she had told him she was unprotected.

He caught it right away, but first he wanted to put her at least a small amount at ease. "You have nothing to fear from me. I am not a witch or a bandit. You travel by yourself? Ysabelle, may I call you Ysabelle, isn't that dangerous? I thought young, unmarried women were to be accompanied by an escort of some kind. Who will protect you on your journey?" He seemed genuinely concerned for her, but she could not decide whether or not to trust this man.

"I am not weak. I can protect myself. That should be clear to you." She arched her eyebrows and waved her hand over his immobile form to prove her point. "But I have no escort. I have no family to care for such things or money to buy them. I go north to find a new home. I have skills and can care for myself," she challenged him, chin lifted arrogantly.

"I'm certain you can do anything you choose."

Surprised by his agreement, she nodded. "Yes, I can. How good of you to notice."

"Ysabelle, look into my eyes. I promise not to hurt you. Please untie me. I travel alone as well. I'm going to Scotland, and perhaps I could accompany you to wherever it is you are going. That is, if we're going in the same direction. I wouldn't want you to travel unaccompanied, unprotected." Adam smiled at her disarmingly, willing her to believe. He hoped his face betrayed his sincerity – it usually betrayed everything else.

She studied him, deciding. He noticed she was chewing on her lip, working her decision over pretty thoroughly. Stepping closer, she nodded to herself; evidently she had made her choice. God save her, she hoped she had made the right one. The pretty girl swung her dagger quickly down at him and Adam flinched away and closed his eyes. Evidently he hadn't convinced her. He braced against the pain.

The lashes binding him came loose and he opened his eyes one at a time.

Ysabelle was laughing at him. "Did you think I was going to kill you? Your fear was displayed all over your face. You looked like a … a … mouse about to be eaten by a cat! You really should try to keep your emotions from showing on your face."

Adam stood up, indignant, his sleeping roll gathering on the ground around his feet. "So I've been told. Of course I thought you were going to kill me. What other reason would have caused you to lunge at me that way? Next time you swing a dirk at me, please be kind enough to warn me first." His sword, still in its scabbard and attached to the belt, fell over from where he had put it in his sleeping bag and clanged onto the ground.

Ysabelle was still laughing. Noticing the weapon, she inhaled sharply and stared in wonder at the beautiful sword. "Oh, my! It's magnificent! I've never seen the like. Of course, I've not seen very many swords."

"Thank you. I like it. It cost me a lot of money."

"Money?"

"Gold. Coin. Money is the word for it where I come from."

"May I see it?"

"The sword? Sure. Yes. Here." He almost fell over twisting to reach for the fallen weapon, and after he handed it to the girl, he busied himself extracting himself from his bedroll. Adam folded the errant sleeping bag, and stuck it in his bag. "Have you got a shelter to sleep in, Ysabelle?"

She handed back the sword, eyes still large with wonder. "I was sleeping in a hole up the hill. It was protected from the wind, though the snow still falls in it."

"Do you have a blanket? Or only the clothes you're wearing? They're quite thin, and it's incredibly cold out here." While he was talking, he had pulled his cloak off and placed it around her shoulders. The fur caressed her face, making Ysabelle feel warm and cosseted – a strange sensation for her. Adam busied himself tying it. "If you will forgive me, I'll keep my gloves. That way I won't miss my cloak quite so much."

She laughed. "It's a fair compromise. I thank you."

"Be careful not to trip, the hem reaches the ground. I'd hate for you to break your neck after I've been kind enough to warm it." Ysabelle laughed again, a warm, throaty, intoxicating sound. Adam found himself wanting to hear it again.

Ysabelle, caught up in his easy humor, smiled and returned his light banter. "Follow me, kind sir. I'll show you to my cottage. There's a fire blazing nicely and you'll enjoy the view. It's quite lovely this time of year." Even in a strange situation, it was difficult to keep her innate humor and whimsical nature from showing themselves. Ysabelle didn't spend much time on the past. Every moment was for living and, if possible, for enjoying.

Adam joined right in. "Then you won't mind my roasting a turkey for both of us to enjoy."

"Not at all. Quite kind of you. I'll busy myself with the bread." As they approached the hole where her meager belongings rested, she stopped, suddenly embarrassed. It was no shame to be poor, but she found herself not wanting to have this man see that vulnerability as well. Ignorance, she told herself. Squaring her shoulders, she pulled him by the arm to the edge of the hole.

"Quite a place you have here," he commented.

Ysabelle couldn't decide if he was laughing at her or not. "Are you making sport of me?"

He smiled at her warmly, she looked so small to him – so vulnerable. "No. This is actually quite a good shelter." She exhaled, obviously relieved at his assessment. She was instantly irritated with herself for caring. Adam, oblivious to the quiet little war being fought between pride and humility right next to him, kept looking at her hiding place – thinking of a way to keep the snow off the two of them. "I think that my bedroll will cover the top of this shelter quite nicely and keep out the snow. We'll have to share body heat, though. I don't want to offend you, but I don't think there will be any other way to keep warm enough out here."

"I'm not sure...."

"I will be quite proper, I assure you."

"But the church...."

"Even the Bible says two sleep warmer than one." Where he had pulled that memory from was anybody's guess, but he even knew the reference.

"No – you're jesting." She was appalled.

"I'm not. It's in Ecclesiastes. Now let's get in there before our lips freeze and we can't argue any longer – although that idea has merit." Adam jumped into the hole.

Ysabelle smiled, he was amusing. He lifted his arms to her, and after a moment of debating, she gave in to the promise of warmth and allowed him to help her in beside him. He pulled his bedroll out of his bag and wrapped it around her, then hauled himself out of the hole to go look for stones to keep their roof in place. A moment later he was back carrying a large stone. Three more trips yielded three more large stones.

"Show me your blanket," he commanded. Ysabelle did as she was told, rather sheepishly as she realized her blanket had holes in it. That blasted embarrassment again!

"Hmm. I see. We'll cover with mine, yours can be the roof. Throw it up to me." She tossed him the blanket and he spread it out over most of the hole and secured three of its corners with the large stones. Adam then jumped into the hole carrying the last stone. After handing the heavy object to Ysabelle, he stretched the final corner out and, slipping the last stone carefully under the blanket, used it to secure the leftover corner. He pulled his arm back into the hole and waited for his eyes to adjust to the darkness. It didn't happen.

"Where are you?" he asked quietly, not wanting to panic himself or her by shouting. It was difficult to keep from feeling smothered. The hole felt so much like a grave. He switched the thought in his mind to a cave – that he could handle passing the night in.

"Right here," came her low, throaty voice from his immediate left. She decided she would take charge of the situation, it would relieve her feelings of vulnerability considerably. "Give me your hand, Adam." She held both of hers out, feeling for him in the dark. Her right hand came into contact with the leather tunic he wore, and his warm hand closed over hers. He had taken his gloves off.

"Are you all right?" he asked gently.

She sighed heavily. "Yes. I'm well. Let us go to sleep. Dawn comes early for both men and women."

"Agreed." Adam sat down, pulling Ysabelle down beside him. "Take my cloak off, Ysabelle." She did so and handed the heavy garment to him, and he wrapped it around them both before he reached for his bedroll. There was the soft buzzy sound of the zipper as he opened the bag completely, then Ysabelle felt his hands gently tucking the warm, soft material around her and then around himself. He was lying so close to her she could feel him from her shoulder to her foot. It was the warmest she had been since she had walked out the door of Nana Inez's cottage.

"Thank you. I haven't been warm in days."

"I'm sorry. It must be very difficult for you – out here alone." Their voices sounded loud in the darkness. Both became quieter as they talked.

"It's difficult, but not impossible. It would be easier if there were more small game to snare. And if it weren't so cold. Of course one would take care of the other." She sounded tired, Adam thought.

Another thought occurred to him. "How long has it been since you last ate?"

"I still have the last of my bread and cheese in my pockets. I'm not hungry."

Adam grinned in the dark, she was a proud one. "You're lying to me. I could see from your thin frame that you were not well fed."

"I do not enjoy being called a liar. I am as well fed as I ever was."

"That I would believe." He was quiet for a moment. "How did you come to be out here alone, Ysabelle."

"I will answer this last question, then I'm going to sleep. The woman who was caring for me threw me out. She was never kind to me and I am well rid of her. Now leave me in peace, Adam."

"Why did she throw you out?"

"Are you rude or simply ignorant? Or perhaps you're deaf?" she asked him, exasperated with him and trying to prod his temper.

He grinned in the darkness. "I'm rude. Now why?"

Ysabelle sighed. "I dropped our rabbit in the fire. Satisfied?"

"And for that you were thrown out of your home?" Adam was appalled. He hated cruelty in any form, any time. And his protective instincts were immediately on alert. No one should treat a child like that, Ysabelle was just a girl.

"Yes. She never loved me. I was a burden she would no longer tolerate." She sounded so matter of fact it broke his heart. She shifted her body to face a small space away from him, trying to withdraw.

"Children should always be loved. She was cruel. It is a credit to you that you're such a strong … woman. How old are you, Ysabelle?"

"Do your lips never shut? Or are you questioning me in your sleep?"

"How old are you, Ysabelle?" he repeated.

"I am in my sixteenth year, as counted by the harvest. I'm not married, have no children, no dowry, nothing whatsoever to recommend me to anyone except my education, and I did not even bring my second pair of shoes with me. I grow extremely tired of this conversation. Please, if I have given you enough information, will you be kind enough to let me sleep?"

His voice was gentle, "I'm sorry. I didn't mean to keep you awake. I just wanted to know why such a young girl would be forced to make her own way in the world. I didn't mean to cause you pain or embarrassment."

She softened toward him. "I thank you for that kindness. Let's sleep now if we can. Agreed, Adam?"

"Agreed, Ysabelle." He shifted his position enough to cushion her. Now they were lying like spoons in a drawer. She felt good, warm and soft, against him. He shook his head against that thought. She was just a girl, for goodness' sake. He kept one arm under his head, and the other at his side. He wanted to put it around her, but knew she would probably have a heart attack if he took the liberty to do so.

She breathed out softly and the two lay quietly for a while. Thinking she was asleep, he jumped a little when she asked, "What was that horrible noise you made by the stones?" Her question came out of nowhere.

Adam laughed out loud. "I didn't think there was anyone around to hear that. It was my victory cry."

"Had you won some sort of victory?" She turned her face toward him, puzzled. They still could not see each other, but Adam knew she was close – he could feel her warm breath on his neck. He forced that thought from his mind. *Jailbait.*

"Of a sort, yes. I had done something, or rather found something I was looking for."

"What were you looking for?"

"This place." His intentional vagueness piqued her curiosity.

"I thought you were going to Scotland. Was that a lie?" she asked him, suddenly wary. He could feel the unease coming off her in waves.

"No. I'm going to Scotland. Actually an island off the coast. But I had to find this place first. It was sort of a ... landmark," he explained. "Where, may I ask, are you going?" He tried to sound nonchalant.

"I don't really know. I'm going north. I hadn't decided where as of yet. To be truthful, Scotland sounds as satisfactory as anyplace else."

"Then we'll go together."

"Adam, I haven't any gold. I refuse to be a burden to any person, and I

101

have no means to pay you to help me." She was stiff as a board now, and if he didn't placate her in a hurry, it would be colder in this cave than outside of it.

He touched her arm gently. "I have enough gold for both of us for the time being, and you are welcome to share with me for as long as it holds out. After that, we'll both be earning our own way. Agreed?"

Ysabelle didn't speak for a moment. When she finally answered him, her voice was tentative, so quiet he had to strain to hear her. "And in return for this kindness, you will expect what of me?"

Adam understood instantly. Evidently the world had not changed all that much in six hundred years. "I expect nothing from you but your company, and at times your assistance. I'll make no demands on you that you will not willingly give – for instance, to help me cook our food or find and snare game. I give you my word. We will travel as brother and sister. Is that acceptable to you?"

After a moment, she answered him quietly, "Yes." Then, as an afterthought, she added, her voice more full of certainty, "And if you are less than honorable to your word, I will carve you a new smile. And don't think I am incapable of doing just that."

He grinned at her back. "Agreed. Good night, Ysabelle."

"Good night, Adam."

Ysabelle was almost asleep when Adam asked one last question. "Ysabelle, what is the name of your king?"

"Edward, of course." Could he truly be that ignorant?

"Longshanks?"

"Heavens no. He is long dead. The Edward on the throne right now is his grandchild."

Adam smiled. "Thank you." He felt her nod in answer. Soon she was breathing deeply and evenly. Adam moved closer to her and was grateful for her warmth. Before long he was fast asleep.

The world was shaking. Adam was lost. It was pitch black. He could feel dirt under him and someone lying next to him. It took a second to orient himself. Oh yes, England and Ysabelle, but what was causing the earthquake? It was Ysabelle – she was shaking like a leaf – shivering from the cold. He wrapped his arms around her and pulled her close to him to warm her. After a moment she was warmed enough to become still again, and Adam was surprised when she cuddled even closer to him. He could smell her, feel her. It was going to be a long night.

He'd have to keep thinking 'jailbait' to get through it without losing his composure. He could only think that after all those years of concentrating on preparing for his journey, allowing himself few thoughts of the opposite sex, he had finally been liberated by his success. But *this* was not the girl to notice. Ysabelle was too young, she was from a different time, a different culture, and he would soon be leaving. She was also beautiful, strong, and resourceful. He couldn't help noticing. As a matter of fact, his whole body seemed to be noticing. Yes, it was going to be a very long night.

Jailbait. Don't forget she's jailbait – and you're not a pig.

Well, maybe he was and maybe he wasn't.

"You can look now, old friend, he's gone." Hugh was tapping Colin on the shoulder.

"'E's gone?" The shorter man blinked his eyes, then rubbed them, then blinked again, looking in the direction of the portal through which Adam had vanished.

"Yes, he's gone. It worked." Hugh breathed in deeply, then let the air out of his lungs slowly, trying to get his mind around what he had just witnessed. "Astonishing!" He could only stare at the place where he had last seen Adam.

"I 'ope 'e's okay." The man looked crestfallen. Colin blinked to keep the moisture collecting in his eyes from overflowing.

Hugh placed his arm around his friend companionably. "Whether or not he made it to the right time, old boy, you know he's in for the adventure of his life. He's ready for it. He's young. He has as much information as he could prepare himself with. How would you have felt at twenty-four?"

Colin sniffed. "Ready to take on the world, I was."

"So is he. Any world."

Colin breathed in deeply and pasted a smile on his face. "Then it's time to go 'ome. 'E'll come lookin' for us when it's all over, I guess."

"I'm certain he will. He's a good boy, Colin. A fine choice for you to adopt as your own," Hugh answered, walking towards the car.

"Aye, that 'e is." Colin turned to follow his friend, and the two men headed back towards the automobile with heavy – and light – hearts.

Adam and Ysabelle set out early in the morning. Between his map and her knowledge, they found their way along fairly easily. They stopped for food and rest just outside a small village along the dirt road. Finding a large tree to lie against, Ysabelle rested herself while Adam went into the roadside town and purchased horses and food for them. Had he any idea what kind of a gift he was giving his traveling companion, he would have been proud of his generosity. But a horse was a horse to him.

He came back, trailing the horses behind him, and Ysabelle leapt to her feet. She was overcome with excitement and gratitude. He was caught completely off guard when she ran to him and hugged him fiercely, almost knocking him over.

"I can never thank you enough. What beautiful horses!" she exclaimed, breathless. She was behind him before he knew it, stroking the mare he had brought for her to ride. This kind man had just given her freedom like she had never known. A horse. Could there be any better gift? Ysabelle made up her mind right then to help him in any way possible.

"Travel is much easier by horse than on foot. Wouldn't you agree, Ysabelle?" Her reaction was confusing to him. It was just a horse.

"Well, of course. It's just that ... well ... you couldn't understand how much this means ... I ... thank you." She dropped into a brief curtsy. He laughed at the unexpected politeness on the heels of her unbridled gratitude. A moment later she joined him, sharing the humor of her behavior.

After tying the horses to a low-hanging branch, Adam laid out their meal for them. He ate quickly. While Ysabelle was eating and refreshing herself, he excused himself and went off in search of a few other things they would need. He purchased saddles and tack, some dried fruit and three loaves of bread, and a few things to make the girl more comfortable.

Adam walked back to where she and the horses were waiting and presented his gifts to her with a bow and a flourish. He had found a slightly worn, but very heavy and beautiful brocade dress in a lovely maroon color. He had bought it at a hefty price from the merchant's daughter. Adam pulled it out from behind his back and presented it to Ysabelle. Her eyes lit up like a child's and she reached out to touch the lovely material. Her eyes misted over and she quickly turned away from Adam. Everything Nana Inez had given her had been a rag, worn by almost every other child in the town before she had worn it. It was the first new, or almost new, dress she had ever been given – and this by a virtual stranger. Kindness for nothing. It was a hard thing to get used to.

She could hardly get the words out. "It looks like something a queen would wear. I've never seen anything so lovely. It will be warm as well, I'm certain. Again, I thank you."

"And it will look lovely on you, Ysabelle. Brown is not the best color for such a lovely young woman." He reached out to stroke her cheek, then jerked his hand back when he realized what he'd done. Turning his back quickly, he began saddling his horse. "It's time we should be moving on. We have a long journey to the coast." Much to his surprise, she picked up her saddle as well and, after positioning the blanket properly on the horse's back, quickly and expertly saddled her own horse as they talked.

"You wish to cross the ocean?"

"No. The only way to my mother's home is by sea. I told you I journey to an island off Scotland." Adam couldn't remember if he had mentioned his mother before or not, then decided it didn't matter.

"Oh. Do you think there will be room there ... um, for an outsider?"

"I don't know. I've never been there. We shall both see." He pulled the girt tight and tested the saddle. This conversation made him feel awkward, like he was walking around with his fly open. Vulnerability wasn't a thing he enjoyed.

"You've never been to your mother's home? That's rather peculiar. Although, if I must think about it, perhaps not. I've never been to my mother's home either. It will be a journey of discovery for both of us."

"Yes, it will." Adam mounted his horse, only then remembering he was expected to help her. Turning to ask if she needed help, he was surprised to find her in the saddle and ready to ride. "Ready?" he asked.

In answer she kicked her horse into a full run. He was hard-pressed to catch up with her. They set a hard pace and didn't stop to make camp until dusk. By the time they had eaten and prepared a place to sleep, night had fallen. The moon rose, full and beautiful.

"It's a sign," Ysabelle told him when she caught sight of the heavenly light.

"Of what?"

"Of our success. You shall find your mother, and I shall find a home. I'm sure of it." She nodded her head, emphasizing her assurance.

"Sounds good to me," Adam responded before he rolled to his side and went to sleep. "Sounds good to me."

Twilight was painting the sky a steely gray when Inez heard hoofbeats approaching. They were coming fast – God save her, it was Randall. She had dreaded this confrontation since she had sent word to him six days ago. Moments later, the cottage door crashed open and a huge hooded figure stood before her.

"You summoned me, madam?" The polite words could not hide the disdain behind them. The hooded man placed his hands behind his back to keep the hag from being so afraid of him she couldn't speak. He hated having to be patient with the weak-minded, especially this old crone. And she was already trembling.

When Randall had brought the infant to old Inez, he had selected her hoping she would inadvertently kill the child and there would be no more complications to the king. The fool deserved what he got, bedding his chambermaid. He certainly had no responsibility to the child, but Edward was of a compassionate nature toward the chambermaid and insisted the child be cared for. Weak-minded fool. The man should have listened to him and disposed of both the child and the woman, but no. He must have this particular woman to attend to his needs, and because she asked, he must have the child tended to. Idiot. To compromise the throne for a woman – it was unadulterated weakness. Randall had no patience for weakness. Yet he was the king, and Randall had promised his very life for the man's protection.

Inez collected herself. He would not hurt her, she was important to the king. "The girl is gone, milord. She left without a word." She faced the man squarely, sure her position with the king would save her from his well-known vicious nature.

"When, exactly, did she leave, old woman?" He towered over her. Trying to control his anger, he counted in his mind, hoping he didn't have to count past a thousand. How he wanted to reach out and snap this woman's neck with one of his hands.

"Six days ago, milord. She was alone, she was." Inez could see his anger, it terrified her. Why he had to be the one to deliver the child to her was beyond her understanding. Facing him now might just kill her through terror alone. Curse him! The stories she had heard of the king's assassin kept floating through her head. Curse those old gossips for filling her head with fear!

"What did she take with her?"

"Nothing. The dress on her back was all. No cloak, no food, no blanket." Inez, of course, didn't volunteer the fact that the girl had no cloak. She thought it might reflect upon her care for the girl poorly if the man noticed her own fur-lined one.

"Then perhaps our problem is solved. Perchance winter has done my job for me. And, Inez, it is *our* problem." Randall had leaned down into her face, glaring.

He scared the life out of her. She understood exactly what he was telling her. Looking at him this close was worse than having him tower over her. He had a huge scar running from above his eyebrow to his chin, straight as a staff, and it turned a vicious red when he became angry. Inez fought to keep her voice from shaking. Jutting out her chin, she practically screeched, "I did my part of our bargain, milord. I raised her. Kept her alive, I did, and even gave her lessons with the parish priest." Curses on that blasted girl! She had brought nothing but trouble, and it wasn't fair to a decent old woman like herself!

He latched on to that. "What kind of lessons?"

"I don't rightly know. I'm sure it was church lessons. You'd have to ask the priest. He's the one what taught her."

"I'll do that. Don't even think of leaving, I'll be back shortly." Randall glared her into submission. He turned, the folds of his rich cloak swirling about him, and he left, leaving the door to the small cottage wide open and the frigid, cutting wind blowing in.

Inez rushed over to close it behind him. He left a chill in the air her small fire couldn't touch. She had heard of him. The old women couldn't wait to tell her all about him after he had brought the infant Ysabelle, named for her whore mother, to her. The thought of the girl made her spit on the floor. Vicious little rat! Now how was such a feeble old woman to tend her garden or make her dinner. How dare she leave poor old Inez alone, and after she'd been so kind to her – feeding the ungrateful wretch, clothing her, making sure she was brought up right in the church. A chill stole over her and she shuddered. Randall always had that effect on her.

Old Metylda had told her that Randall had slaughtered women, children, babies. He had no heart. He had eaten dragons for breakfast. He practiced black magic. He was the son of the devil. Of course, he was loyal to the king, but he always liked to do things his own way. Florie added that once, when he had been told to get some information from a Norman duke and the man hadn't been forthcoming, he had skinned the poor man alive. Randall had gotten his information, but the duke had not survived. The king had reportedly been angry, but nothing had happened to his favorite "get it accomplished" man. Some said even the king feared him.

Inez put no stock in the stories those old crones had told her. It was rubbish, that. If he was that evil, he would have killed the baby instead of finding a place to raise it. He was loyal to the king, she was sure of it, for he made sure the child was cared for.

Grabbing up her cloak to warm the chill from her old bones, she convinced herself of the excellent care, well adequate care, the ungrateful girl had been given. Inez had done a good job, for sure. Given her best, was it her fault the ingrate was so horrid, so rebellious? Of course not. Who could deal fairly with such a vile little rat? The girl deserved whatever Randall had in store for her. Inez puffed out her lip and nodded her own agreement. Rotten filthy ingrate!

With no prelude the cottage door crashed open, shocking the old woman. Randall stood there, fuming, staring at her with nostrils flaring. The man hadn't even knocked. "It would seem she had more lessons than would normally be given to a girl of her station."

"She's a bastard child, daughter of a whore, she has no station," Inez spat viciously.

His hand snaked out and cracked across her cheek. "I have no time for small minded talk. She is the daughter of the king – she has a station. That is the reason she presents a problem. The priest has prepared her well, in every way that could be taught. He has made good use of the last ten years. You, my good woman, it would seem, could not even be bothered to keep your eye on what lessons were being taught. Exactly what did you think your wages were paying for? You have been worse than useless, you have been detrimental to my plan. Be sure the king will hear about your behavior." He stepped toward her, eyes flashing, filled with violence.

She dropped to her knees, "Mercy, milord!"

"If it were not expressly against His Majesty's wishes, I would dispatch you here. However, regrettably in this case, I obey my king. The girl Ysabelle already has six days' travel?" The man held his fists clenched at his sides, Inez noticed blood on his knuckles, it was not dry.

"She does, milord. But she is on foot." Inez paused, took a deep breath, then continued, her voice barely a squeak, "Sir, does the priest still breathe? He is sorely needed here."

"He will live." He waved aside her concern with his hand as he would a fly. "Which direction did the girl take?"

"I did not see, milord." She bowed her head, terrified of what he might do to her for her ignorance.

"Useless...." he mumbled under his breath, then he was gone. Relieved, Inez went to close her door, looking out first to make sure Randall had gone. She caught sight of the dust from his horse. He was headed to the North, in the direction Ysabelle had gone. She hadn't wanted to protect the girl by not telling him her direction, she was simply angered by his bullying – so she hadn't told. He had chosen the right way in spite of her. It wasn't fair. Nothing worked out for her. At that moment, she remembered the poor priest, and remembered the kindnesses he had done everyone in the village. Someone really should tend his wounds.

Sighing, Inez fetched her needle and thread, her herb bag, and some clean strips of cloth. She tied on her beautiful fur-lined cloak and her fur muff before heading out the cottage door to find the priest. Making her way to Father Corey's tiny but adequate abode, Inez called out to him through the door. Inez was answered by a quiet groan.

She entered through the low door to find the man, crumpled and bleeding, on the dirt floor. When she rolled him over to assess his wounds, the poor man groaned loudly. On his back, she could see that his face was torn and bloody, his left arm was broken, and when she touched his chest, it felt as though he had several broken ribs. Poor cleric – he had obviously been beaten severely. Crossing to relight the fire, Inez heard the poor man groan again. True, he was going to live, but it would surely be a long night.

EIGHT

They had no idea they were being followed. They rode into the port town of Hythe late in the afternoon, four days after their journey together had begun. Hythe was one of the four port towns in the area that laid claim to being a Cinque Port, a confederacy of south-east coastal towns with the same occupation – supplying ships and crews to Edward. In exchange, of course, they were granted special privileges and charters. It made sense to Adam that this would be the first place to try and hitch a ride to Scotland.

Averaging forty miles per day, they had come the hundred and fifty miles or so without incident. Most of the terrain hadn't been overly rough, and a majority of their travel had been quite easy. Adam felt he had been patient enough keeping such an easy pace, but by the time they had reached the town, he was practically crazed with anticipation. After trading a piece of his gold for a large amount of the currency in use, he went straight to the docks. So much could be bought for so little here – information, passage, confidentiality. Evidently the king didn't pay his sailors all that well.

By the time Adam reached the place he had left Ysabelle waiting, he had secured them passage on an arms ship that was heading up the coast to Dunwich to pick up its escort – a warship fully decked out for battle. The sailor assured him he could find a small vessel to charter at Dunwich to take him as far North as he wanted to go. The man assured Adam that anything could be had for enough gold. Adam was beginning to believe something his old history teacher, Prof Daniels, used to say – history doesn't repeat itself, people never change.

Ysabelle wasn't quite as excited to be at the port as Adam was, but she was game for adventure, so after they secured enough supplies to last them the short sea journey, they found a room to hole up in until daylight. The woman who owned the small boarding house eyed them suspiciously, but decided that their similar colorings marked them as brother and sister enough to let them share a room. The room they slept in had no furnishings, so again the two slept in their blankets on the floor. They were awakened in the middle of the night by the door opening a crack and the old woman peeking in, making sure there was nothing going on between the 'siblings.' All was quiet. The woman smiled and shut the door without a sound. Both Ysabelle and Adam had been sleeping deep when she had opened the door, but for the rest of the night, both slept fitfully – waking in plenty of time to get them to the boat. It was set to sail at dawn.

They arrived before first light, and the man Adam had talked to previously was waiting for them. He introduced himself as Forster. He was small and wiry and kept looking around nervously and licking his thin, weather-cracked lips.

"Follow me, and don't make a peep." He showed them to the far end of the hold where the extra necessities were stowed away until needed. There they would hide themselves away and wait until the ship docked at Dunwich. On their way through the hold of the ship, they passed huge stacks of longbows and bundles of arrows. There was also an assortment of swords and maces and an impressive variety of other weapons of murder and mayhem. Where there weren't weapons there were chests – twenty-five in all. They were closed and locked, surrounded with heavy chain.

Forster lowered his voice conspiratorially and said with a wink, "Them's full of gold and other treasure, they are. Straight from the king's treasury, that. Some of it came from his barons as well, but you're lookin' at the king's gold. Headed across the sea to help defeat the Norman dogs. Quite a sight, eh?" They both nodded, eyes wide. He paused and looked around for witnesses – then led them to the very end of the hold. "Ah, here we are, younguns."

Behind a small partition made by the skeleton of the hull itself, there was a smallish area filled from top to bottom with huge coils of rope, wound around and around like enormous spools of thread. Forster installed the two behind the stacked spools. "Stay here and keep quiet. As long as there ain't no unforseen circumstances and the wind is wiv us, we'll reach port no later than tomorrow night – maybe sooner if fortune holds. I'll come and get you when we dock, and from there I'll show you to me friend. He owns a small boat and would be pleased to take his share of your boy's gold." He winked at Ysabelle.

"If you got a light wiv you, feel free to use it, but keep it dim. The rope and the wood 'll keep you from bein' seen." He patted the huge u-shaped wooden frame lovingly. "We sailors come up and down often, so keep your lips tight together. And be on your guard. There's none of the crew what would hurt you, we've all got families of our own and understands how things are, but we've got a fancy britches aboard that'd stretch your necks for the sheer enjoyment of it. He's a mean one, that." Forster nodded.

The wiry sallow-complected sailor stowed their belongings with them behind the rope and as an afterthought asked the brother and sister if they had food and water enough to last them. They assured him they did, and he left the tiny room in a hurry. Adam lit the oil lamp they had brought with them and they waited. Ysabelle insisted on lighting three matches herself and watching them burn to her fingers before Adam called a halt to the fire play.

"You're worse than a little kid," he whispered, taking the box of matches from her. "These are dangerous, Ysabelle, they're not toys."

She took issue with his lecture and ignored him completely for a good ten minutes as punishment – ostensibly straightening her meager belongings and wrapping them up tight in her blanket. But the trip was far too long to keep her irritation up, so with a sigh, she gave up her display and turned back to her traveling companion.

It wasn't long before Adam and Ysabelle felt the large ship lurch and begin to move away from the dock. They could hear the voices of men, some shouting orders, some repeating them, some just shouting. Every now and then they would hear men going up and down the ladder into the hold, and two or three times they heard footsteps pass in front of the rows of rope behind which they were hiding. Each time they held their breath. But then the footsteps would pass by and they would both sigh with relief. The day passed slowly. Adam pulled out a deck of cards he had brought from home and taught Ysabelle how to play gin. Their relationship had shifted slightly. At first there had been a kind of tension – sexual, Adam had thought at first. But as the journey wore on, he had felt like a caretaker of Ysabelle, very much like the older brother he was pretending to be. Now it was as though he truly had a sister. There was only camaraderie now, and even a sort of platonic love.

Adam had grown very close to her during the few days they had been together. The constant closeness had built for them an intimacy greater than either one of them had experienced before. They were comfortable with each other – with all of the built-in teasing and enjoyment of the siblings they were supposed to be, but lacking the hostility a long history of competition can instill. There was a lot of good-natured ribbing between them, and they had an instinctive trust of each other. She attributed it to their similar pasts, he believed it was because of her fine character. She would grow to be a wonderful woman, there could be no doubt of that. Too bad he wouldn't be around to see it. Of course, by the standard of her day, she was already a woman. That was tough for him to imagine. In Adam's world, she was a child.

As they sailed, they quietly whispered to each other of their pasts. Adam, of course, left out the part about being from another time and his mother's kidnapping. To Ysabelle, he told the story of being raised by his father, a builder of great buildings, because his mother lived in a distant country and had been forced to leave him as a six-year-old. She thought his mother was heartless, but he explained that the country had needed her. She had been given no choice in the matter and she had been very important to that country's survival. His father wasn't permitted to go with her, so as an adult Adam was going to go find her and live with her, since his age had finally made it possible. She didn't know he was coming, so it would be a surprise.

All of his explanations aside, Ysabelle still thought his mother heartless. Any woman who would leave her child.... She stopped the thought before it could take her where she didn't want to go.

She had to ask. "But how do you know she will accept you?"

"Of course she'll accept me," he said without a hint of hesitation. "Why wouldn't she? She loved me very much as a child, I remember, and my father told me so – and he had reason to be unkind." He seemed so sure.

"Not every parent accepts their child," Ysabelle told him sadly, her voice catching in her throat.

It was very telling. Adam grieved for her, her pain, hidden behind her pride, was almost palpable. "I'm sure that's true of some, perhaps those who don't know what they're missing, but not of my mother. You'll see ... if we find her."

Her eyes grew large. "Then you don't know where this island is?" she looked worried – she had unconsciously grabbed his hand.

"Vaguely. But don't worry. We'll be fine," he tried to reassure her.

"And if we don't find this mysterious island?"

"We'll find it. Trust me." That was that. Adam didn't want to discuss it anymore, so he returned to his hand of cards. Ysabelle left him in silence for a short while. Then, as a diversion for them both, began to recount her own childhood to him. As she spoke of the past, shock rippled through her listener. Adam had never personally known anyone who had been treated so cruelly.

Ysabelle laid down her hand and called gin, grinning broadly. As Adam shuffled and dealt another hand, she continued her painful tale. She had been whipped, ten lashes, for being late from her lessons, even though she had been helping the parson and several others get a carriage out of the mud. For her entire life she had slept on the floor, while her mistress had slept in a fine feather bed bought with the money intended to go for her care. Ysabelle had no cloak while Inez had a fine one with fur lining. She had been whipped, fifteen lashes, for burning dinner – even just a trifle. Of course, she was quick to defend her lack of skill to Adam. Ysabelle was a fine cook, she

113

declared to him – it was just that she had begun making dinner at four years of age.

She still wore the scars from when she had pulled young vegetable plants instead of weeds in the garden as a five-year-old. Fifteen lashes had been her punishment for that mistake. Inez had once cut all her thick, dark hair off – a great shame for a female of any age – when she had cried at the merciless pulling of her tangles during a brutal hair brushing. Ysabelle had been four.

Adam listened to the recollections of her childhood in silence, trying to pay attention to his hand, but failing miserably. Punching Adam playfully in the arm, Ysabelle called gin yet again. Adam smiled, collected the cards once more, shuffled them, and dealt another hand. She was quite the card shark, and losing to her this much was beginning to get on his nerves.

The deck above them had been fairly silent for a great while, with only the occasional shouted order to adjust a sail here or inspect the rigging there to interrupt the sound of the water lapping on the hull. The rhythmic sound had lulled the two into their current contemplative mood.

Watching his young friend from beneath his eyelids, Adam's heart went out to her. Ysabelle had learned to be very tough indeed, poor girl. Despite his childhood trauma, he had been so loved, so cared for. Even though they didn't relate terribly well, his father had always loved him. No question. This sweet girl, through no fault of her own, had been treated so cruelly. He couldn't ignore her story or shrug it off to the way of the world, his heart wasn't the least bit hard – another gift from his mother. They continued to play cards for hours, changing games several times through the quiet hours. Adam had to refill the oil in the lamp twice.

Sometime in the night, neither was sure exactly when – but the lamp had been filled for the third time – the ship came to a halt. They heard the creak of the huge winch letting the anchor down and there was enough shouting to wake the dead. The few sailors who were belowdecks went charging out of the hold, swords drawn. Then came the noise of fighting – the ring of steel on steel.

"This could not possibly be good," Adam stated, worry evident in his voice. Ysabelle nodded, not knowing what to make of their situation. He looked around, then dimmed the lamp to a faint glow. "Hide back there," he pointed, indicating where the ship's stern came to a point behind the stacks of rope. "I'm going to go see if I can find out what's going on up there." He kissed her forehead. "Be as quiet as you can. Don't even breathe until I get back," he whispered to her.

Ysabelle obeyed, but whispered just as Adam disappeared around the corner of the row of spools, "Be careful, Adam. Please." He heard her desperation clearly. She sounded as terrified as he felt. So much for courage. Adam desperately hoped courage was an action thing, not a feeling thing. Otherwise he would have to reconcile himself to being yellow all the way through – he was completely terrified. It was one thing to read about something, it was entirely another to step into it physically.

"I will. Promise. I'll be right back, Ysabelle." He moved away from her and the supply of rope, and as his footsteps receded, she became aware that she was totally alone in the faint darkness of the hold. She could still hear the shouting clearly, punctuated by the loud pops of the sails and the sound of steel hitting steel.

Seconds later a spool of rope slammed to the ground somewhere in the darkness in front of her. She crouched, waiting. There was no greeting, no call. Had it been Adam, he would have put her fears to rest as soon as he got close enough to call quietly. Ysabelle put out the lamp immediately. She heard footsteps, huge and booming. It must be a giant.

One by one, the spools of rope on top were being knocked off the coils they rested on. Row by row they toppled. Each time one of the huge coils hit the floor, Ysabelle's heart skipped a beat. The second row started to fall, one by one, to the floor. The huge thumping sounds they made as they hit masked the unbearably loud pounding of her heart. Someone was looking for something, she prayed it wasn't her. She put one hand on her dagger and fumbled in the dark with the other for the hilt of Adam's sword, which he had left behind with their things. Finding it, she held it in a death-grip. *Please don't let me have to use these*, she prayed desperately, knowing that anyone she faced would surely be much more skilled than she.

Whoever was after her began to topple the final row of spools – her last remaining shield. Ysabelle's eyes grew round with terror. She consciously steadied her breathing, making herself be quiet and trying to still her wildly beating heart. She visually searched her surroundings desperately, looking for some way, any way out. There was nowhere she could go. She was trapped in the far corner of the hold – rope on one side, hull on the other, enemy between her and freedom. Ysabelle drew her dagger and waited – hands trembling, heart racing.

One by one the coils fell. She caught a glimpse of the hand pulling them down, it was huge! Dear God, help her! She was being searched for by a bear! The third spool of rope fell – there were only four left between Ysabelle and exposure. *Adam, where are you?* The fourth hit the floor with a resounding thud. The noise was getting louder as her enemy got closer. The fifth one toppled. Ysabelle pulled the sword from its sheath exactly when the coil hit to muffle the ringing noise. She raised the weapon in her right hand up in front of her at an angle, readying the dirk in her left.

Getting herself into ready position as Father Corey had taught her, she waited, barely breathing. On the balls of her feet, ready to spring at the intruder, she held her breath waiting for the last two spools to fall. Number six hit the floor. If they hadn't been so huge, she would have already been visible. The last spool fell, exposing her, vulnerable now in her feeble hiding place.

Ysabelle sucked in her breath sharply. Sweet heavens, it was a giant. He was at least a head and a half taller than she was, and wearing a black mask about his eyes and the upper part of his face. His weapon was drawn and at the ready, his massive shoulders a knot of hard muscle. The power radiating off him could have reached across and knocked her off her feet without him ever having to strike a blow.

A child was standing in front of Gray, holding a sword in her hands and trembling violently. No it wasn't a child, after all, it was a young woman. A stunningly beautiful young woman. He found himself reacting to this young beauty physically and was instantly disgusted with his revolting lack of discipline. Staring at the weapons in her hands and reminding himself what mayhem they could do to his person, the man pulled his thoughts under control. *A woman. What the devil was a woman doing in the hold of this ship?*

He couldn't fight a woman. And she was definitely a woman. He guessed she had looked like a child to him because her head hardly reached his shoulders and she stared him straight in the chest. He lowered his sword. Opening his mouth, he was about to tell her not to be afraid, she was in no danger. He never got the chance.

She shook her head to recover her wits and lunged at the giant. She thrust her sword at his chest, keeping her dagger ready to thwart his return blow. The giant was completely taken off guard. She connected with the mail on his chest.

"Oh no ye don't, lassy!" He recovered himself like lightning – bringing up his sword and deflecting her blow before it could penetrate further. He grabbed her right wrist with his free hand, squeezing until the bones ground together and she dropped the sword with a shout. Ysabelle promptly slashed at his arm with the dirk in her left hand, slicing partway through his studded leather and mail gloves before he dropped his sword to grab her free hand.

"Blast ye, woman!" he shouted at her. "Those were my favored gloves!"

An iron grip held her fast. The man squeezed her newly captured wrist until she could no longer stand the pain and she dropped her dagger. He quickly spun her around so that her back was toward him and crushed her to his chest – pinning both of her arms completely – with one powerful arm. Her struggles seemed to mean nothing to him.

"Be still, lass, or I'll have to make ye a wee bit uncomfortable." Ysabelle stilled herself. She wasn't sure what 'uncomfortable' meant to him, but she was relatively sure she didn't want to find out. The interloper spoke with a Scottish brogue. Of course he would be one of the unwashed heathen Scots, she thought, then immediately chastised herself for thinking about something so insignificant. It was fitting, though – everyone knew the Scots were barbarians. She was such a fool! She never should have agreed to come with Adam. Ysabelle stomped on his foot as hard as she could just for being Scottish. He crushed the air out of her in return.

"I don't want to have to do that again, lass. So behave yerself." The giant bent them both double to pick up both swords and her dagger with his free hand. He sheathed his own sword, then shoved her dirk and sword into his belt. He took a length of rope from his belt with an efficient, powerful movement and, gripping her wrists in one hand, skillfully tied her hands behind her back. Then the huge man effortlessly forced her across the room and through the doorway. As they passed the now empty hold, Ysabelle began to understand what was happening.

"I understand now. You're a pirate, aren't you?" She asked boldly. Pirates always killed everyone. It was common knowledge, so she had nothing to lose. "A pirate and a heathen Scot."

"I am. How kind of ye to notice. I am at yer service." She straightened up, angry. She wasn't trembling and begging for her life, she was furious – ready to slash his throat. How interesting. He was amused.

Ysabelle could hear the laugh in his voice – how irritating. She snorted. "A pirate with manners? Please, just be the brute I'm certain you are and kill me now. I have no need of your manners. It's rather like a pig wearing velvet." Her chin jutted upward and she turned to look at him with fire in her eyes, challenging.

He laughed out loud at her insult. "Well, lass, I've never heard it put quite that way before. Tell me, am I a pig because I'm a pirate, or because I'm a heathen Scot?" The underlying threat was there as he waited for her to insult him again.

"Truthfully, I've never met a Scot before. So I suppose you're a pig because you're a pirate. Although I understand there's only a trifling difference between the three."

"I'm not sure if ye're honest, brave, or foolhardy. How refreshing. Not somethin' I've encountered before in the English." He leaned down to her ear and said in a low whisper, "Ye don't belong on this ship, girl," he told her. "Why are ye here?"

"I'm not a girl. I was traveling to Dunwich with my companion. From there we were going to an island off the coast of Scotland. Little chance of getting there now, I suppose."

He laughed again. It was rather rude of him, she thought, since he had asked the question to begin with. "More honesty? Ye're awfully forthcoming with me, lass. Why not lie? I'm but a vile pirate. Or a pig wearing velvet, whichever ye prefer," he added as an afterthought, eyes twinkling with amusement. This young woman was a delight. Irritated with himself for noticing, he suddenly frowned.

She could not see his frown, she was too busy being annoyed with him. "Why, indeed? What has a dead man to lose by telling the truth?"

"A dead man? Not by my accounting. Unless I'm sorely mistaken, lass – or blind as a new kitten, ye look like a woman to me." He prodded her up the ladder to the deck, engaging her in conversation the entire way – perplexed by his own behavior. Blast her for being so beautiful. He immediately corrected the direction of his irritation. There were many beautiful women at court, the appeal in this woman was in her demeanor.

Ysabelle had a feeling he was enjoying her terror, although she wasn't truly terrified any longer. His foolish banter had put her at ease, at least for the moment. Now she was just angry. Brute. When they reached the upper deck, he shoved her through the small trapdoor.

"Whatever does it matter how I speak to you? Everyone knows pirates never take prisoners. If I'm to die, be certain I will speak my mind first." The deck was freezing, the wind whistled around them. Ysabelle began to shiver, even though she was still wearing Adam's heavy cloak.

"Speaking yer mind may singe my tender feelings. What ye say is quite true. Pirates definitely have the reputation of not taking prisoners. Perchance I'm not an ordinary pirate."

"Of that I'm sure that every pirate is certain." Blinking after her hours in the dark hold, she looked around the deck. It was brilliantly lit up by at least fifteen oil lamps. They were hanging from pegs all over the deck. Everything stood out in stark relief against the dark night. At the stern end of the deck sat every sailor – bound hand and foot – guarded by a handful of armed, masked men.

The crew's weapons were heaped in a pile in the middle of the deck. Forster was among them, sitting towards the back of the group. They were unusually quiet – she hadn't heard the men say anything in less than a shout since she had been on board, but they weren't uttering a peep now. Evidently having their lives threatened quieted them a bit. Forster looked at her with pity. Adam was sitting against the central mast – tied to it actually – alone, also bound. He smiled when he saw her. A man tied and sitting with the sailors, but in very fine clothing, began to shout at the giant when he saw him. Ysabelle turned when she heard his shrill voice shatter the quiet.

"YOU THERE! DUNCAN! I know who you are! I know and I'll tell everyone who'll listen! Baron Duncan, you're a traitor to the crown and I'll see you hanged! Mark my words!"

"Gag that man!" the giant ordered one of the pirates guarding the men. It was swiftly done.

Ysabelle took it all in with wonder. Baron? In a pig's eye. He was as likely to be a baron as she was to be daughter of the king. Turning to look her captor in the eye, she held her head high and said haughtily, "I believe you delude yourself, Scot. I highly doubt you are anything but an ordinary pirate. I doubt there is anything extraordinary about you but your size." She caught sight of Adam and caught her breath.

She turned to him accusingly, "Why is my companion separated from the others? Has he done something particularly heinous that would aggravate a pirate that is not ordinary? Is it because he had the gall to stow away on a ship that was taken by you? Is he to die in some special, horrible way you have reserved for innocents?" She whirled away from the giant, catching him off guard. She glared at him, her maternal hackles raised – protecting her pup – something she cared about.

It should have been amusing, but for some reason her defense of the bound man angered her captor unreasonably. "He was yer companion? Does he mean something to ye, lass? Is he yer husband?" The giant pirate, unconsciously, had drawn his sword. When he realized what he had done, he put the weapon away.

"No, he's not my husband! It's nothing like that. He's my brother," she stated emphatically. "He's not a soldier or a sailor. He was a stowaway, like myself. We are equally guilty, pirate, and we should die together!" She had seen the malevolence in the man's eyes – a violence that had no rhyme or reason – it had appeared out of nowhere the minute she had asked the man about Adam. It was terrifying. Why did he hate Adam?

Still free for the moment from the giant's grasp, she ran over and plopped herself down next to Adam. "Call me foolhardy, I don't care what you think of me. He goes nowhere unless I am with him. If you think I lie, test me. I will throw myself in front of a sword aimed at his heart. We die together, or not at all," she said passionately, chin jutting upward in defiance.

He simply stared at her – a perplexed look on his face – as if he couldn't quite decide what he wanted to do about her.

"Ysabelle, no!" Adam shouted. He would have leapt to his feet had he been able. He was not about to be responsible for her death, and if there was a chance for anyone to come out of this alive, it was a woman. She might be able to play on the sympathies of the pirates. She was beautiful, strong, brave.

"Close your mouth, brother! Do not be foolish!" she ordered. She eyed him meaningfully.

Brother? He looked at her strangely. Well, if she thought there was a reason to carry on this charade, he would be happy to comply. "As you wish, dear sister." He winked at her.

She nudged him with her elbow in return with a you'd-better-behave-yourself look on her face. There was nothing to do but sit and wait to see what would happen to them. Their odds were not good. Adam had not felt this helpless since his mother had disappeared.

The giant, glaring at Ysabelle since she had sat down beside her brother, had watched their interchange and was still staring at the two of them, nostrils flaring, color high. They were not brother and sister, he was sure of it. Gray paced the deck, lithe and powerful like an enormous panther. His dark hair gleaming in the lamplight, that was exactly what he looked like – a huge cat, compelling and dangerous. Struggling with some unknown battle, he unconsciously berated himself while he paced. It was difficult for Ysabelle to even look away from him – he confused her. She hated her weakness. She would be strong – for Adam, for herself.

Ysabelle whispered out of the corner of her mouth, "Why are you separate from the rest?"

Adam whispered in return, "I'm not sure. They nabbed me from behind as I was coming out of the hold. Took my dagger first thing, then dragged me over here and started shouting for the big one that brought you up. That huge one over there, I mean. The one who keeps staring at you. He stared me up and down and asked where I'd been hiding. Of course, I wouldn't answer him. His face turned white when he looked at me. It wasn't fear, his reaction was … strange. He ordered me to be bound here until the 'Gentleman' could see to me. Don't ask me what that means. At that point he went looking for anyone else who might have been hiding along with me in the hold. Why is my sword in his belt? And is that your dagger as well?"

She blushed. "I attacked him with it. Needless to say, he bested me. It was, however, my first real sword fight, next time I'll do better. I had only trained a few lessons with Father Corey. And yes, he's got my dagger as well." Adam began laughing uproariously, drawing the attention of the giant pirate and practically everyone else on board. The pirate scowled fiercely.

Adam tried to stop himself, but he was close to hysteria. His own reaction sickened him, but he couldn't stop laughing. There was something ludicrous about her defending her swordplay against a seasoned fighter.

Gray, consciously deciding to ignore the two for the time being, turned away to sort himself out. His reaction to her was wrong – completely out of character. He hadn't noticed a woman since Abigail's death. But he was having trouble keeping his eyes off this woman. That was breaking his vow, and he would not willingly do that. There was no other way, he would have to distance himself until he could determine what was wrong with him. Besides, there was much to do. The Gentleman would be here any second to survey his work. He began dividing the booty into halves.

Ysabelle kicked Adam. "Idiot, stop your laughing! You'll get us both killed!" Her voice softened toward him. "Besides, my losing at swordplay is not that funny. I rather expected it," she admitted.

Her sincerity struck him as funny and he began to laugh again. "I'm afraid it is. Besides, I laugh when I'm nervous, and I tend to get nervous when I'm about to die. Don't look so serious, sister, at least you won't be homeless anymore." Unable to help himself, he began to laugh again.

"Laughing at danger is a deplorable habit we shall have to break you of – if we live long enough, that is. Don't you think that giant over there, the one that had such a strange reaction to you, looks a trifle familiar? He stares at you as if he knows you." Ysabelle kept glancing at the enormous man who had captured her, trying to figure out why he seemed so … well, like she knew him. It was impossible, of course, for her to know him. Her entire life had been spent in her tiny village, and he was definitely not a local. Still, he did look very familiar.

The giant pirate was now joined by an even taller man – if it was possible – at least a half inch taller and just as broad, who came up from below decks. Ysabelle could tell by their camaraderie and appearance that they were either brothers or similar looking friends. She guessed brothers. They spoke in low voices for a moment, then nodded in agreement. The slightly larger man turned to look at Adam and Ysabelle, then turned back to his companion and whispered to him while nodding vigorously. The two giants and their cohorts then turned their attention to a small rowboat crossing the short distance between the ship they were on and the enormous sailing ship that was pulled alongside them flying the Jolly Roger. Every now and then Ysabelle's captor would turn and stare at his two captives as if drawn to them. What was it about that man that seemed so familiar? He still hadn't bothered to secure her to the mast. He had allowed her to stay where she was unfettered.

Her eyes opened wide in surprise. "I know what it is! He looks a bit, maybe even more than just a trifle, like you, Adam! Look at his hair! It's as dark and as red as yours – red like blood! Now that's not something you see every day." She nodded with her head, and Adam followed her gaze. She was right. The giant did look somewhat like Adam. Except for his size, of course. The man had six inches on Adam – both tall and wide. He must have felt their gazes on him, for he turned his head in their direction and caught their stares. Gray stared back, a puzzled look on his face – as though he was trying to figure something out.

Adam interrupted her thoughts. "He stares at me as if I were a three-headed fish. But worse than that, he stares at you as though he'd like to swallow you. Don't push him, Ysabelle. I think he could be dangerous to you – or worse."

It was her turn to laugh. The melodic sound bounced around the hushed deck. The giant's head came up swiftly to look at her. His stormy gray eyes held her gaze for a long moment. "He *might* be dangerous to me? Adam – you've gone daft. Of course he's dangerous to me! To you as well, for that matter."

He lowered his voice. "That wasn't what I meant, and you know it. Be *careful,* Ysabelle." Their hands, still tied behind their backs, were almost touching. He reached over with his hand and squeezed hers.

The giant had the instincts of a cat as well, for he noticed the slight gesture. Immediately he pulled away from the side of the ship and stalked up to the two of them. Grabbing her by the upper arm, Gray hauled Ysabelle to her feet and angrily dragged her away from Adam. He sat her down on the deck at his feet and glared at her – willing her to submit. She would have kicked him, but remembered what Adam said and restrained herself.

There was the thump of the small dinghy on the side of the ship and Gray's attention was turned to the water once again. Up and over the side of the ship came not a masked, but a hooded pirate – quite a bit shorter than the enormous men waiting for him. Both of the huge men on deck bowed slightly to their superior. Directly behind the hooded pirate came a tall, blonde masked man. Even masked he was obviously very handsome. Ysabelle could not help looking at him. He was beautiful – if a man could be beautiful – and this one was. The giant noticed her notice and stepped between Ysabelle and the blonde man. She had to keep herself from laughing – the poor giant was totally irrational.

She couldn't help but stare at the small pirate they were calling 'Gentleman.' Such a tiny pirate leading a crew of giants. It was fascinating to watch, like a mouse leading a group of cats. But this was no mouse.

Obviously in control and respected, the leader made short work of directing his crew.

"Pull the ship alongside. Haul the dinghy to the rear and secure it. Get this booty aboard and quick. As soon as it's done – signal the waiting ship and leave." His speech was concise and full of authority. Immediately his men hopped to.

The pirate ship was drawn so close in that the two ships were practically touching. The haul from the hold-half of it still piled at the bow end of the deck, half now in the middle of the deck where it was easily accessible – was taken by pulleys onto the pirate ship's deck. Funny thing, though, she noticed, they only took the half. The rest was left piled at the bow instead of moved to the pirate ship. Straightaway a group of pirates waiting on deck quickly stowed the pilfered booty in their hold. The diminutive pirate had the total obedience of his crew. Ysabelle was entranced.

"Sir!" the giant called out to get his leader's attention. When the small pirate finally turned toward his giant crewmember, the enormous man signaled for a private conference. The two spoke in whispers for a moment – surprise and shock registering ever so briefly on the leader's face. Immediately he turned to look at Adam. Ysabelle couldn't read the leader's expression, but she had the feeling it was taking great amounts of control to keep whatever emotion was threatening from showing.

The hooded pirate crossed the distance between him and the captive in a few strides, authority radiating in his walk, and dropped to one knee in front of Adam. Staring into Adam's face for a full thirty seconds, the rogue captain made his decision. Without a word he regained his feet, recrossed the deck, and signaled to the one man who was even bigger than the giant. Ysabelle was still of the opinion that the two were brothers.

The small, lithe captain snapped his fingers impatiently. "Take him across to the ship. Put him in the hold under lock and key. He goes with us," the leader commanded.

"Captain, the girl goes as well," the giant said, loud enough for all to hear. Adam looked up quickly at the giant, assessing the threat to Ysabelle. He wasn't sure how he would accomplish it, but he felt like he must keep her safe. He had talked her into this idiotic trip, after all.

The leader whirled around. "Are you in charge now, boy?"

Boy? Ysabelle didn't see any boys around here. If that hulking thing over there wasn't a man, she was stumped to know what one was. But as long as he was battling for her to accompany Adam to whatever destiny was waiting, anything they said between them was okay with her.

"No, sir. I do not wish to challenge ye on this. That notwithstanding, sir, she will accompany us." The leader looked up and studied the giant's face for a long moment. There was no give in his expression.

He sighed heavily. "You may have her." He turned to the blonde man, "Take her over."

"NO!" the giant shouted. His leader stared at him, obviously shocked. Gray used his discipline to pull his voice down to a reasonable level and began again. "I'll take her to the ship. She'll not be goin' with him." His brogue became quite thick when he was angry. The leader had a slight burr, but nothing like the giant. Ysabelle hadn't yet heard the brother speak.

The handsome blonde man bowed deeply to both his superiors. "As ye wish, milord." He addressed the giant with a grin. Glaring at the handsome man, the giant waved him away. The leader again studied Gray's face. Shrugging his shoulders, the captain turned to walk away.

The giant stopped his superior by gripping his shoulder. The captain turned and craned his neck to look the man in the eye. "I've never asked anything like this of ye before. Ye know that."

The hooded pirate nodded. "That's true. It's why I've allowed your request." He started to turn away, then changed his mind. "But tell me … why now?"

"Truthfully … I don't know. But thank ye for this concession. It's important to me." The man was speaking almost tenderly to his leader. It was most strange, this emotion between these men. Ysabelle was caught, spellbound, watching the curious interplay between the two. It was as if they were all a large family. Not a rough, cruel family – not like most of the families she knew – but a tender, loving one. The kind of family she had often dreamed of belonging to. She shook her head. That image was so incongruous with the pirate image ingrained in her mind that the poor girl was becoming more confused by the moment.

Her strange captor walked over to her, extending his hand to her in an almost gentlemanly fashion. "Get up, lass," he spoke warmly, kindly, confusing her even more. The giant leaned down and pulled her to her feet, gently – much to her surprise, and began to herd her toward the side of the boat that was closest to the pirate ship. When Ysabelle looked down over the side, she saw a deep chasm with only a few feet of water separating the two ships. The dinghy that had carried the leader had been pulled to the rear of the pirate ship and was trailing by a rope. Good thing too, for it would have been crushed, so close were the two ships. Two men were hoisting it up to its resting place, hooked just under the railing at the stern.

The giant lifted her by the waist and, whistling shrilly to get the attention of a crewman standing opposite him on the other ship, held her effortlessly

124

out over the water and placed her into the waiting arms of the crewman. Ysabelle closed her eyes, holding her breath until she was safely across the steep drop. She finally took a deep breath when she was safely on board the pirate ship. Without a word, she was tied to the mast and told to be still.

She had a good view of the taken ship's deck, and while she waited for only God knew what would happen to her, she watched as Adam was attached to one of the pulley ropes by his belt. Ysabelle prayed the belt would hold as he was slowly and somewhat painfully pulled across in a much less gentle fashion than she was. His bruises would not face for more than a week, she was certain. Still, he was here with her. To his credit, his face – for once – betrayed nothing. Adam was using every ounce of control he possessed to keep it that way. He knew that in this time, strength and weakness were the only things that counted – both physically and mentally. Adam looked up from his humiliating position and winked at Ysabelle to ease her. It worked.

She sighed with relief. It made her feel safer, somehow, even though they were both still in grave danger. Or maybe it was just that she felt less alone. *Quit being selfish*, she chided herself. For whatever reason, she was grateful for Adam's presence – even when he bumped down hard onto the deck and winced in pain. He lay there for a moment panting, catching his breath. When he had recovered his breathing some, he sat himself up as best he could and gave Ysabelle a rousing smile. There was no need for her to be worried about him as well as the situation they were in. If he could do nothing else, he could at least attempt to put her at ease.

The pirates came next – almost twenty of them – hand over hand on the two pulley ropes tied to their own rigging, back across to their ship. The small one, the Gentleman, was the last across, but made the trip with no less ease.

Once on board their own ship again, Gentleman gave the order. "Cut her loose! Weigh anchor, mates! And look lively, we're sailing for home!" The anchor winch began to clank as the crew hurried to obey their captain.

Momentarily, they cut loose from the king's ship. The pirates cheered. Ysabelle was horrified, setting the ship adrift with the men aboard and no one to navigate or steer it. Then she realized that the other ship was still anchored, giving them a faint flicker of hope that someone would find them. In the next instant, there was a great booming noise from behind her. The noise was so monstrous, Ysabelle thought the world was coming to an end for a moment. Another ship, she hadn't noticed it before, had been standing not too far off the bow. Hearing the signal, the ship began moving in. The pirate ship lowered the Jolly Roger and attached a new flag to the pole, although they did not raise it.

Ysabelle was surprised when the pirates sat off at a short distance and waited as the new ship came alongside and boarded the king's ship, taking all the prisoners and the remaining booty and transferring them to their own deck. Once their mission was accomplished, that ship cut loose as well, and headed north – sails full and churning up quite a wake. The other rogue ship was flying the Norman flag.

On board the ship that held her hostage, Ysabelle looked on as the new flag of the pirate ship was raised. It was an odd banner – showing an elephant facing a lion in what she supposed was an attack stance – although she could not imagine an elephant in such a position. She half-wondered if the flag was some sort of jest.

As the pirates watched the unfolding drama from the railing, Ysabelle found her voice. "What's to be done with the poor sailors? Will they all be killed?" She addressed her question to the back of the giant's head, but the leader turned and answered her directly.

"The crew will be marooned on an island that will sustain them well enough until they are found. They will be in good company, there are four other ships' crews there." The Gentleman seemed quite pleased with himself. Even though she thought him a vile creature, she couldn't help but notice what fine bone structure the conspicuously short man had. He almost looked feminine. Ysabelle's attention was turned from her study when Adam was rescued from his awkward position on the deck by the giant and dragged over to rest by her.

"Are you all right, Adam?" she called out to him warmly as he fell to her feet with a thump.

Looking up, he flashed her a meaningful smile. Gray saw it and frowned viciously, rethinking Adam's resting place and dragging the captive back to his feet and toward the hold. "I'm fine, Ysabelle. Be careful. We'll be okay." Gray roughly turned Adam over to his brother, who half-dragged, half-pulled him toward the stairs.

The captain watched closely, taking in everything. "Stop, Alane," he called. "Bring the prisoner to me." Alane did so.

The captain inspected him thoroughly, walking in a circle around him, head moving up and down. "Boy," he ordered, "tell me your name."

"Adam Talbot, sir."

The captain flinched as if struck and all the color drained from what was visible of his face. The hood had fallen backward a bit, exposing a small amount of the captain's chin and neck, and what little Ysabelle could see had grown markedly whiter. Adam noticed the pirate's reaction as well. Strange.

He stared at the small man, a puzzled look on his face. Why on earth would the mention of his name cause the captain fear? Perhaps there was someone from this time who possessed his name and was notorious for some reason. Still....

The captain cleared his throat. "Take the prisoner below and secure him. Keep him separate from the crew. Bed him down. Shackle him securely. It won't do to have him wandering about the rest of the night waiting to cut our throats." Nobody moved for a moment. "Now, sir!" the captain shouted at Alane.

Alane eyed his captain, an unreadable expression on his face. His jaw set rigidly. "Aye, sir!" He took the prisoner below, resurfacing from the hold a few minutes later.

Her bravado was at an end. Katharine had to get all of this away from her before she lost all her composure in front of her men and fainted. It couldn't be! It just couldn't be! She felt weak in her knees. "Gray, Alane," she called, "Come to my cabin immediately. We must speak privately."

"Yes, sir!" they answered in unison.

As they crossed the deck to the captain's quarters, Gray saw Percy approaching the mast where Ysabelle was tied. He stopped short, turning to address the handsome blonde man. "Stay away from her, Percy. There's nothin' for ye there, man."

"By all means, milord," his second answered with a curt, mocking bow and a gleaming smile, switching directions in a single graceful move and heading for the bow where he seemed to have immediate business to attend. He couldn't help himself from grinning, though. There was something to this strange fascination of Gray's – Percy was sure of it.

Gray and Alane followed the captain almost to the stern where the captain's quarters were located. There was a low door there and, hunching their shoulders so as not to bump their heads on the doorframe, the two men stepped through it after their captain. Through it lay a short companionway with one door on each side and one at the end. Behind each of the three doors was hidden a small cabin belonging to one of the three. The two men followed their captain down the companionway and into the captain's cabin-into their mother's cabin. Once inside the Gentleman Pirate's cabin, Gray always found that name quite humorous, Alane turned and shut the door with a bang.

Once the door was shut, the captain pulled off her hood. The two men took their masks off as well and stuffed them into their belts without a word. The air in the small room was icy, and Gray crossed the room to add more wood to the small stove.

Alane was the first to speak. "Well, Mother?" Gray looked up from his task in anticipation of her answer.

She sank heavily into her desk chair and exhaled loudly. "Sweet heavens, it's him. There's no doubt about it. It's him. I can't believe it! He's here!"

"Told ye!" Alane shouted.

"I told ye, little brother," Gray returned. "I saw him first, remember?"

"In a pig's eye!"

Dropping her head to rest on the desktop in front of her, Katharine vented her frustration on her sons. "Not now, boys, please! I must think. Gray, did you see how much he looked like you? It was amazing. Except for his size, he could be your twin." She stared at her hands, which were twisting in her lap. She hadn't felt this uncertain in years. "If he's here, he's here for only one reason – to find me. How can I explain to him why I was absent for the greater part of his life?"

"If he didn't know that already, Mother, he wouldn't have come. He couldn't have come. He has to have the letter. Surely ye must realize that! Think, woman!" Alane came around the desk, approaching his mother slowly and kneeling in front of her. He placed his hands on her knees and looked up at her tenderly. They had no secrets between them. The truths of their lives had always been stranger than fiction, and none of them doubted any of the others. She covered his hand with hers and smiled as she gazed into his eyes. Gray was instantly behind her, lending her his support, both his large hands on her shoulders. She leaned her head over to rest on his forearm. He said nothing, waiting for her to speak.

"I never expected…. Gray, he really could be your twin!"

"I already have one of those, mother, and I'm sure Annabella would not appreciate bein' replaced. Even by a brother."

Katharine rubbed her forehead with both of her hands and shrugged out of her well-worn cloak, in truth it had belonged to Garrett, the fire in the wood stove finally warming the air a degree or two. "Gray, you understood my meaning. I had no idea his hair would be as dark red as yours is. He was so … young … such a small child … when I saw him last. He looks to be your age as well, Gray. Well, except for a few hundred years." She tried to smile at her joke, but failed miserably. Turning to Alane, she pleaded for his acceptance, "What did you think of him?"

Alane winked at her, grinning wickedly. "Well, Mother, he's certainly much better lookin' than old Gray. Certainly stronger, cuttin' a much more manly figure, and I'm sure he's a better chess player. How could he not be? All in all, I think we could just throw Gray overboard right now and replace him with Adam. It's been a lifelong dream of mine, for sure."

Gray's foot snaked out from behind his mother's chair and toppled his brother onto his backside with a grin. "Mine as well, my wee little brother. I could think of nothin' more peaceful than to be rid of yer incessant teasin'. But I'm sure ye would only jump into the ocean and drag me back so ye could continue to harass me for the rest of my natural days. Yer jealousy is not becomin' to ye, wee laddie. It's high time ye grew up and recognized that."

Alane scrambled to his feet, glaring at his larger brother. Quick as a wink, a mournful look replaced his glare as he teased, "Tis true. Harassin' ye is my most favorite form of entertainment. Has been since I was but wee boy. Ah, youth!" He sighed dramatically as he continued, " However, big brother, much as I would like to debate the virtues of throwin' yer worthless carcass overboard, I have duties to attend to. The first, of course, is to go see what ye find so dazzlin' about that young woman out there. Pretty creature that she is, I don't know that I've seen ye captivated by a woman in years." With a wink, Alane turned to leave.

Gray leapt from behind the chair onto him with a ferocious shout. "The devil ye will!"

Their mother was standing over them in a flash. "Gentlemen!" Her soft command called their attention to her. They looked up from their positions on the floor, hands still about each other's throats, to find a sword perched a scant inch above each of their exposed necks. "I will not allow grown men to act like children in my presence. Feel free to carry this childish tussle out on deck, but you will leave my cabin behaving as the gentlemen I had always hoped you would become. A mother's dream – dashed to pieces by her own children. Tis a pity. Humor me, boys."

They nodded their hasty agreement and stood to their feet. The two men busied themselves straightening their appearances. They always knew she wouldn't kill them or even do to them what she threatened. The bite of it was, they were never sure what she *would* do, if they pushed her hard enough. It was her edge. She knew it and she used it.

She waved them away. "I have to think. Leave me now, boys. I'll call for you in a while, when I've had some time to think. Alane, don't let them treat Adam harshly." They bowed politely and as one her sons turned to leave. "Gray, wait a moment. What is it about this woman? I've never seen you react to a woman at all since Abigail, and now you seem to have gone daft. Why this one? Why is she here?"

"She was traveling with Adam."

She lifted her brow skeptically. "Is that why she's here, now?"

"Aye."

She sighed and shook her head knowingly. "Gray, lies do not become you, son. I am your mother, not one of your men. I know you. Now – the truth."

He sighed, "Nay, Mother. She's here because I want her here."

"Obviously," she answered. "Now, why?"

"I don't know, mother. There's somethin' about her … it's hard to explain … well, she pulled a sword on me."

"Admirable. I've seen the need many times myself."

"When I found her hiding place, she engaged me in a fight. She was shaking with fear. The woman did passably well, I might add, even though she was terrified."

"A compliment from you as well. Interesting." She looked at him piercingly, willing the truth out of him.

"After … when she realized the danger was past, she sassed me. It was astonishing. No woman, and few men, has ever talked to me that way. She was honest. When I addressed her, she didn't cower or tremble. She didn't bat her eyes or simper at me like the women at court. She's brazen and … courageous. I liked it … I liked her."

"Don't forget her beauty, big brother," Alane added, elbowing Gray in the ribs. "She's quite a sight to look upon, isn't she now, old sot?"

Gray punched him in the shoulder none too gently and awarded his younger brother a fierce scowl. Alane ignored the blow and winked at him, irritating him even more.

"And?" Katharine pressed.

"I want her, Mother. I imagine I do at any rate. I'm not really sure. After Abigail, I never thought I'd want any woman again. I promised myself … I don't know how to feel. Granted, I haven't had much practice at feeling in the last few years."

"Then we definitely keep her. At least until you decide whether you truly have feelings for her … or just a bad case of indigestion," Katharine smiled. Her son – the one with the heart of iron, the one who had closed himself off from the world of love – was caught. He was fluttering about like a wild thing searching for freedom, but he was caught. As the boys left the room, Alane whispering insults to his brother, they heard their mother's parting comment.

"Yes, boys, it's been a red-letter day."

Alane grinned as he gently shut the cabin door.

NINE

"When did they leave, old woman?" Randall was standing, full of anger and violence at missing them again, over the broken form of the old woman. She hadn't resisted him, he had simply been so enraged at failing to overtake the girl and having to leave that crone Inez untouched the he hadn't been able to help himself. The old woman would live – he had left her that and was feeling quite proud of himself for it. He wasn't usually so contained.

"Two days past, milord. They was leavin' on a ship what left at dawn. Don't know for where. Don't know what the ship's name was. Just know they was leavin'." She burst into sobs again. "Please, milord," she begged, "It's all I know. I swear on me 'usband's grave."

"Perhaps you didn't like your husband, old woman," he said with a wicked smile.

"Oh no, sir!" she protested. "I wouldn't risk my soul for a girl I don't know. I only gave them quarter. I only gave them quarter!"

"You should pick your boarders more carefully in the future. What did this man look like? The one traveling with her."

The old woman painfully pulled herself up to lean against the wall before she answered. "Her brother? He was tall and handsome, that. He had thick dark hair and pretty gray eyes. He was dressed right elegant, he was. She was as well. Dressed in rich brocade and velvet, what. I thought they was nobility, in all them fine clothes and all, milord. The young man even paid me in gold."

"Let me see it," Randall commanded. She slowly and agonizingly got to her feet and walked across the stuffy dark room. From behind a loose board, she took a small box. She fetched the treasured piece of gold and handed it to the king's man. He studied it carefully, taking a similar piece from his pocket. It was identical to the piece he had liberated from the merchant.

He threw the woman a coin and pocketed the piece of gold. Randall gave the woman a once over, wishing he could finish what he started with her. The terror in her eyes as she read his look was so enticing to his murderer's soul. With a sigh, he turned and left the small house without so much as a backward glance and went in search of a loose tongue at the shipyards.

When Gray and Alane stepped back out onto the deck and into the biting wind, Gray expertly evaluated the sails and the rigging with his eyes. The lanterns that had lighted the deck had all been extinguished but two, and they cast an eerie glow and wildly swinging shadows across the deck. Even in the dark, he expertly assessed the status of the ship. The sea was choppy, but not violent. Campbell was on watch, Boyd was aloft. "Take in the starboard!" he ordered, breath pluming out white in front of him.

"Aye, sir!"

Gray watched intently until it was done. Alane continued on without him, needing to check on a slight course correction with the helmsman.

"Sweet heavens, you're twins!" Ysabelle shouted. She was still tied to the central mast, shivering violently. Her legs were asleep and she was almost numb with cold when the brothers exited the companionway. "But that couldn't be, or Adam would have known you. Of course he told me he didn't know his mother. I've divined the truth now! You're Adam's brother, but he doesn't know it." She turned and eyed Alane. "And you're his other brother – and he doesn't know you either!"

Alane grinned and walked on. Gray stopped dead in his tracks when Ysabelle addressed him. He turned to look at her, focusing his complete attention on her. Immediately, warmth flooded her body, and she knew she was blushing. She felt like a bird caught in a trap, immobilized by his intense gaze. Determined not to show him weakness, she straightened her shoulders and looked at him squarely.

Her stare was scorching. Every time the beautiful woman looked straight at him, Gray felt hot all over – like he was standing in the summer sun. He returned her scrutiny with his own, and she forgot what she had been talking about.

"Oh my...." She could so easily fall into the storm in those eyes. She shook her head to clear the squall inside it. "That's why you didn't kill us, isn't it?"

"Ye're right in part, lass. It's why we didn't kill him."

"He doesn't know, does he?"

He shook his head. "Nay, he doesn't."

The import of his first statement dawned on her. "Well then, sir, if that's the reason you didn't kill him, what's the reason you didn't kill me?"

Gray had no idea what to say. It felt as though his brain had seized up and his tongue had become leaden. Then he remembered her words to him on the *Laney*. "If ye'll remember, sweet one, ye told me ye were his sister. Wasn't that the truth?"

She was so nervous her mind didn't even register the endearment. Her eyes telegraphed her lie to him before it came out of her mouth. "Of course I'm his sister. We've been together forever."

He was disappointed by her lie, but only for a fraction of a second. He leaned down until he was eye to eye with her and asked, "Then what, sweet lass, is yer family name?" Gray grinned at her – amused, knowing she was caught.

Ysabelle glared him to cinders. Blast that man! Adam had only mentioned his family name one time – when they first introduced themselves – and she couldn't for her very life remember it. All she could remember was that it began with a T. Attempting to kill him with her very eyes, Ysabelle glowered at her captor. He had her and he knew it. The giant looked so smug. She knew that any answer she gave him would be verified and would have given her extra pair of shoes to replay their sword fight and do a bit of damage this time. Not too much, of course, she wouldn't want to add any more scars to his handsome face, but arrogant men were more often than not well served by being knocked into the dirt now and then. She grinned imagining the look on his face at his humiliation, then scowled because there was no way to accomplish it.

Gray watched, fascinated, as her emotions flitted across her face. She settled on anger. The frustration on her face was priceless. He battled with himself, reining in his desire to irritate her further just to watch her face disclose all of her feelings. He grinned at her and bent down again so he could look her in her dazzling green eyes.

Ysabelle tried not to become rattled at his nearness, but she was weak. He was close enough that she could smell him. Much to her consternation, he smelled good – all wood smoke and leather and soap. She begged God to make him stink, then promised to serve penance for her request if it would only be granted. She needed some help here.

"Ye lie, lass," he whispered, his nose touching her own. The dog had the audacity to wink at her. Then he straightened up to leave.

She tried to think of something to say that would keep him there. "You, sir, have more character defects than the devil himself. I would ask, my large brother, if you insist on leaving me tied to your lovely mast, would it be too much to ask such a gentleman as yourself to have my hands tied a trifle lower so that I might sit down? You see, despite the many luxuries on board, my legs have fallen asleep and my wrists hurt a bit, of course it's fortunate that I'm numb with cold for I can't feel either discomfort. In England, it's unfitting for family to be treated in such a manner.

"However, being a Scot, it's entirely possible that you haven't been trained as to proper behavior for family members, or dogs for that matter.

133

Would you pray be kind enough to take the time to allow me a modicum of comfort? It's not as though I had anyplace to escape to, I would have to be able to swim better than Triton himself to remove myself from your odious presence. Even a man as thick-skulled as you can see that." She lifted her nose haughtily toward him, baiting him into more conversation. Irritated with herself for wanting to talk to him further, but unable to keep herself from goading him further, she tempted the man into another inane discussion.

Gray laughed out loud. By the saints, she was a daft woman! She had the nerve to insult him. Wealthy, powerful men didn't even dare speak to him in such a way! His sweet Abigail had always been so gentle and accommodating, nothing like this beauty. His father had been constantly amused when Katharine insulted him, and his son had thought him quite crazed to allow a mere woman to speak to him in such a manner. Gray never understood it until now. It was good to deal with an equal, very good.

He feigned shock. "Do ye mean to tell me, lass, that ye're uncomfortable tied to our mast? With family, we are honor bound to use ropes rather than irons. I thought we were being quite kind, the last prisoner we had was dangled from the rigging until we decided what to do with him. We threw him overboard and dragged him behind the ship all the way to port. Of course he had no family ties to us."

After considering for a moment what he had just told her, she decided he was bluffing. She tilted her head all the way back to look him in the eye and gave the cad her fiercest frown. "I'm not at all uncomfortable, kind sir." Her words dripped sarcasm. "This is entirely enjoyable. Here I am, without even my cloak, pleasured by the full impact of the wind and, on occasion, spray as well. It's enjoyable to have my wrists rubbed raw and my feet and hands numb with both cold and sleep. I thank you for your consideration. This journey has been an absolute delight, and I will be looking greatly forward to booking passage aboard this vessel again in the future." After glaring him to cinders, she turned her head away from Gray, dismissing him. She breathed deeply to calm herself. Why she had ever felt the desire to speak to this knave was a mystery. She had never before been tempted to commit murder, but there was a first for everything.

Seeing her immediate need for warmth and feeling quite the villain for not thinking of it before, Gray removed his own heavy cloak, the lining rich with ermine fur, and placed it around her shivering shoulders. He tied it securely under her chin, his knuckles brushing her jaw several times intentionally as he did so. He looked into her emerald green eyes, fascinated. This young woman was such a novel creature – insolent but novel. Grateful for the warmth and encompassed in the softness and masculine smell of his cloak,

Ysabelle was tempted to put away her pride and thank him. She restrained herself and proudly kept her head turned away from him.

Unwilling to be dismissed, Gray pulled her face back to him with his forefinger and leaned down close enough that their noses were a hairsbreadth from touching. Being this close, he badly wanted to kiss her, just to taste her soft lips for a moment. With great difficulty, he restrained himself. "Nay, lass. *You* are the delight. I'd have saved ye from the Normans just for the sheer enjoyment of it. Although I fear ye'll be quite disappointed to learn it, I have to tell ye the truth. We don't kill our conquests. We allow them to safely live out their lives." He grinned broadly at her.

Knitting her brows together in irritated disbelief, she nodded and agreed with him. "That is a disappointment. It might cause me to think of you in a better light." She screwed up her face, obviously thinking. She made her decision. "Nay. There's no danger of that."

His laughter bellowed across the deck, drawing the attention of the few crewmen who had not retired to belowdecks for the night. "I'm sorry to say I am unable untie ye, lass."

"Why ever not?"

"Well, now, sweet lass. It's just that pirates have a code of ethics I'm duty bound to follow. Rule number six clearly states – a pirate can never untie anyone without bein' introduced first."

She glared at him. "Ah, yes. I had forgotten the age-old code of pirate chivalry. By all means, I would hate to violate the sacred trust of a band of thieves. Kind sir, I am called Ysabelle of...." she faltered, "Well, it's not really important where I'm from. I'm not going back, so I'm not from there anymore, am I? You may call me Ysabelle. Yes, that's it – I'm simply Ysabelle."

Gray studied her face. She looked so lost and alone as she abandoned wherever her home had been – like she'd abandoned her very life. He wanted to hold her close to him – make that forsaken look go away. "Very well, simply Ysabelle. I'm simply Gray."

"Like your eyes," she said softly, gazing up at him. When she realized she had spoken that thought aloud, she blushed and lowered her eyes.

Her blush was the first sign she had given of her young and innocent nature. She had only shown him a fierce combativeness up to now. It was charming. "How kind of ye to notice. I was named for my eyes when I was just a newborn babe. My mother seemed to think they were noteworthy." He moved to her side, but not before she saw his self-satisfied grin. "Now, Ysabelle, since we have become friends, if ye'll turn a wee bit to the side, I'll happily see to ye comfort."

She would put up with his insolence, she decided, if he would only let her sit down and rest. Huffing her opinion of their 'friendship', Ysabelle turned as he instructed. The ribbon having coming undone, his cloak fell away from her shoulders and lay in a puddle of fur and fine wool on the deck. As he was loosening her bonds, she yawned. It had been a long time since she had enjoyed a good night's sleep. Gray noticed and frowned. She had dark smudges under her eyes as well. How long had she been traveling, he wondered.

When she was loose, Ysabelle stretched her arms above her head. It felt as though every muscle she had was coming awake with pins and needles. Wanting to help her hands awaken, she rubbed her wrists. A lusty yawn forced its way out of her mouth, drawing Gray's attention back to her tired, drawn face. He leaned down for the cloak, then tied it securely about her neck, his hands again stroking her jaw intentionally as he worked to fasten the heavy garment.

She tried, unsuccessfully, not to notice his caress. The skin where he touched her was on fire – she could hardly breathe. He stepped back from her, noticing her breathlessness, and smiled arrogantly. He watched her as she sank down and settled herself on the deck, repositioning her hands more comfortably behind her, waiting to be retied.

When Gray stooped down, Ysabelle held her wrists out to him, but instead of tethering her, he scooped her up effortlessly into his strong arms and carried her across the deck. He pressed her tightly against his hard, muscular chest and glared defiantly at the stunned faces he passed, faces of men who had never witnessed him even notice a woman in the last six years, and carried his prize through the small doorway at the end of the deck. Ysabelle was so surprised at the turn of events that she forgot to struggle. She almost forgot to breathe, but when she did finally fill her lungs, his wonderful masculine scent – intoxicating in its nearness – floated about her.

Gray carried her the short length of the companionway before reaching his destination. He opened the door on the left to a small, furnished cabin and, crossing to the long, narrow bunk across the room in one huge, powerful stride, he dropped her roughly upon it. Turning to light the lamp that was hanging from a peg on the wall, Gray then added wood to the small heating stove that inadequately warmed the cabin in such cold temperatures.

Ysabelle must have looked shocked, for when the light filled the room and he looked at her face, he laughed. The man laughed at everything she did, she thought with irritation. In response, she instantly made her expression serene. "Thank you, sir. Perhaps you are more than an ordinary squalid pirate, after all. Or is this a last consideration before my execution?

Should I request a last meal?" she baited him.

He nodded serenely.

She blanched, her eyes round. Ysabelle breathed in sharply. "Truly? Oh heavens! Please milord, If I've offended you–"

He cut her off with a bellow of laughter. "Of course ye've offended me! Ye've the tongue of an asp, woman! Ye should be grateful I'm a patient man with women, for ye could tempt a saint to violence. Were ye a dragon, I would be cinders by now and ye would be unfortunate enough to have my sword run through yer gut. I simply wished for a wee bit o' politeness in return. I had high hopes that ye possessed manners of some sort, although I must confess I wasn't sure if anyone had ever taught ye proper conduct. Courtesy was given. I thank ye for it. And ye may call me Gray, Ysabelle. Tis my name, so please be kind enough to use it. Enjoy a good night's sleep, lass." He walked to the end of the bunk and opened his sea chest. Pulling from it his sextant and charts, he closed the lid, straightened up and turned to go.

"Wait!"

Pausing with his hand on the handle of the cabin door, Gray turned. He said nothing, just waited.

"What will happen to Adam?"

His eyes narrowed on her face and he crossed the room in one great stride to stand in front of the narrow bunk. "And why do ye ask me that, lassie? Do ye have some special feelin' for him, sweet Ysabelle? Ye would be wise to tell me no." He had become angry in a flash – towering over her, menacing. His face was set like granite.

This man could scare the scales off fish, if he had a mind to. She wasn't going to let him know it though. With all the control she possessed, she kept her face impassive. "I care for him, of course, but I'm more concerned about his well-being." Her offhand remark eased him somewhat, a fraction of the tension drained from his clenched jaw. She continued, "He seeks to find his mother. Perchance you could help him – if you are indeed his brother as I thought."

"Don't ye mean yer brother as well, lass?" he asked her, waiting for the lie.

She sighed heavily. "Nay, milord, I do not. Lies are much too laborious for me. I have such a difficult time remembering them." She sat up high on her knees so she could look him eye to eye. It was more like eye to chest, so she craned her neck back. Ysabelle surveyed him critically.

Gray stared back – a man could get lost in those pretty green eyes. "We are brothers, lass," he admitted.

She nodded. "Thank you for being truthful with me. I'll afford you the same courtesy, it's not as though I had much else to surrender. I'm not Adam's sister. Of course you were already aware of that, although we do appear enough alike to fool many. We did not meet until less than a week ago. He agreed to travel with me and protect me on my journey – I was alone, you see. I am poor. I have no money and no dowry – nothing to recommend me except that I have an adequate education. Now you know the truth of it." Her jaw lifted defiantly, yet when he made no move to retaliate for her lies, she was puzzled. Ysabelle studied Gray's face carefully. "Yet, even so, I don't think you mean to kill me. You would have done so many times over for my forward tongue if that had been your plan. And you most certainly would not have comforted me. In truth, I was pushing you to it, in order to see what kind of man you were. I know I have sorely provoked you."

"Provoked me? In truth, the Almighty has had less provocation from the devil himself! A mighty risk, lass, seein' that ye were playin' with yer life. A bit foolish, don't ye imagine?" He looked at her strangely, trying to ascertain why a woman with so much to offer would think she had nothing to lose.

She dropped her eyes sadly. "Nay, milord. Dying is no risk. I am settled as to my eternal soul, Father Corey saw to that." Bringing her head up to look him in the eye, she told him the truth of her life. "Living under cruelty is a far greater risk. I know that to my very bones." She stretched out her arms expressively, and the cuffs of her sleeves pulled back to reveal scars criscrossing up and down the inside of her forearms.

Gray's eyes softened as his brow clouded over. Anger ignited in his eyes as he saw the evidence of cruelty done to this woman. A muscle in his cheek began to twitch reflexively. He reached out with both his hands and touched her scars gently. "And who was cruel to ye, sweet Ysabelle?" he asked softly, his voice a contrast to the granite in his eyes, staring at the permanent reminders of her cruel life.

Too late she pulled her arms out from under the scrutiny of his gaze. Embarrassed, she pulled her cuffs down hurriedly, wrapping her arms about herself. "It's of no importance now," she said stiffly, still looking at the floor. "I'm not from there anymore."

Gray raised her chin to face him and leaned down to her. He pulled her back to her previous topic of conversation. "When ye provoked me, did ye find yer answer? What kind of man am I, Ysabelle?" He arched his eyebrow, intensely curious as to her opinion of him.

She folded her hands in her lap and stared at them for a moment. She raised her eyes to his face again, uncertainty mottling her expression. "I haven't yet decided. You're different from any man I have known before – I know that much. And I don't think you're a bad sort, except for the piracy, of course. Other than your tendency toward thievery, which is a sin according to the church, I suppose you're a decent enough man. Adequate, after a fashion." Uncertainty was replaced with brazenness as she challenged him with her eyes to argue with her assessment.

He smiled at her evaluation. "Adequate? High praise indeed." He stroked her cheek absently as he spoke. "Again such honesty. Ye're quite different from the women I've met before, lass. Except for my mother and Abigail, I've had less than a wee bit o' interest in dealin' with most women before. I've no patience for their games."

She nodded gravely ... knowingly. It was an unusual reaction to Gray's mind, but then, everything about this woman was unusual.

She understood. Except for Liza, Ysabelle had no great amount of enjoyment for the games and trickery of the women of her village. "Games and intrigues are a waste of precious time, I must agree."

"Ye certainly speak yer mind, Ysabelle. Have ye always been so unguarded?"

"Unguarded? Certainly not! Though I'm young, I'm not so foolish as to leave myself unguarded and vulnerable. Never mistake being forthright with being unguarded. I have walls enough to scale that a thousand knights could never accomplish it. I will not lie to you, however. I'll not cower either, sir. I've been under a fist for long enough. And I've a fine enough mind to make my own way in the world – a man's world such that it is. So, don't fool yourself, I'll not subjugate myself for money or favor. I intend to stay free – or die trying. Life is far too short to choose anything else." Her expression was arrogant, but there was fear behind her eyes.

Gray wondered for a moment what such a pretty lass had to fear, then remembered all the English of his acquaintance at court. Then, of course, there were the scars he had seen, and if there were scars on her arms, there were likely many more on her back and legs. Such cruelty. It made even his hard heart bleed. He knew exactly what she had to fear. It took such courage for her to challenge him. He held her very existence within his hands as far as she knew, yet she opposed him. She was literally taking her life in her own hands, or rather having it stolen away by him, and prodding him as well to see whether or not he was trustworthy enough to handle it. He was trustworthy – she would know that soon enough. Ysabelle would know, he would make sure of it.

"I would never ask yer freedom of ye, Ysabelle," he said tenderly, taking her completely off guard.

"You have already done so, sir." Glaring, she waited. She was expecting a fit of temper or, at the very least, a lecture or a slammed door. Instead, Gray reached down and tenderly caressed her forehead, trailing his fingers down her cheek. Then he turned and headed out the door.

"Gray," she called his name, and his heart leapt.

Get it under control, man! He turned again. "Aye?"

"Thank you."

"It's a pleasure, lass." He turned and shut the door, leaning against it until he recovered himself.

Ysabelle heard the lock turn, but she didn't care. She was safe and warm for the time being. In a bed – of all places. She rolled around, savoring the luxuriousness of the bed – it was soft and warm and safe – and the kindness of the man who had given it to her. She was being allowed to sleep in a bed for the first time in her life. It didn't matter that it was, by definition, a bunk. It was an indulgence she had never been afforded in her life. It shouldn't have been such an important thing, but Gray had no idea what he'd given her. Warmth and safety, luxury, freedom to speak without the threat of the whip. Mulling their conversation over in her mind, Ysabelle fell asleep.

The huge, well-muscled pirate who was leading him to his pallet among the coils of rope was fairly decent. He didn't indicate any basic hostility toward Adam, didn't even speak a word in fact, although the man kept looking at him strangely. He was still wearing his mask, but even so, Adam could see the resemblance between him and the giant who was keeping such a close eye on Ysabelle. He was worried about her, to be sure. The giant pirate hadn't really looked at her indecently, but he had shown such an irrational possessiveness over her that Adam was very concerned.

It was so frustrating to be held down here. Not much to look at, although he had looked with interest at the long benches fitted with enormous oars for the ship when he had passed them. Sails up top and oars beneath, and the ship was quite huge. It seemed to be somewhat Norse in its design. There was no more time for thought when his captor shackled his hands and hooked the chain to an iron ring on the ceiling where Adam would have a heck of a time getting it free. At least there was enough chain for him to lay down. He was going on almost three days without any decent sleep to speak of, and if he was going to be able to use his mind or body, he would need to get some sleep now.

Stretching out on the thin pallet, Adam was lulled by the rocking of the ship. It reminded him of deep sea fishing with his dad in the Gulf of Mexico. The memories flooded back, and they were good ones. They would go out on his grandfather's boat, carrying ice chests and several poles apiece, and spend the hot days talking and the cool nights drinking beer and speculating on world politics, the economy, anything and everything. Sometimes Joe would bring his small telescope with him and they would see what they could discover in a most unscientific manner.

Joe had taught Adam the art of using a sextant and charts, a skill Adam had difficulty mastering, but eventually he got it. He was beginning to realize that he had a lot more in common with his father than he had realized. He had been given his mother's looks and passions, that was true, but he had also done some things with his father that were very special indeed. Things that he now missed. His memories warmed him, allowing him to make himself comfortable in this strange, dark place.

"Sorry, Dad," he mused aloud. "I judged our relationship unfairly. You were always there for me, even if you didn't understand. Thanks. I hope to tell you that in person soon. I miss you, Dad. I hope I'm not in more trouble than I can handle."

Alane, who had been standing just out of sight, smiled at the young man talking aloud. He was definitely his mother's son. Katharine did it all the time. It was a habit neither Gray nor Alane had picked up, thankfully. Not wanting to impose on Adam's privacy any further, Alane turned and headed back through the hold.

It was truly amazing, this turn of events, and the chance of it was incredible. To have Adam stowed away on the king's treasure ship that was pirated by them, it was just amazing. Alane went looking for Gray, shaking his head in wonder over it all.

Adam looked around at his prison in the hold, and he was mad as a hornet. He again found himself stuck in behind the extra rope. Except for his guard, who was completely ignoring him, he was totally alone. There was no reason for his isolation, either, as he saw it, for they had passed at least fifty hammocks slung from the beams with almost as many crewmen occupying them- sound asleep. He could have easily been given one of the hammocks and slept with the men, but the captain had ordered him to be kept privately. Thanks a lot, Cap'n. Appreciate the accommodations, sir, and thank you very much.

Inside he wondered what fate awaited him, he had read enough of pirates in his numerous college history courses to know he should worry. Adam was more than a little surprised he had survived this long. He felt guilty as well, for Ysabelle was still tied to the mast on deck when he had been dragged by, probably blue with cold. He hoped she was still tied to the mast, instead of in the giant's bed being used horribly by him. There was no choice, he had to find a way out of here, if for no other reason than to save that poor girl he had talked into traveling with him to Scotland from a horrible fate.

He lay on his pallet and looked at the iron ring his chain was fastened to, willing it to fall open and release him. A plan occurred to him, and a slight smile curved his lips as he allowed himself to drift off for some much-needed slumber. He set his mind to wake him when the ship became quiet.

Katharine was supervising the stowing of the treasure in the hold and she snagged Alane as he came by, needing all the help she could get moving the huge, heavy chests with the few crew that were awake. Percy was feverishly trying to lift a particularly titanic chest, and Alane bent down to lend a hand.

"Milord Alane," came Campbell's voice from behind them, "Yer turn on watch, man. I'm hittin' me berth. Bretane's up after ye. Boyd's aloft, inspectin' the riggin'. Watch out for 'im, though, sir, the riggin's singing in the wind, and he's bein' flipped about at a good snap." Alane grunted his assent, and after placing the trunk where Katharine indicated, he stood and took his leave. He passed Gray headed in the opposite direction and they eyed each other playfully, each man deciding there was no time for sibling rivalry for now and continuing on his way.

Gray was going to check on the disposition of the commandeered longbows and various weaponry before he bunked down with the crew. He whistled for attention as he passed his mother in the hold. She was still helping the men inventory the treasure. "I'm keepin' her, Mother," he told her, grinning like an idiot.

"I already knew that, son. Have you told her yet?" She motioned for a chest to be moved to the far wall. Its contents had been counted and marked in her log. Percy and Douglas grunted with effort, but couldn't budge it.

"Nay, I haven't." Gray laid down the charts and the sextant he had been carrying under his arm and bent down to assist Percy and Douglas with the chest. It was incredibly heavy – probably filled with his very own gold.

"Be careful when you do, she seems like the sort who might take her dagger to you. It's one of the reasons I like her." Katharine chuckled to herself. Seeing the navigational instruments Gray set down, she asked, "Have you checked our heading yet?"

"Course is laid and helm is steady, sir." Gray gave his mother a dirty look when he and the others finished moving the chest. He didn't like to be questioned as to his duties. He redirected the conversation back to the topic of Ysabelle. "And I'm sure Ysabelle would be more than happy to take a dagger to me. In fact, she has already done just that. Exactly the reason that I took the weapon away from her. She was much more skilled with it than the sword – cut my favorite pair of gloves all the way through. I'll be careful, she's a wild one, that." He grinned again, letting his mother's unintentional insult slide.

His smile was contagious. Katharine smiled at the change the girl had effected in her usually stoic son. "You may have her, Gray – and with my blessing. I happen to like you this way." She finished writing down the figure from the finished chest, then asked, "Where will you sleep tonight, what's left of it anyway? You've given away your room, I see."

"Aye. I'll sleep with the men, I'm sure there will be a hammock about that won't be bein' used. But first I'll go harass Alane for a while. He could use a bit of excitement to pass the time, ye know how the wee lad always likes a bit of fun." He never missed the opportunity to slight his brother.

Katharine smacked him playfully on his armored chest. "I don't want to hear any wrestling. I'll go to that lovely young thing up there and give her a sword, I will. So behave yourself, Gray." He nodded and walked toward his brother's cabin, still whistling.

Katharine quietly walked to the bow and peeked around the extra coils of rope. Adam was sleeping soundly on his pallet. He had managed to get comfortable enough to sleep despite his shackles. She waved his guard away for a moment of privacy. How she wanted to run to her sleeping son and fold him into her arms. Instead, she stood silently and watched him as he slept. He breathed slow and even, his sleep peaceful even in this tense situation, just as hers would be. He was handsome, and he still looked like her, except for his deep red hair. In this light it looked black, like Gray's. It fascinated her that he looked so much like Gray. She used to tell Garrett how much their oldest son reminded her of Adam, but she had thought her memory softened by time.

He was here now. She hoped she would hold him soon. And maybe, if she was lucky, Katharine could reclaim at least a small part of him. She couldn't possibly restore all they had lost as mother and son, but she could have some small part of her lost child – if he was only willing.

The tears that had been threatening since she had first seen him tied to the mast on board the other ship began to flow. They were different than the ones she had shed when she realized she had lost him for good, or the tears she had shed every now and then just because she missed him so terribly. They were better, healing, but the pain was the same. The intensity of the ache had never lessened, time had not dulled or healed this wound. It had just given her a life and more children to love. But time and all its compensations – love, home, children, happiness – could not replace Adam. They only balanced the ache a bit with a sweet joy. A broken heart mended still remembers the pain. For the first time in a very long time, she allowed herself to grieve for her lost child – her first child. Her beloved Adam.

When he had seen her last she had been a young woman of twenty-six. Now she was old. By the standards of the day forty-nine was ancient, but she lived by the standards of the time she had left and because of that she was still a young woman – both in body and mind. Her only regret was that he wouldn't get to know her Garrett. Truth be told, though, if he got to know Gray, he would know Garrett. They were like peas in a pod. And yet he would need to know Alane to know Garrett's playfulness. Together the boys made their father, and Katharine was never happier than when they were at home together. They made everything so light. She wanted Adam to see that light, the one that had drawn her, had allowed her to stay and not die of loneliness for her son.

She couldn't help herself, she stepped up to the side of the cot. He slept like the dead. She wondered if he was a slow waker, as she was. Stroking the air around his face so as not to wake him, she could almost feel his skin under her fingers. Having him here was like having a child die, and then having them restored to you. Katharine never thought she would see him again, yet here he was. Young, handsome, strong – here. Dearest God, if it was possible to ever say thank you enough – Thank You. For my son. For another chance. For the love I've had and the love I want to give Adam. Thank You.

She wiped her cheeks with her fingertips and turned to go. Not quite able to leave him yet, she turned, kissed her fingers, and placed them softly on the lips of her sleeping child. Then she went up to the captain's cabin go to bed. Katharine lay awake until dawn, planning what she would say. She scrapped conversation after conversation, finally deciding to just tell him she had always loved him. And until the stars fell from the sky, the earth rolled up its continents, and the angels closed her eyes – she always would.

Adam woke later, the ship fairly quiet around him. Leaning his head around so he could observe without being observed, he saw there was no guard in sight. He stretched, yawned wide enough to hurt the muscles of his face, and stood. Eyeing the chain attached to the ceiling of the hold, he decided to give his simple plan a try. He began to climb, hand over the short distance the chain would allow to the other hand. His weight training had done him good service, for after struggling just a bit, he finally made it to the top and looped the fingers of his left hand through the iron ring. He deftly unhooked the chain and, as silently as he could, dropped to the floor.

Carefully, silently, he made his way along the coils of rope, and peeking around the last one, he checked the alleyway that led between the piles of cargo that had been stowed. From a bundle of swords, nowhere near as nice as the one he had purchased for himself, he pulled one that had a grip he thought he could handle. He then pulled a dirk from a small box full of them as well. Passing through piles of bows, arrows, maces, iron-studded gloves and the like, Adam eyed all the weapons critically, then decided to stick with what he had.

He crept along, trying to avoid loose or squeaky boards, doing his best to remain silent, and listened for any sign of movement ahead of him. He passed the oars and benches next and, seeing no one, moved up the short ladder to the next level of the ship. He poked his head up over the floor carefully, for this was where the men slept, and slowly took in the open space hung with hammocks. It appeared that all the men belowdecks were asleep. Adam watched for several minutes just to make sure. Although he looked for them desperately, he didn't see either of the giant men languishing in any of the hammocks. Of course, if they were of the highest ranks among the crew, they might have cabins of their own up near the captain's cabin.

Adam made it through the sleeping crew undetected, and was about to climb to the deck when he had the good fortune to hear an approaching crew member coming down the narrow steps. Ducking into a dark corner under the stair, Adam held his breath until the weary man passed. He gave himself several minutes before coming out of his hiding place, and was grateful for his foresight, for shortly after the first man retired, another went topside to take his place. Evidently the watch was changing.

Several minutes later, Adam appeared on deck. It was still pitch-black out, but the edge of the sky – which of course had to be east – was beginning to lighten just a bit. There were three men on deck, two at the stern manning the tiller, and the other hanging in the rigging watching the sea and the horizon. Staying in the deep shadows, Adam crept toward the mainmast, but it was unoccupied. He breathed a sigh of relief, for if Ysabelle had been there, she would have been frozen through. Since he had already been the length of the ship belowdecks, he decided to try the low door that led to the captain's cabin.

By the time Adam had followed the shadow of the railing to be even with the door, the sky was beginning to lighten. Panic set in. He checked the three men on deck for the thousandth time and made a run for it. He was inside the door and closing it softly behind him in less than three seconds. He had only expected to see one door, but instead there were three. He closed his eyes and quietly turned the handle to the door on the left. Bingo! It was locked! It had to be her prison, none of the crew would lock their door.

Digging through his pockets, Adam pulled out two slim four-inch pieces of metal, and got to work. Lock picking was not his forte, but given enough time and patience, he should be able to dispatch these simple locks eventually. The problem was, he had neither the time nor the patience for delay. The sun was going to rise any second now, and with the sunlight would fly their chance for escape. The tumblers moved and he was inside. A dwindling lamp barely illuminated the inside of the cabin. There was a form sitting up on the bed. It was small, but he couldn't make out the features well enough, and because of the slight stature of the captain, it was entirely possible that he had intruded on the man's sleep. It took a moment for him to decide whether or not to call out Ysabelle's name, but with the sun rising, there was no more time anyway.

He took a deep breath and whispered, "Ysabelle! Wake up!"

The grating of the key turning in the rusty iron lock woke Ysabelle from a sound sleep. She rubbed her eyes and sat up quickly, impatiently waiting for the door to open. It was taking a long time. Whoever was opening the door was having a lot of difficulty with the lock. Finally the door swung open. Adam stood there, illuminated by the last flickering light of the wall lamp. Her face fell. It took Ysabelle a moment to realize she was sorely disappointed. It took a moment longer for her to realize that she had been hoping to see Gray's outline filling the doorframe.

"Ysabelle! Wake up!" he whispered harshly.

She didn't answer, groggy at first. When she realized why Adam had wakened her, she was unsure of how to proceed.

He was in a panic. "Wake up Ysabelle, we're getting out of here." Adam had somehow gotten hold of a sword, it was tucked in his belt, and he was holding in his hand an assortment of metal pieces. Ysabelle surmised he had used these to open the lock on her door. His whisper cut through the semi-darkness. "Come on! Let's move, girl. We've only got one chance at this."

She panicked. If they left, she'd never see Gray again. Even worse, if they left, Adam would never know he'd been taken by his own brother. Perhaps his mother was close by. After all these years, she knew what it would mean to her to find her true family – she wasn't about to help him lose his.

"What do you mean, we're leaving?" she shouted at the top of her lungs. *Dear heaven, let Gray be close enough to hear her, and let him be paying attention.* The man had been paying enough attention during the last few hours for ten men – let him be listening now!

"Be quiet, Ysabelle! Do you want them to hear us?" Adam whispered again, his agitation evident.

"NO! Of course not! I don't want to wake anybody up!" she shouted

146

again. *Please, let one blasted pirate on this whole dashed ship have ears that work!* If she had been at home, her entire village would be on the run by now, what was wrong with this group? Pirates were supposed to be alert, for decency's sake.

"Ysabelle, if you don't shut that mouth, I'll shove my cloak into it!" he shouted in return. What was wrong with her? Had she lost her mind? She had been a meek little mouse the entire time they had traveled, acting as though she were afraid of her own shadow. Now she had metamorphosed into a cheerleader complete with her own megaphone? What in the world was going on?

"Touch one hair on her lovely head and ye'll have me to deal with, boy!" The booming voice came from directly above and behind Adam. He could tell by the sound that whoever made it was enormous and standing directly behind him. Adam drew his sword with a flourish and turned, ready to do battle. He was leaving, and nobody was going to stop him.

Adam stopped cold. He was facing the giant man who had ordered him tied to the mast of the king's ship. And he was staring at his own face. Dear God, this could only mean…. Stunned, he forgot to breathe for a moment, barely keeping hold of his sword. He took a great breath of air through his nose while his mind worked feverishly on this shocking development. Adam's mind was busy reading a tabloid headline – "TWINS SEPARATED AT BIRTH!" There could only be one explanation. He was staring into the face of his own brother. How had he been this fortunate? How had he been this stupid? Why hadn't he noticed it before – when he had spent what seemed like hours tied to the main mast of the king's ship? Did the man have any idea? Holding his hand out in front of him in a 'stop' gesture, Adam slowly slipped the sword back into his belt, careful not to make any sudden moves.

He cleared his throat nervously and tried to catch his breath. He closed his eyes, inhaled deeply and exhaled slowly to gain control of his riotous emotions. "Do you know me?" Adam asked cautiously.

"I do," the giant who was wearing Adam's own face answered.

"My name?"

The big man stood stonefaced for a moment and then sighed. "Yer name, my good man, is Adam Talbot. Ye are my brother." Gray didn't know what else to say to this man he had heard about his entire life, but never met.

Adam blanched. He inhaled sharply, tried to pull himself together, and kept talking. "Do you know my mother?" His voice quavered with emotion like a schoolgirl's, and he hated himself for it. His only desire was to keep it together long enough to find out where his mother was and talk to her.

"Aye. She's my mother also. Of course I know her." His Scottish brogue was charming to Adam's ears. For a moment he wished it was his own.

"Will you take me to her?" He felt like he was going to faint. His whole life had been spent bringing him to this moment.

"I will. Leave Ysabelle alone, for now. No harm will come to her, ye have my word. Ye may talk to her later, but neither of ye will be leaving this ship at present. Follow me."

"She's here? My mother's here?" he was incredulous.

"Aye." Gray paused, he narrowed his gaze on Adam, warning him. "And she's been agonizin' over how precisely to meet ye again after all of these years. I love her, so ye'd better be kind, no matter how ye feel towards her." Gray turned his stormy eyes upon his newfound brother.

"She knows I'm here?"

"She does."

Adam reeled. Between the information he had been given in such a short time and the intimidation tactics of the giant in front of him who was wearing his very own face, there was more than his brain could handle. He spoke haltingly, "I … will be as good to her as I possibly can … I love her, too, or else I wouldn't have come … traveled, um … all this way … to find her."

Gray accepted his answer after a moment of consideration. He nodded without a word and turned to proceed.

"Brother.…" Adam mused behind him. Gray turned in time to see Adam unconsciously reach out for him. He didn't see the action as weak, he understood it. It would have been how he would have felt upon discovering he had another brother. Gray loved his brother Alane as much as anyone, and more than most. Aye, he understood. Gray held out his arms and embraced Adam.

Ysabelle watched from the bunk. Eyes misting, she couldn't watch anymore. It was such an … intimate moment. And they were being so – well … caring. She had seen that kind of caring to some degree in Liza's family, and even experienced such a wonderful thing directed at her from them in a small way as a close friend. But she had never been given the gift of tenderness that Gray had just given Adam. Ysabelle had never even seen a man behave in such a way. Not even Father Corey had shown such feeling, and he was the kindest man she knew, although she had to admit she'd never seen him with his family.

"Ysabelle, lass, go back to sleep," Gray called out to her, and when she lifted her face to answer him, she realized too late he would see her tears.

She was weeping, he realized. It stunned him. Gray could not fathom why, but her tears moved him unbelievably. "Go on now, sweet lass." His voice was so incredibly tender when he spoke, it made her cry all the more. She nodded and snuggled down under the covers, pulling them over her shoulder to hide her tear-streaked face. He gently shut the door. The lock did not turn this time.

Gray returned to the task at hand. Looking Adam full in the face, he asked, "Are ye ready now, brother?"

He could only nod his agreement. He didn't trust himself to speak. Gray put his hand on Adam's shoulder and lightly propelled him toward the cabin door at the far end of the companionway. "Then come and meet yer mother, Adam."

"May I have a word with His Majesty privately?" Randall, no longer dressed in his black assassin's garb, was on one knee before the throne. His red velvet coat and pristine white ruffled shirt made him look quite the noble gentleman.

The king nodded knowingly. "Let us retire to my private sitting room, my good man." Edward rose and led the way to his private apartments, where many a woman had been shown his private favor. Once they were safely away from listening ears, the king motioned for Randall to shut the door and sit down. After making sure the guard was stationed outside the door to protect his king, he complied willingly.

"Now, Randall. What is this all about?" Edward slapped his trusted friend on the back and motioned him toward a chair.

"Well, Your Majesty, it's the chambermaid's daughter–"

"My daughter," Edward interrupted him.

"Of course." Randall sighed deeply, then continued, "In any event, the child Ysabelle has run away from the home she was being raised in. She was reported to have fallen into company with an apparently wealthy young man of unknown origins, and both were seen to board your treasure ship, the *Laney*, before it left out of port at Hythe. Of course, your majesty is aware that the ship was sacked by the Gentleman Pirate and the crew spirited away to some secret place. When the ship was found anchored some distance up the coast, there was no one left aboard. Therefore it must be assumed that Ysabelle and the young man accompanying her were taken with the crew."

The king absorbed this information. His face betrayed nothing. The news, of course, wasn't overly upsetting. Edward himself had never even seen the girl; however, he did feel a responsibility toward her mother – his own sweet Isabella. Even the mention of her name made him feel warm. There was no way around it, the girl would simply have to be found.

"Randall, you've no choice but to find her."

"Your Majesty, with all the honor and respect due to my liege lord, I have looked exhaustively for the girl. The trail ends at the ship of the Gentleman Pirate." Randall didn't want to prick the king's anger any more than necessary, the man was so unreasonable when he was riled.

Edward smiled condescendingly. "The solution is simple, old friend. Find the lost crews. If my daughter is among them, you will bring her safely back to a place where she might be employed. You did see to her education, did you not? She is capable of working for a decent living, of course?"

"I did, of course, see to her education, your majesty. She was very well educated," he answered ruefully. And then some, thanks to that busybody intellect Corey.

"Well then, the child should have a position befitting her education. Keep her far from here, of course, old friend. I would not want to offend Her Majesty the Queen. When she gets her back up, I might as well occupy Hades itself. But see to it the child Ysabelle is properly installed, either by employment or marriage, in a comfortable place, Randall. Have I made myself clear to your understanding?" Edward nodded to himself, this was a very good plan.

"Your Majesty, might I be so bold as to ask you a question?"

"I am of the opinion you just did." The king laughed at his own small jest and proceeded, "Of course you may, old friend." He was still chuckling.

"Why, my lord, when there are so many others who could see to this task, have you chosen me?"

"Do you mean to say why am I boring you with such a frivolous unimportant assignment when you could be happily murdering people and causing mayhem in high or low places for the crown instead?"

Randall inclined his head and raised his eyebrows in answer. Edward was far too frank with his wording. Randall preferred to think of his business as seeing to the balance of power and keeping it where it belonged – with his king.

"Well, Randall, old friend, it's simple. It's really your own fault, you know. You've been a loyal friend to me since we were only but children. Remember the lashing you took for me when I plucked the jewel from the handle of my father's favorite sword and gave it to the dairymaid for a kiss? You never broke that confidence, even though it took a month for the wounds on your back to heal. I trust you. A king can say that of very few – including his own wife." His lips bent ruefully at the thought. "You do my bidding even if you disagree with it, and you do it well. If anyone can find my daughter, it will be you. I would assume the missing crews of the lost ships would be pleased to be found as well. And of course, your success will make me quite popular among the port towns for having found their husbands and sons. I must tell you – I enjoy winning. But don't fret, Randall old friend. There will be plenty of killing and maiming to do when you return. Some of our enemies are hatching a plot against me even now. They will be your next project. If you make haste, you can have your hands bloody within a fortnight." The king dismissed him with a wave. Randall gave the obligatory bow and retreated in frustration.

Randall left the royal apartments wishing he had blood on his hands right that moment – Edward's. *Find her.* Indeed. It was all that sillyheaded chambermaid's fault. Blast that Isabella! The king was daft where that foolish woman was concerned. He actually felt tenderness for her! It was disgusting really, allowing your heart to rule your head. Edward was getting soft, and Randall had no liking for it.

He left the palace mulling over where to look first. If he were a pirate, where would he stash a crew? That was simple, at the bottom of the ocean. But this pirate was as soft as Edward had grown to be. The fool thought not killing his victims would show respectability. Softness and foolishness, all of it. *Silly women's thinking.* Randall shook his head in disgust. It was truly of no consequence. Once the crews were found, at least there would be a description of the rogue and it wouldn't take long before he would be discovered. Then his neck would be stretched on the gallows, gentleman or no. Perhaps Edward would even allow Randall to do the honors. It would only be just, in that he was wasting his valuable time looking for a girl he would already be in possession of if it weren't for that fool pirate.

Aye, he would ask to do the honors. Perhaps he would be fortunate enough to get to hang the entire crew.

TEN

The low door opened on a dimly lit cabin. Adam was confused, this was the captain's cabin, why was his mother here? Half-formed images began flashing through his mind – the slight figure of the captain, the way the man reeled when Adam gave him his name, how thoroughly the Gentleman Pirate had studied his face when he was tied to the mast of the other ship – he was beginning to understand. The captain, the Gentleman – it was his mother. Katharine Talbot – no, Duncan, he reminded himself – had turned pirate. What on earth was going on? Adam's mind reeled under the weight of his questions and his emotions. He felt like a field mouse trying to lift a barbell.

Searching the room with his eyes, trying to find her, he found a slight figure in the very back of the cabin. In the dim light of an oil lamp, it was hard to make her out. She – his mother – he kept telling himself, was sitting in the window seat that looked out from the stern onto the ocean beyond. The window was partially iced over, but had been cleared in the middle. An apparently beautiful woman, her face half-turned away from him and long, gray streaked hair tumbling down her slender back, was staring out at the lightening sky.

"Gray–" She turned as she spoke, and when she saw who stood in the doorway, she snapped her mouth shut and stared at Adam wide-eyed. Moisture collected in her blue eyes, and a small tear slipped over the lashes of her left eye, and she brushed it away briskly with her fingertips. Katharine turned back to the window to collect herself, but instead found herself sobbing unrestrained.

"I'm sorry –" she tried to apologize for her unseemly behavior, but her voice was a croak that wouldn't leave her throat. "Adam...." she tried again, her voice a hoarse whisper.

He was overwhelmed by her emotional response to his presence. He couldn't allow her to suffer any longer. "Hello, Mother. It's been a very, very long time." Adam stepped toward her, but then stopped, hesitating. She still hadn't moved from her place on the window seat. All of a sudden doubt overcame him – maybe her tears had nothing to do with missing him, maybe she wouldn't accept him. For the first time since he was given the safety deposit box telling him of his mother, Adam was unsure of how to proceed. "Mother?" he asked timidly. *Please, God, let her accept me.*

Hearing the uncertainty in his voice, her heart broke for her lost child, and Katharine again assumed the role of mother to a small child. She stood confidently and moved across the small cabin toward him, arms open, a smile curving her lips – encouraging him to come to her. "Adam. I never thought this day would come. I've missed you every day of the years I've been gone. Since you were six. Here, it's been twenty-six years, but you don't look old enough for the time to have passed equally for you. How old are you now? Twenty-three? Twenty-four?" He shook his head yes, unable to speak. "Adam, may I hug you? Did you come to find love?" She hesitated and her voice dropped to an almost inaudible level. "Or revenge?"

Adam fell into his mother's arms. *Thank You. Thank You.* His mother loved him still. She *had* missed him. *Thank You.* Adam could not stop the tears that rolled down his face. In his heart he was a six-year-old boy again, desperately wishing for his mother to come home.

She enveloped him with her small frame. Both sobbed deeply, uncontrollably. "Adam. Sweet Adam," she whispered, over and over again, into his hair as she stroked his head, his shoulders, his back.

Gray, eyes misted over, slowly backed from the room and shut the door silently, leaving them to their privacy. He stopped in the companionway and, resting his forearm against the hardwood wall, dropped his head upon it and gathered his emotions into something he could reason with and understand. Chest aching, throat tight, he allowed the emotions to come. Relief mixed with a deep sadness, and even a very small and quickly gone jealousy reared its head for the attention his mother was lavishing on her firstborn son. Gray, always so secure, even battled for the briefest of moments a small kernel of displacement, but more than anything else, he felt an intense, overwhelming gratefulness. *He came. Thank you.*

All of his life, although he knew his mother was very happy, anyone who knew her intimately knew that there was a small, hollow place in her soul – a place that grieved for the son she had lost to the cruelly selfish plan of a scheming bishop. Taken arbitrarily and without warning, there were no good-byes, no hugs and kisses – only empty longing for a child she would never see again. Katharine had loved her husband Garrett and three children completely, but in the deepest part of her soul there had been a grief that had lessened a bit with time, but never healed. Perhaps this man, who had entered their lives in such a striking manner, could heal that grief now. Maybe he could give Katharine back her whole heart and a new peace to enter her old age with. She certainly deserved that small happiness, after all she had given to their family of herself.

Gray breathed in deeply and blew it out slowly, collecting himself, and stood straight again to go check the condition of the sea with the rising sun. Raising his eyes, he saw Ysabelle standing timidly in the doorway watching him, an unreadable look on her face. He wondered how long she had been standing there, he hadn't heard the door. He stepped toward her, compelled by a reason he couldn't articulate, and she closed the distance between them with two steps of her own. He reached out for her, and she accepted his embrace willingly. Gray's head dropped, resting his cheek on the softness of her dark hair.

Ysabelle wrapped her arms about his lean waist and held him tightly, saying nothing, not moving – willing him comfort, wanting to ease the pain she had seen etched around his eyes. She simply listened to his uneven breathing, wishing she could see his face. Several minutes later he straightened up again and gently pushed away from her. Looking up into Gray's stormy eyes, she was completely caught off guard by the meltingly tender look he gave her. She reached up to his unshaven cheek and caressed it, her gaze warm and soft. His whiskers felt rough against her hand, sending a chill down her back and warmth down her arm.

Gray bent his head down to look into her wonderful green eyes. "May I?" he said simply.

Sweet heavens, this man moved her. Unable to maintain the rules of propriety she had never had any understanding of anyway, Ysabelle answered by stretching up on the tips of her toes and gently touching her lips to his. His strong arms wrapped around her waist tightly and he crushed her to him, almost suffocating her with his grasp. His mouth devoured her – giving of his overwhelmed emotions, receiving from her the comfort she freely offered, radiating his need for her sweetness, her gentle acceptance, through every inch of his body that touched hers. When he finally pulled away from her, he was shaken and angry with himself – realizing the vulnerability he had shown. Her eyes looked up at him lovingly, glazed over with passion and tenderness. She couldn't remember how to breathe. Wanting to frown, but wanting to keep that look on her face, Gray smiled at her indulgently. Ysabelle was precious, this feisty wee beauty without an ounce of pretense, who had offered him an ocean of compassion.

"A thousand knights?" he whispered into her ear, the warmth of his breath snatching from her lungs the tiny fragments of air she had left in them. "I think not." His warm lips kissed the soft place of her ear gently. Turning his back on her, Gray stepped through the low door onto the deck and shut it behind him, leaving Ysabelle to recover herself.

She sighed deeply and sank back against the wall, completely overwhelmed. What had he meant about a thousand knights? The arrogant words she had spoken to him earlier floated back to her on the currents of her mind. *I have walls enough to scale that a thousand knights could never accomplish it.* She laughed at her own foolishness. She had meant the haughty words at the time, but had no idea how artfully the giant man with the stormy gray eyes would get behind her defenses. Gray had known he had breached them as well, which was extremely irritating, but she had felt the beating of his heart against her chest when he had held her close. Gray had not been unaffected by their kiss. He had been a bit breathless himself, and she knew it. Ysabelle grinned to herself, knowing that his vulnerability would cost his peace of mind far more than she was suffering.

Walking back through the door of the cabin, she sat down on the small bunk and turned her attention toward the small sea chest that rested at its bottom. She stroked the top with her fingertips. Made of a highly polished dark wood and heavy brass bands, it was really quite fine. *No, I shouldn't. It's rude.* She started to reach for the latch, then drew her hand back, willing her body to obey her years of training.

You're the child of a whore, and no better than a whore yourself.

Well, since I'm no better anyway.... Deciding she would do penance later, she reached for the latch of the polished wooden sea chest and opened it. The inside was neat and the contents well ordered. Charts, maps, two pairs of trousers, and five clean white shirts. Woolen socks and a heavy woolen sweater. A nightshirt. A dress. *A dress?* How strange. Ysabelle moved it aside, careful not to disturb it, and kept rummaging. An embroidered linen square. Someone had quite skillfully embroidered a man, a woman, and an infant – standing together on a grassy slope in front of a small manor house built of stone. The work was exquisite. A pang of longing shot through her. Some man was keeping these things to remind him of a love. What other possible reason could there be to hold such things in a sailor's sea chest? His wife must be very happy indeed, to be loved so well.

Panic tore through her – what if this chest belonged to Gray? *Sweet heavens, no! Please, God, I'll fast for a week as penance for my intrusion if You'll only make this chest not belong to Gray.* But he was an honorable man, she was sure of it. Of course, every pirate sailing the seas was honorable, she mocked herself. And then of course there was the question of how many otherwise honorable men take mistresses? The answer made her want to weep. Too many. Why did she think he was honorable? Because he had kissed her? Because she wanted him to do it again? He was a pirate, a thief, a traitor after all. It was all too much, Ysabelle consciously dismissed all thoughts of the man from her mind. Instantly Gray invaded her mind again, thoughts of him taking down all the strongholds she had carefully constructed against sweet-talking men.

Sighing, she carefully replaced all of the items in the sea chest exactly as they had been when she found them and closed the lid. She latched it, then sat back on her heels and looked at the confusing box. It wasn't his. It couldn't be. Looking around the room, she saw a few books on the small shelf above the bunk. She stood and climbed into the bunk to examine them. Taking down a title that looked somewhat interesting, she began to read. *Thank you, Father Corey, for teaching me how to occupy myself.*

Inez had left the small rectory, the door clicking shut behind her, and Father Corey pulled himself up on one elbow, grimacing in pain. His eyes immediately searched the mantlepiece that shadowed his hearth, making sure the stone which kept his papers hidden had been left untouched. Those papers revealed Corey's true name and origin, something he might find necessary to reveal in the near future. Randall had known Corey was not what he appeared, but didn't know enough to know he should kill him.

It was Corey who had been the priest in attendance at the birth of the babe Ysabelle. It was he who had been sent to this place by the queen to insure Ysabelle's safety. Evidently Her Majesty did not find Randall trustworthy, and no matter whose belly the child had come from, Phillippa was a softhearted woman and insisted that the child be cared for and watched over. So Father Corey, the queen's personal confessor, was sent to attend to that very task. It had not been a troublesome assignment, he reminisced, not until now. The beating had been bad, it was true, but compared to the beatings he had taken at the hands of Bishop Cooke, Randall's had been child's play.

And the girl, Ysabelle, had been such a delight. She had showed such spirit, such intelligence, she had rather reminded him of his first and only love – sweet Katharine. The highlight of his lonely days, the young girl even looked somewhat like the woman in his memory.

Of course, Katharine would never have returned his feelings, did not even know he possessed them. And he had another calling, in any event. He had learned enough in the service of the vicious Bishop Cooke to be careful, but he had learned that there was another, far greater side to the priesthood. One he longed to return to and embrace.

The priest straightened up to an almost sitting position, grimacing at the pain that shot through his every limb, his arm reaching for the special liniment that was hidden under his mattress. As he rubbed the muck on his wounds, he reflected on the woman who had shown him so many things he had never forgotten. Katharine had showed him how to make the ointment when he had been a resident on Ellshope.

He had learned many things while there that had been integral to not only his survival but his life. He had trained with Master Duncan's men, learning swordsmanship, becoming an excellent marksman with a bow. Although he already had known to read and write, he had been given the time to expand his knowledge far beyond where many even imagined the human could imagine. All of his learning had been the gift of Katharine. She had many reasons to give him over to a horrible death, but had begged her Garret, a good and fair man to be sure, to allow him to join their ranks.

So much had he enjoyed his stay there, yet when he had found his heart was calling him elsewhere, Katharine had not been surprised. She had embraced him, blessed him, and given him a pouch of gold to assist him in his travels. He left the torture and the bliss that was Ellshope, using the gold to take him to a small monastery in Wales, where he could finally concentrate on his future. Who could have known it would lead him here?

He palpated his bones, beginning at his knees since that was where the blows had begun, and very gingerly working his way up to his neck. He didn't move his hands any higher, there was nothing he could do to fix the damage done to his face anyway. So far, he could tell that he had a broken leg, which would have to be set – God help him, four broken ribs, and thank heaven they had not punctured his lungs, and a broken collar bone. He would set the leg tomorrow, when he could think more clearly and be able to stand the pain.

Ethan looked around, trying to decide what to do. If Randall was after Ysabelle, it could only be to kill her. It wasn't as if he hadn't already done so by leaving the girl with that old witch Inez. He crossed himself in repentance for his uncharitable thought, then decided he needn't repent for the truth. It was because of her that he wouldn't be able to leave, and unless Ysabelle had traveled far by now, only God could save her from the devil himself.

Mustering all of the strength he possessed, Ethan raised himself from his sickbed, trying to walk the length of the room to his wooden chest. Before he had taken three steps, he collapsed back onto his bed in agony. He would try again tomorrow after he had set his leg. Somehow, he must reach Phillippa. Ethan said a blessing over Ysabelle for safety, then one over the queen for her goodness, and fell into a dead sleep on his small bed while his body began the healing process.

"I've been looking for you since Dad gave me the safety deposit box on my eighteenth birthday. He said the letter from the English Monarchy came the year after you were taken. But I had always maintained to him that you were alive." Adam was sitting on his mother's bunk, telling her how he had finally reached her. They were side by side, Katharine and Adam, holding hands while they talked.

"And how is Joe?" she asked. It seemed like she hadn't heard that name or talked of him familiarly for a thousand years, but with the appearance of Adam, her old life had come flying back to her like the wind in the sails on deck.

"He's fine. Dad hasn't really changed much in the last eighteen years."

"It's only been eighteen years for you? How odd."

"Not really. It's possible I used the portal differently than you did, or maybe time is not constant between the doors. In any case, Dad and Lily got married shortly after you disappeared. They were good to me, honestly. Lily was a good mother to me, and Dad was a good father. I always knew I was loved. But I have to tell you that there always seemed to be a hole there – it was like I had a really hard time finding anyone to understand me. Dad said it was because I was so much like you – although I cannot for my life imagine why you turned to piracy. What brought you to where you are today, Mom?"

She smiled, remembering how it felt to be called 'Mom' by him. It bathed her in warmth. Wrapping her arm around his shoulders, she began her story, "Well, I guess it started with Garrett's, my husband's, death. He was a wonderful man, you would have loved him – strong, intelligent, resourceful." Her eyes misted over as she remembered the love of her life. Adam watched her, seeing her happiness written all over her face, and was grateful.

She continued her story. "When I met him he was stealing me – the would-be queen – to irritate the English government. He was successful. The feud between him and them went back years, to the death of his family at the hands of raiding English soldiers. Anyway, in order to secure the letter for you, he had to agree to a truce with the English. I thought giving in to peace with them would kill him, but he cheerfully did it for me. We lived happily for twenty-four years, almost twenty-five. I couldn't have asked for more from any man – except perhaps more time.

"When he was set upon in ambush and killed by a turncoat Scot working for the English, my sons and I decided to take up the feud again. Both of my sons, Gray and Alane – oh, and I have a daughter, Anabella, as well, had been made barons by Edward III for their vast wealth – did I mention that Garrett was a vastly successful merchant?"

"No, your glowing praise of him omitted that." Adam was amused, she could very well be a teenager in love, the way she gushed about her husband. Even her eyes warmed when she spoke of him, he had made her happy. *Thank you, Garrett.*

"Well, the boys took their inheritances, which were substantial, and parlayed them into great wealth. Edward could hardly keep his hands off their gold, so he gave each a barony, knowing he could tax the life from them. It's a small price to pay, however, for the information they acquire. They are both much favored at court and are privy to all manner of information from the loose lips of the courtiers. They use their position to spy for the Scots and the Normans, who are allied against the English.

"Even as we speak, the English are devouring the Norman countryside and raiding the Scottish border – burning, killing, raping – all the things that make them so beloved by their enemies. So we sack their treasure and weapon ships, making sure they don't reach their destinations. We do try not to kill anyone. We're not out for revenge, or at least that's not our first purpose, we're simply out to ensure that they fail. And to make sure that Gray's and Alane's contributions to the royal treasury don't actually do any good." Her eyes gleamed with mischief as she explained.

"And the name 'Gentleman Pirate'? How did you come up with that?" Adam couldn't contain his smile.

She looked a bit sheepish. "Well, that's my own little joke. If you knew the people of this day, you would know how literal they are in their thinking. They would never consider a pirate to be a woman, but the name would cement it further in their minds that I was a man. It's silly really, but I enjoy my joke privately. I could hardly call myself 'The Nineties Chick who Robs Boats.' Some of the men of this age – not Garrett or my boys, of course, I trained them better – would never consider a woman capable of creating a thought, let alone engaging in piracy. It's rather fun to prove them wrong and laugh while they scratch their heads." A smug smile quirked her lips at the thought of fooling some of the men she had come to know and loathe.

She was so animated as she spoke, her eyes so dazzlingly clear, it was clear to Adam that his mother enjoyed her life of piracy. She was an adventure junkie. If there were bungee cords in this time, she would be the queen of them (dressed as a man, of course.) Yes, they were definitely cut from the same cloth.

His eyes warmed as he gazed at Katharine. "Mom, I'm so glad you found … er … happiness. I know you were so alone when I was a kid. No family, no roots, maybe a couple of friends. It's weird, really, thinking of you here. But to think of you home and alone and unhappy – only living to raise me –

that's weirder. I would have liked to have our lives turn out at least a little differently, but I'm not sure how I would do that and still give you the happiness you deserve." She squeezed his hand.

"Well, it's rather a moot point now, isn't it?" Katharine leaned over and hugged him. He was so handsome, had grown so tall. He would blend into her family without a question if he so chose. She ultimately hoped he might make that choice – the choice to stay. In the back of her mind, where the truth always stood guard over fantasy, she knew better. Sighing, she turned the subject. "Were you happy growing up?" she asked hesitantly, her voice low, not sure if she wanted to hear that answer.

"I was. Lily and Dad were very good to me, I'm a partner in his construction company now. And then there were always Grandma and Grandpa, and don't forget Uncle Tommy – he was forever taking me on camping trips and out on his boat. I grew up well. But you were always in the background. I had dreams, Mom." His eyes searched hers, to see if she understood what he was telling her.

She did. "About the wolves?" Adam nodded. She took a deep breath and jumped in feetfirst. If he could believe in time travel and a magic ring, he could certainly believe in dreams they had shared. "I had them, too. The dreams about the wolves, I mean. Or sometimes I would have dreams where I was calling to you at the top of my lungs, but you couldn't hear me. It was as if there was a, a...."

"An invisible barrier," he finished for her. "I know. I remember it. The dreams were frustrating, and sometimes terrifying. But then, after about a year and a half, I had a dream about you where you were safe – sitting in a great green meadow and playing with twin babies. One of them looked like me in my baby pictures, and at first I thought it was me, but then I knew it was not. As soon as I saw Gray's face – I knew. I knew I had a brother, I knew I would find you, I knew the dreams hadn't been just dreams. I just knew."

Katharine nodded knowingly. "When I saw your face, on the other boat, you know, I thought someone was playing a cruel joke on me, or that time had muddied my memories." Katharine shifted back to rest on the paneled wall behind her while she spoke. Her face warmed with amusement as she remembered her own shocked behavior. "I was afraid I would faint, and I haven't done that since I was pregnant and managed to get overheated – tough to do in Scotland, let me tell you. It's pretty darn cold all year. And when you told me your name, I was sure I must be losing my mind. I even looked around to see if everyone had heard the same name I did. The boys knew instantly. They recognized you right off. It's fortunate that you look so much like Gray, or we might have marooned you with the other sailors and we would have never found each other. The whereabouts of our island, Ellshope it's called, are well-guarded." Reaching over to stroke Adam's cheek, Katharine's eyes misted over again. *Thank You, thank You.*

Adam captured her hand in his, and leaned back against the wall himself. It was as if they'd never been apart. The conversation flowed easily, and again he felt like he was six and they were talking in her bed in the morning while she slowly surfaced from sleep. "When you were taken, Mom...." he hesitated, she squeezed his hand reassuringly, telling him to go on, "did they hurt you? I had more than one dream where a huge gray wolf took a pretty big chunk out of you. It made me crazy with worry. The psychologist Dad dragged me to said it was normal aftermath of my trauma, but I still worried."

Katharine searched his expression, trying to decide whether or not to be truthful with him. But he was a big boy, no – a man, she decided, and could handle the truth. "Babe, the gray wolf in your dreams, I'm sure, was Bishop Cooke. I used to dream about him sometimes in the same way. And yes, more than once he took a pretty good chunk out of me, but nothing permanently damaging. My body healed and my soul remained untouched. He just hurt me, nothing more." She watched as his face first fell, and then showed relief. He was definitely hers, she still had trouble keeping her thoughts off her face. Garrett said he never had to ask how she was feeling, he could simply look at her face and tell.

"Did you know I would come?" Adam raised his eyebrows, waiting for her answer.

"I didn't think you could, with the ring broken. How ever did you manage it?" She absently stroked the inside of his forearm with her fingertips like she had done when he was a child and he was sitting next to her while they talked.

Adam began his explanation with his eighteenth birthday and Joe's disclosure to him of the letter, the ring, and all of the reports from Scotland Yard verifying the age and history of both. He spent the next half hour telling her of his college education and preparation for this, his search of England and Wales for someone to fix his ring, and how he eventually made it through the portal at Stonehenge to her. Katharine listened intently, amazed that he had found another ring and been able to figure out how to use it.

"Astonishing!" she told him when he had finished his tale. "And you just happened to travel north on the ship we attacked. Our lives were definitely working in our favor, wouldn't you say, Adam?"

He grinned at her assessment, so much like he himself saw the world. "I would. I'm so glad I found you." They leaned in to hug each other at the same time, accidentally bumping heads. Laughing, they tried again, successfully this time.

Katharine stood. "Well, let's go introduce you around. All of the crew are my men from Ellshope, most are the sons of the men who served with Garrett. I would like them to meet you, and you have yet to be introduced to Gray and Alane properly. It will be only a few hours more until we get home." Adam stood and straightened his clothing a bit, already used to the feel of the strange clothing. "Are you ready, son?"

"Tally ho! Lead on! And all that rot!" Laughing, they headed for the small cabin door.

She turned to go, picking up her dagger and sliding her sword belt into place on her hips before she walked out the door. It was so rote, such habit. Adam arched an eyebrow in surprise and she looked around and caught his expression.

She laughed self-consciously and explained, "It's just like picking up your car keys here. You know, like that old credit card ad – you don't leave home without them." Adam laughed out loud and Katharine joined him. It was kind of funny, when you thought about it from his perspective.

Adam's eyes were warm with affection as he followed his mother out her cabin door.

Ysabelle had worked herself into a genuine panic. In her mind she had already been dragged to the altar, married against her will to a brutish husband who dragged her about by the hair and demanded that she rub his smelly feet, and forced to spend all her waking hours cooking and cleaning an enormous home – all enormously pregnant. Ridiculous as even she recognized her thoughts to be, she could not shake the images in her mind.

She had no desire to trade her freedom for life under the thumb of a man – any man. Not even a handsome, sweet, tender– What on earth was she thinking? She had been around long enough to know that marriage changed a man from a kind and gentle suitor to a demanding and tyrannical husband. All married women said so. Thank you, but no. If she was going to be someone's servant, he could by heavens pay her to be so. A married woman gave up her soul for free. Ysabelle would die a thousand deaths before she would trade a life under Inez's heel for slavery somewhere else.

You're nothing but a worthless whore. Your mother was a whore, and you will be the same as her.

NO! I am NOT a whore! Inez is wrong!

With these thoughts battling to seize the fortress of her mind, Ysabelle decided to rebuild the walls she had allowed Gray to scale. Ashamed of her weakness where he was concerned, she chided herself for letting him break her defenses down in such a short time and with such little effort. He and his handsome face be hanged! She had already told him she was no man's for the taking. He would be wise to remember that, she huffed to herself as she made the narrow bunk she had slept so poorly in. Ysabelle wondered who it belonged to – who had been kind enough, or more likely ordered, to give up his bunk for her. Whoever it was owned the mysterious, and truly mournful, sea chest she had crudely rummaged through.

These were pirates, she reminded herself. There was little kindness here. The bunk probably belonged to whoever had been on watch last night, and Gray had known it to be empty. So the owner loved his wife, so what? She hoped the man who slept here didn't have lice. Shuddering at the thought, she scrunched her face in disgust and scratched her head absently. She looked at her fingernails just to make sure there was nothing under them and then shuddered again.

Finishing her task, Ysabelle decided to try and find a way off this ship. All of a sudden, Scotland wasn't looking like such an appealing place to go. Maybe she could find a ship going to those fabled countries of the north, where snow and ice reigned and the men and women were fabled to be giants. Vikings, she thought they were called. Thinking of giants brought Gray back to her mind – his tenderness, his vulnerability. Tears pressed against the backs of her eyes. She shook her head involuntarily, wishing she could clear that man from her mind completely.

Ysabelle hated having this blasted soft spot concerning him. It was just because he had shown her a little kindness, something she simply wasn't used to. Gray wasn't extraordinary, he was just a man. No, he wasn't even a man – he was a pirate, and she would do well to remember that. He didn't deserve any feeling from her. He hadn't earned it, and with any luck, he would never be able to do so. The fact that he had wormed his way into her heart so easily made her curse her own weakness.

Ready to face the demon who had stolen her freedom away from her, she stepped out into the companionway. Leaving her timidity behind her, Ysabelle boldly strode out onto the deck. She had taken less than three steps when she looked up to see Gray striding across the deck to meet her. He was wearing the most wonderful smile on his face – gentle and tender – it made her warm inside. Even his eyes smiled at her. The crinkles around his eyes echoed what his smile told her – he was very pleased to see her.

It was almost Ysabelle's undoing, but she was no small child who could be charmed with a bit of a sweet. She had made up her mind, and by all that was decent, she wasn't going to back down now. She shook herself to dissipate the spell he cast on her so effortlessly. By all that was sacred, it was going to take more than a kind act and a handsome smile to turn her head. She glared at him defiantly.

Gray faltered for the barest of moments, confused. Then a smile tugged at his lips as he realized her game. He was an excellent chess player, he would most certainly win this trifling game with such an inexperienced opponent. She would be his – willingly, even happily. He would make her love him, and he would be as happy as he had been when.... The very thought of Abigail brought feelings of guilt. He was at fault. If he hadn't been such a big man, she and their son would still be alive. It was selfish to think he could have another woman. No, not selfish – murderous. Why should he believe any woman could have his babe? It was insanity to think he would be allowed happiness with the sin he carried around his neck.

Faltering, he stopped midstride. To want her was wrong. She was an innocent, he was a murderer. He tried to change his mind about the beautiful girl in front of him attempting to glare him to ashes. His eyes probed hers for the truth under her facade of combativeness. She turned away under his intense gaze. It didn't matter. He decided to leave her be. She didn't deserve to be hurt by him, and that he would surely do. He would do the honorable thing and turn around. He would leave her alone and let her go find a nice young man to love her. Yes, that's what he would do. She would live happier, not to mention longer, without him.

She stared at him, watching in confusion as his face turned dark. His jaw set, his eyes grew cold, and he turned away from her. She shouldn't have been hurt, but she was. Ysabelle had already decided to do the very same thing to Gray, but the force of his rejection sent her reeling. Tears pressed at the back of her eyes as she struggled to contain her emotions.

Turning to the rail to avoid his head-on emotional assault, Ysabelle pressed the heels of her hands to her eyes. She jerked them down, realizing that the gesture was far too telling. Clearing her throat, she attempted to ask him a question over her shoulder, but her voice stubbornly refused her. Blast! Even her own voice was on his side, trying to defeat her! Ysabelle cleared her throat and began again. "Where's Adam?" she asked hoarsely, unwilling to look at him – hoping to anger him by asking after her friend when he clearly wanted her to be interested in him.

He halted his retreat at the sound of her voice. Battling himself over the proper thing to do, he knew it was best to walk away from her. Aye, that was the best thing. He turned around to her anyway. Her back was to him as she stared out over the rail. The slope of her shoulders telegraphed her hurt to him, even though her back was ramrod straight. She tucked her hair back over her shoulder, for the wind had been whipping the strands into her face. The gesture, so feminine, so graceful, was Gray's undoing. The devil with the proper thing! He wanted her, she wanted him, and by all that was right and just, he would have her! His decision finally made, he would get it done, no matter what lay in his path – even if it was the devil himself.

Ysabelle glanced at him over her shoulder to make sure he watching her, then she tossed her head at him – her face a mask of indifference.

He knew this ploy, the women at court played games like these, but were much better at it. He felt hopeful that her ineptitude at game playing meant it was a foreign thing for her. Another reason for him to care. Refusing to be baited, Gray reached for her. Grasping her by the waist, he turned his sweet lass around and forced her chin up so she would look at him. Those emerald green eyes looked everywhere but his face. Amused, he stilled her face between his huge hands, forcing her attention on him completely, and kissed her thoroughly. He released her as soon as he felt her return his kiss eagerly, submitting to her own desire.

When she drew back from him, eyes wide, his self-satisfied grin piqued her temper. How she would like to reach out and wipe that arrogant grin from his handsome face. She shouted at him, "That wasn't at all fair!"

"Tis true," Gray chuckled. "However, my sweet Ysabelle, neither is yer wee game when ye know fair and certain that ye were likin' me overly much only a short hour past. Nothin's changed – except that ye've let yer fear grab hold of ye, and I refuse to suffer for it." He turned – keeping his infuriating smile in place – and, grabbing her hand, pulled the angry woman across the deck to the bow, glaring at his back the entire way. They made their way – she reluctantly, he eagerly – toward a small knot of crewmen, Katharine included, who were talking to Adam. The captain was introducing her son to her men.

Still dressed in her captain's garb, Ysabelle recognized Katharine immediately as the Gentleman Pirate. "Sweet heavens! It's a woman! Your captain's a woman!" she shouted at him, as if he didn't already know. "What manner of pirate are you that you give your loyalty to a woman? You take orders from a woman?" she asked, gaping, incredulous at the scene laid before her. No man she had ever heard of served a woman – at least no man that she'd ever known. A spark of hope jumped within her.

He squeezed her hand and offered her his most charming grin. "The best kind of pirate, sweet lass. And she's me mother. How many men dinna obey their mothers? My mother has a habit of drawing a sword when she's riled. Not the kind of thing a man takes lightly." She felt her chest tighten at his grin and silently cursed the weakness of her flesh.

Gray turned his attention to the modest group and cleared his throat loudly. All eyes turned to him. "Mother, may I humbly present to ye Ysabelle of – ah, well, pardon me, that would be simply Ysabelle – to ye. Ysabelle, may I present Lady Katharine Duncan of Ellshope – my mother." He bowed low, first to Katharine, then to Ysabelle – his courtly manners impeccable – mocking the girl's irritation with his arched eyebrow and wicked grin.

"How lovely to meet you, Ysabelle. You may call me simply Katharine. I have always preferred comfort to convention myself," Katharine told her, giving Gray a reproachful look. She reached out to the girl with both her hands and her eyes, offering total acceptance with both.

Ysabelle was overwhelmed. The woman could have ignored her, could have said nothing, been cold and appraising, or even neutral. But no, she had to be warm and inviting. Saying the one thing that would put Ysabelle's heart at ease and make her want to like the woman. Like Gray, she seemed to instinctively understand what a person wanted or needed and then graciously offer the same. Again Ysabelle found herself lacking her voice. She stood there – eyes wide, mouth working – no sound coming out.

Gray stepped in to help her. "I would assume that her lack of voice would indicate that my sweet Ysabelle is overwhelmed to make yer acquaintance, Mother. It's always difficult to meet one's future mother for the first time. Especially when one doesna want to be wed." He looked at his trapped dove and winked at her, drawing a withering glare.

"Ysabelle, I would also like to present ye to my second in command, Percival. Percy, may I present to ye my sweet Ysabelle." Percy bowed low and kissed her hand, a mischievous gleam in his eye.

Ysabelle pulled her hand away from the man's grasp quickly as she found her voice, "I am not your sweet anything, sir. And it is lovely to meet you, Lady Duncan. Percival." Ysabelle dropped into a perfect curtsy.

She regained her feet and turned to Gray, hands on her hips, chest heaving with anger. She advanced toward him until they were standing toe to toe. Craning her head back so she could look the presumptuous knave in the eye, she fairly shouted at him, "You, sir, are an arrogant cad. If you think I would even consider marrying you, you have the mind of a … a.…" *Please let me think of something horrible!* "Well, you have the mind of an ignorant sheep!"

It was the worst thing she could think of, and it sounded ridiculous. Wanting to come off scathing, she had come off the fool instead. Blast that man and his impudence! Ysabelle turned on her heel and stalked across the deck, back toward the door to the cabins.

The wind brought her final comment to the ears of the onlookers and Gray, "…that man is as stubborn as a donkey's backside.…"

166

Riotous laughter followed her, but she wasn't so foolish as to think the men were laughing at Gray. He hadn't just made an arse of himself, she had. Face burning with shame, Ysabelle jerked open the companionway door and then slammed it roughly behind her.

"If the lass only knew she was sleepin' in yer cabin, Gray, she'd probably burn it right down to the hull itself!" Alane bellowed with laughter. "Did ye see the look she gave ye? If a man could die from a glare, we'd be callin' for a priest to be givin' the last rites to ye, man – be sure o' that!"

Katharine smiled broadly. "Aye, Gray. I definitely like her. She'll be more than a match for you, if you're able to gentle her into loving you. And you're as arrogant as your father was, saying such insufferable things! I pray you had enough sense to remove any weapons from your cabin before installing the poor girl there. Even so, she may find some way to strangle the breath out of you. You'd be wise not to close your eyes in a sound sleep for a night or two." Now she was laughing as well.

Adam simply looked back and forth between the closed door and his brother, trying to make sense of the exchange. When had Gray proposed? When had he had time? And if she had accepted his proposal, which was beyond Adam's imagination, why was Ysabelle so angry? Maybe this was one of the reasons he hadn't dated much – he just didn't understand women at all.

"And I thought I was the only one who dreamed of murderin' you for pleasure," Alane called out, winking at the small knot of men watching the scene, ever the thoughtful brother.

"No," countered Percy, "on occasion ye share that luxurious fantasy with me." The sailors erupted into coarse, bellowing laughter.

"She had murder in her eyes, she did," Campbell called helpfully from where he was hanging in the rigging, rebraiding a frayed rope. His body convulsed with his silent laughter, almost causing him to lose his leghold and tumble to the deck.

Percy couldn't refrain from comment either. "I'm not sure I've ever inspired that kind of emotion in a woman. How fascinating. Perhaps I should seek lessons from ye, friend, as it would save me many of my face cloths." Gray glared at him.

For the most part, Gray remained unaffected by the rude comments and laughter around him. In truth, he had a broad smile on his face. He had enjoyed her unrestrained display of temper. In his experience with people, the greater the resistance, the greater the loyalty when the heart was finally won. She would love him – body and soul. He would see to it, and have a lot of fun going about winning her.

Katharine slapped him encouragingly on the shoulder, "Take heart, son. I've seen that expression on my own face in the looking glass when dealing with your father on more than one occasion. Rest assured, she'll be giving you hell, she will," she lowered her voice conspiratorially, "that is – if she ever speaks to you again." She couldn't help herself, she broke out into peals of laughter. Seeing her stoic son in this position concerning a woman was incredibly funny. He had always prided himself on being unaffected by the gentler sex. Right now he appeared to have been ravaged by a gale, and a blue norther at that.

Alane slapped him on the back. "Well now, ye've got yer work cut out for ye, big brother. If ye've a mind to make any inroads with the lass, however, I think ye'd better be gettin' to grovelin' with haste. Or we might find ye swingin' from the yardarm by the ties on her gown . She looks stout enough to do ye harm. And that would definitely be a tragedy for me." He looked over at Adam and winked. "Or maybe not, now. Seein' as how I've got a new brother, I suppose we could do away with yer surly presence. Don't ye agree now, Adam? Why don't ye go orderin' the lass around again and see what she does to yer scrawny hide, big brother?" Alane headed for the tiller, laughing to himself. "Just be sure to call me first, so I can warm myself with the blaze, it's freezin' out here," he called over his shoulder.

Gray was getting fed up with his brother's needling. "If ye're so cold, my wee laddie, why don't ye go to blazes? I hear it's warm there all year round. And I'm sure the company would suit ye very well. Many cads and fools and the like."

"I'm sure ye're right, brother. And of course, I have the assurance that we'll be seein' each other again. Ye seem to be a bit distressed, brother. Is there any way I might be able to help restore yer peace of mind? If it's the lassy that's disturbin' ye, I'll be happy to take her off yer busy hands and then ye can return to not carin' about anythin' but money and lands and annoyin' our fine monarch. It's a sound plan, don't ye agree, men?"

All the crew that was on deck at the time had been enormously enjoying the display the two brothers were putting on, but this last bit of amusement at the expense of their invincible first mate pushed them over the edge. The hooting and laughter were more than Gray could take. He had held his temper at their jeering as long as he possibly could. His eyes flashed violently at his audience, and he strode to stand in front of his brother.

Alane held his hands out in mock surprise. "Did ye have something ye wanted to say to me, Gray?"

"Aye, I did, little brother."

"Well, by all means, tell me what it is."

"Happy to." With that, Gray's fist smashed into his brother's jaw, knocking him backward three steps. He lost his footing and landed on his backside.

Alane rubbed his jaw and grinned up at Gray. "Well said."

Gray turned away from his amused audience and strode boldly to his cabin to confront the enemy without a backward glance.

Adam turned to Katharine, "Doesn't he have to *ask* her, at least?"

She smiled enigmatically at him. "Not here. Men of this...."she paused, unwilling to share her secret with the men who were standing close about them on the deck. "Men of this area take wives any way they please – they buy them, woo them, steal them, ambush them. On occasion they even court them." She grinned.

"You've got to be kidding! I thought there were elaborate courtship rituals, asking for hands – you know."

Katharine shook her head knowingly. "I remember what I was taught in college. The reality of life here is somewhat different. A pretty bride is a prize – and Ysabelle definitely qualifies on that count. In England, among the very wealthy, it is as you were taught. In Scotland, and among the more earthy, lower classes, courting's a bit ... shall we say – wilder. Some highlanders have been known to lie in wait and kidnap a bride meant for another man. Now, of course, this does cause hard feelings and often war, but sometimes a man is willing to risk it for a particular prize." She strolled to look over the railing, and Adam followed her. This was intriguing.

"And how was it with you and Garrett, mother?" He arched his brow, looking more like a perturbed father defending his daughter's honor than a curious son.

She laughed at his response, remembering. It had been such a long time ago. "He simply informed me that he was keeping me. That was exactly how he said it. 'I intend to keep you.' I didn't understand at first. I thought he was crazy. And when I finally did get it, I flatly refused. But he was a persistent sort – he eventually won. It took a good while and much argument to convince me." Her smile turned sad, and Adam watched as her eyes grew moist under the sweet memories of her dead husband. Breathing in deeply, she blew the air out in a stream to dispel the mood that was threatening to engulf her. "Gray will do the same. He's set his heart on her, and I know him well enough to know that he'll get what he wants. I've never seen Gray this stirred up before – in truth, I was beginning to wonder if he would ever find a woman he was interested in marrying. He's not so much as blinked in the direction of a particular woman since Abigail – until now. There's a history there that I'll share with you at another time. Your Ysabelle must be quite a special creature. Women have been chasing Gray for years, but he never even looked at them. Some said he had a heart of stone. Now he has all the appearances of a smitten puppy." She reached both of her arms over her head, stretching the stiffness from her shoulders, and then threaded her arm through Adam's. Together they took a turn of the deck.

"You seem restless, Mom. Are you okay?"

"I haven't heard that word out of another mouth for twenty-six years," she paused, then leaned over and kissed him on the cheek.

"It's only been eighteen in my time," he added.

"Interesting. I'd like to pretend I have a clue as to why. In answer to your question – yes, I'm okay. But I'm restless as well. At home I get up in the mornings and run three miles before the morning meal, you know, breakfast–"

"Still?" he interrupted.

She nodded. "Still. In the afternoon I run the steps to the parapet where the lookout stands. My people used to think I was quite daft, but after all this time they've grown used to me – sort of. They still think I'm odd, but then, I'm used to that. I always was odd – especially in your time."

He laughed out loud. He was odd himself, always had been, but that was all right with him. With the help of the internet and chat rooms for people of like interests, it was now easy to find others like yourself and enjoy their oddities as well. "Odd is good, Mom. But you're a big girl – I'm sure you know that." He looked at her inquiringly, brow arched, expectant.

She squeezed his arm with her own and answered him as they continued walking the deck. "Of course I know that. At times, however, it can be quite uncomfortable. You should have seen how the people of Ellshope reacted to me at first."

"I'm sure they were warm and welcoming. Especially when you told them what to do. Is there anything you really miss from home?" His brows arched inquiringly.

"You mean besides the child I lost for too many years?"

He grinned and squeezed her hand. "Yes. Besides that."

"Chocolate, cheeseburgers, and sunglasses," she answered without hesitation.

"Sunglasses?"

She nodded. "And about now, I would love to see an optometrist. I'm afraid I'm having to hold my books at arm's length, and unless someone puts me on a rack soon, I'll be quite unable to read without someone holding anything I read across the room."

Adam laughed aloud. "If you continue with your secret activities, you may get your wish. The rack, I mean."

"Too true, too true," she agreed. "I wish I could have all the time with you that I lost. There's so much I want to know."

"We have almost twenty years to catch up on by my count, Mom. I hope you'll give me the time it takes to tell your story." Adam chuckled, thinking of her in a world so foreign to what she was used to. "You must have cut quite a figure, with all your knowledge and freedom versus their ignorance and captivity in the church and feudalism. I'm a little surprised you weren't burned as a witch," he joked. He turned pale when she answered him honestly.

"I almost was," Katharine replied with a girlish giggle, remembering. "Had it not been for Garrett's clear thinking and the isolation of the island we lived on, saving us from the demagoguery of the outside world, I'm sure the people would have given in to ignorance and prejudice instead of listening to reason. Garrett even allowed me to teach the women of the island to read and write, a skill even many nobles lack at this time. Such foolishness is left to priest and scribes for the most part."

"I'm sure you set the place on its ear. What else did you change? You remember the old line from Star Trek, 'It is impossible to observe without changing.' I'm sure that you couldn't possibly have left everything as it was," Adam stopped at the railing and searched the horizon. He'd never been so far out that you couldn't see land before. It was invigorating. The wind and the spray and the frigid air energized him.

"It's beautiful, isn't it?" his mother said quietly, a contented half-smile curving her lips. Adam nodded, at a loss for words. "Star Trek – I hadn't thought of that in years. Does it surprise you to know that I don't miss television at all? I have to tell you, though, in all sincerity, I love it here. I love the peace of where I live. It would seem a contradiction, but even with the wars that constantly come and go and the feuds that are almost a living force between the clans of Scotland, life here is tranquil. The people here work extremely hard, but they know how to laugh and play as well. They can also play baseball and volleyball, thanks to some intensive coaching on my part. Both the men and the women love it. And they like to play golf – only they don't call it golf – they dig little holes and hit stones or balls made of skin into them. It's not nearly the country club set your time is used to, but it's a lot of fun."

He smiled at her warmly, the small dimple on the left side of his mouth – an exact replica of his mother's – pressing the skin into a tight attractive dent in his cheek. She reached up and touched it with a knowing smile. Adam sighed, "It sounds like you found your element. I'm happy for you. I found

171

mine as well, in the company of two old odd duck professors of history in Wales. I look forward to telling them all about this grand adventure. They'll never believe the pirate bit."

Katharine froze, her hand in midair. "Do you mean you won't be staying here?" She tried to keep her breathing even. Only having just found him, she was nowhere near ready to let him go again.

"Don't worry, Mother. I can't leave for at least half a year. The solstices, remember?"

Exhaling with relief, she pulled herself together. She began to walk again, pulling him along with her. "So I get you for six months? Thank heaven. It's not nearly long enough, but it's so much better than never having gotten to see you again at all. I thought you might turn right around and leave me. And after I've only just found you again." Tears welled up in her eyes, and she backed them down again with extreme concentration.

Adam stopped, sensing her emotion, and hugged her fiercely. "You won't get rid of me that easily. Not this time. There's no bishop around to help you escape me, no matter how challenging I become." He laughed, trying to lighten her mood, and the tightness in her chest began to ease.

Thank You, God. "Well, so much for my great plans to wiggle out of my responsibilities again," she joked.

"I hate to spoil all your fun, Mom, but I'm glad I found you." Tugging on her arm to resume their walk, he turned the subject back to a less emotional one. "So what else did you introduce these people to?"

"My people," she corrected. "Well, you would be surprised how ingenious they can be. They just lacked the ideas to work with. Free thinking is not exactly encouraged in this time period. With just a smidgen of help, they can be quite inventive. On Ellshope they now have bicycles, indoor plumbing, much more modern medicine than the rest of the known world–"

"No doubt due to your love for the medical books you were always poring over when I was a kid."

"Precisely." Katharine turned to him, flashing him a warm smile. "You do remember me well. Much better than I would have expected. Thank you. Only love would allow such a memory."

Nodding, he answered, "I committed every detail of you to memory after you disappeared. And I couldn't forget your face, you were always in my dreams. Go on."

"The medicinal knowledge was the most helpful. While the rest of Europe was ravaged by, and is still suffering through, the plague, we have remained largely healthy. The mortality rate of women in childbirth hit rock bottom on our island – the things they did to a woman right after she had a baby would have turned your blood cold. The church dictated everything that had to do with childbirth. They said that if a woman didn't endure enough pain during birth, then she was in league with Satan and both she and her baby would be condemned to death. The Sins of Eve – the dictate was called. The church also insisted that the midwife pack the birth canal with a mixture of mud and leaves. If the poor woman was lucky, she wouldn't contract a septic infection. But if the woman was unfortunate, and you wouldn't believe how many succumbed to childbirth because of this foul practice, and died from the infections the ignorance of the church caused, they had to be buried in unconsecrated ground – condemning them to hell. Astonishing! When I discovered this horrible practice, I started conducting classes on pregnancy and childbirth."

"That had to have been an earful for these people. And they didn't burn you as a witch? How forward-thinking of them." What a backward place to be full of information, he thought. Again he blanched at his mother's response to his joke.

"No, it was when I gave a drowned boy CPR and brought him back to life that they wanted to burn me for being a witch. Now that made for a tense moment or two, I'll tell you. I was brought before the warriors of the island and made to explain exactly what I did and why. Only after I had shown them how to find their pulse and explained the CPR procedure did they decide I might not be a witch. It's a good thing I was a foreigner, or they would not have believed me. I explained that in my country, many educated people had this information."

"I'll bet you could almost feel the flames."

"It was close all right. By the time it was all over, I was sure my hair was singed." Mother and son laughed heartily, calling the attention of the crew members on deck. They smiled at their captain's laughter and bent back to their chores. Katharine's face grew thoughtful, her voice quiet. "If it hadn't been for Garrett, they probably would have killed me anyway."

He heard the anguish in her voice. "You loved him very much, didn't you?" She nodded sadly. "How long has he been dead?" he asked cautiously, not wanting to hurt her further.

"A year now. It doesn't seem to get any easier, though. I still miss him all the time. It seems so hard to believe that he's gone. He was such a strong man, even in his fifties. He was a warlord and a merchant. Quite a man. But a turncoat Scot felled him in an ambush. We're all itching to find the snake and kill him." Her voice grew hard like a blade, saturated by a quiet violence that was chilling. Adam had never heard a woman speak this way before. She sighed heavily. "But Garrett made me promise him before he died that I would not be the one to exact vengeance. That's Gray's job."

"Why is vengeance a necessity?"

"It is the way of this place," she said simply. They stopped at the railing again, looking out over the stern. Adam and Katharine remained quiet for a while.

"LAND HO!" rang out above the deck, shouted by a man hanging high in the rigging.

Campbell approached, hat in hand. "Cap'n, sir, Ellshope's in sight."

Katharine turned, her persona metamorphosed back into the feisty pirate captain right before Adam's amazed eyes. "Very good, Campbell. Have Alane check the heading, order Berclay to hold the tiller fast, take in the starboard."

"Aye, sir." He turned on his heel and was gone, shouting orders to the men.

Katharine turned to Adam to tell him they were almost home, but stopped short, caught by an unreadable look in his eyes. "What?" she asked, eyes narrowed on his face.

"I was just thinking how well your life here seems to suit you. It was a bit of a surprise." He spread his hands wide, and the memory of Joe making the same motion when he was explaining various things struck Katharine hard.

"Joe always did that."

"Did what?"

She repeated the motion as a slow smile spread across her face. "I had almost forgotten everything about him. You brought him flying back to my memory with that one gesture. Funny, the things you remember," she mused. Straightening, she pointed at a small dark spot on the horizon. Adam eyes searched for the place she was pointing out. "We're almost there. We'll reach the island in about two hours, and I've got to get busy. You can follow, or go get your own things together. I believe Gray has possession of your sword. Knock before you enter his cabin – I have no idea how persuasive he'll have been with young Ysabelle. He does have a way, you know," she said with a laugh, and she headed back to talk to Berclay at the tiller.

Adam gave his mother a last look and then went in search of his leather bag and weapons.

ELEVEN

Randall stood at the bow of the ship, peering through the cold mist that blanketed the water as far as the eye could see – which was about six feet. There was a crewman beside him, failing as miserably as Randall was to see what lay before them. Another crewman hung from the rigging, hoping against hope that the mist would burn off when the sun rose, but the sky had been leaden for over two hours – so he knew the sun had already taken care of its morning chore of rising and it hadn't helped a bit.

It looked as though they were in for a blow – the water was as smooth as glass – it barely could be heard slapping against the hull of the small ship – a sign that a dangerous squall was imminent. The air was still, but full of energy. As he stood watching for any sign of land, Randall's skin was awash with pins and needles. The feeling of the charged air on his skin made him suppress a shiver. The sailors on deck were waiting, anticipating the coming squall, ready to man the sails if needed. For the moment, they were all in and tied securely. If the wind got hold of a sail during a real titan of a storm, they would be hanging in shreds, and more than likely the ship would capsize.

Wariness saturated the deck. Captain Abyrnathy, hanging from the rigging, called down to his first mate Keyth to climb up and help tie off the last sail. Immediately he set to the task, his heavy woolen sweater caked with ice, his beard and mustache white with frost. The rest of the crew were similarly attired by mother nature. The men on deck were stamping their feet and blowing into their hands, praying for something to happen so that at least they would be too busy to think about the cold that seeped through their bones.

Some sought shelter in the hold where they slept, but except for cutting the biting wind – which at the moment was still, there was hardly any respite there. The small stove in the captain's cabin and the stove belowdecks were thoroughly inadequate to heat the men's sleeping area, and the crew had been sleeping in their woolens and cloaks, curled together on the floor in front of the stove for warmth.

Randall was freezing. He had come prepared for cold, but this was *cold*. If hell had been cold instead of warm, he would be able to credit himself with finding it. He was almost ready to tell Abyrnathy to turn the ship around. This search to the north had been futile. He had been almost sure of his hunch, and time had taught him to trust his instincts, but this time he had been wrong. There were so many islands off the coast of Scotland it would take months, possibly years, to check them all for the lost crewmen. If the sailors from the ransacked ships had been dumped up in this Godforsaken part of the ocean, they were sure to freeze to death anyway. As he turned to look into the rigging for the captain, he heard a sharp intake of breath to his left.

"LAND HO! HARD TO STARBOARD, MATES! WITH SPEED!" The man went scurrying back to help the helmsman with the tiller and Randall saw, unmistakable, looming out of the mist, a huge cliff face that would surely have crushed the ship within moments if they had been underway with full sails and even a breath of wind. As it was, he was uncertain as to whether they would be able to turn in time to save them from a horrific wreck on the enormous rock face ahead.

Instantly on deck there was a chorus of shouts and what seemed like a brilliantly orchestrated dance of foot falls as all of the sailors scrambled to save their ship from becoming several tons of firewood. In seconds, Captain Abyrnathy swung down, hand over hand, from the rigging and leapt to the deck from almost twenty feet up in the elaborate tangle of ropes. He landed lightly on his feet, and immediately began shouting orders to the scurrying sailors.

"HARD TO STARBOARD, HELMSMAN!"

"AYE, SIR!"

"UNFURL THE PORT AND MAKE IT FAST!"

"AYE, SIR!"

"BRING HER AROUND, QUICK AS YOU CAN!"

"AYE, SIR!"

"You'd best be prayin', mates!" Abyrnathy suggested, in a voice loud enough to hear, but not loud enough to be taken as an order. "Clearin' this here piece of land will take a right lot more than we can give her," he said under his breath. The sail caught the wind, snapping its obedience sharply, helping the tiller turn the ship more quickly. There was no sign of any shift in the ship's position to the side as of yet, and they were still coming dangerously near to the huge wall of rock – the mist parting before them as if to give them a healthy glimpse of their impending doom.

Even so, a chorus of subdued "Ayes" rounded the deck, and as Randall looked around, wide-eyed with disbelief, he watched the crewmen as they stared at the monolith in front of them, their lips moving in silent petition to their Maker. Was the world completely peopled with idiots and fools? He had thought himself to be among men who took their work seriously, men who held their own destiny in their hands. They had no need for prayer to some mythical God.

Looking up, an involuntary gasp escaped his throat. There was less than a few hundred paces between the huge wall of rock and the ship. Slowly – painfully slowly – the ship was turning to the right. It didn't appear as if they were going to make it in time. Randall was tempted to hold his breath, but instead decided to thrash the captain for the stupidity of his men. Better to be doing something, certainly.

Irritated, he turned to address Abyrnathy. "What nonsense is this, Captain?"

"Randall, we're in serious trouble, man. You'll be hard put to find a sailin' man who doesn't believe in prayin' to his Maker in tough spots, and this is as tough as they come. I was thankin' the good Lord Himself for keeping the water calm or we'd be dead on that wall already, sir." He paused and looked the man up and down. With a look of disdain, Abyrnathy added, "You might try throwin' a word or two that direction yourself if you want us to clear that there rock face." His Scottish burr was thick.

Captain Abyrnathy, seeing on the Englishman's face Randall's distaste for him, was hard-pressed to remember why he'd taken this assignment. If it hadn't been so hard to put food on his table at home, he never would've ventured north this time of year and with this vile Englishman, only assignments were scarce right now and his family had to eat. And it was a noble task to find the poor sailors who had been marooned by the Gentleman Pirate. Yes, it was a good thing he was doing, even if it was in the company of a well-known evil like Randall. He said another quick prayer, then again turned to make sure the tiller was hard over. There were four men, including Phillippe, the helmsman, leaning on it – the hardened wood was groaning loudly under their weight.

The huge rock face loomed enormous over them, only a few paces between the bow of the ship and the rock. But they were turning. Slowly, but they were turning. Abyrnathy could see it was too late, though. They were going to hit, not head on, and maybe they would glance off without much damage – but they were going to hit, nevertheless.

"BRACE YOURSELVES, MEN! WE'RE GONNA HIT!" Abyrnathy shouted. Each sailor grabbed on to whatever he could to brace for the coming impact.

Randall, holding the railing in a death grip, stared at the sheer cliff in a daze. Was this how it would end then? If he leaned over the bow, he could reach out and touch the edge of the monster about to devour them. Blast Edward!

There was an enormous splintering sound, then the grinding of wood on rock as the ship finally completed its turn, only far too late. The front of the ship buckled upward, as though it was opening at the bow on a hinge, throwing Randall and three other crewmen backward onto the middle deck. It happened so fast they couldn't catch themselves, but landed on their backsides as the ship lurched to the side, finally clearing the wall of rock. However, the damage was severe.

Water began to shoot up from the gaping hole in the bow.

"MAN THE PUMPS! BAIL AS WELL, MEN! HELM, HARD OVER! GET US AS CLOSE IN TO THE LAND AS POSSIBLE AND BE READY TO SWIM FOR IT!" Abyrnathy grabbed one of the buckets from the deck and began to bail feverishly, as did several others. The remainder of the crew jumped through to the hold and manned the pumps, buckets, and anything else that would bail water. It did little good, but as they rounded the rock wall, they saw that there was a natural cove, and beyond it – a beach.

Through the thinning mist, there appeared to be dwellings dotting the sloping hills beyond the beach. The beach itself was dotted with what looked like hundreds of men, evidently drawn by the clamorous noise of the ship scraping against the rock face of the island. As the bow of the ship drew nearer the beach, it sank, inch by inch, into the water, the pumps losing the one-sided war they were battling. The men watching, both on the ship and on the beach, were silent – nothing more could be done.

Abyrnathy stood, stonefaced, as he watched his ship founder. Randall was furious, until it occurred to him that the men on the beach were in all probability the ones they had been searching for. Looking around, he could see that there were merely a few hundred paces between the ship and the beach. He turned to the captain.

"Salvage what you can, including tools. We'll fix her up here using the resources of the island and, if these are the missing men, take them home with us when the repairs to the ship are completed." Randall turned a smug grin to Abyrnathy. "It would seem your God didn't hear your feeble petitions, Captain."

Abyrnathy turned his attention from the sinking bow, his look incredulous. "He dumped her in a lagoon where she could be repaired, gave her scores of able-bodied men to fix her, and the use of the wood and resources of this island in the mean time. We were further kept from smashin' ourselves into firewood on the cliff, and founderin' in the deep. You, my eminent sir, are a fool if you believe the words you have just spoken." Abyrnathy turned his back to Randall, and began to shout new orders to his men.

"DROP ANCHOR! IT LOOKS LIKE WE'LL BE STAYIN' ON HERE A WHILE, MEN!"

"AYE, SIR!"

"STOW OR TIE ANYTHIN' THAT'S LOOSE AND PREPARE TO ABANDON SHIP! GRAB TOOLS AND BELONGIN'S AND SECURE THEM, MEN! SEE TO YOUR POST! WHEN ALL IS SECURE, LOWER THE DINGY AND HEAD FOR THE ISLAND! LUCIAN, MAN THE DINGY!"

"AYE, SIR!"

He turned toward Randall. "If you have any plans of stayin' warm durin' the time we're here, you'd best be fetchin' your things, Randall. The hold will be fillin' up in a hurry – so you've not a lot a time."

Randall smiled sardonically. "It would appear that we have a great deal of time, Abyrnathy." He turned to go find his cloak and belongings.

Abyrnathy dismissed the assassin from his thoughts and concentrated on the matters at hand. He helped Keyth tie off the sail they had opened, and when the scraping of the boat on the sandy bottom caused all of the men to stop their work and listen, he turned to the helm.

"Bring 'er up, Phillippe. Bring 'er up and stow 'er."

"Aye, sir!" Immediately he began uncoupling the fasteners on the tiller. The three sailors who had been leaning on the helm with him helped him hoist the huge oar-like rudder up to the deck and secure it. Then they went below to gather their few belongings. There was a splash as the dinghy hit the water, then Lucian nimbly climbed down the rope ladder into it. Immediately following him were seven sailors. Three of them grabbed the free oars, and Lucian set the pace with his own.

"PULL!" The oars hit the water in unison and stroked from the bow to the stern.

"PULL!"

In another five minutes, they had gained the beach, and everyone save Lucian stepped into the frigid water. Lucian stowed the other two oars, put himself to the first two, and rowed back to the ship for his next load.

Abyrnathy watched with satisfaction as the first men to shore recognized their friends and colleagues. The sailing world was small, and it had been a great tragedy to lose four crews. He said an earnest prayer of thanks for the Gentleman Pirate – at least he left the crews alive. As he turned back to survey what was left of the deck, he sighed sadly. She was a lovely ship. He shook himself from his small indulgence in self-pity, and inspected the

179

damage. The bow would have to be rebuilt entirely, half of the deck would need repaired or rebuilt, she would have to be resealed, and he hadn't even checked the hold yet. With any luck, and decent weather, she would be complete by spring. Three or four months. It was a good thing they had all the spare hands.

Lucian made several more trips between ship and shore, the last including Abyrnathy and Randall, along with Keyth and Ulric, the last aboard. They rowed for the beach, pulling in time with each other, until the bottom of the small dinghy scraped the sand as the water shallowed. Abyrnathy and Keyth jumped into the water and pulled the small craft up to the dry ground. Randall had a strange grin on his face as he stepped out of the boat.

"What are you findin' so amusin' about all of this?"

"I was simply congratulating myself on such a fine success. Too bad nobody will know. It's amusing, don't you think, to find the men only to be lost ourselves?"

"Aye, it would be," Abyrnathy answered, "if we were truly lost. I hate to disappoint you, man, but we can rebuild. It should take a few months, but you'll be back in your own benighted land before summer."

Randall arched his eyebrows and sighed. "Then I suppose I will not have to look forward to the pleasure of your company for the rest of my natural life? Tis a pity."

Abyrnathy gave the man a hard look, then turned to go meet his fellow sailors. Randall heard his parting statement, "Aye, tis truly a great pity."

A knock sounded on the cabin door. She turned toward the sharp sound. Ysabelle considered calling out something rude, go to Hades came to mind, but if it wasn't Gray, she would be totally embarrassed. Instead she waited to see who would enter. Then she'd tell whoever it was to go to blazes. In truth, she was looking forward to doing so. Freedom was intoxicating.

The handle turned, the tumblers clicked, and the door opened inward. Gray stood hunched in the doorway, shoulders and head filling the frame, a strange look on his face. He looked – was it possible? – sheepish. He cleared his throat.

"May I come in, Ysabelle?"

"That would depend upon your purpose, sir. If you intend to begin ordering me about, then no, you may not come in." She stood with her hands on her hips, defiance set in every line of her face.

"I had another purpose in mind, lass. My father taught me how to handle women, and I would like to apologize to ye for my ungentlemanly behavior on deck."

Her face hardened at the word "handle," then softened again at the word apologize. She almost smiled with satisfaction, then caught herself in time. He still had some punishment yet to come, and by the stars, she was determined to give it to him. She drew a deep breath and looked at him expectantly. "Come in then, milord. And you may apologize to me for your rudeness, your tyrannical ordering me about, and your insane proposition that I wed you. You may begin."

Her face was a haughty mask of superiority – she had obviously overcome any fear she had of him. Gray attempted to control his laughter and, after a brief internal struggle, was partially successful. He gave a strained smile and made a strangled sound in the back of his throat. She thought he was swallowing his pride and was extremely proud of him for doing so. He thought she was amazingly smug, but enjoyed her intriguing game even so. It was good to see her so sure of herself with him – a small beginning of trust. She knew he wouldn't hurt her.

"Well?" she demanded imperiously. "Are you having difficulty finding the words, sir?"

Giving a slight bow, Gray began. "Sweet Ysabelle, I am not called "sir," I am called Gray. I would be beholdin' to ye if ye would call me by my given name. I believe ye called me an arrogant cad. I thank ye for yer keen eye and excellent judge of character. I am both arrogant and a cad. However, on yer way to yer cabin, I also believe I was compared to the backside of a donkey – there I would have to conclude that ye missed the mark. Donkeys are far more rude than I. And nowhere near as clever. And yes, I would like to apologize for sayin' to ye what my mother called 'insufferable' things. Please accept my apologies for embarrassin' ye in front of yer future mother. She's a wonderful woman and took exception to the way I introduced ye to her. She thought I should inspect yer person for weapons in order to spare my hide – somethin' I readily agreed to do." His mischievous grin broadened as he reached for her.

Ysabelle immediately backed up a step. "Don't you touch me! I have no weapons – remember, you took them from me on the king's ship. And why do you persist in saying that Katharine will be my mother? We are no relation, and will not be. Please understand that."

"I will not. And ye'll find me to be quite thickheaded when it comes to things I've set my mind on. Have I made myself clear, lass?"

"Perfectly, milord. And you'll find me to be quite thickheaded when it comes to things I've set my mind on. And I have set my mind on freedom. I will do as I choose, when I choose, and answer to no man." She leaned her head back and set her jaw mutinously. "Have I made myself clear?"

"Perfectly. And ye are almost correct. Ye will do as ye choose, when ye choose, and answer only to me. Tis an excellent proposition I offer. If ye were to be a tutor or a governess, ye would answer to an entire household. If ye were to take a position in some other business – no doubt because of yer … femininity … ye would start at the most inferior position, never be allowed to advance, and never be given a raise in wages. A cold truth, but a truth, nevertheless. I am offering ye a position as my wife–"

"The wife of a pirate, and what good would that do me, except to guarantee that I would be a widow at a very young age with no one to care for me?"

"Ah, so that's it? The lass is lookin' for security. A home as well – didn't ye tell me that when we first met?" He stepped towards her, she stepped back, feeling the wall against her back and knowing she was quite trapped. He placed one hand on the wall on either side of her head and leaned in close enough to make her blush.

She shifted her weight from one foot to the other uncomfortably, searching for some route of escape. He saw to it there was none. "I did. And you have far too sharp a memory for my comfort. I have no interest in taking what I need from you."

"If ye have needs, lass, why not take them from me? I'm offerin'. I don't see anyone else steppin' up to do so. I'll not exact from ye a price which ye cannot afford to pay. After all, ye'll have to find a home, food, clothin' … love … somewhere. Why not let me give them to ye? There is nothin' I wouldn't deny ye, Ysabelle."

She looked confused, sad as well – as if she were going to cry. She dropped her chin to her chest so he wouldn't see her cry. Why did he have to offer her this? Why now? And why couldn't she just allow herself to reach out and take what she so desperately wanted to have?

Gray's heart melted at the tears he'd seen in her eyes. His voice was soft, almost a whisper, "How have I hurt ye, lass?" He tilted her chin up with his finger and kissed the trail of the tear rolling down her cheek. "Tell me so that I won't do it again. I've my heart set on ye, Ysabelle, and I want ye to come to me willingly."

You're the child of a whore, and no better than a whore yourself.

I'm NOT a whore! I'm not a whore! I'm not! She shook her head back and forth, the battle raging. Gray watched her struggle with some unknown demon, wishing he could help her.

No money in the world is worth keeping you another second!

I can be loveable, blast you, Inez! It was you, not me! How could you be so cruel? She peeked up through her lashes to Gray's face. He stood over

182

her, eyes gazing steadily at her face, waiting patiently for her to come to terms with herself and then him. She looked tortured, her eyes pleading with him for comfort. He dropped his hands from the wall to Ysabelle's shoulders, then drew her in close, resting his chin on her hair. Patiently he remained still, offering silent comfort, offering his strength, offering himself to her.

He wants me, Inez, he might someday come to love me.

Inez's voice rang through her head, as if she had heard and was rebutting all of Ysabelle's arguments. *How could I possibly love something defiled and filthy? You're not fit to walk on the dirt of my floor! You know what you are!*

"NO!" she shouted aloud.

Undeterred, Gray pulled her closer. "Yes, love. Ye'll be mine. And I'll be yers. And we'll be happy. Ye'll have a home, and food, and clothing, and love." Ysabelle began to cry again. He leaned away from her and tilted her chin up toward him again. "And Ysabelle, ye'll be a baroness. For I am an English baron – with title, lands, money. Does that not appeal to ye, sweet?"

A baron? Ysabelle cleared her throat. Surprise showed on her face. "A baron? How could you be a baron? An English baron at that! You're a Scot. And you're a pirate! Pirates are of low character and breeding. Everyone knows that." She looked at him, incredulous.

"Well, I'll have to become better educated so that I can behave properly and accordin' to my station." He grinned at her, then pulled her close to him again. Cradling her hear against his chest with his hand, he asked her again, "Ysabelle, ye haven't answered me yet, sweet lass. Will ye come to me willingly and be my wife?"

Her eyes blazed against his humor. Such an arrogant, frustrating man! "I'll be wed to you, sir, when pigs sprout wings and fly off to the south in winter!" She pushed back from his chest and glared her most wicked scowl at him, then slapped his chest for good measure.

He would not let her go. "I've heard tell of a special type of boar in the highlands that does precisely that. It's a legendary creature, and only the most educated know of its existence." His devilish grin spoke his intent before he hauled her up against him and kissed her again.

"Now, since we have established that there are flying hogs, will ye give me yer pledge?"

The man was completely daft! She couldn't imagine why he was allowed to run around loose instead of being locked up in a dungeon somewhere. Studying him thoroughly, Ysabelle could not help but laugh at the ludicrous look on his face. She took a deep breath and sighed, then she mumbled something against his chest.

His smile deepened indulgently, "I seem to have missed yer answer.

Would ye mind repeatin' it for me?"

Huffing in frustration and embarrassment, she nearly shouted, "I said I'll wed you, you crazed man!"

"Ah ... the right answer at last. It will save me endless hours convincin' ye that I'm right. And as my men and all who serve me will tell ye, I'm always right." Her eyes were flashing fire at him. My, but she was pretty when she was disgruntled. Unable to help himself, he kissed the bridge of her nose. "Ye won't regret yer decision, sweet lass."

She backed away from him with a glare. "Aye, but you might!" She ducked around him and headed to the door.

He caught her before she even got close to escape and dragged her back around to face him. "Never," he said, and he surprised her with a kiss. His mouth angled over hers and was at first just a brush on the lips, which was his intention. Although as he smelled her lovely womanly scent and tasted her soft mouth, he lost his discipline totally.

Unable to breathe or think, Ysabelle found herself responding in kind to this strange but powerful man. He held a control over her she did not understand. It terrified her, this power he had. He made her feel completely wanton – the warmth from his touch spreading through her like wildfire. After a few moments, when he realized in a panic that he should back away from her or he would have his wedding night here and now, he withdrew quickly and turned his back on her to compose himself.

She stood, eyes glazed with passion, confusion reigning on her face, not understanding why he was rejecting her. Was it all true then? Was it only a matter of time before he realized what he had done to himself? Gray turned back to her. The tender look in his eyes was so warm her fears were soothed, and she smiled up at him euphorically.

"Truly?"

He kissed her again. "Truly."

Her brow furrowed. "Do you give your word? You will not regret this decision?"

He couldn't contain his laughter. "On my honor. I will never regret ye." She smiled beatifically up at him and squeezed him tightly around the waist. He kissed her again, then released her and headed for the door. Opening the small door, he turned back for a moment.

"Ysabelle?"

"Yes, Gray?" she answered, her face still beaming.

"Have ye ever heard the pirate code of honor?" he asked, shutting the door. He left her glaring at the closed portal. No doubt she was calling him a donkey's backside, or a goat, or a pig in velvet right now. With that thought in mind, he stepped onto the deck, whistling one of his favorite tunes as he headed for the tiller.

TWELVE

"STEADY NOW! STEADY NOW BRETANE, MAN! EASY INTO HER, BOYS!"

"AYE, SIR!"

"EASY! EASY! NOW, TIE HER OFF, MEN!"

"AYE, SIR!"

Katharine went to talk to Bretane at the helm while Boyd and Campbell leapt from their precarious perch on the rope ladder on the side of the ship to the natural rock pier to make her fast.

Gray went to stow his instruments and charts as Alane went below to see that all was made ready for their departure. The men passed down the gangplank to the waiting hands of Boyd and Campbell, and once the heavy wooden walkway was steady on the ground, it was made secure to the side of the boat.

Entering the small companionway, Gray didn't hesitate to knock and then open his door. Ysabelle was sitting on the bunk, looking despondent. Crossing the small cabin in a long stride, Gray knelt, opened the sea chest, and stowed his navigational instruments. When he closed the polished wooden lid, he was met by the enormous, shocked eyes of Ysabelle.

"Have ye seen a spirit, lass? Ye look as though ye've had a wee bit of a shock." A mischievous smirk played about his lips. "Would ye be needing' comfort? I would be happy to assist ye."

She nodded no vigorously and stood to her feet. Trying not to look as though she were escaping, she eased backward away from Gray. Perplexed, he stood as well and followed her. She would not allow him to know she had seen the hidden dress and the linen square embroidered with a picture of what she was certain were his very happy, not to mention ignorant, wife and child. What kind of a cad would not only propose marriage to a woman, but announce his intentions in front of his *mother* yet, and be married to someone else? Sweet heavens, what had she gotten herself into?

Gray moved to take her into his arms, but when he reached for her, she slapped his hands away from her waist. "Now what game is this, Ysabelle? Ye've already given yer consent to marry me, why in paradise won't ye let me touch ye? Ye behave as though I carry the plague." She tried to duck away from him, but he was far quicker. He caught her easily and held her secure. His grip like iron, it was surprisingly gentle. It was obvious he wasn't about to let her go, although he was being careful not to hurt her. He hauled her up to his chest, wrapped his arms around her, ignoring her struggles, tilted her face up to his own and kissed her thoroughly. "Now what the devil is wrong with ye that ye won't even look at me? Have I hurt ye in some way I am unaware of?" She shook her head again. A fierce scowl clouded his face, and he leaned down until they were eye to eye. "Ysabelle, talk to me!"

By the stars, he could be intimidating. One of his scowls could blister the sun itself. He was back to the way he was when she had first met him, blustering and scaring the devil out of her. He even looked like the devil at this moment, with his dark hair glowing red in the lamplight and the frown wrinkling up his features. All the man needed was a scythe and he would look like the picture in Father Corey's Bible. Of course, this thought made her grin, which only made his scowl fiercer, which caused her to begin to giggle. Throwing his hands up in the air with a sigh that could have capsized the ship, he turned and went to sit down on the bunk. Ysabelle was doing her best to get herself under control, except the picture was still in her head, and Gray looked so disgruntled. She had forgotten what the entire scene had been about to begin with.

Exasperated, he shouted, "I don't see what the devil is so amusin', Ysabelle. Ye could drive a man out of his mind." He crooked a finger in her direction and patted the mattress beside him. "Come here, Ysabelle."

Memory flooded back to her about why she had been upset in the first place. She shook her head no. He shook his head yes, and the look on his face suggested she had better obey. Hurrying to placate the man, and angry with herself for doing so, she sat down on the bunk, although she was so far away from him that she was half hanging off the small mattress. He reached out and, hooking his arm about her waist, hauled her up to his side. Before he spoke, he took a moment to pull his temper back under his control.

Speaking softly so as not to spook the girl further, he gently prodded her. "Now what in paradise is this all about? Or do ye know?"

She shook her head sadly. In truth, the girl looked as though she were about to cry. "Yes," she whispered into her lap, "I know what it's all about. You do as well, you just don't know it yet."

Did the woman even hear what she had just said? Gray rubbed his temples in an attempt to maintain his patience. "Ysabelle, I can't possibly know if I don't know. Please, try to make a wee bit o' sense."

She whirled on him – eyes flashing, agony on her face. "I make perfect sense! It's you who don't make any sense! What kind of a man would propose marriage to a girl, offer security to a girl – especially when that is what the girl needs more than anything – then practically bully her into saying yes against her better judgment and all her good sense, when he's got a … a…." She choked on the words. Tears began to pour down her face. She stood and began to pace the small expanse of floor.

Gray looked at her, incredulous. What in blazes was going on? "A what, Ysabelle? What, exactly, do ye think I'm hiding from ye?" His voice was soft, soothing. His blood pounded in his temples, causing his head to ache with the effort he was making to stay calm. Making this woman speak sense was going to kill him or make him daft.

This man could exasperate the saints! He had the impudence to sit there on his – sweet heavens she'd been sleeping in his bed! She shook her head to drive that thought away.

He stood and crossed to her. He took her by the upper arms and held her still. "Look at me!" he commanded. Slowly she raised her face to him. "When I have a what?"

Never mind discretion, the man wasn't deserving of the gift. "A family!" she shouted. "You have a family! I know I wasn't supposed to, only I saw the dress and the embroidery in your sea chest! I wouldn't have – I mean to say that I know better – save I was in this small cabin for so long and I read the only book of interest, and … well, I'm sorry for my presumption…." Ysabelle hung her head in shame. Then she recalled again why she was angry and laid into him again. "But by heavens, you should be sorry as well! Lying to me! Deceiving me! Offering me what you were not free to give!" She dropped onto the bunk, exhausted and in despair. Her head dropped into her hands and she began to cry in earnest. Between her sobs she choked out, "How could you?"

Gray stood, perplexed, and watched the lovely face of the hurricane that had just cut a swath through the room and landed on his bunk. He finally understood what she was talking about, and was even mildly irritated concerning her intrusion into his privacy, although he was more than a little amused at the wild, crazed outburst she had just displayed. My, but she was strung a pinch tight. Of course, her upset could only mean one thing, he hadn't bullied her after all – she cared for him. One doesn't have a fit of lunacy over something one doesn't care for. Grinning like an idiot, Gray dropped to his knees in front of her – finally understanding her and wanting to give her comfort.

"Sweet Ysabelle. Look at me, lass." His voice was gentle. His huge hands reached out and caressed her shoulders. When her head slowly came up to look at him, he captured her face between his palms and stroked her cheeks while he gently explained. "I don't have a family, Ysabelle. I *had* a family. I was married, six years ago, to a young woman named Abigail." He took a deep breath. Even after all this time, it never got any easier to say. "She died in childbirth along with our babe. The dress is hers, as is the embroidery. I carry them because I treasure them. Although no less than I will treasure ye. Together, ye and I will make a new embroidery – a new picture. A new life for ye, a second chance for me. Do ye understand, lass?"

Relief washed over her face, and on its heels came a deep sadness. She couldn't help but feel sorry for this man who had loved so deeply and lost. Her hope for a future came rushing up from the depths of her, and she impulsively threw her arms around Gray's neck and embraced him fiercely.

After a moment, he laughed and gently loosened her arms. "Ye'd like me to breathe until our weddin', would ye not?"

She blushed pink, then laughed at her own behavior. It was a wonderful sound to Gray's ears – free and lighthearted – the first glimpse he had seen of the girl beneath the heavy yoke she carried. He stroked her jaw with his knuckles, then drew her to him and kissed her. Pulling back, he remembered why he had come into the cabin in the first place.

"Ysabelle," he looked warmly into her emerald eyes as he held her, "we're home!"

At the top of the hidden rocky path, Garen was waiting with a contingent of warriors to greet them. He turned to Katharine first. "All is well, milady. Nothing out of the ordinary occurred during yer absence. The rest will be given upon report after the evening meal."

She smiled and inclined her head to her second in command. "Thank you, Garen. As always you are efficient and capable. When the ship is taken to the cove, send a wagon and several strong men. The chests aboard are quite heavy and will take several strong men to winch them up the cliff. Be sure the weapons are in good repair and then see that they are added to our stores."

"Milady." He bowed his head quickly, then surveyed the rest of the first group off of the ship. For the briefest of moments his eyes flitted over Gray, Percy, Alane, Campbell, and stopped at the two strangers. His eyes were wide as he curiously looked over first Adam, then Ysabelle, then Adam again before he asked, "And the prisoners, milady?"

"They are not prisoners, Garen. This is my long lost son Adam. I have not seen him since he was six years old and now he is returned to me. You will make him at home here and treat him as you would any other member of my family. His visit will not be overly long – he will be with us for almost half this year and then he will be forced to return to his home."

Garen turned to Adam and bowed crisply. "Welcome to Ellshope, Adam. If ye have need of any thing, feel free to ask whatever yer request of me."

Adam mimicked the soldier's bow quite well. "I thank you, Garen, and look forward to learning all I am able to about my mother's home."

"I will be happy to assist ye." Garen cocked an eyebrow in Gray's direction, the silent question hung between the two men. The soldier's eyes were drawn back to Ysabelle, it was hard not to notice the woman.

Gray drew her up to his side possessively, causing Percy to snicker and Garen's eyes to widen. "This is Ysabelle. She is to be my wife."

Garen actually took a step backward in surprise. He blinked in astonishment, taking a moment to find his voice and another moment to ask a somewhat coherent question. "When?" he asked simply.

"As soon as the chapel can be made ready and Father Clair can say the mass."

"As ye wish. I will have someone fetch him as soon as we return." Garen bowed courteously and turned to take the lead on the way home.

A thought struck him and he turned to Gray. "Milord Gray, the manservant Desmond from yer holding in England had come. He awaits yer return impatiently and says he has an urgent message for ye from the court of England's king."

"Do ye know what the message is?"

"Nay, I do not. But he's waiting in the great hall to speak to ye. He's taken up vigil there every day for the last four days. He's driving old Hilde daft. Keeps her from setting the tables proper and is always telling her how a proper English table is laid. She's ready to cuff ye – once for hiring the old boor, and again for letting him come bother her."

"He's harmless. Opinionated, but harmless." Gray considered this news – any word from court meant hassle. He wanted nothing to do with Edward or his court for now. There was his wedding to plan, Ysabelle to win over and marry, his honeymoon to carry out – the thought made him smile. Edward be hanged! He wasn't going back to court until spring. He gave Ysabelle's waist a gentle squeeze. She looked up at him tentatively and half-smiled. There was fear behind her eyes, although she was doing her best not to let it show. The determined set of her jaw made him smile. They walked on.

As they marched down from the rocks, the land opened out before them. The beauty of Ellshope was as breathtaking to Ysabelle as it had been for Katharine the first time she had seen it. The green of the island heather, surrounded and protected by the steep, forbidding cliffs that made the island look like no more than an inhospitable rock to the eye of any sailor, were a combination that never failed to astonish visitors. Even though it was the dead of winter, the island was a lush green. Much to her surprise, on their way through a huge field Ysabelle even saw a few vivid purple wildflowers. She gasped in surprise and Gray smiled indulgently.

"They're the heartiest of the flowers. However, in the spring, this field looks as though God slipped and dropped a rainbow upon it. The beauty of my home is something I always look forward to returning to." He grasped her hand as they walked in company with a group of warriors – Katharine, Adam, and Alane included in the company. Percy kept making chortling noises behind Gray, until Gray turned around and fixed him with a withering gaze. Still, it only served to cease the rude noises; even so, Percy couldn't keep the grin from of his lips.

Dusk was falling, and within half the span of an hour what was left of the tired, simple group was tramping across the lowered drawbridge. Other soldiers had dropped from the group one at a time as they passed their homes outside the walls of the enormous castle. The smells floating from the windows of the small stone cottages as they passed by made all of their stomachs rumble with hunger. All manner of dinner smells were wafting through the air – meat roasting, stews simmering, black bread baking. Mothers were calling children in from their play, and the sounds of the preparation for evening filled the rapidly cooling air. There was no snow on the ground, but the air carried the smell of snow and the slight wind was chill.

Even in their cold and fatigued states, both Adam and Ysabelle wondered at the beauty of the place. Even here, where the small cottages dotted the soft, grassy meadow, it looked like a five-star resort to Adam. The sky was a beautiful darkening blue, the grass was unbelievably green – it looked painted in fact, there was a lake that he could just see, and a waterfall that poured into it. His dad, an avid golfer, would have given his house to be able to play a round here, and would have been happy to part with two hundred dollars a night to stay in one of the quaint roughhewn cottages. He couldn't have taken it for longer than a day, though, or he would go through severe withdrawal from his business phone. Maybe it was just because he had been raised in the desert of Arizona, but to Adam the landscape here was amazing.

Ysabelle tried not to look astonished as well, although it was difficult to keep her mouth shut when all around her was such splendor, both in nature and manmade. England had been pretty, but this place was breathtakingly beautiful. And it would soon be her home. She sighed at the thought of living in this wonderful place. The slight smile that played about her mouth turned to a frown when she remembered that she would have to get married to live here. *Married.* She suppressed a chill. Gray noticed and absently pulled her closer to warm her. His unthinking kindness helped her subdue her fear.

Adam turned to Katharine, "It's pretty chilly here, Mom. I know it's the middle of winter, but when does it start to warm up?"

She laughed, "I wondered the same thing when I arrived – also in the middle of winter. The answer is – never. Scotland is freezing most of the time. We have a slightly more temperate climate than on the mainland because of the ocean's constant temperature, but only slightly. When I first came here, Garrett bragged of the gentle, livable climate, although to tell you the truth, I've never seen it. It's January, give it a week or two and you'll be knee deep in snow." She wiggled her eyebrows at him, Groucho-style – something she hadn't done in years. Adam gave her the obligatory laugh. An old memory shared and enjoyed. It warmed him considerably. He was still hungry though.

Ysabelle could have eaten Gray's sea chest, she was so hungry. She looked around and caught Adam's eye and he winked at her. Gray had kept them fairly separate during their walk, still ill at ease with their close relationship. Adam had been far too busy paying attention to his surroundings to notice. He was enthralled as Ysabelle was. They both looked like children on Michaelmas. Wide eyes and huge grins of wonder visited each of their faces as each new beauty of the island revealed itself. Ysabelle audibly took in her breath more than once. Gray was enchanted. Such enthusiasm was hard to come by in the jaded women of Edward's court.

Every time she would see something new and fascinating that they were passing, Ysabelle would grab his hand and point furiously or start dragging him towards whatever she wanted a closer look at. Adam had a bit more control, Gray noticed, although his reactions were quite similar to Ysabelle's.

Adam and Ysabelle both forgot their hunger as they passed through the drawbridge into the lower bailey and received their first full view of the castle itself. They both took in their breath sharply at both its size and beauty.

"It's gorgeous, Mother!" Adam couldn't help exclaiming.

"Thank you, Adam." Katharine couldn't hide the look of pride on her face. "I've always thought so."

"Your home is beautiful, Lady Duncan," Ysabelle agreed.

"Just call me Katharine. I've never been much of a lady – ask anyone." The soldiers escorting the group broke into agreeable laughter.

Ysabelle looked questioningly at Gray. He winked at her in return, then nodded his head in agreement with his mother. As they trooped from the lower bailey through the upper bailey, Ysabelle smiled. Perhaps there was hope for her yet, if he was used to an informal and unconventional woman, it was possible that he wouldn't look on her so harshly when she failed him. She would fail him, she was sure of it. At least in a working relationship, when the employee failed, their pay was taken away. If she failed at this undertaking, she would lose all she would gain – home, family, love. *Family.* Never a word to be taken lightly in Ysabelle's mind, she liked these people, immensely – piracy aside – and if she decided to love them and become a part of them, it would kill her to lose them. She cautiously studied the curious band from beneath her lashes. They were good people – Adam's people. *Adam.* Would she lose the friendship she had gained with him as well? *No!* She wouldn't have it. She would do everything right, she decided, then she would lose nothing. Squaring her shoulders, she faced the entry to the castle and her new life.

As they approached the stone steps leading up to the door of the castle, four hunting dogs came racing around the corner and playfully attacked the group. Ysabelle actually squealed with delight when one of the hunting dogs – happy to see anyone at all – ran directly to Ysabelle and jumped up, placing her enormous paws on Ysabelle's chest, and licked her face enthusiastically.

Gray laughed and pulled the dog away from her. "Down, Cleo! Ye'll have to find something else to eat, old girl." The dogs hopped around joyfully and accepted affectionate pats from Katharine and Garen. Cleo wiggled up against Adam's leg, showing her affection for the stranger, and then promptly laid down on top of Percy's boots.

Alane clapped him on the back. "Well, Percy, if all those wenches don't work out for ye, Cleo will always be waiting. She was yer first love, ye know. And what more could ye ask for in submission? She's lying at yer feet! What a gift. I've never had the good fortune to find a woman nearly so accommodating." He looked over at Ysabelle and winked playfully at her.

Percy grinned at Alane in return and leaned down and gave the dog a good scratching. "Yes, there's always old Cleo. At least she'll warm my bed without demanding a wedding. Good old girl." He patted her belly affectionately, then straightened back up – a warm smile bending his lips. "Although I've half a mind to go to Lady Ullswater's holding and look up that sweet gypsy girl Gray and I met up with on our way to Ellshope." Ysabelle waited for him to expand on the subject, but he didn't, causing her great frustration. Gray noticed the frown on her face and grinned. Jealousy perhaps? He hoped so. It would mean she was softening toward him.

Katharine walked to the bottom step and turned to address them. "Gentlemen, thank you for your escort. When all of the personal items are taken inside, feel free to go to your homes. I will expect you in the great hall for the evening meal and reports in one hour's time." The six-man escort bowed their heads as one, then began toting the few items each person had carried off the ship with them inside. Katharine turned and led the way into the entry hall, all of them careful not to get in the way of the soldiers, and down the steps into the grand hall. Ysabelle looked around her with great curiosity as she had never been inside any home grander than the dairyman's cottage.

Adam was as fascinated with the castle's interior as Ysabelle was, and as Gray and Alane were giving directions for which chest went in what room, he slowly and methodically walked the perimeter of the hall and looked at every detail. The sconces on the walls held candles, illuminating light-colored rock walls and the polished wooden adornments. A large, round table, draped with a colorful plaid runner and an exquisite candelabra, sat in the middle of the floor surrounded with eight heavy chairs. Their seat cushions matched the table runner. Against the far wall, which was also a stone staircase that disappeared somewhere above them, was a small table where several more candelabra were stationed awaiting use. Hanging above the polished wooden table was a beautiful tapestry. Adam paused a moment to examine it more closely. Each piece of furniture was ornately carved and polished to a bright shine. There was nothing crude or rough about the pieces that decorated this home. Except for the bare rock walls, it was quite luxurious. A fireplace, large enough for Adam to stand in almost upright, was burning a log as large as a pig. Reflections of the flames danced on the walls as the fire hissed and popped and warmed the large room.

As soon as he heard voices in the entrance hall, Desmond scuttled out of the great hall, where he had been pacing and called his lord's attention. "Milord Duncan, I have an urgent message for you from the king. May I have a moment of privacy with you so that we may discuss it?"

Gray nodded his assent and followed the man back into the great hall.

Katharine leaned into a darkened hallway between the fireplace wall and the stairs and called for someone named Bessie, then turned and smiled solicitously at Ysabelle. "Would you care for a bath before the evening meal? I'm sure it would make you feel ever so much better." She waited, praying that Ysabelle wasn't one of the English who didn't believe in bathing. Her very first campaign among the uneducated peoples she came to live with was to teach them to bathe daily.

Ysabelle was overjoyed. "I would be so grateful. I haven't had a bath in.... Well," she blushed, thinking how she must smell, "I'd rather not say. However, I would love to wash." Gray looked over her head and gave his mother a grateful smile for making the girl feel at home.

Turning as Bessie, a woman in her mid-thirties with extremely dark hair, contrasting richly with her ivory complexion, entered the room, Katharine caught sight of the woman and hugged her warmly. "Hello, Bess! I've ordered a bath for our young guest here, and I wish for you to see to her comforts before our meal. Hilde and Dora can handle the preparations of our repast without you, I'm certain."

"It'd be a pleasure, Katharine. Tis good to have ye home again. My father frets over ye while ye're away. He wants to see to yer safety as he used to when he was captain of the warriors." She dropped her voice conspiratorially. "I *hate* it when he broods, he's even worse than my mother in one of her moods when he gets this way."

Katharine nodded knowingly. "He always was. When he and Garrett worked themselves into a snit at the same time, they would make me, and everyone else on the island, miserable. I'll send McGrath to fetch your parents up to dinner, that should improve their dispositions. And how is William? And wee Cora? Are they well?"

She nodded. "Aye, they are. Cora talks incessantly, and won't sit still long enough to learn her household duties. She'd much rather be out fetchin' branches to make bows and arrows with her father. She's getting to be quite a shot, she is. Father has her out huntin' rabbits for our stew tomorra. The two of them make me daft, truly! Cora even wishes to shave her hair off, just like her father. She thought him quite fetchin' when we were warrin' with the MacCannes – wouldn't leave his bald head alone." She sighed dramatically and threw her hands up in the air. Katharine laughed and agreed with her. Ysabelle watched the two women with interest. The servant was treated as an equal. Never before had she seen that. Although, in truth, she had to admit she had only been in the presence of those who had servants a few times – only they had been cold and superior to their underlings. These women were obviously friends. It was astonishing.

Katharine caught Ysabelle's eye and waved her over. She pulled her to the bottom of the stairs, out of earshot of the men, so the girl wouldn't be overly embarrassed by her questions. "Ysabelle, do you have any other clothes to wear after your bath?" Ysabelle shook her head sadly, it must be obvious that she was poor.

"What about clean underclothes and stockings?" she whispered. Ysabelle blushed bright red and continued shaking her head.

Giving her a squeeze around the shoulders, Katharine was quick to reassure the girl. "Don't let it worry you, I'll not embarrass you. I'm sure I have something suitable that will fit you quite well. I'll have Bess lay a gown and some clean underthings out for you. She'll brush your hair as well and help get you ready for the meal. She's a wonder, and I'll wager that when she's done with you, the queen of Scotland herself will fight her envy. Now how does that sound?"

Ysabelle kept her head lowered. Shame would not allow her to raise her eyes to the kind lady. "I'm afraid you've been ill-informed, madam. I am not a gentlewoman. I am a poor girl, no better than a servant, from a small village with nothing at all to recommend me to you. I will be happy to work for my keep. I am an adequate hunter, and I can clean as well. I'm not a terribly sound cook, though, mistress. I am not worthy of these kindnesses you bestow upon me."

An inelegant snort caused Ysabelle to look up sharply. Katharine was grinning at her. "I'm not a gentlewoman either. I come from common blood, a family with no name or title, and you are as welcome here as I am. And I speak to you truly when I tell you that there are few things in my experience better than my servants – I trust them with my life and I love them like my family. So if you're truly no better than they are, you're plenty good enough for this home. Now, follow Bessie and don't give me any further difficulty, or I'll force you to wear a crown and have everyone address you as 'Your Highness'."

Ysabelle blushed again, not sure whether to laugh or worry. She laughed. Katharine's eyes crinkled with delight. "That's more like it, Ysabelle. You will laugh while you are here, and often at that." Katharine tilted her head up and assumed a very commanding stance. "I am the mistress of this household and I insist upon it. Understood?"

Ysabelle laughed again, blushing pink. "Thank you, Lady Katharine. I am truly grateful."

"Then quit calling me Lady Katharine. I'll get out my crown and make you kiss my ring, and don't think I'm not determined to do it! Now, up the stairs with you!" Katharine gave her new charge a motherly swat on the seat.

Ysabelle nodded gratefully and followed Bessie, who was waiting, wearing a charming grin.

Gray, his brow knitted together in frustration, came back into the entrance hall just in time to hear Ysabelle's laugh. He smiled instinctively. That sound was one he would like to hear more often. Desmond, his mission completed, retreated from the castle at a brisk pace. Gray frowned at the man's back, his look of frustration returned to knit his brow.

Katharine noticed her son's distress. "Is there a problem, Gray?"

"There could be. I'm not certain." He shook his head. "Desmond's message is an inconvenience, nothing more. The king has summoned me back to court immediately. But I will stay long enough to wed."

Katharine smiled apologetically, then turned his attention to Ysabelle. "She is a beauty, Gray. She has definite potential. I decidedly approve."

Grinning at Ysabelle's retreating back, Gray nodded his agreement. "That she is. I'm indebted to ye, Mother. She's quite a resistant wee bit of a thing, though, isn't she now? Gettin' her to soften towards me could take some time and no small amount of effort. Although she's smilin' now, and laughin' as well. It's a delightful sound – isn't it?"

Adam grinned at his older brother and answered before Katharine could. "It is. When I first met up with her, I would swear she didn't even know how to smile. She was so serious, carrying the weight of the world on her shoulders. Determined to find herself a home and an occupation. Did she tell you how we met?" Gray shook his head no, and waited for the explanation eagerly – hoping it would shed some light on this wildcat of lass he found himself taken with.

Katharine interrupted them before they could get carried away with their conversation. "Let's hear his story in the great hall, where we can pour ourselves a drink and listen in comfort." They all agreed and followed her into the giant room. Three long tables were situated in a u-shape, all with clean linen cloths on them and flowers arranged in their middles. An enormous fireplace took up the entire wall opposite the entryway, a fire burning brightly within it.

"Wash your hands, gentlemen, while I pour each of you a goblet of wine," Katharine ordered. Adam followed Alane, Percy, and Gray to a pitcher and washstand in the buttery. The men remembered their manners and let their guest refresh himself first. When everyone had washed the travel dirt off of themselves, they all sat down at the table nearest the fireplace and waited for Katharine to seat herself. She came to the table carrying a tray with five goblets and a pitcher on it. Putting one goblet in front of each man and one in front of her own empty place, she then poured wine into each cup from the pitcher. Before taking her seat, she returned the tray to the buttery – leaving the pitcher on the table.

Gray looked at Adam expectantly. "Didn't ye have a story to tell us, brother?"

Adam grinned, recognizing the anticipation on his brother's face, and began to tell the story of how he and Ysabelle came to meet. "Meeting her was a rather nerve-racking experience. I woke from a sound sleep to find myself tied to the ground, and this little wisp of a girl kneeling over me with her dagger in her hand – ready to do me serious bodily harm."

Gray laughed. "Well, if that just doesn't sound like my sweet lass. She

197

would have been happy to gut me when I found her in the hold on the king's ship. It was a good thing I was quite a bit larger and much more skilled than she was, or I would've been meetin' my Maker then. She looked like a cornered animal, she did."

Adam nodded and grinned. "She had the same look when I ... um ... met her. It took me a while to convince her I meant her no harm. Then, when I found out she was traveling alone–"

"She was travelin' alone?" Gray interrupted him. "Why in all of heaven was a young woman travelin' without an escort or some sort of protection?" Instantly angry, he fought to keep his thoughts controlled. Imagining what could have happened to her if Adam hadn't come along was agonizing.

Breathing deeply, Adam launched into an explanation of how Ysabelle had come to be in the field above Stonehenge where they met, just as she had explained to him on their journey.

Gray interrupted him as soon as he heard where they met. "She was in that Godforsaken place? At night? All alone?" He had half risen out of his seat. Adam held his hands up, trying to placate his mammoth brother.

"Yes, only if you'll give me a minute, I'll explain how she came to be there."

He told the assembled group about Inez, about Ysabelle being thrown out of her home for dropping the rabbit in the fire, about the old woman shouting her shame to the entire village....

"Does the lass know who her parents are then?" Alane questioned.

"No. The old woman didn't tell her, if she was even privy to the information."

Percy jumped in then. "Knowing some of the parents I've come across in England, she's probably better off not knowing her heritage. At least this way she can imagine her origins were pleasant and happy."

Gray nodded, rubbing his chin. "So that's why she's from nowhere. I wouldn't claim that heritage either." Alane and Katharine nodded unconsciously.

"So after I convinced her I wouldn't do her any harm, we decided to continue on in company. She didn't have a destination in mind, and since we got along well together–"

"How well?" Gray growled.

"Cool your jets, brother–"

"What Godforsaken words did ye just say to me?"

"I apologize. Our languages are quite different and I forget you don't understand my tongue. What I meant to say was, Ysabelle and I do not have an improper, or even mildly threatening, relationship. If you want her, you may have her – provided you will treat her well."

Gray leapt to his feet, his chair flying out from under him and skittering across the floor. He was inches away from Adam's face in a split second. "I'm certain, brother, that since ye are not from this place, ye do not understand that ye just insulted me gravely. I am waiting to hear yer explanation and apology of such conduct." He controlled both his anger and his tone as he spoke softly over the table. The quiet in his voice was more threatening than a shout.

Backpedaling, Adam held his hands up in surrender. "I meant no insult. I merely meant to say that I have become quite fond of Ysabelle...." Gray breathed in deeply, his eyes slits, and waited for him to continue. Adam took a gulp of air and went on, "I mean that I feel quite *brotherly* toward her and am only out to insure the best for her future. In my ... home ... many men mistreat their wives, and I only wish to ensure this does not happen to my Ysabelle."

Gray breathed out heavily and took his seat. "I forgive ye yer insult. However, I will remind ye she is not yer Ysabelle, but my Ysabelle, and ye will spend time with her only when others are about."

Adam grinned. "Now it's my turn to be insulted. I would not intrude on your plans or your relationship with your intended. I am trustworthy."

"Perhaps. However, here it is improper for a pledged woman to spend time with an unmarried man unescorted. Therefore, I'm sure ye would want to be proper. Isn't that correct, Mother?" Gray glared at his mother, willing her to back up his outrageous statement, but his back was up and he would have his way.

She nodded slowly and winked out of the corner of her eye to Adam. "It is so. Adam, please continue with your tale. It's most interesting."

The conflict narrowly averted, Adam breathed a shade easier and went on. He spoke of how inadequately she had been fed and her threadbare clothing. He told of their journey leading up to their stay on the king's treasure ship and the outcome which everyone knew. As he was finishing his recounting, two women came into the great hall carrying trenchers and goblets and, working around the small party, set the table for the evening meal. They set almost fifty places by Adam's count, filling glasses with wine and placing huge loaves of steaming black bread in the center of each table. Large platters with butter and cheese were placed by the hot bread, and bowls of honey – including the comb – were set on the tables as well. Adam couldn't help but notice the incredible aroma of the food. His mouth was watering as he spoke and it took great concentration to finish the story. The next half hour was going to feel like an eternity.

Following Bessie, Ysabelle had been taken to a beautiful and elegantly appointed room containing the biggest bed she had ever seen. It had a carved wooden headboard and ornately carved posts. The canopy was of damask, and the matching curtains surrounding the bed were tied back at the corners. Two polished wooden chests sat on either side of the bed. The wall to her right was taken up by an enormous fireplace, already burning bright with a large fire. Except for at Father Corey's, it was the first fire she had enjoyed that she didn't have to lay.

Bessie put the candelabra down on the chest closest to her and motioned for Ysabelle to sit down at the dressing table. She obeyed, and while she was getting comfortable on the embroidered tapestry-cushioned stool, Bessie leaned out the door into the hallway and let out a shrill whistle. She crossed the room and stood behind Ysabelle, picking up the brush from the dressing table and pulling the leather tie from the girl's hair.

She introduced herself as she brushed, prattling on about the castle and the Duncans and how much Ysabelle would enjoy being a guest here. Behind her conversation, two soldiers came up carrying a round tub, and then made several trips up and down the steps carrying huge buckets of steaming water. Bessie braided Ysabelle's thick dark hair, then twined it into a lovely bun on top of her head. Satisfied, she held the mirror up to the girl so she could see her work.

"It's lovely. Thank you."

"Yes, it is. I do good work, don't I?" She turned to the soldiers just finishing the filling of the tub. "Thank ye, men, I'll call for ye when we need the tub retrieved."

She turned back to Ysabelle. "So lass, why is it ye are here visitin' us this time of year? Most people go to visit in the spring and summer. Ye're English aren't ye? Many English find it too cold for their thin skins hereabouts. They find Scottish weather inhospitable, although we all think it's lovely."

Ysabelle had no trouble following the girl, and she didn't become upset at the insult. Scots felt about English the same as English felt about Scots. "Aye. It's true that your climate is a bit inhospitable to many. But I will be living here." She swallowed hard, not wanting to let the confession out of her lips. She spoke the dreaded words. "I'm to marry Gray."

Bessie dropped her brush. "Ye're to what?" The surprise on her face was comical. Ysabelle was determined not to laugh and embarrass the woman. She laughed anyway. Bessie scrounged around the stool for the brush and came up triumphant.

Ysabelle and Bessie laughed together. "Aye. You heard me rightly. I've been told I'm to marry Gray. He's … well … he's insisting upon it and even though I tried to dissuade him–"

"Ye tried to dissuade him?" Bessie's mouth hung open, incredulous.

"I truly did."

"Have ye lost yer senses, lass? Can ye not see? The man is as handsome as God ever made. Are ye completely daft?"

Ysabelle couldn't help but smile. "I suppose I must be. To tell you truthfully, I have always seen being wed as servitude without pay. My experience is limited, of course."

"Have ye been married yerself, lass? No, I suppose ye haven't. Ye're a young one at that. Well, I can tell ye.… Do ye know about Gray? I wouldn't want to tell ye somethin' that wasn't my place.…"

"I know he had a family. A wife and a child who died during the birthing. Is there more?"

"Not to the facts, but to the man – yes. He loved his wife dearly. Doted on her, in fact. They had loved each other since they were but wee children. She was the daughter of his mother's closest friend. When she died, it was as if something in him died as well. A piece of him, we all thought it was his heart, grew cold as stone that day, and we thought he'd never love again. Ye must be somethin' special to have gained his notice, not to mention his interest. All the simpering lovelies at court beg for his attentions, they simper and bat their eyes, only he never even looks their way. What on earth did ye do to snare the man?"

"To tell the truth, I'm not certain. I can't imagine why he's interested in me. I even tried to kill him. Of course, I thought he was intent to do me harm at the time."

Bessie laughed and unbuttoned the fasteners on Ysabelle's dress, then lifted it over her head. "Well, that would do it. He grew up under a woman who knew her own mind – it would only be sensible for him to desire a woman who did the same. Get in the bath, lass," she ordered. Pausing for a moment, she asked, "Did ye truly try to kill him with yer sword?"

Ysabelle nodded earnestly as she slid into the hot water. Bessie's laugh floated through the room. Ysabelle closed her eyes and sighed contentedly as the water covered her. Another first – in Inez's home there had been only a small bowlful of freezing water and a harsh cloth that rubbed skin raw. To the poor girl the tubful of warm water was the epitome of luxury. Growing up in Inez's home, she had only been allowed to take a bath when Inez was done, and the old woman had never left the tub until the water was almost cold. She wouldn't allow the girl to heat any more water – it was, of course, a sin to waste. It was especially a sin to waste good, hot water on a gutter rat.

The water was always dirty and cold by the time Ysabelle got in it, but even so – she had loved taking baths. The warmth of the water was like hot cider in her belly, it made her want to curl up by the fire and sleep.

Bessie excused herself and left the chamber. The water was so warm, Ysabelle instantly relaxed. She began to hum as she washed. She scrubbed her hair with the lovely scented soap, then concentrated on cleansing her body. While she washed with the soft cloth, she hummed, then sang her lullaby. Silly that an infant's tune soothed her in such a foreign and grown-up situation.

Far away, long ago –
Someone, somewhere loved me.
Once upon a better time,
I was someone's child.

And someday I will find
Someone destined to love me.
Once upon a better time,
I'll be someone's love.

Gray was walking down the corridor, passing by her door for no less than the fifth time in as many minutes, when heard her sweet voice floating through the stagnant air in the hall. He couldn't help himself, and was happy for the excuse, so he stopped to listen.

It was a child's voice, really, or maybe just a child's need – for a home, for family, for love. A cornered wildcat on her exterior, it was strange that when alone and unguarded she sounded so young, so innocent, so vulnerable. It was the first time he had been allowed to see her longing, her need. The childish lullaby showed a heart that had not been hardened, no matter the cruelty inflicted on it. As illogical as it seemed, instead of being a testament to her weakness, the fact that she hid her vulnerability behind a fortress built on caution was a testament to her strength. He was moved by her – her words, her voice, her vulnerability, her very being. And had she any idea he was listening, she would have snatched his sword and run him through.

Desperately wanting to walk away from his growing vulnerability toward this strange girl, Gray moved closer to the door instead. He knew he shouldn't, but couldn't help himself. Holding his breath, he silently opened the door a crack.

I'll have to remember to thank Bessie for oiling the hinges often.

Ysabelle's eyes were closed as she nestled deeper into the warm water.

She hummed contentedly to herself as she soaked. Her thick hair hung down the outside of the wooden tub, pooling on the floor like gossamer. Face flushed with heat, she pulled her right leg out of the hot water and hung it over the side of the tub, allowing the chill of the room to cool her body a little.

Gray drank in her beauty, again struck by her innocence, her well-hidden vulnerability. He stared at her for the longest moment, then with monumental effort forced himself to noiselessly back out of the chamber. Quietly he edged the door closed.

Bessie appeared at the top of the steps as he turned from Ysabelle's door. She was concentrating on straightening out the hem of the gown she was carrying, evidently for Ysabelle to wear after her bath. When she saw the direction Gray was coming from, her mouth dropped open. Her free hand flew to her hip and she took a deep breath so she could give him a good setting to for infringing on the young woman's good faith.

Before she could utter one reprimand, Gray caught her eye and silenced her with his finger in front of his lips. He shook his head knowingly and gave her the silent command to keep quiet. Pursing her lips together and attempting to glare him into more fitting behavior for a man of his character, she nodded her assent curtly. He smiled broadly in return and headed for the stairway. Unable to stop the warmth that spread through him as he thought of his beautiful captive, he grinned all the way down the stairs.

A moment later, when Bessie came back through the door, Ysabelle slowly opened her eyes to see that the older woman was holding a glimmering gown of luminous green silk and a pristine white sheath for her to put on underneath.

"The evening meal will be served soon. It's time for ye to get out, sweet girl. I take it yer bath was satisfactory? Nothing to bother ye, dear?"

"Nay. It was most peaceful, and the first time I've been truly warm in what seems like weeks."

Smiling over the girl's honesty, Bessie again told her to get out of the bath. "I've a warm cloth to dry ye with, it's been sitting in front of the fire."

Ysabelle sighed loudly and grumpily mumbled something Bessie couldn't quite hear.

She took exception. "No grousing now, Ysabelle, I'll make certain ye get another warm bath tomorrow night," Bessie promised, realizing from the girl's face what a luxury this experience was. "Now, up ye go."

Ysabelle obeyed, allowing the woman to towel her off, telling herself she would only indulge in the kindness this once. It would be a sin to step out of her station for more than just a moment. She allowed Bessie to slip the sheath over her head and tie the narrow silk ribbons that held it in place. Next came the beautiful gown. As the servant woman fastened the ties of the lovely frock, she cocked her head to the side and considered the pretty picture in front of her.

She snapped her fingers. "Just a moment, I have an idea," Bessie said, then disappeared from the room. In less than a moment, she returned with an incredibly beautiful braided gold-colored belt, which she slid around the tilt of Ysabelle's hips. Considering the girl again, she mumbled, "Just one thing more...." and disappeared again.

When she returned, she was holding several strands of pearls. Ysabelle's eyes widened when she saw them, and grew even larger when she realized the woman was intending to add them to her ensemble. She started to protest, but Bessie motioned for the girl to hush, then twined three strands throughout her braided hair and the remaining two strands around her slender neck. Satisfied, she pronounced Ysabelle "finished."

"Ye're as beautiful as a princess, lass. Lord Gray will hardly be able to catch his breath."

"You flatter me, Bessie. I'm nothing more than a servant girl. I have no station, no title, no money, no dowry. I cannot fathom why Lord Duncan would fancy me. And I'm sure his attention will turn, once he realizes what a poor bargain he has made for himself." She shook her head sadly, and Bessie grieved over the insecurity underneath. Unwilling to be too unguarded, Ysabelle slapped a serene expression on her face, squared her shoulders, and smiled up at Bessie.

She attempted to encourage the girl. "Lord Gray is an excellent judge of character. If he has deemed ye the woman he is to marry, be sure he is more than certain of his choice."

Ysabelle just shook her head. "Then the man took one blow too many in battle."

"Well, in any case, follow me, lass. The evening meal will be served momentarily." Bessie took hold of the girl's shoulders and steered her toward the stairs. She heard the bell calling the warriors to their meal, and attempted to push the girl a wee bit faster.

"Come on now, Ysabelle. Ye're going to the evening meal, not a hangin'. Be a good girl now and smile pretty."

Ysabelle possessed a steel that was not evident, and she resisted enough to slow the woman down. Getting hold of herself, she straightened her back, squared her shoulders, and marched down the stairs like a queen. No one would tell her she was unworthy of the dirt she walked on this night.

Just as Adam got to the point in his story where he and Ysabelle were captured by his very family of pirates, Cook came in and announced that it was time to eat. Following her were the two servant girls carrying four platters heaped with large portions of steaming meat surrounded with vegetables. She nodded, satisfied, as the women placed the platters at intervals on the tablecloths, then turned to go get the puddings and tarts. Percy excused himself and left the table, and moments later Adam heard the ringing of a large bell from outside. Shortly thereafter Percy returned and took his seat, followed quickly by a trickle of soldiers. They came in groups and singles, but within five minutes, every seat at all three of the tables was filled.

Garen stood and proposed a toast to the homecoming of their mistress and her sons, followed by a rousing cheer from the warriors. They all gulped their wine and slammed their goblets down on the table, following their drink with a cheer.

Katharine nudged Adam with her elbow. "They used to belch after their toasts, but I put a stop to that right away." He grinned, imagining what that would have been like.

Gray stood. "Here's to us!"

Alane jumped to his feet. "Who's like us?"

Percy finished. "Damn few, and they're all dead!" Every warrior shouted his agreement. Adam stifled the belly laugh that threatened. Giving him a you'd-better-not-laugh look, Katharine joined in with her men's cheer.

At that moment, Ysabelle appeared at the entrance to the great hall. Every eye was on her, every mouth was hushed. The men stared. Several of the giant warriors took their breath in sharply. Gray, beaming with pride, strode across the room, hand extended. Ysabelle, encouraged by the gesture, walked toward him, attempting to keep the smile on her face. The men's reaction to her had her shaken, though. Worried, she looked down at her dress to make sure she hadn't spilled something on it.

"Ye are so incredibly beautiful this evening, love," he told her in hushed tones as he reached her at the top step and took her hand in his. "I am honored to call myself yer intended."

She blushed pink. "Thank you, milord." It occurred to her that it was the dress and all the fussing he was praising, and that chafed her. After all, a pig in velvet was still a pig. She looked him straight in the eye and challenged him, "What if I told you I was a poor woman with nothing to offer you?"

"I would tell ye I was a very rich man with everything to offer ye." He kissed her hand and then turned to take her across the room to the place he had waiting beside his own.

She didn't budge. No man felt that way, they married for dowries and titles and lands. She decided to shock him out of his juvenile fancies. "What if I told you that I was the bastard child of parents I didn't even know? That I was the child of a whore, and because of that I was no better than a whore myself?" She braced herself for his rejection, her jaw set, ready to defy his denouncement of her character.

"I would tell ye that I will give ye children with a name that they can claim. I have chosen ye. Ye have agreed to become my wife. And Ysabelle, I will not allow ye to go back on yer word."

"You would marry me against my will?"

"I would convince ye that I was right."

She tilted her head and considered him. "I am not so easy to convince."

"I believe we have already had this conversation. It ended with yer agreement to marry me. Ysabelle, I will tell ye that when I make a promise, Hades itself will not stop me from accomplishing it. That said – I can promise ye that I will love ye no matter what ye may tell me about yerself, no matter whose child ye are, no matter where ye are from. I will love ye if ye cost me my fortune and my title. I give ye my pledge." He kissed her lips, long and passionately, taking her breath away.

She took a moment to get her pounding heart under control. "You lie," she announced, turning her back to him and preparing to leave the room. Hunger be hanged.

He grabbed her arm, turning her around quickly, and kissed her again. He whispered fervently into her ear, "Ye are mine. Ye agreed and I will not allow ye to change yer mind. No matter what, no matter where, no matter when. I will love ye. I have pledged myself to ye. I am more than strong enough to fight all of yer dragons, Ysabelle.

"Understand me, lass, ye are the woman I chose. Even if I am evil, I have given ye myself. If I am evil – I give ye permission to slit my throat. If I am not evil, I give ye permission to love me. I know it will be difficult to believe for a woman who has never been safe, but please know ye are safe with me. As simpleminded as it may seem, I have affection for ye, sweet Ysabelle. I will love ye with all of my heart. If ye will accept me. Please, I fervently beg ye to accept me."

Ysabelle stared into Gray's stormy eyes. He was begging her for acceptance, for love. She cleared her throat. "I accept you, love," she whispered into his ear. Gray nodded. He clasped his future wife to him.

"As I accept ye, my love," Gray whispered into her ear.

"Thank you," she whispered back. "If you will truly love me, then I will try to love you."

"Then be prepared – for you will be the happiest woman in England or Scotland."

"That I will believe when you have accomplished it." He laughed, and pulling her by the hand, dragged her across the room to their seats. Curious eyes followed them to their seats.

Alane, ever helpful, pointed out the obvious. "Ye sure took yer time convincin' the sweet lass to come and eat." He flashed Ysabelle a watch-me-drive-my-brother-daft grin and needled his brother further. "I'd be hard-pressed to believe that she wants to sit at table with ye. Would ye rather sit with me, lass?"

"No, she would not!" Gray growled at him. Adam and Percy grinned. As they began to fill their trenchers with food, an elderly couple entered the hall. The man, tall and thin but well muscled, even though he looked to be in his sixties, had a shock of white hair and was missing an arm. His wife, a beautiful woman with fire in her eyes, looked about her until she spotted Katharine.

Katharine, noticing the two, stood and beckoned them to the head table. "Lance, Magenta, we were saving places for you. Come and eat." The man named Lance smiled broadly at his mistress and, pulling his wife by the hand, strode across the crowded room. Several soldiers called greetings to him, a few even got up from their seats and embraced him as he passed by.

Gray and Alane stood, happy to see their father's dearest friend, and embraced him happily. "Lance, old man, have ye taken on any armies single-handedly recently?" He laughed at that, then turned and bowed to Katharine. She inclined her head to him and embraced his wife.

"Lance, we have guests. I would like for you to meet my son, Adam, and Gray's intended, Ysabelle." Lance's eyes grew wide with surprise. He didn't know whether to stare at Adam or Ysabelle first.

"It's a pleasure to meet both of you, although I'll admit, it's also quite a surprise."

Katharine turned to Adam. "Lance was the captain of our soldiers until Garrett was attacked and killed. He lost his arm in that battle. Twenty-five men ambushed them, six walked away, although Garrett was killed and Lance lost his arm. He stepped down after Garrett's funeral because he felt he could no longer fulfill his position, only he stayed on as our chief advisor. Even now, Lance trains our younger soldiers. He is invaluable to us." Lance inclined his head to her again, acknowledging her praise.

"Please," Alane came to his rescue, "sit down before my mother feels the need to tell of all of yer victories in battle." He winked at Ysabelle. "Mother loves to tell the stories of our father's cunning. Stories of our former captain

207

are almost as intriguing to her. Be careful when she gets ye alone, ye may find out more of our interestin' island than ye could ever want to know." Katharine gave Alane a mock glare and laughed. Lance and Magenta took their seats beside Garen.

Lance turned to Gray and Alane, "And how long will you be with us? Your mother suffers from a stern countenance when you are away." Katharine nudged him under the table, and he grinned mischievously at her.

Alane answered first. "I have no immediate plans. Except to defeat my brother at capture the queen. He seems to be distracted enough by the beauty sitting beside him to give me an edge in our game."

Gray shook his head. "I could be in a deep sleep and beat ye, brother. But in truth, Lance, I am forced to bring up an unpleasant topic by yer question. We have all been summoned to the court of King Edward immediately. We are to arrive within the next six weeks, giving us no more than three weeks before we must set out for London. As long as the weather doesn't turn threatening, the trip will be tolerable."

"All of us?" Alane's eyebrows shot up, surprised.

"Well, unless we are to anger the king, ye and I have been summoned. And mother, Edward has requested, rather strongly, that we bring ye to court along with us. He didn't threaten me, exactly, although the threat was implied."

Katharine considered the implications. "And for what purpose, Gray, have we been summoned?"

"The reason remains a wee bit vague. Although Edward did express to me his desire to meet ye the last time I was at court. He said his reason was curiosity, I had no reason to doubt him, yet no reason."

"Is it possible our ... activities ... have been discovered?"

"It's possible, although not probable. Unless the ... cargos ... of our business trips have been found, I cannot see how we could have been found out." He rubbed his chin thoughtfully. "Mother, I can make my apologies to the king and simply tell him ye refused to leave yer home. He thinks of ye as an old woman and would consent to that excuse."

"And have you face possible retaliation? I think not. I'm a grown woman, Gray, and I take responsibility for my own actions."

"As do I, although I would not want to put ye in the path of danger."

"Mother, listen to reason...." Alane interjected. Adam and Ysabelle listened intently.

"Reason would dictate that I make sure of my sons' continued happiness. I will not hide behind any man, even if that man is my son."

Gray leaned toward her, trying to sway her with the truth. "Mother, even if ye could have some impact on any possible proceeding, ye are a woman, and although permitted to give testimony, it will bear no weight. Ye know that as well as I."

She nodded. "True. However, neither am I willing to allow you to take responsibility for my actions." She matched his frown with one of her own. Gray backed down, knowing his mother was too stubborn to listen to any more arguments.

Alane sighed. "It's possible that Edward merely wishes for us to return for his enjoyment. His niece has been after my dear brother for the past year. I highly doubt she'll be pleased to meet his wife." He winked at Ysabelle, making her blush.

"The woman can be hanged for all it would matter to me. I'll not change my mind." Gray turned to Garen. "Have ye spoken to the father?"

"Aye. Father Clair said preparations could be made in no more than a week's time. The women will begin making the chapel ready first thing tomorrow. Eloise herself is taking charge of the decorating."

"Eloise? How did she hear so quickly?"

"I told her." Katharine announced, turning to Ysabelle and smiling gently. "I wanted to be the one to bear the news. I didn't want her to hear from anyone else on the chance she would feel ... slighted." She shrugged. "She was excited for you and will come to meet Ysabelle in the morning."

Gray turned to Ysabelle. "Eloise was my wife's mother. She and my mother have been close since Katharine first came here." Seeing the panic on Ysabelle's face, he was quick to reassure her. "Eloise wants only the best for me. She will like ye. Trust me." Ysabelle looked as if she didn't believe him.

Katharine turned everyone's attention by calling for each commander's reports. Ysabelle and Adam sat listening as each man in turn gave his mistress his report. Repair work on the wall was going as scheduled. If all went well, it would be completed by the time the snows came. The new roof for the stables was almost completed, although a young soldier who was not being cautious had fallen through a rotted section of the old roof and broken his arm. His arm would be mended in the course of a few weeks. The crops were harvested and put up in the new barn for the winter, the soap that had been curing was now dry and ready to use, and the animals that had been butchered were smoked and ready for storing as well. With the dead of winter almost upon them, it was of the utmost importance to have everything ready so there would be plenty for all throughout the cold months ahead.

Adam was fascinated by what he was hearing. Reading history was one thing, living it was an entirely different and fascinating proposition.

"Excellent work, men. I suggest we suspend training drills for the next three weeks so that all hands can take part in the work on the wall and the stable roof. The more men, the quicker the tasks will be done. Agreed?"

"Aye," chorused its way around the room. Katharine nodded and dismissed the men. As they filed out, they each bowed their heads to their mistress and wished her a good night. By the time all the men had left, Ysabelle was having difficulty keeping her eyes open. Not wishing to be rude, she didn't ask to be excused, but listened for another half an hour as Katharine, Gray, Alane, Percy, Garen, and Lance discussed the possibility that their piracy had been discovered and what to do about it.

Adam and Ysabelle simply sat quietly and listened to the discussion. She propped her head on her hand and was soon sleeping soundly. Gray saw her slipping from her stool and scooted closer to her, bracing her with his large body, so that she wouldn't fall. Soon she was draped across him, sound asleep. The men dropped their voices so as not to wake her.

It was decided that Katharine and her sons would indeed venture to England and if necessary, face any charges leveled in their direction. Adam spoke up then, insisting that he would go as well. Alane and Gray attempted to sway him, but his mind was set. Gray and Ysabelle would wed in three days, then the assembled family and their escort would head for England and King Edward's court. It was decided. Everyone excused themselves from the table.

"Adam, if you'll follow me, I'll show you to your room. Gray, please settle Ysabelle for the night and meet me in the library. Alane, you as well. We have much to discuss concerning our upcoming journey."

"Aye, mother." Gray gently lifted Ysabelle into his arms and carried her up the stairs to the small guest room. He laid her on the bed, covered her, and kissed her goodnight. He considered locking the door, then changed his mind. She had agreed. She wouldn't run away. He turned to make his way up to the next floor and the library where his mother, brother, and Lance would be waiting to plan their strategy.

When he entered the room, a large map was spread on the huge table in the center of the room. Lance was already pointing to where he thought they should station their own soldiers and their allies troops in the event they had to fight their way out of England.

"I don't believe we've been discovered. I see no reason to call for our allies troops."

"Milady. We must be prepared in the event that Edward is aware of your activities. He will have you hanged if you've been discovered. I cannot allow that."

"And I cannot allow our men to die because I felt the need to annoy the king of England."

"Our men would be disgraced if they weren't allowed to come to your aid."

Gray interrupted their argument. "Ye won't win this one, Mother. He's even more stubborn and headstrong than ye are. Remember, Father has only the reputation for taming ye, but Lance tamed Magenta the tigress." Lance glanced at him and flashed him a knowing smile.

"Aye, I did. And I will not give on this point. If you insist on following your sons into the lions' den, I insist on having men ready to shoot the lions. Garrett would have my hide if I allowed you your way now."

She sighed heavily and nodded her reluctant agreement. "I suppose you're right. I will allow it, only you must be sure they are well hidden. I do not want any battles unless they are absolutely necessary."

"It's rather difficult to hide an army," Lance objected.

She gave him a hard look. "I'm certain that you will accomplish it."

"Aye, milady."

Alane spoke up. "Then it's all settled?"

"It is. Lance, hurry the work on the wall and the stables. Set the women to preparations for the warriors who will accompany us. All must be done within the fortnight." She looked at Gray and Alane, who nodded their agreement.

Lance bowed. "As you wish." He turned and left the room.

"Gentlemen?" Katharine arched her eyebrows, waiting for their challenge. They offered none.

"So be it," she said. "I'll see you in the morning. Good night." She left the chamber.

Alane looked over at his brother. From his pocket he pulled a chess piece and waggled it in Gray's direction, waiting for an answer to his silent question. Gray grinned broadly and reached up to the top shelf of the bookcase on his left and pulled down the chess board. They seated themselves across from each other at the table and began their game.

THIRTEEN

The next week passed for Ysabelle in an exciting but exhausting blur. She had never known anyone who had even attended such a fancy wedding as was being planned for her, so the flurry of activity took her by surprise. She was taken to an immense room full of exquisite materials and told to pick eight bolts of fabric that she liked. It was like choosing between jewels. She had never seen anything so fine in her life. Brocades, silks, charmeuses, woolens – all the choices made her dizzy. Gray hadn't been exaggerating – he was definitely a man of wealth, if the fortune of his family home was any indication.

After the noon meal, the busy bride was led to the master chamber where Katharine and Gray were waiting. The two were sitting in cushioned chairs beside the fire, ready to start the afternoon of choosing materials and styles for the gowns that were to be made. Bessie started in measuring Ysabelle every which way, then pinning and poking and having the girl choose ribbons and weaves and all manner of buttons and cords.

When Ysabelle looked to the spectators for mercy, Katharine explained that a girl couldn't get married without a trousseau, and it was her job to see that Ysabelle had one. She tried on slippers and riding boots, gowns, and chemises. Gray sat in the cushioned chair in the now-crowded sitting area and nodded his approval or disapproval of the different choices Bessie would offer. With each new option, Ysabelle's face showed more and more strain, and when she started looking truly fatigued, he called a halt to the process. She smiled at him gratefully. This was all so overwhelming.

"Go ahead and sew what we already decided upon and surprise Ysabelle with the last two gowns. Have ye the proper measurements for the wedding gown?"

"Aye, milord Gray. I'll set Cora and her cousin to work on it immediately. We'll have everything ready for yer departure in a fortnight's time. Well enough?"

"Aye. Thank ye, Bessie. The lass looks tired. I'm thinkin' to have her meal brought to her in her chamber."Gray looked in the direction of Hilde, who had been helping with the whole process.

She hopped to her feet, eager to help, not to mention ease the cramping in her legs from the last hours of kneeling on the floor. "I'll be fetchin' it for ye, milord. We wouldn't want to tire the lass out. Be sure to have her dress warmly for bed tonight, there's a chill in the air this evening, and we wouldn't want her to catch her death."

Gray stood and stretched his massive arms upward, almost touching the ceiling. The chair he had been sitting in had put quite a cramp in his back. He reordered his clothing and held out his hand to Ysabelle, who gratefully took it and allowed him to lead her from the room.

As soon as they were out of earshot, she turned to him and whispered conspiratorially, "Thank you for rescuing me. Bessie and your mother are hardly dragons, but I was definitely a damsel in distress."

He laughed at her jest. As they approached her room, she held back. "Gray, I don't really want to go to bed as of yet. Might we walk in the courtyard or find a book and read together?"

His eyes widened in surprise. She wanted to spend time with him. "It would be a pleasure, lass. Pick yer poison – a walk in the courtyard or a book in the library?"

Ysabelle grinned at his choice of words. "I'm feeling rather daring tonight, milord. Why not both poisons? Let's walk before it gets too chill, then retire to the library and read."

He hesitated. She still looked tired and drawn, with dark smudges under her eyes and lines of fatigue around her mouth. "I'll strike a bargain with ye, love. We'll take a turn about the upper and lower bailey, if after we've done so ye will allow me to read to ye in yer room while ye eat yer evening meal and ready yerself for bed."

"Is that proper?" she asked from beneath her lashes. She could hardly breathe at the thought, and her face was reddening at the mere idea of having the handsome man in her chamber, let alone while she was in her bed.

He nodded. "Completely, lass. We'll leave the door open and remain in the sitting area by the fire. Agreed?"

She smiled up at him. "Agreed," she said with a nod. Placing her arm through his, she followed him down the stairs and through the kitchens to the rear door. Pausing to gather their cloaks from the hooks in the entry hall, Gray placed Ysabelle's about her shoulders and tied it securely under her chin. Pulling her through the back hallway, they passed through the kitchens to the rear door. As he pushed it open, a gust of icy wind caught hold of the heavy door and almost ripped it out of Gray's hand.

"The wind's up, lass. Are ye still wantin' a walk?"

"A brisk bit o' wind should never stop a walk."

"I see. Well what about sleet and snow?"

"They merely make the walker move more quickly." She grinned. "Although, if you feel daunted by some overly brisk weather or are afraid your frail body might become chilled...."

"Then I'm certain ye'll be more than happy to lend me yer cloak." He winked at her and pulled her into the courtyard.

Gray took her on a tour of the grounds, from the herb garden to the practice field, where the soldiers drilled every day. After showing her the housing for the soldiers in training, he led her over to the repair work on the wall and showed her the progress that was being made. Although she wasn't particularly interested in some of the more mundane affairs concerning the castle, she enjoyed listening to Gray's voice as he explained all about his home. The pride in his voice warmed her and the cadences of his speech soothed her frazzled nerves.

Almost three quarters of an hour later, the two reentered the kitchens and headed up to Ysabelle's chamber. Hilde had already brought the tray with Ysabelle's dinner on it into the room and laid out a meal for two on the small table between the sitting area's chairs. The fire had been laid and lit and was burning brightly, hissing and popping its way through the wood.

Gray seated Ysabelle, then took his own seat and served the venison and black bread onto first Ysabelle's trencher, then his own. They ate, Gray finishing first, at which point he excused himself from the table. When he returned shortly thereafter carrying a book he hoped would interest her, she was finished with her meal. He stepped into the hall while she changed into her nightdress, and when she called for Gray to come back, she was snugly settled under the covers of her bed, brushing the tangles out of her hair. Gray installed himself comfortably in his previous seat before the fire and began to read aloud. Finishing her evening routine, she sank back into the soft pillows and closed her eyes. Less than ten minutes later, she was sound asleep, and Gray quieted his reading and listened to her slow, even breathing. After a time he stood and, after blowing out the candles by the bed and stoking the fire so that the logs would be settled safely in the grate, he left the room, shutting the door quietly behind him.

Gray went to bed fully satisfied with the way his life was unfolding.

They ate breakfast together the next morning, went riding before lunch, and ate lunch in – of all places – the tower. At Ysabelle's request, they ate a lunch of bread and cheese in the highest room in the castle, fulfilling her desire to see the island from a great height. There was also her confession that she had never been in a home before that had more than one floor, and

214

she had always wondered what such a place was like. She was beginning to laugh now and then when she was with Gray, which made him jest with her even more, simply to hear the glorious sound over again.

Ysabelle made Gray take her all over the castle, from the root cellars to the turrets. Her exclamations of wonder made him smile, feeling like he was giving her gifts. When he took her to the cliff that overlooked the waterfall, she instinctively grabbed his hand in her excitement. Her face was alight with her exhilaration. She was so excited she took her shoes off in the chilly weather and stuck her feet beneath the frigid water, just to feel it on her skin. Gray began to suspect he was grinning like an idiot whenever he was around her, a conclusion that was confirmed by his most gracious brother Alane.

Alane and Adam were becoming thick with each other. Alane was performing much the same service for Adam that Gray was for Ysabelle. The only difference being that once Adam had seen all of the castle and grounds, he insisted upon spending his spare time with Lance and learning the fighting skills of the soldiers. In return, he showed Lance a few of the finer moves he had learned in his years of fencing. Much to Adam's surprise, he was able to teach the old warrior a thing or two. He drilled with Lance and Alane every day for the three weeks they remained at Ellshope, spending his mornings drilling with the two men or assisting the soldiers in their repairs and his afternoons visiting with his mother.

Katharine was amused by the fast friendship between Alane and Adam. It was as though they had grown up together, they even developed a rivalry between them – constantly attempting to best each other in their drills. Adam bested Alane with the sword almost every time, but had quite a hard time mastering the bow. Alane taught his new brother how to play capture the queen, and hang it all if the boy didn't catch the fever for that annoying sport. Their last game ended in a wrestling match, during which Katharine was forced to pull rank – and her daggers – on the two to make them finish their childish antics out of doors.

Adam showed the soldiers an easier and quicker way to build and support the new roof that was being built for the stables, incorporating his vast construction experience and their materials, and the new roof was finished within six days. Under Garen's supervision, all of the soldiers that had been working on the roof then transferred their efforts to the repair of the wall. Finally, the day before the wedding, seven days after Katharine and her men returned to the island, the wall was finally finished. With the preparations for winter snows completed, the evening meal that night was a free-for-all of celebration. Wine flowed freely, and the men boisterously celebrated the completion of the building, Gray's wedding, and Katharine's son coming home. Adam was already a part of them, having worked side by side with the men and having helped them make short work of the stable repairs.

The rabbit stew was delicious that evening, and Gray was quick to point out that Ysabelle had been the one to bag the rabbits during their hunting trip that day – boasting of her skill with her bow. Ysabelle just picked at her food, however, and since she normally had such a hearty appetite, it invited comment.

"Is there something troubling ye, lass?" Garen was the first to ask. "Ye've eaten hardly anything. Ye should be celebrating, ye wed on the morrow!" His statement brought a loud cheer from all of the soldiers within earshot, who were already far along in their cups.

Ysabelle smiled weakly, apologizing for her behavior. "Please forgive me, milord. I am not myself this evening. Perchance all of the excitement has overwhelmed me."

"Aye, you do look overjoyed, sister." Adam winked at her. He had picked up the burr of his brother Alane and was enjoying speaking with it.

"That she does," Alane agreed. "If she looked any happier, she would be ready to go to her closest friend's burial." He chuckled at his own joke, earning him a kick under the table from his older brother, causing him to laugh even harder.

"Please forgive my brother's manners, love. He was raised by the wild pigs that roam the woods." Everyone at table laughed then, even Ysabelle, breaking the tension.

The nausea that had threatened to overwhelm her eased a bit, and she ate a small piece of black bread with honey. *I'm getting married tomorrow.* Instantly the nausea was back.

"Lady Katharine, may I be excused. I believe I shall do ever so much better tomorrow if I'm well rested."

"Of course, child. Although I must warn you, I believe Bessie is in your chamber waiting to have you try your gown to make sure it's right for tomorrow. And we'll have the tub brought up in the morning so that you may prepare for your wedding mass then, agreed?"

"Yes, thank you. That will be most agreeable. Good night." As she turned to leave, Gray caught her by the hand, questioning her with his eyes. She shook her head to reassure him and fled the room. He stared after her thoughtfully, wondering what was troubling her. Not that he should be overly concerned, of course. The lass had agreed to wed him and that was that. He had no doubt that after the ceremony she would come to her senses and become more reasonable. After all, her strange behavior was no doubt caused by nervousness. Everything would be fine.

Alane began telling a joke about King Edward's court, and Gray pulled himself back to the present just in time to laugh politely over the jest he had not heard. What ever the jest had been, reminded Adam of several blonde jokes he had heard, and he retold them making the English the butt of the joke instead. The warriors laughed uproariously at the insults to the English, which touched off a string of humorous stories from all around the room.

Katharine finally called a halt to the party. If the group didn't return to their homes and go to bed soon, everyone would sleep through the wedding feast tomorrow night. She turned to Gray and lifted her finger to her lips in signal – and he let out a shrill whistle – one of the few things she had never been able to master.

"Gentlemen, it is time to end our evening. We will finish with a final toast and then every man is expected to go to his home –"

"So we can do it all again on the morrow!" Bretane shouted, nearly falling off his stool. His shout was met by the enthusiastic cheers of his fellows.

"Aye, so that tomorrow ye will be able to remain awake throughout the wedding and the celebration after. To Ellshope – life and liberty!"

"LIFE AND LIBERTY!" the men stood to their feet, repeating the pledge with their closed fists over their hearts, draining their cups. Between the wine and the humor, by the time the room cleared, the warriors' faces and stomach muscles were sore from laughter. They all bowed respectfully as they filed out of the great hall and headed for their homes.

Katharine turned to her sons. "Tonight I'm going to behave like your mother and tell you to go to bed. I expect to see a groom without shadows under his eyes in the morning."

"Aye. I'm already sound asleep," Gray answered as he stood and left the room.

She turned to Adam and Alane, who were wearing mischievous grins and doing their best not to look her in the eye. "What have you got planned, boys?"

Adam feigned shock. "Me, Mother? As a guest, I can assure you that I will behave in only the best and most decorous of manners."

"I can see that by the evil grin marking you two devils' faces. Hear me, gentlemen, if you do anything to cause difficulty or annoyance at your brother's wedding, I'll take you to the barn and use my new leather whip on you."

Alane grinned broadly and held up his hands in mock surrender. "Aye, Mother, we'll be good."

As she turned to go to bed, she heard Alane's quiet remark, "Ye won't be able to find us, in any event."

She turned to glare at him, but her frown turned to a grin when he winked at her and smiled innocently. That boy could drive a saint to curse! Oh, how he was like his father. She sighed deeply and retired for the night.

The chapel was full of rich green ivy. A canopy of fresh purple flowers, the only kind that could be found this time of year, was suspended above the altar, and two cages filled with white doves were sitting on each side of the chapel, waiting. They were to be released at the close of the wedding ceremony. The upper bailey was a rush of activity. Hilde and Dora and a few recruits were busy setting tables and filling them high with food for the wedding feast. Eloise was absorbed in her task of draping everything with fresh green tree boughs and iridescent blue silk ribbons. The sun was shining brightly, giving its blessing to the day. The wind was still, and everything was in readiness for the much awaited wedding.

Everything, that is, save the bride.

She refused to come out of her room, had barred the door, in fact. No one knew quite what to do about it either. Gray was pacing the library, waiting for his mother to come and tell him how to persuade Ysabelle to come out of her room. She had been holed up in there since last evening, when she had excused herself from the meal and retired to her room. Bessie had been waiting abovestairs to have her try on her wedding gown and the distressed lass had burst into tears during the fitting. Both Bessie and Katharine had tried to comfort the girl, only she kept muttering something about servitude and getting paid and freedom to choose and how nothing was fair – to her or to Gray.

Gray was pacing in front of the fireplace in the library, warring with himself. He didn't want to wed the girl by force, although then again he did, too. *Blast!* He wanted her to come to him willingly, although by heaven he wasn't above coercion. If he could only get hold of what the problem was, he was sure he could find a way to fix it. *Devilment!* He thought they had all this straightened out already. The woman was making him crazed! She wouldn't even talk to him to tell him what was wrong.

"Blasted unreasonable woman...." he muttered as he paced.

Adam stood in the corner with his arms folded across his chest, eyes alight with interest as Gray wore a groove in the floor. Alane had been enjoying the show as well, but was banned from the room for his rude remarks after Gray nearly drew his sword on him. Gray was driven to distraction and that knave Alane had been pricking his temper with every word. It wasn't until Alane called Gray 'henpecked' that Gray had actually lunged for him. It was hard for Adam not to smile, to see a giant of a man like Gray reduced to the agitated state he was in by a slip of a girl like Ysabelle. He knew she would see the humor in the situation if she could get past her panic. Gray would have been able to see the humor as well if he had been anyone save the groom.

There was a knock on the door and Katharine entered, a broad smile on her face. Gray looked up, face full of anticipation. "She has agreed to come out. She won't tell me whether or not she'll marry you, but at least it's a start."

"She'll marry me, by heaven! I'll not take any other answer from her." He started for the door, a murderous look on his face when Katharine stopped him.

"Son, I feel I should offer you a bit of advice. Your Ysabelle does have a fondness for you, but you've been very purposeful and determined with her. Give her a choice, let her feel she's in charge of her own future. It will be easier for her that way."

Gray just looked at her, not saying anything. Then he pulled his arm free and went to find his reticent bride. When he found her, she was sitting in front of the fire in the entrance hall, wearing her wedding gown – so stunningly beautiful she took his breath away – and looking like she was ready to bolt. His chest tightened at the sight of his future wife – at least she would be if God had any favor for him at all. Her long dark hair, curled and draped with pearls, floated around her like a cloud. The long, iridescent light blue dress shimmered in the dancing firelight as it flowed around her gentle curves. Sitting on the tilt of her hips, a braided silk belt in a vivid royal blue was slung, its fringed ends hanging down her front. Just peeking out under the hem of her dress were beaded slippers in the same color as the dress. They were made of silk as well, with just enough heel to let Ysabelle stand as tall as Gray's shoulders. She had never looked so lovely. Gray worried for a moment that his heart might burst from his chest – so hard was it beating.

He approached her carefully, not wanting her to scramble for the door. Ysabelle looked small and fragile, although her back was straight as an arrow and she held her head high. Everything in her demeanor shouted 'challenge'. His shoulders sagged and he steadied himself for the coming confrontation. She was defying Gray to force her to marry him, he supposed, and for the first time, he wasn't sure if he was willing to do that. Immediately he knew better. The devil if he was going to let her go – Ysabelle was going to marry him, and by all that was holy she would be happy doing it!

Then Ysabelle turned toward him and smiled – tentatively at first, then radiantly. A spark of hope jumped in him. A decision had been made – she had made up her mind, it was clear. He prayed that she had decided to marry him. He couldn't possibly – no, he absolutely refused to – let her go. She held up her hand, silently commanding him to halt. Her hand trembled and she quickly clasped them behind her back.

Gray stopped midstride, confused. She composed herself for battle and looked straight at him. She had to crane her neck backward to look into his eyes. His heart leapt in his chest. When she focused on him like that, he could scarcely force himself to breathe.

"I have come to a decision, milord," she explained with a nod. The look in her eyes was impossible to read.

Gray crossed the room to stand in front of the fireplace and waited, doing his best not to shout at her. His throat hurt from the strain. She was maddeningly quiet, she just kept looking up at him with those great green eyes of hers as if she expected him to read her mind. Unable to stand the suspense anymore, he blurted out, "Well?"

"Well what?" she asked, eyebrows knitting together, irritated at his impatient tone of voice.

Gray rubbed his forehead and sighed, shaking his head. Leaning back on the mantlepiece, he took a deep breath to gather his wits. "Have ye come to yer senses and decided to marry me, Ysabelle?"

She brightened and smiled up at him sweetly, but for just a moment. Her face clouded over a fraction of a second later and she started twisting her hands in the ends of her belt. "Oh, yes, that. I have decided that if you're foolish enough to want me, I'm foolish enough to say yes. That is, if you still want to marry me when you fully understand everything. Only before you decide to wed me, milord, I must be perfectly honorable with you. I have made it no secret – I won't be a good wife to you. It's only just and right that I tell you that directly." She acted as though she were giving him a very grave confession. He kept his face impassive.

"And why might that be, lass?" He arched his eyebrow, curious.

"Because I can't possibly give you what you want." Her eyes dropped down to her hands, which had abandoned the belt by now and were now knotting and unknotting nervously in her lap. "I refuse to be shackled. You see, I wish to be free. And if I marry you, I will insist on being so. I'm sure I'll make you angry time and again."

"Ye will?" He kept the smile from his face, knowing she would become offended if he were amused at her uncomfortable confession.

"Most certainly. I always made Nana Inez angry. After I left her home, I promised myself I would not allow anyone to control and dominate me ever again. Even a man such as you, milord. And husbands wish to control their wives." He should understand that – he was a man, wasn't he? – but instead he looked thoroughly confused. The man was obviously not getting it. How blunt did she have to be?

"They do?"

"Well, of course they do! Everyone knows they do. Even your man Percy said they do!"

He smiled at her answer, and she gave him a disgruntled look. He put his hands behind his back, not wanting to seem threatening so that she could finally get out what had been bothering her. "And?" he prodded.

Making fists with her hands, she planted them on her hips, stood, and stuck out her chin defiantly. "And nothing. I know men want submissive wives, and I'm certain I cannot be that to you. I wouldn't want to lie to you concerning my character, or rather lack of it, and you seem to ignore the hints I've given you."

He straightened up and leaned toward her. "Like when ye tried to carve me up like a roast goose? Aye, lassie, ye're a subtle one, ye are." The maddening male had the audacity to grin at her.

Ysabelle gave him her fiercest frown. "No, I'm not subtle. You're daft! I know what I am and in a moment you will as well. Nana Inez was always quick to instruct me as to my flaws – I'm rebellious and slothful – you might as well know that right now. Furthermore, I sometimes burn the food I cook, and I often drop stitches when I sew or weave. Once I dropped an egg in the neighbors' henhouse when I was gathering eggs for baking – although I did serve my penance of a week without bread – and at times I get my face dirty and don't rush to cleanse it. Often I don't even care.

"I have forgotten more of the Holy Scriptures than I have remembered – something which exasperated Father Corey to no end. Even worse, I sometimes forget to say my prayers before I go to bed, and every now and again I have been known to say extremely unladylike words – like when I was chased by the dairyman's bull, Horace.

"You seem to be an honorable man where women are concerned, and I wouldn't want you to get less than you bargained for. I am not, and I'm certain of this, willing to do what I'm told, stay where I'm put, or keep my lips shut. I'm certain you will find living with me intolerable. A reasonable man would go no further with this foolishness." Ysabelle sank back into her chair, exhausted from her confession.

Gray laughed. "I was already aware of many of these … traits … in ye, Ysabelle."

She sucked in her breath. "You knew?" she asked, incredulous.

"Aye, lass." He nodded slowly to punctuate his answer, then crossed his arms and leaned back against the mantle again, a broad smile curving his lips.

"And although I've always considered myself a reasonable man, I must confess – where ye are concerned, that trait seems to desert me."

"Then why in heaven would you want to marry me?"

"Call it a character flaw of my own. I don't find bein' with ye intolerable at all. For that matter, I happen to relish my time with ye. I find I enjoy ye immensely, Ysabelle. And we've already decided this question of marriage, have we not?" Smiling warmly at her, his tenderness waged a full-scale war on her defenses – laying siege to her mind, enveloping her senses.

Straightening away from the mantle, his eyes met and held hers. His gaze was so intense, she felt like she was standing in the sun. She dropped her eyes. Still she could feel his eyes on her, waiting patiently, the full force of his will encompassing her – threatening to overcome her. Ysabelle mulled his words over for a moment. This could be her future. Home, family, comfort, as opposed to searching for those things for the rest of her life and perhaps never finding an offer nearly so good. He was a good man, she decided, it would be a sound match. And she did want to have children, didn't she? Of course she did.

Ysabelle stood. Taking a deep breath, she squared her shoulders and looked Gray straight in his stormy eyes. "Yes. I believe we have at that."

"So ye're ready now, Ysabelle?" He extended his hand to her.

She placed her small hand into his large one and nodded, smiling up at him. "I am, Gray."

"Ye won't regret this, lass," he promised her.

Grinning, she nodded. "Aye ... but you might."

He moved closer to her, taking her into his arms and kissing her. He had only been meaning to seal her decision with a brief kiss, but ended up losing himself in her instead. It was just that she was so soft and giving. She felt so good in his arms and she smelled incredible. A man could be overcome easily by these sensations.

After a moment of resistance, Ysabelle surrendered the fight and melted into him. He was so warm, and so strong. She felt safe with him. God save her, he could destroy her mind with just one kiss.

Several minutes later, the sound of a throat clearing resounded behind them and startled them out of their sensual stupor. Gray pulled back from the woman in his arms, thoroughly affected by their encounter – his heart was slamming in his chest and there was perspiration on his forehead even though the room was chilly. Ysabelle stood dazed, her eyes glazed over and her lips a bit swollen and pink. The man had taken all her senses from her. She shook herself to clear away the flustered feeling. Smiling in an arrogant, self-satisfied way, Gray congratulated himself on a job well done.

Turning in the direction of the noise, he was mildly irritated to see his brother Alane standing at the bottom of the steps. "So – are the two of ye goin' to finish this in the chapel, or are we goin' to have to seek penance from the Almighty for yer lustful behavior?"

Ysabelle blushed, Gray smiled broadly. "It seems the chapel will find a use today after all."

"Well, it's about time. At least by my measurement." Alane winked at Ysabelle. "Ye'll have to forgive my brother's poor manners, Ysabelle, he rather loses his faculties when ye're about. Ye must have quite a high opinion of our family, in that I was raised by wild pigs and my brother is of an unsound mind. What a gift to us that such fresh and unspoiled blood as yer own is marryin' into our frightful wee family." He smiled warmly and held out his hand to her, "If ye'll come with me, lass, I'll show ye to where the women are waitin' to fuss over ye. They're all cooin' and cluckin' like a bunch of hens, waitin' to pluck ye silly." She smiled gratefully up at him and took his arm. Glancing back to see Gray smiling tenderly at her, she returned his smile, then followed his brother through the small hallway and out the rear door toward the chapel.

When they entered the stone chapel, Ysabelle was immediately stolen away from Alane by Eloise, who couldn't seem to stop telling her how beautiful she was and what a lovely bride she made. The girl was pulled along through an alcove door in the nave of the chapel into an anteroom where Katharine, Bessie, and a looking glass were waiting. She saw her reflection and stifled a gasp. The woman in the mirror couldn't possibly be her – that woman was so … incredibly beautiful … and she … well, wasn't. It was as if a princess had taken her place for the day.

"Aye, lass, ye do look lovely." Eloise seemed to read her thoughts.

"It must be the dress. The material is so exquisite." Ysabelle still couldn't accept what she was seeing in the glass. "And so is your handiwork, Bess."

"It's kind of ye to say so, and now that I see the gown on ye, I'd be hard-pressed to disagree with ye. However, to be truthful, I have to say that ye'd be beautiful wearin' a hauberk and armor. Lord Gray chose well for himself." Bessie was nodding and beaming as she circled Ysabelle, surveying her handiwork and making certain everything was just so.

"Aye, lass, Bess is right in thinkin' so. It's the beauty within the dress that's captivatin' to the eye." Eloise instructed her, then leaned over and fluffed Ysabelle's hair. "Yer hair is just lovely hanging down around yer shoulders in those curls. And ye must be very happy indeed, yer face is absolutely radiant." Ysabelle felt her face heat.

Katharine joined in the fussing, pulling out a brush and separating her curls so they would hang in ringlets. "I'm pleased you changed your mind, Ysabelle. I think you'll be content you did. Gray has grown up to be a wonderful man. And you'll never lack for anything, including his devotion."

Ysabelle stood quiet, willing her knees to quit knocking and her heart to slow down its frantic beat. It kept threatening to leap out of her chest and run for the hills. Eloise pinched her cheeks to add color, and told her to bite her lips as well. Ysabelle obeyed. That done, Katharine brought out the wedding veil. It was a beautifully crafted piece of snow-white lace, sewn to a wreath of the fresh purple flowers Ysabelle had seen growing in the field and intertwined with a deep green ivy and a white winter flower as well. It was quite lovely. As Katharine set the headpiece on the girl's head and pulled the snarled strands of her hair free, she cocked her head to the side and looked the girl up and down. Satisfied, she nodded her head vigorously toward Bessie and Eloise. They nodded their agreement.

Beaming, Katharine lifted the short veil and kissed Ysabelle on her cheek. "Welcome to the family, Ysabelle. I hope you'll be happy with us, although that will most assuredly be better accomplished if we keep Alane locked in the tower."

"I'm certain I will. And Alane's not harmful, but rather amusing. Especially the way he infuriates Gray. Thank you for your kindness."

The older woman nodded. "Do you need anything else?"

"I don't imagine so. May I ask who will be giving me away?" Ysabelle knew such things were done, but had no idea who would be the one to do it for her.

"If you have no objections, since your father ... um, was unable to be present, my husband's dear friend Lance has requested the honor."

"I have no objections. In fact, I found him to be a very pleasant man."

"He took an instant liking to you as well. And he is overjoyed to see our Gray wed again. Everyone is eager to see Gray wed. Even Gray. I'm grateful for the change you've brought about in him. I must warn you though, he can be a hard man when he desires to be. But don't be troubled, he's always just." She patted Ysabelle on the shoulder, then mumbled as she turned away, "Now if I could only see to Alane...."

Ysabelle smiled. Poor Alane, he was for it now. He'd be wed before he had the time to make a jest about marriage.

A knock sounded at the door, and Eloise hurried to open it. Lance stood at the entry, grinning like an idiot. He made a stately bow to the three. "Ladies, if you'll take your seats, I'll be more than happy to escort this young lass to the altar and assist in getting this wedding underway."

Katharine, Bessie, and Eloise nodded, dropped into hurried curtsies, and quickly left the room to take their seats in the chapel proper. When he looked back to Ysabelle, she was wearing her rabbit-in-a-trap look. Lance took her arm and draped it through his own, patting her hand gently and attempting to soothe her.

"When my Bess got married to her William, she looked almost as terrified as you do, lass. I don't believe that she was quite so pale, though." He chuckled low in his throat, a sound that ended up being contagious. Ysabelle giggled once, then again, and soon she was having difficulty keeping her peals of laughter quiet enough not to be heard at the altar. It wasn't that anything was humorous, she just couldn't help herself. Giving her time to control her hysterics, Lance freed himself from her iron grasp, looped his arm around the girl's shoulders and gently held her until the hiccups of terror subsided.

"Feel better, lass?" he asked, keeping the grin from his face so as not to hurt her and cause her unstable feelings to erupt again. If she exploded into laughter anew, she might well begin to sob, and sweet heavens how he hated that! It didn't matter why a woman was crying, it was his experience that it was always the nearest man's fault. Thanks to his sweet Magenta, he carried enough guilt, thank you very much.

Finally controlling herself, she bent to the difficult task of composing her expression. She wiped her eyes and nodded her head. "Aye. I believe I do." As he opened the low wooden door of the anteroom and pulled her into the foyer, Ysabelle pulled on his arm and caused him to stop. "Lance," she whispered, "if I swoon, please catch me."

He nodded, careful to keep his face straight. She nodded too, satisfied that all contingencies were prepared for. As the bagpipes began their chorus in the nave, Lance began pulling Ysabelle toward the altar. With each step she became more and more resistant, until he was practically dragging her up the aisle by her arm.

In the front stood Gray, waiting for her to reach him, a puzzled look on his face. Watching the tug of war between Lance and Ysabelle as they made their way up the aisle, realization of why the struggle was occurring caused a smile to tug at his lips. He tried not to smile, but the scene they were making was comical.

Alane, standing up beside the groom, was openly grinning at the tussle. My, but she was a timid thing. Gray would run her right over if she didn't come up with some spirit soon. Although the lass was holding her own with Lance. Perhaps she had some mettle in her after all.

Finally the two reached the altar. Lance was out of breath and Ysabelle was disheveled – her veil hung askew and she had lost one of her slippers.

Gray smiled graciously at her, surely the woman had completely lost her mind. Her appearance reinforced the notion, as her eyes were wild with fear and her hair tumbled about her in all directions. Lance pried her arm from around his and gratefully handed the woman over to Gray, who was careful not to let go of her hand. He was certain that if he did, she would lift her skirts around her knees and run for the ship.

Attempting to soothe her frazzled nerves, he leaned over and whispered, "It will be over very soon. In just a few moments we'll be man and wife."

"That's what I'm afraid of," she whispered back. Her voice was not as quiet as his, though, and Alane, not to mention the entire front row, overheard the exchange. He couldn't help himself. He leaned over so that she could just see him and put his fingers around his left wrist to form shackles. Ysabelle's eyes widened and she turned quickly and headed back down the aisle.

Gray intercepted her flight in two short steps and hauled her up tightly against his side. Together he half-dragged, half-coaxed her back to the altar, where the priest was standing and waiting, an incredulous look on his face. The holy man's mouth hung slack, and his eyes bugged out slightly. Could it possibly be true that someone would *not* want to marry Gray? Unbelievable.

Glaring at his poorly behaved brother, Gray turned to the priest. "Please proceed, Father."

The priest turned to Ysabelle, "Is that acceptable to ye, lass?"

Ysabelle took a deep breath and nodded. The father turned to Gray and asked him to recite his vows. Still holding Ysabelle pinned to his side, he did just that. When the father turned to Ysabelle for her to recite her vows, Gray thought perhaps this wedding was going to get done after all, so he released his tight hold on his bride. All of the color drained from the girl's face. She gulped huge breaths of air in an attempt to steady herself, only instead of helping her gain back her poise, the breaths made her sway on her feet. Without warning, she fell to the floor with a thud.

Gray was at her side in an instant, and the chapel was completely silent. Was she dead? No, she was still breathing. He gave her a gentle slap on her cheek. Nothing. Another slap, a bit harder than the first, made him feel like and ogre, but didn't bring Ysabelle around. Gray sat back on his heels, considering what to do. After much internal debate, he finally decided to carry her back to her room and try marrying her again tomorrow. As he placed his arms under her neck and knees to lift her up, she opened her eyes, smiled at him sweetly, and said, "I'll marry you."

"Ye will?" he asked, surprised.

"I will," she said, to the priest this time, then she climbed out of Gray's arms.

"Very well, lass. She said she will, clan!" A loud cheer went up from the audience. "Gray, kiss yer bride, and somebody, let the doves loose."

Alane moved to the cage on his side of the small chapel, and Eloise made her way to the other. The groom pulled his bride to her feet, then swept her into his arms and kissed her. While Gray ravaged his bride in front of God and kinsmen, the doves were released to make their way to the skies, celebrating the union with their beauty and sweet cries.

It wasn't until Alane tapped his brother on the shoulder that he pulled back from kissing his bride. Ysabelle's knees buckled and her legs dropped out from under her, and Gray had the gall to catch her and grin as she blushed charmingly up at him. He kissed her again for good measure and thought for a moment that he might not be able to wait until the wedding festivities had ended.

"Ysabelle?" His voice sounded like a caress.

"Yes?"

"Pigs just sprouted wings!"

The fire that ignited in her eyes was exactly what she had needed to take away her fear. She planted her fists on her hips and made to shout at him. Aye, she was fetching when she was angry. Gray considered taking her directly to his chamber, until Percy grabbed hold of his arm and dragged him out into the festooned courtyard for the wedding feast.

Alane was at least a bit accommodating to his brother, in that he scooped up the bride as soon as she was abandoned by Gray and pulled her alongside him to the feast. It was the last time they saw each other until the end of the evening.

The gaily adorned tables were laden with sweetbreads, tarts, cakes, and sweetmeats. The wine and ale flowed like water, and by the end of the evening, when the huge bonfire was dwindling down to embers and the dancing was concluded, Ysabelle had taken so much wine for herself she couldn't have told the difference between herself and her husband. At first, she had refused the wine and would only drink water. But she had been so nervous she didn't even taste the wine when Alane handed it to her, watered down of course, and told her it was punch.

When the dancing started, he was sure to keep her away from her husband. Ysabelle danced with Percy, Adam, Alane, Garen, Lance, and a young soldier she didn't know named Dugal. Each time she became thirsty, Alane was by her side with a refreshment without her even having to ask. Every time Gray would approach to cut in on the dance, or at least get close to his bride, one of his friends would whisk her away. His face grew darker and more frustrated with each passing hour.

"Well, sister, it appears that yer husband is becomin' a mite vexed." Alane had once again appeared at her side, cup for her in hand. "Shall we see if we can pique his temper just a bit more before I turn ye back over to him?"

Ysabelle giggled and nodded. For some reason, the thought of annoying Gray by paying attention to his ill-behaved brother seemed absurdly humorous. She was feeling a light-headed euphoria that was only enhanced by the fun she had dancing, so when Alane offered up his hand to her – that mocking smile on his face – she took it and was rollicked through the grass and around the great fire. Between the wine, the fire and the dancing, few of the revelers even thought of being cold. Even the children were dancing in happy circles around the adults, sneaking sips of wine and taking treats from the tables.

Though it seemed strange to her, Ysabelle noticed that Alane was most solicitous of her comfort all evening, much to his brother's dismay. He kept bringing her all manner of cured meats, always accompanied by a drink to wash them down with as well. She was surprised at his thoughtfulness, the foods were so salty after all. Constantly refilling her punch cup, Ysabelle's new brother was forever at her side, ready to bring her something else to eat and, of course, a bit of something to wash it down with. Even when she was certain her stomach could hold nothing else, Alane reminded her that the women of the island had helped prepare this great feast and that she wouldn't want to slight any of them.

After a while, and many cups of now undiluted wine, Ysabelle was in no shape for her wedding night. She was completely sotted, and if he'd done his job well, he had assured his brother of a totally miserable – probably messy – wedding night. Certain that he had accomplished his goal, Alane signaled to Adam and Percy to allow Gray to find his wife.

When Gray finally broke away from the men surrounding him with congratulations and advice on how to handle new wives, his gentle wife was reeling from drink. The poor thing was leaning against the sweets table, her eyes having difficulty focusing on anything, and praying she would be able to stay standing long enough to reach her chamber, where she could gratefully throw up. One of the many things she had eaten must not have agreed with her, or she was certain she wouldn't be feeling quite so vile.

Gray had been visually checking on Ysabelle throughout the evening, both to make sure of her well-being and to make sure that Alane was well behaved, if that was possible. He wasn't overly concerned. Although Alane could be difficult, he was loyal to Gray, and therefore basically trustworthy.

It was just that he had such an errant side to him.…

During the evening, many of the inhabitants of Ellshope had come forward to wish Ysabelle well. Gray enjoyed watching the reactions of his people toward her. Without exception, the islanders accepted her and welcomed her to them. She had been hugged, patted, kissed, tightly embraced, squeezed, clasped, welcomed heartily, slapped on the back, and cried over.

The only holdout wasn't an islander at all, but Gray's manservant, Desmond. It was clear to the baron what his servant's obstacle was. Ysabelle's lack of pedigree offended the man, and with great difficulty he kept his opinion, although not his facial expression, to himself. Gray knew him well enough to know how much it bothered him that a baron would marry a commoner, especially when there were so many beautiful women at court who would have happily given him lands and titles, not to mention their virtue. He made a mental note to have a discussion with Desmond later about his inhospitable attitude. Gray would not allow Desmond to color the opinions of his own household in Penrith concerning his new wife.

Steadying herself against the table, Ysabelle blanched as the bailey started spinning around her. She could feel her grip loosening, her body sliding from the side of the table, tilting at a perilous angle toward the ground. Adam, who was out of breath and recovering from his last dance, saw her condition and rushed across the courtyard to get to her side, only he wasn't fast enough. Her husband was the one who came to her rescue, or at least one of him did. When he approached, she had difficulty deciding which one of the three husbands she was seeing was actually Gray. After a moment, she decided to pick the one in the middle.

He came toward her, reaching her just as her legs fell out from under her and picked her up into his arms, promising her in fervent whispers that in a day or two, she would be herself again. She was going to disagree with him – she was just fine, thank you – but passed out instead. Pulling her soft body to his chest, he gently carried her through the courtyard toward the castle and the wide stone staircase leading to his own room. He had ordered her few belongings to be moved to his chamber earlier in the day and now was grateful for having done so. He had no inclination to be disturbed on or have to wait for his wedding night.

His mother had been kind enough to furnish both gowns and underthings for her new daughter, and after seeing the condition of the brown cotton dress and woolen stockings Adam had found her in, he was grateful for that as well. Katharine had given the girl a wardrobe fit for a queen, and a queen was exactly what Ysabelle looked like in the clothes. The green silk gown was his favorite.

To Gray's mind, his Ysabelle was the most beautiful, exasperating, wonderfully exhilarating creature in all of Scotland and England combined. But he really didn't believe it was her looks that had drawn him to her – it was her character. Any woman who was brave enough to challenge not only him, but the dictates of propriety, and risk her own happiness to tell him the truth about herself was a woman worth having. And as their lives together unfolded, he looked forward to unraveling the mystery that was his Ysabelle. She was going to be a frustrating delight to live with and get to know – when she wasn't driving him daft. He pulled her up against him possessively, savoring her closeness.

Ysabelle moaned pitifully, fighting her nausea. She regained consciousness long enough to complain, "Everything is spinning around my head, Gray. Please make it stop." She nuzzled her head into the crook of his neck.

"I will, sweet lass. I will. Although it may take a wee bit o' time. And yer head will hurt a bit in the morning. Is yer middle botherin' ye, Ysabelle? Ye look a trifle green." He pulled her closer to him, not even breathing heavy as he mounted the stairs.

She nodded against him, bumping his chin with her forehead. "I can feel the sweetmeats I ate wanting to come back up. I'm afraid I'll embarrass myself in front of you if I'm not able to keep my wedding feast down." She lifted her head and gazed drunkenly into his eyes. Even through her haze, she could see the gentleness and compassion in her husband's expression. "I know you won't remember this in the morning, since you've had so much to drink with the other men – you know, I saw all of the toasts that were being made to you. And since I'm sure you're sotted from the wine, I'll tell you how I feel about you. But only if you promise to forget what I say to you." Her words slurred together as she fought to keep her eyelids open.

"I promise," he lied.

"Well, to be completely truthful, I think I'll like being married to you. And even though Nana says I'm not any better than a whore myself, you might even like being married to me. I know that I told you I would make you angry – however, I'm sure I'll try to please you as well. I find I want to make you happy, which can only mean that I've completely lost my faculties. You've been so kind to me, and even though I'll never admit it, I think that eventually I'm going to love you."

He tenderly rubbed against her head with his jaw as he carried her. "I think I'm going to love ye, too, Ysabelle."

She sighed deeply and snuggled up closer to him. "I think you might, but not if you can keep your head about you. Thank you for wanting to marry me. Don't tell anyone, but I'm grateful. But tomorrow I'll probably take a dirk to you anyway. I can't let you believe I like you."

"I won't tell. However, I'll be sure to be prepared so that ye don't hurt me." He kissed her fore head.

"Gray?"

"Yes, love?"

"You're a handsome man."

"And ye're a beautiful woman."

She became quiet again, and by the time he reached his own chamber door, he was sure she was asleep. As he placed her on the soft bed, he debated whether or not he should undress his bride. Deciding she would be far more comfortable in her nightdress, Gray unfastened her gown and pulled it over her head. He took in his breath sharply, knowing immediately he should have let her sleep in her gown. He was no blackguard, and would not even consider taking advantage of a drunken woman, although he was going to pay dearly for his restraint. Just as, he decided, his unrepentant brother would. Cursing Alane for his cruel jest, not to mention the headache sweet Ysabelle would have tomorrow, Gray pulled off his wife's shoes and stockings. Even her feet were soft and shapely. Leaving her in her chemise so as not to torture himself any further, Gray leaned down, kissed his wife gently on the lips, and covered her with his blankets.

Gray undressed as well, climbing into bed beside the unconscious Ysabelle. He pushed the tangle of curls off her face and gazed at her. This precious beauty now belonged to him, and he to her. He smiled, he liked the thought of them belonging together. She was going to make his life interesting, and it was high time something did. He had no idea how true that would be. He settled himself under the covers, blew out the candle, and pulled his wife to him. Settling her back to his chest, spoon-fashion, he breathed in the scent of her hair, touched her satiny skin, and sighed deeply. It was going to be a very long night.

FOURTEEN

Randall had not returned. There had been no word of his ship from any port in the six weeks since it had set sail, and no one had seen any one of the sailors who had been with him. Edward, however, was not one to give up on his friend. Every now and then the man would get himself into a tight spot, except he always found a way to get out of whatever scrape he was in, and would eventually come dragging back to the palace – assignment completed, demeanor as sullen as ever.

Edward was most certain he would see his old friend again. Although in any event, he would have seen to his promise to Isabella, and that was enough for him. That mincing fop Alistair wasn't around to muck up court either, and as long as the sailors stayed hidden, Edward would not have to put up with the stench of his cousin's stepson. That favor was becoming interminable nevertheless, so that even if Alistair was to be ransomed from death, he would not be allowed at court again.

"Milord," Phillippa interrupted his thoughts.

"Yes, my sweet?"

"Did you not order the Barons Duncan to court?"

"I did, my sweet."

"Have you had a return message from them? Our sweet niece is determined to have Baron Gray Duncan for her very own. Her mother already has the wedding planned and in readiness." She was a trifle worried, Gray was obviously not a man who would allow himself to be forced into anything, particularly marriage.

Edward could see the worry lines creasing his wife's lovely face, and he reached out his bejeweled hand to pat her arm. "Rest well, my love. I am certain the baron will come. He will be especially curious as to my demand for the presence of his mother." He chuckled. "Of course, one's mother must be present at one's wedding, mustn't she?" He grinned meaningfully at his docile wife, squeezing her hand.

She blushed, "Yes, milord." She paused, "Only are you certain–"

"Now, now, sweet. All will be well. I am prepared to make the good baron an offer no man in his right mind would refuse. Add to that fact that the request is coming from the baron's overlord, and I'm sure he'll be more than happy to comply." He smiled sweetly at his queen. She had pleased him so on the night when he had needed her – the night Isabella had left him forever. She had been good and giving, comforting and pleasing to him. The very thought of their passion made him react to her physically.

"Sweet."

"Milord?"

"I will be visiting your apartments this evening. Be bathed and ready for me."

She bowed her head submissively so her husband wouldn't see her triumphant smile. "Yes, milord. Please be kind enough to excuse me, milord. I wish to make ready to please you this evening."

"Of course, sweet love. My dulcet one. I will be looking forward to our visitation." Edward inclined his head toward her, indicating that she had his permission to leave. She curtsied low and stepped from the dais, swinging her hips provocatively as she left the throne room. Turning to give him one last look over her shoulder, she was pleased to see that his lips were bent in a sensual smile and his eyes were set on her retreating back. She returned his gaze for a moment, leaving him in no question of her desire. Tonight she would rid him permanently of his other entanglements with her love.

Progress on the ship was going slowly. Abyrnathy seemed to be pleased with the pace of the work, although Randall's impatience was driving him daft. He would assist the men when it was a task he was capable of, and pace when it was not. It had taken all of the almost one hundred fifty men on the island to tow the ship to where it would not be pulled out to sea by the tides. Cutting the timber had been extremely time-consuming, but at least then Randall had felt as though they were making progress. But Abyrnathy wouldn't allow the men to build with the green lumber and the waiting had almost killed Randall. He could feel the veins on the side of his neck bulge every time he was again told to 'wait.'

Worse than waiting were the interminable hours with nothing to do. After they had built themselves suitable quarters, at least they were a trifle more comfortable. Sleeping on the beach had been positively beastly. Randall didn't like to think of himself as a man who needed comforts, but this experience was wearing on his person and his self-confidence. He was certain if he didn't leave this horrid place soon, he would be as much a blithering idiot as the men he was forced to associate with every day. Abyrnathy wasn't so bad, of course, at least he possessed an education and a keen wit. It was just that the man refused to speak to him concerning any concept save the weather.

Finally the sailors had begun the rebuilding process. It was maddeningly slow. Without the proper tools the work took days longer than it would in a shipyard. Things that would normally be performed with tools had to be done by hand or with makeshift devices. Randall couldn't help his frustration, he had rarely been confined with other people for more than a week before. And this island was blasted confining. It was made worse by the fact that the heathen sailors rarely bathed, and Randall was a man who liked order, neatness, and cleanliness – none of which he could have in this freezing cold Hades.

"Abyrnathy!" Randall strode up the beach to where two men were planing a piece of lumber.

Abyrnathy looked up from his tool, eyebrows raised, waiting for the man to get to his reason for interrupting him.

"What can I do to speed our progress?" The frustration of standing idle had worn itself thin early this particular day.

The captain grinned. "You can fetch water from the stream for the evening meal. Boyd will see to it for us. Or you can go about snaring some kind of game to put in the water, generally the men like it better with a little something in it."

"I meant with the rebuilding."

"I know what you meant, man. Unless you have uncovered some previously unknown carpentry skills, the answer remains the same."

Frowning fiercely, Randall sighed angrily and went to fetch his bow. Blast! He hated doing menial chores. That was what God made serfs and women for. Entering his shelter and grabbing his bow and quiver, he stalked into the trees in search of game.

The pounding in her head was fierce as Ysabelle slowly groped her way to consciousness late the next morning. This was not her room nor her bed. Confused and desperately wishing she could remember something from last besides Alane's laughing face, she looked around, attempting to gain her bearings. Nothing. She rubbed her eyes. Still nothing looked familiar.

Realization hit her like a fist.

Sweet heavens, I'm married.

Swallowing hard, Ysabelle forced the panic into retreat. This must be Gray's room and ... God save her, she must have slept with her husband last night – and she didn't even remember it! She was going to do a month of penances for this great night of sin. First she had become violently ill, though in all honesty she had no idea how it had happened. Then her mind had completely deserted her and allowed her to make a fool of herself – on her wedding night, of all times. Perhaps it had all been so frightening – she had heard of such thing before – that her mind had decided to overlook the entire night.

Holding her head, Ysabelle, climbed to the floor. She took a deep breath, bit her lip, and whipped the sheets back from the mattress – if Gray had bedded her, there should be blood. Nothing!

What in blazes had happened last night? How had she ended up here? And what if this wasn't Gray's room after all?

God help me! What shall I do?

Who could she ask? Who could she trust? She certainly couldn't question Gray. It would insult him grievously to think she was so feebleminded or he was so inadequate that she had no memory their first night together. But who else would know? She sighed heavily as she realized that she would have to think of some cunning way to question her husband. *Husband – of all things!* She crossed herself. God save the foolish and weak-minded! She was disgusted with herself for having joined their ranks.

Rising far too quickly, she held her head as she sank back to the bed. Her head hurt like she'd spent several days in Hades. The squeak of the door hinges sounded like a trumpet as she looked up to see Gray enter the chamber – an enormous, irritating smile on his handsome face.

"And how is my sweet wife this day? Does it feel any different to be a married woman?"

"Kindly lower your voice, it feels like arrows piercing my head. I don't mean to be rude, husband, but I think I'm going to–" She cut her sentence short as she rushed to the garderobe and threw up the contents of her stomach.

Gray was instantly behind her, holding her head and her waist, keeping her balanced and steady on her feet. When she was finished, he picked her up and tucked her snugly into the bed. After wetting a cloth, he poured a cup of water for his ill wife and took both back to the bed. He wiped her face with the cool cloth and gave her a sip of the water. Sitting down beside her, he gazed down on her sympathetically and smiled gently.

"An auspicious beginning to our marriage, love."

She grimaced at him through her blinding pain, trying to give him a fierce frown.

Seeing her pain, he changed his tack. "Does yer head hurt badly, lass?" he said quietly.

She winced away from the near shout of his voice and closed her eyes. Beginning a nod, she cut it short as soon as she realized how painful any movement of her head was.

"Poor Ysabelle. Have ye ever had anythin' to drink before?"

"Is that what's wrong with me? I thought I had contracted some grave illness," she grinned and was instantly sorry, "or had a severe reaction to being married."

He laughed out loud, which made her wince and grab her head. "I'm sure that couldn't possibly be what ails ye, sweet lass. How could an intelligent woman be anythin' but overjoyed about bein' married to me?" He leaned close enough to whisper in her ear. "I know for sure marryin' ye has already been an adventure."

"I'm not sure what you mean by that, but I'm sure I'd become annoyed with you if you explained." She gave him a stern glare for good measure. This man was the devil, and her head was aching more with every sentence of their inane conversation.

"Aye, lass, there's no doubt about it. Now, answer my question. Have ye ever had anythin' to drink before?"

"Only a sip of wine at a wedding once when Nana Inez wasn't looking. Oh, and the dairyman gave me a skin of ale to keep me warmer while I traveled from my home. But it tasted vile, so I dumped it out and filled the skin with water. Oh!" She placed her hand on her forehead and begged God to take her now. She would repent for all the sins she had ever committed and do any penance if He would only make her head feel better.

Gray stood up, shaking the bed. Ysabelle groaned again. He leaned down and tucked the blankets under her chin, kissed her forehead, then the bridge of her nose, then her lips. "It's not yer fault, sweet. My ever-thoughtful brother Alane thought he would have a bit of fun by getting ye sotted and ruinin' our weddin' night. He'll be gettin' a surprise before long that just might cause him a wee bit o' needed repentance. Sleep til ye feel better, love. Then go down to the kitchens and have Hilde fetch me. I've got to help Mother, Adam, and Alane prepare for our journey to London. We'll be stoppin' at my, I mean our, home in Penrith on the way to court in order to leave yer things and take on supplies. Ye'll get to see the castle I'm buildin'. It's quite a beauty, although it pales in comparison to its mistress."

Ysabelle opened one eye and looked at him oddly. "Do you mean to say that you don't live here?"

He laughed. "No, of course not. I live in England. I'm the Baron of Penrith, one of Edward's favored barons. I have a home there, and am buildin' a castle."

She laughed out loud, then winced at the noise and the pain of her own outburst. "You're one of Edward's favored barons, yet you pirate his ships and maroon his men? How favored do you think you'd be if he but knew?"

"I'd probably be a wee bit taller after he was done stretchin' my neck. Then ye might pass out while kissin' me." He winked playfully at her as she blushed pink at his familiarity. "Whatever made ye think I lived here?"

Ysabelle lifted her shoulders in a feminine shrug. "How in blazes did you begin your life of piracy? And against your own king yet?"

"Ye see, Ysabelle, I am first and foremost a Scot. Edward was never my king. I simply had enough gold and land that he would've done anythin' to get his hands on it. He offered me a barony so that at the very least he could tax my wealth. He wanted my gold, I wanted the information I could get at court, so I accepted his generous offer. It was a tidy arrangement and worked well for me and my purposes. That is, until now."

She gave a loud unladylike sigh. "I hate to ask, for it pains my head so, but why has your arrangement changed as of now?"

He smiled warmly at her and came back to the side of the bed. He sat down beside her again and stroked her face while he answered her. "I'm a married man now, lass. And if I'm favored by God, I'll soon be a father as well. What kind of a rogue would I be if I were willin' to risk the lives, happiness, or welfare of my family for a petty feud? We never allowed married men to go along on our … shall we say … business trips for the same reason." She stared at him, shock on her face. "I myself would never do that to my wife. I've somethin' to lose now. I never did before."

His explanation surprised and warmed her. He cared about her welfare – he really was going to take care of her. When she smiled sweetly up at him, she took him completely off guard. Leaning down impulsively to kiss her, Gray intended to just brush her lips in a thank you, but as soon as he touched her, she went all soft and willing on him. He deepened the kiss, gently ravaging his young wife until she groaned quietly in the back of her throat.

Thinking he had hurt her, he pulled back quickly and looked into her eyes. They were misty with passion. It stunned him that he had that effect on her. Pulling himself together for the time being, Gray leaned down and kissed her briskly on the forehead.

"Come find me when ye're feeling better, love." And he was gone.

She shouldn't have felt abandoned, but she did anyway. Ysabelle stared after her new husband, wishing he would come back and give her more of the same. She had the most wonderful warm feeling resonating through her. It was like sitting in front of a warm fire and drinking hot mulled wine at the same time. And oh, she wanted him to kiss her again.

But sweet heavens, her head hurt. As Ysabelle rolled over, a wave of nausea hit her and sent her back to the garderobe. When she lay back down, she savored the feel of the cool sheets and the warm blankets against her skin. She was almost immediately asleep.

Adam was standing in the loft of the huge stable barn, adding a brace to the last of the eaves that he had seen were lacking support. Even though it was frigid outside, Adam and his brother were stripped to the waist, sweating freely. Alane was holding the brace while Adam pounded it into place with a mallet.

Ever since he had been here, Adam had silently blessed his father's patient teaching in construction concepts. They had become infinitely useful during this trip. Finally getting the brace set firmly in position, Adam picked up his tunic and wiped his face with it.

Following suit, Alane then pulled his tunic back over his head. "Adam, did Gray say anything to ye about last night?"

Adam shook his head. "No. Not to me anyway. Why?" He gave his brother a cockeyed grin. "Are you worried?"

"Well, normally I wouldn't be, but in the past when I've caused my brother a wee bit o' discomfort, Gray has already exacted his revenge on me by now. Havin' to wait for it only means I'm in more trouble than I had supposed. His temper must be kindled to an unbelievable burn this time. By the by, Gray's no fool, he must know we were all in league together, so ye'd best watch yer back as well. He can be evil, that one, when he's riled." Alane punctuated his lecture with a shout as the flooring gave way beneath him.

Adam took a step and then ended up in midair as well. *God help me!* he shouted silently in his mind. It had to be thirty feet to the ground, frozen ground at that. He heard a murky splash seconds before he too was engulfed in foul-smelling water. Holding his breath, he struggled to the top of a large tank filled with what smelled like sewage. As he broke the surface, he heard Alane laughing at the top of his lungs. Clearing his eyes, he turned to see Alane neck deep in the stuff as well, laughing his fool head off.

Adam looked at him for a minute before he started laughing as well. "Revenge?" he asked.

Alane just nodded as he laughed until tears rolled. "I riled him this time, that's for sure. No other reason he'd dump us in the fertilizer."

Adam blanched. "You mean—"

"Aye!" Alane erupted into fresh peals of laughter. "He's sure done for us this time. Ye're bathing in a fragrant concoction of pig dung, compost, and only God knows what else."

Gagging, Adam heaved himself up and over the rim of the tank. Alane followed him, but when Adam bent over and retched, Alane couldn't contain himself any longer. He laughed until he thought his heart would fail him.

"Oh, brother! Ye're a foul one, ye are! We'll have to wash in the lake. There's no way Mother will let us inside her home like this. Yet another well-exacted revenge. I forgot to mention it to ye, Gray is one to be reckoned with when he's riled."

Looking up, it was obvious that the beams had been sawed through. Adam sighed. "I suppose we'll be responsible for repairing his work as well?"

"Aye, yet another revenge. Gray always was excellent at the sport. He always did finish our petty games with great flair."

Adam took a halfhearted swing at Alane, missing him by less than an inch. "You could have told me that before I agreed to go along with your plan. I have a particular aversion to freezing lakes."

"As do I. But I have a much bigger aversion to facin' my mother and acknowledgin' my sin in the condition I'm in. Ye've obviously not crossed her or gained her disfavor since ye've been here."

Adam smiled wickedly. "Except for my alliance with you, that's true."

Alane laughed again. Grabbing Adam's arm, he pulled him out the stable door toward the lake. "Aye, there is that, brother. But ye're a better, more entertainin' soul for knowin' me."

It was only a short distance, thank goodness, for the wind might as well have been made of ice. Of course, it was warm in comparison to the water. Alane had to push him in to get him in the lake. Seconds after he broke the surface, Adam was certain he felt his heart stop. He pulled himself from the frigid water and ran for the stable as fast as he could. The wet clothes that were pasted to his body felt like they were frozen to his skin and still reeked of fertilizer. At least his cloak was yet dry and undefiled. If he was lucky, Angus, the stable master, would let him borrow a tunic and breeches. He heard Alane crashing through the underbrush behind him and poured on all the extra speed he could muster, not wanting the instigator of all this mischief to gain Angus' only spare pair of breeches.

Adam got to the stable mere seconds before Alane, and was therefore the beneficiary of the only spare garments about. After stripping off his wet clothes and dressing himself in Angus' dry ones, he threw on his cloak, grateful for the warmth the fur and heavy wool offered.

"I'll be sure to send Gray out with some garments for you, brother. I'm certain he'll be most gracious, seeing the awkward situation you find yourself in." Alane had stripped his foul garb off as well.

Alane, disgruntled that he had lost the race to the stables and been cheated of the pleasure of torturing Adam further, simply grunted at his brother and wrapped his cloak around his naked body. Angus did his best to keep a straight face, he was one of the young masters after all, but eventually it became too much for him and he let go with his own hoots of laughter. Alane huffed indignantly at the man, and, with a whirl of his cloak, marched out the stable door stark naked and headed for the front door of the castle.

When he slammed the heavy door open, Alane was greeted by a gathering of servants and relatives, including Adam – the traitor – who clapped and cheered loudly at his most undignified appearance. Undaunted, he bowed to them all, marched right past them and up the stairs to his chamber. There was a hot bath waiting for him, no doubt the work of his mother, and fresh attire laid out on the bed. Far be it from Katharine to keep him from his just punishment, but he smiled at the knowledge that she'd always see to his comforts afterward, whatever sound thrashing he had received.

Stepping into the bath, he sighed deeply, satisfied with both his own jest and the sound retaliation he had been able to share with the unsuspecting Adam. *Aye, life is good.*

Belowstairs, Gray had thanked everyone for their participation in his revenge, something they always enjoyed assisting with, and sent the servants back to their duties smiling broadly. Evening the score with Alane, even just a wee bit, always put the household in a fine mood. Bess and Hilde left the entrance hall laughing, as did Desmond and Percy.

"Adam, there's a bath awaiting you in your room, son." Katharine couldn't keep the grin from her face when she told him, "You smell a bit … shall we say – ripe."

"Aye, that ye do, brother. Spending time with Alane can be offensive to the senses – or haven't ye noticed?" Gray was grinning wickedly at him, a satisfied look on his face, his gray eyes sparkling.

Adam grinned in return. "That I did, but I'll have you know, I salute you your vengeance. It was far worse than our cruelty to your poor wife." He turned to Ysabelle. "My apologies, Ysabelle."

She nodded. "Apology accepted, Adam. Now you should probably head up to that bath if you want to be presentable by the evening meal. It may take that long to wash the stench away." She grinned mischievously at him.

"As you wish, milady." Adam bowed low before he headed up the stairs to his own chamber and waiting bath.

As he reached the top step, Gray called his attention from behind. "Adam, did ye find the lake a bit cold for this time of year?" His eyes sparkled with merriment.

Adam grinned good-naturedly. "Aye brother. It was a bit cold for this time of year. It was sweet smelling, though, which made me grateful for the cold water."

"I simply wanted to make sure ye had enjoyed all of the comforts of our home."

"My eternal thanks to you, brother, for giving me an extraordinary view of Ellshope."

Gray inclined his head, wearing a mocking smile. Candlelight glinted off of his white teeth and, combined with his black-red hair, made him look to Ysabelle very much like the panther she had compared him to on the king's ship. Heavens, that seemed like years ago. So much had happened.

Her husband turned his wicked smile upon her, and the instant his eyes locked with hers, she blushed. The look he gave her was altogether possessive. This was the man she had met before – the pirate, the panther – powerful and beautiful and more than a trifle dangerous. She shivered at the thought.

His smile warmed, softened when he caught her shiver. "What are ye thinking, love?"

She grinned diabolically. "I was thinking how very much you looked like a predator, a panther to be precise, when you smile that way, husband. I am certainly pleased that I was not the person on the receiving end of your vengeance. I do pray I never manage to offend you so." Ysabelle broke into laughter. "He did smell vile, did he not?"

Gray's laughter joined with hers. "He did at that, lass. Shall we go refresh ourselves before dinner?"

All the ruddy color her laughter had put into her cheeks promptly drained out again. She swallowed. "Together?"

His grin was mocking her. "That is the usual way of husbands and wives. Don't ye agree, wife?"

She squirmed under the title and breathed in deeply. "I suppose it is. Though I'm not sure – I've never been married before."

Grabbing hold of her arm, he gently steered her toward the stairs. "I have and it is. Trust me, sweet love." He gave her a swat on the backside to get her moving, causing her to jump and run for the stairs. When he gave chase, she couldn't help but put on more speed, laughing and squealing until she reached the top, at which point her drink-ravaged body caused her to slow down and catch her breath. Gray had her then. When he grabbed her waist, she squealed and giggled, slapping at his hands and breaking free. She ran down the hallway to what had been her chamber, dashing through the door laughing breathlessly, attempting to get the bar into place before Gray could catch her. As she slammed the door, he caught it with his foot, forced it open a bit, and slipped inside, an enormous predatory grin on his face.

Ysabelle backed away, not certain if she should be afraid or not, but there

241

was no question as to whether or not to be nervous. Her new husband was approaching her at an alarming rate – a gleam in his eye that scared the devil out of her. *Dear God, give me strength to handle whatever is about to happen!*

Stopping abruptly inches in front of his young wife, amused by her rabbit-in-a-trap expression, Gray pulled her into his arms. Ysabelle tried to push back, but he would not allow her to move away from him. He took hold of her chin and brought her face up to his, planting his lips firmly on hers. It took less than a second for her reservations to melt away, leaving only hunger and desire in their wake. She kissed him back passionately, leaving him shaken. Without a word, Gray scooped Ysabelle up into his arms. She wrapped her arms around his neck and cuddled close to him.

Leaning down so that their foreheads were touching, he whispered, "Ye're in the wrong chamber, wife. I've no intention of allowin' ye to sleep separate from me." With that, he carried her from the room.

On his way through the door, he glanced down at her face. Her look of surprise caught him off guard. He stopped. "Is there somethin' wrong, Ysabelle?"

"Well, uh...." she stammered out, "I thought that only poor couples shared a bed." Her face felt like it was burning, she knew she was blushing, and she hated that this man had that power over her. She was used to considering herself unflappable. Father Corey had always chastised her for her saucy tongue and lack of proper modesty.

The rogue actually laughed out loud. "And where would ye be gettin' that fool notion, lass?"

She stiffened in his hold and pulled her arms away from his neck, crossing them over her chest defensively. "Because poor married couples only have one bed, of course! I thought that when couples had more than one bedroom, that the husband preferred only to visit his wife when ... well, you know." She was as red as fire now, but Gray couldn't help himself. He laughed so hard he almost dropped her.

By the time he carried her through his chamber door, he had pulled himself together enough to answer her preposterous statement. "Ysabelle, it may be that way among the English, but it will never be that way with me. Even when ye are angry with me, I will not leave our bed." He placed her on the bed and leaned over her, a hand on either side of her, his face so close they were breathing the same air. "Do ye understand, wife?" He kept his tone low, but the command was there all the same.

She nodded, still blushing. Sweet heavens, he was a possessive one! His eyes were narrowed on her face, his gaze so intense, it felt as though he could see right through her skin. Ysabelle shifted uncomfortably, trying to think of some way to distract him without reminding him they were on his bed.

Adam was kind enough to distract him for her. After knocking briefly but loudly on the door, he slammed it open without waiting or permission to enter. There he stood, wearing a mischievous grin, and announced, "I thought it would be a good idea to let you know that it's time to go down for the evening meal." He winked at Ysabelle, she sighed with relief. Gray wanted to strangle her for being so happy to see his brother. "Just in case you were too busy to notice," he added, his grin broadening to show his dimple.

Gray shot him a fierce glare. "Evidently, brother, ye didn't spend enough time in the fertilizer tank. We could remedy that one, to be sure."

Adam held up his hands in mock surrender. "No, but thank you for the kind offer." He thought fast. "I just wouldn't want our sweet Ysabelle to miss another meal. If she's going to be traveling with you for the next month, she'll need her strength."

Feeling like a cad for not seeing to her needs, Gray backed down a bit. "Ye're justified in yer intrusion then, Adam. Now go away." He glowered ferociously at his brother. Adam obeyed, instantly disappearing from the doorway. Turning, Gray offered Ysabelle his hand, trying not to notice how relieved she looked at the interruption. Couldn't she at least pretend to be excited about being married to him? He hadn't forced her, had he now? He sighed heavily and stuffed his frustration down again.

Taking her hand and looping her arm through his, he escorted her down to the meal. Tomorrow they would leave before daylight, and he still had not had a proper wedding night. He brooded about it all during the meal, wishing to heaven this blasted evening was over so he could take Ysabelle upstairs and ravish her. All he could think about during all of the endless, pointless talk was how soft her skin would be, how desperately he wanted to make her his. Would the dolts at these tables never cease their senseless prattle? If it would not have incurred his mother's wrath, he would have paced the floor while he waited for the meal to end.

He was looking like a caged beast again, Ysabelle thought, ready to spring. He looked every bit as dangerous right now as any beast of the wild she had ever read about. She wondered what the man was thinking about that put him in such a pensive mood. Could he be worried about tomorrow's travel? Had she displeased him in some way? She began wringing her hands. It was going badly already – the man must have finally realized he was sorry he had wedded her.

Gray noticed her agitated hand movements out of the corner of his eye. Bending to whisper in her ear, he asked, "What's botherin' ye, sweet love?

Ye're making a muck of yer skirts."

She looked down and saw all of the wrinkles she had twisted into the fabric of her gown and immediately quit her nervous motion. "What are you thinking about, husband?"

"Do you always answer a question with a question?"

"Do you?"

He smiled then. She had no idea the effect she had on him, or she wouldn't be taunting him right now with her banter. His eyes softened as he looked at her, and she began to feel somewhat less nervous. He couldn't possibly tell her what he was thinking about, wishing, *dying* to have – even though he desired to do so in great detail. His sweet wife would surely swoon on her stool if he did. He lied instead. "I was hopin' ye would like our home at Penrith."

"Thinking about your home puts you into a dark mood?" Her eyebrows shot up, surprised.

"Nay, lass. Thinkin' about ye not likin' my home puts me into a dark mood." His expression was unreadable, but he kept his eyes hidden beneath his lashes, and Ysabelle didn't think he was being totally forthcoming with her.

"And if I tell you I'll be proud to live wherever you take me, will you be happy then?"

"I will."

"Then I'll be happy wherever you take me."

He smiled at her warmly. "Then I suppose I shall have to take ye with me."

She cast him a glance from under her lashes. "Are you certain you'll be happy to take me with you?"

At last he understood. He slipped his arm around her waist, pulling her and her stool close to him. "I'll be overjoyed," he whispered reassuringly, pushing her curls back from her face in a tender caress.

"Promise?" she whispered, her face turning crimson.

"I give ye my word." He gave her a gentle squeeze just for emphasis. "Of course, ye'll have to promise to give me an endlessly difficult time or I won't be the least bit content with ye." She nodded, breaking into a luminous smile. That was an order she could easily obey.

"See how easy it can be to be submissive, wife?" His smile warmed her, even while his words chafed her, made her want to disobey – by being sweet and docile. Infuriated by her own reaction, Ysabelle thought even now, the scoundrel might be clever enough to trick her into dreaded submission. She kicked him under the table just for being clever. He squeezed her waist, thoroughly enjoying her irritation.

Adam watched their interplay and smiled. He could rest easy. His brother did give Ysabelle his consideration and affection, she would be well taken care of. Adam, still in a jaunty mood, nudged his young friend under the table. She looked at him quizzically, he winked at her and gave her an affectionate smile. Ysabelle beamed in return, nudging him back underneath the table and winking at him. Adam laughed, causing Gray to pivot his head in his brother's direction, raising his eyebrows in silent inquiry. Alane took that opportunity to jump into the hushed fray, hating to be left out of anything.

"Gray, seems ye've been too preoccupied to play a good game of capture the queen with me since we've arrived home with yer young beauty there. I've a right to a rematch, as I was the unhappy loser in the last contest. It's yer duty to assuage my pride. What say ye?"

He shook his head firmly. "Nay brother, I have other things to attend to on this evening."

"What could be more important that givin' yer rogue brother a sound trouncin'? I'll even make it a public humiliation, if that would make it more appealin' to ya."

Gray looked at him squarely, fixing him with his gaze. "Sorry to disappoint ye, my benighted brother, but my sweet wife's company is far more appealin' than yer ugly face. All ye have to do is look at her and know why I'd rather spend my time with her."

Smiling knowingly, Alane sighed heavily. "Aye, she is a beauty. I guess if our places were reversed, I would rather spend my time caressing my lovely wife than pummeling my ugly brother. Tis such a pity though, nay, truly, a great villainy, that such a triflin' matter as marriage could keep ye from yer sworn duty to beat me into submission. I do believe ye're gettin' soft in yer old age. Or could it be, dear brother, that ye fear defeat at my most capable hands?"

"Now, Alane, don't start–" Katharine began.

"Mother," he interrupted cheerfully, "it's a fair question to ask, as I'm such a formidable opponent, ye know." Katharine shook her head and rolled her eyes, vanquished for the moment.

Gray smiled smugly and rose from the table, taking Ysabelle's arm and pulling her to her feet as well. "Nay, brother. I don't, nor would I ever, fear competition with ye. I fear never bein' able to spend time alone with my wife if ye have yer way, and I don't know how I would go about dumpin' ye into the fertilizer tank again on such short notice. So I'll have to be takin' my leave of ye for the night. Perhaps inspiration will strike me before mornin'.

Mother. Gentlemen." He bowed to his mother and strode from the room, dragging Ysabelle in his wake.

Alane gave a dramatic sigh and, loud enough for Gray to hear, called to Adam. "Ah, such cruelty, and from my own flesh and blood yet. Tis a pity, that. Seems as though I'll be forced to divert myself with ye, brother. Though truly, ye're not so entertainin' to harass as me oldest brother. A pity, tis truly a pity that all that talent and exasperation is wasted within a single man."

"Aye, it is, dear brother," Adam agreed woefully, imitating his brother's burr. "Shall we then?"

"Aye. We shall," Alane agreed with a nod. He stood, bowing to his mother. "If ye'll be so kind as to excuse us, Mother, we have an important duty to attend to."

She sighed, unable to contain her laugh. "By all means, gentlemen. And do remember, although I am aware of how sorrowfully short your memories are, you ARE gentlemen." They both bowed, hiding their smiles, and headed for the library.

Katharine stood and addressed the warriors. "Men. Tomorrow we begin what will no doubt be a dangerous journey. Believe me when I say I am grateful for the discomfort you will suffer for the next two months – both because you will be away from your families and because we are venturing forth in the cruelest part of the winter. I thank you for your sacrifice. I will see you in the morning."

A chorus of "Aye, mistress," circled the hall. Katharine, satisfied, bowed her head and left the company to their talk while she went to her chamber to rest for the long journey ahead of them.

Katharine had seen to it that there was a bath waiting for Ysabelle in her former chamber to save her the embarrassment of taking her first bath as a married woman under her husband's alert and watchful gaze. The girl would be shy enough without adding that discomfort to her evening. Ysabelle took her leave of Gray in the hallway, promising to return to their chamber as soon as she was finished with her bath.

Laid out on the bed was a beautifully embroidered white silk nightdress and wrapping robe, with matching slippers. The embroidery was done in the same purple as the wedding flowers, and it encircled the neck and the cuffs of the sleeves of both gown and robe. Ysabelle disrobed and stepped into the hot water, letting its warmth soothe away the rough edges of her fear. She scrubbed herself clean, washing her hair with the lovely, exotically perfumed soap that Katharine had provided. When she was finished with her bath, she spent a time in front of the fire drying her hair and separating her curls into ringlets. She stepped into the gown, wrapped herself in the robe, pinched her cheeks, and headed for her husband's chamber. She would please him if it killed her, and to hear the other young brides talk, it probably would. Endless tales of the pain and muck of the mating ritual had passed among all the young women of the village. Too late to change her mind now, she was a married woman. She took a deep breath, squared her shoulders, and stepped into the hall. It took all the courage she possessed to walk the corridor. Pure bravado allowed her to step into Gray's chamber.

Gray stood bare-chested in front of the hearth, using a poker to move the hottest coals into the proper position. When he was satisfied with his work, he bent and hefted a huge log onto the fire. He shifted the log a trifle, then stood and turned to wait for his wife.

Ysabelle was standing in the doorway, in the most splendid gown and wrapper. She had calmed herself and now felt quite composed. She was certain she didn't look the least bit embarrassed.

Gray smiled as she turned and barred the door. Her blush was obvious even in the dim light. What a glorious creature she was!

Ysabelle came toward him, stopping halfway across the room. She just wanted to look at this man, her *husband*, for a moment before she got so close to him she couldn't breathe. His body was magnificent. She had watched him as he moved the logs, admiring the powerful muscles in his shoulders and back, thinking what a handsome physique he possessed. His arms were strong and hard, his chest and back a wall of corded, solid muscle, his strength obvious to anyone who was looking. Feeling ridiculous, she found herself hoping that no other woman was.

When he turned to lean against the mantle, he was so gloriously handsome. His stormy eyes were gazing at her, almost through her, his dark hair glowing bloodred in the firelight. His body was so strong, even in its relaxed state, that she reveled in her own good fortune. This glorious being was hers. Only God in heaven knew how it had happened.

As he looked upon his sweet wife, Gray could hardly breathe. She was glorious. Her long curls floated around her graceful shoulders, her hips swayed seductively as she walked toward him, her hesitant smile told him she wanted him even though she was afraid. What more could a man want? He moved away from the mantle, standing to his full height, and Ysabelle stopped in her tracks. Her eyes grew large and for just a moment, he saw true fear in her eyes. She quickly lowered her gaze to his chest, not wanting him to see the vulnerability lurking behind her eyes. Gray closed the distance between them with one stride, wrapping his gentle wife in his arms. He simply held her tight to him, waiting for her body to relax against him. When he felt the tension ease out of her muscle by muscle, he pulled back from her enough to tilt her face up to his. The tenderness in his eyes took Ysabelle's breath, and her fear, away. His mouth settled on hers and he began his gentle assault.

Ysabelle first resisted, then yielded, then found herself craving his closeness, demanding more of his gentle, maddening touch. Overwhelmed by her response to him, she was frightened and deluged by the enormity of it all. Yet he had promised to keep her safe, hadn't he? She forced herself to become calm. That was blasted hard when her heart was pounding in her ears and her body was on fire. This man drove her senseless! The only soothing thought she could find was that from the look on his face, he was reeling from her touch as well.

Gray was afraid she just might kill him. If his heart beat any harder, it would leap out of his chest. He could hardly contain himself, he wanted, no, he needed her so badly. It had been so long since he had felt this alive, so long since he had felt loved. No, he wouldn't fool himself into thinking she loved him, but she bore him affection, and that was enough for now. The rest, God willing, would come later. When he kissed her again, her uninhibited response to him made him frenzied to have her. He fought to keep himself calm. He must, for her. He would not be an animal and hurt this precious woman in his arms.

Together they moved to the bed, and for just an instant, Ysabelle had to resist the urge to bolt from the room, but all thoughts were stolen away from her when his mouth settled possessively on hers. All she could think of was Gray – his hands, his mouth, his caresses. When he took her robe and gown off of her, she hardly noticed. He was so gentle, so loving, so full of tenderness. She gave her husband the gift she could give no other, herself. There was pain, but as it ebbed from her, elation and a wonderful feeling of warmth and almost a radiance surrounded and encompassed her. And just as she thought she could feel no closer to anyone, her body flew apart, leaving in its wake contentment, affection, and the one thing Ysabelle had never had in her life – a sense of belonging.

Gray kissed her again, wondering at the moisture in her eyes. She was smiling so beautifully up at him. *Mine. Ysabelle is mine. Thank Ye, God, for second chances. Please don't take this one from me.* He lay down beside her and pulled her back to his chest, holding her close. His arms tightened around her waist as he pulled her to him. He held her, breathing the scent of her hair, feeling the soft of her skin, grateful to be alive to receive this gift.

"Gray, I can't breathe."

He chuckled and loosened his hold. "My apologies, love, I was simply delightin' in bein' close to ye. Ye feel so good against me."

She smiled to herself. "And you against me. Thank you."

"For what, love?"

"For giving me more than I ever dreamed I could have."

He frowned and tried to keep the disapproval out of his voice. He had been the one to promise her all he had, he should not be angry that she thought about that now that they had consummated their marriage. He had lured her with his wealth, and the comforts it could provide her, he had no right to be disturbed. "Yes, I am very wealthy. Ye will never lack."

When she turned to face him, his heart stopped beating. Her eyes were so warm, so full of affection. She reached up and touched his face, caressing his cheek with her fingertips. "Nay, husband, you misunderstand me. I'm not grateful for your wealth. I've never had it before, and it doesn't matter now. I said thank you because I'm grateful for you, for the closeness and affection you just gave me. If I never lived another day, this would be enough."

Relief flooded him – it was him she wanted, not his money. He chastised himself silently for how easily she could move him, vulnerability was not a feeling he enjoyed. But she wanted him.

Thank Ye, God, fer my second chance .

Squeezing her tightly to his chest, he whispered in her ear, "The best is yet to come, love. The best is yet to come."

Ysabelle snuggled closer to him, resting her head on his shoulder and curling her leg around his. Could there be anything better than this? They fell asleep holding each other – content and happy in their new life.

FIFTEEN

"Wake, love. It's time for us to begin our journey home."

Ysabelle's lids fluttered open to see Gray's handsome face. "Home?" She rubbed her eyes.

"My home. Remember, love?"

She yawned loudly. "Oh. Yes. I believe so. We leave now?" She looked around him to the window, only to see utter darkness outside it. "Is it morning?"

"Aye, lass. And we leave as soon as ye're dressed and ready. I tried to give ye as long as I could to sleep. I kept ye up far too late last night." He grinned.

At the mention of last night, Ysabelle's face instantly heated. She dropped her eyes from his intense gaze and instinctively pulled the coverlet up all the way to her neck.

Gray pulled her chin up so that she could not avoid his eyes. "Ye're my wife. Ye'll not be embarrassed in front of me where yer body or our bed is concerned."

He looked so serious. She could hardly keep from laughing. What a ridiculous decree! "I won't?" Her eyebrows shot up.

"Of course not." He nodded as though that was the last of the matter. "Ye're my wife."

She nodded her agreement. "Well, thank you for ridding me of all of my constraints with one simple decree. You are truly amazing, husband." She kissed his cheek.

Gray blushed. He actually *blushed* as he realized how ridiculous his order sounded between them. As if he could order her to cease being flustered in front of him. Better that he ask her not to breathe. The woman was always flustered in front of him, and blast it if he didn't adore that girlish trait of hers. "I apologize. I realize that I must have sounded...."

"Pompous? Arrogant?" she tried to be helpful.

"Yes, thank ye," he said wryly. "I believe arrogant is the proper answer. I appreciate yer assistance, truly I do. Would ye like to insult me further or are ye finally ready to rouse yerself and dress for our journey?"

She blinked, trying to remember what he was talking about. As realization finally came back to her, she was hit by a burst of energy that always accompanied any thought of a journey for Ysabelle. She sat up quickly and started to crawl out of bed. The tenderness hit her by surprise. Each move brought pain. She grimaced, then quickly changed her expression to a strained smile when she saw Gray watching her intently. He frowned.

She smiled brightly at him. "Don't frown so. I'll dress right away. Thank you for waking me. I'll be ready in less than a moment," she promised. Ysabelle hid her discomfort as she slowly climbed out of bed, kissed Gray on the cheek, and stood to her feet. Getting out of bed and walking were agonizing. Ysabelle quickly brushed her hair, then tossed the brush into the top of a carrying bag Gray had produced from the foot of the bed. Folds of material were visible from the opening. It was clear that Gray had packed her gowns for her.

Reaching for the gown that was laid out for her over the back of one of the chairs by the fire, Ysabelle noticed that it was the deep blue heavy woolen gown Katharine had insisted she have, citing the cold of winter as the reason. Ysabelle was grateful now, knowing how cold it would be outside, especially on the water. As she stepped into her gown, stockings and shoes, Gray fastened the buttons down her back and kissed her neck gently. After tying the belt that hung from the tilt of her hips and securing her dirk there, he pronounced her "ready."

He handed her a cupful of hot mulled wine. "This will warm ye. The outside air is bitter this morning."

"Thank you." She took a sip. It tasted good.

Ysabelle drank it gratefully, feeling the warmth of the wine as it poured down her throat and caught fire in her belly. Not having eaten, she immediately felt the gentle effects of the wine. Ysabelle studied her husband thoughtfully. She noticed that Gray was wearing his chain mail and leather – battle gear. Just a hint of a frown passed over her face as she finished off the cup, wondering what danger might await them on their journey. No, she had to be honest with herself, she was worried what danger might await him. The warmth spreading through her belly allowed her this honesty. She cared. Another frown washed over her face as she realized that was the truth. His gentleness had won her over. And she had thought herself so impenetrable. Sighing, she gave up a brief silent plea for Gray's safety to her Maker before banishing the disturbing thoughts for the time being.

Gray looked into her eyes, trying to read her thoughts. Her face kept bending itself into frowns, then quizzical expressions, causing him to think perhaps she was still befuddled by sleep. That, or the daft woman was mad.

"Are ye well, love?"

She nodded, smiling, afraid to speak and allow her voice to betray her unsteady thoughts.

"Then shall we away?"

She smiled sweetly up at him as she looped her arm through his and tossed her head playfully, giving him a sidelong glance. "I suppose we shall. Are we ready then?"

He slowly trailed his index finger down the side of her face as he answered her thoughtfully. "Aye, lass. The warriors are all assembled in the courtyard, almost ready to ride for the ships. We're taking all three to accommodate the men and the horses. We haven't done that since we were feuding with the Kirklands." His expression was wistful as he remembered that victory. His father had led that charge and they had defeated their rivals swiftly and with no loss of life. Ah, the days of his father.... Gray pulled himself back to the present and smiled at Ysabelle warmly. He leaned down to kiss her lips. Such warmth, such softness. How he longed to.... He shook himself, putting on his mantle of discipline only with great difficulty. She had the disconcerting ability to make all of his discipline leave him without so much as a spoken word. All the men were waiting, and there was simply no time for dallying.

Reaching for their cloaks, Gray first put on his own heavy black one, lined with rich mink trim, then he wrapped Ysabelle's deep blue woolen cloak about her shoulders. The mink lining matched her auburn hair so exactly it was difficult to tell where the cloak ended and his young wife began. He pulled her hood up and over her hair, smiling as he touched, for the briefest of moments, the small tendrils curling riotously around her face, then tied the cord securely at her throat. Gray's gaze was full of warmth as he kissed the bridge of her nose, then her chin. She returned his affectionate gaze and smiled. Wrapping his arm around her waist, he led her out into the corridor, down the stairs, and out to the waiting horses.

"I'll not untie you until I know you will not harm me. Again, sir, I ask you to tell me your name." Without moving any closer to him, she waved her dagger in his direction for emphasis.

"I'm Adam Talbot. It's my pleasure. And do you also have a name, miss?" Adam grinned at her.

"Of course I have a name. What a ludicrous question." She stared at him, her gaze narrowed on his face.

"Would you be kind enough to tell me what it is? I prefer to deal with people by name. It's not as if I can do you any harm tied up like this."

"Well," she paused as she considered whether giving him this information could harm her, "I suppose. My name is Ysabelle. Where do you come from? Your accent is strange."

A loud crash in the corridor brought Adam to instant wakefulness. His eyes flew open as he realized the rollicking commotion in the hall was the sound of preparations to leave. They were going to London and no one had bothered to wake him! Panicking, he tried to sit up. He couldn't move. He and his blankets had been tied to his bed. The light filtering in from the corridor allowed him to easily take in his situation. He had been bound with thick rope, starting at his shoulders and crisscrossing down his body, culminating in a large bow tied to the bedpost. Tied to the bow was a note which simply stated,

You'd better hurry. Alane.

As if to punctuate his note, Adam heard Alane's voice in the hall. "Aye, Mother, I've woken him. He'll be along in a moment." There was no doubt that Adam was the him to whom his brother referred. He couldn't help but smile. What a royal pain in the neck. And of course it had been Alane's idea to share a bottle of port during their nightly game of capture the queen. Come to think of it, Alane refilled Adam's glass twice as many times as he did his own. There would be hell to pay, and he looked forward to giving it to Alane, but he'd have to get loose first.

One of his feet was out of the covers, allowing him a slight movement. Adam wiggled his toes in the direction of the loose end of the bow. He tried to grasp it with his toes. It slipped away. He grabbed at it again. It swayed out of his reach. The noise in the hall was receding. Most everyone had left their living quarters. Time was running out.

Blast you, Alane! You are in so much trouble! He tried again to grab the free end of the bow, this time catching it in the valley between his big toe and second toe. He pulled gently – nothing happened. He improved his grip as best he could and pulled harder. The rope moved just a bit. He tugged as hard as he could and the knot pulled free. The ropes around his ankles eased enough for him to work them loose, and slowly but surely he extracted himself from his bonds.

He leapt from the bed and dove for his clothes. Tugging on his pants, he grabbed his shirt and cloak and headed for the door. At the last minute, he remembered he needed the rest of his clothes and his pack, but when he threw open the wardrobe, it was empty. As he flew out the door, he hoped

Alane had stolen his remaining clothes and taken them with him to return after humiliating his half-brother, or Adam was going to smell pretty rank by the end of this journey.

The castle was silent except for the sound of clanging pots and pans coming from the direction of the kitchens. Adam's breath sounded loud in his own ears as he rushed down the stairs, throwing his shirt over his head as he ran. Not stopping to tuck in his shirt or put on his cloak, he dashed out the door and down the stone stairs only to discover his horse, pack tied to the saddle, tied to a post just to the side of the steps. He was up and into the saddle in less than a second, and he spurred his horse into a gallop, enormous grin on his face.

Alane had better watch his back.

The courtyard was lit brightly with torches positioned every ten feet or so along the wall. It was wall to wall horses and armed men – huge men, loaded with all sorts of strange and terrifying weaponry, fierce-looking and readied for battle. There were so many warriors they filled both the upper and lower baileys and spilled out into the grassy meadow beyond. They looked savage and overpowering. Ysabelle could not even imagine any army, even Edward's formidable soldiers, defeating this staggering force.

Gray handed Ysabelle the fur muff he had carried out for her hands, made sure it was in place and that she was warm enough, then effortlessly lifted her into her saddle.

A frown suddenly creased his forehead, erasing the contentment there. "Do ye ride, wife?" It had just occurred to him that she might not be an accomplished enough rider to handle the journey ahead of them.

"It's a bit late to ask, don't you think?" Just the hint of a grin hovered around her lips, waiting impatiently for her composure to break and give it opportunity to emerge.

"Aye. And I'm hopin' ye ride, lass, or this journey will be most difficult for ye. Or perchance for me, as I would be forced to carry ye most of the way." He placed his hand over hers on the pommel of her saddle, "Don't tease me now, sweet wife, or I'll be forced to take ye upstairs to discuss it privately." He wiggled his eyebrows at her, grinning wickedly.

She laughed at his play threat, then shuddered in mock fear. "We can't have that now, can we? Rest easy, husband. I ride."

He nodded, sighing in exaggerated disappointment, and squeezed her hands tightly. He then turned and mounted his stallion in one fluid motion. He raised his hand in signal to Garen. The captain, ever watchful, nodded.

His young wife leaned toward him and whispered, "Are we going to war,

Gray?" Ysabelle's brow knit with worry.

"Not as yet, love. Only a precaution against danger that might await my family."

Her eyebrows raised. "All this–" she waved her hand to encompass all of the warriors spread across her filed of vision, "only a precaution?"

"Aye."

"I see. I can only say that I'm pleased that you're not certain there will be danger for your family. I would hate to see the entire Norman and Scottish armies together rallied behind our small party heading for home. We would be most difficult for Edward's forces to overlook." She crossed her arms over her chest and gave him a mischievous grin.

"Aye. That we would. That has been a bigger thorn in Edward's side than even the Gentleman Pirate. Our forces rival his own. Twould make it difficult for him to turn on me. I command the largest force of the best-trained fighting men in all of England."

"You forget yourself, husband. We are not in England."

"Nay, we're not, wife. And in Scotland, a wife who challenges her husband is forced to ride upside down with her heels in the stirrups instead of her toes." She didn't know whether or not to believe him until a rich grin spread across his face as he winked at her. Then he turned towards the head of the enormous party and shouted toward Katharine. "Madame! All are present and accounted for. Proceed when ready!"

A small figure dressed in breeches and a man's heavy cloak at the very far end of the lower bailey nodded its head and raised a closed fist in answer. From where they were, Ysabelle could see the long, gray-streaked hair of Katharine above the man's clothing she wore as she shouted, "Advance!"

The word echoed through the upper and lower bailey as countless soldiers began their trek across the wooden drawbridge and through the endless meadow that surrounded the dwellings on Ellshope. The sound of horses' hooves echoed throughout the valley where the people of Ellshope lived and waited as the formidable warriors, Ellshope's husbands and sons, left for England in the dead of night – the dead of what would soon be the most bitter part of winter.

Wives and mothers watched solemnly from their cottage windows and prayed that their men would be victorious – that they would return to their families after this mess was over. Despite their warriors' legendary ability to vanquish enemies, every wife and mother silently begged her Maker to return her precious loved one to her quickly and on his own two stubborn, masculine feet. The same prayers floated upward every time the men left for battle.

Ysabelle watched as the amazing procession bottlenecked through the gate to join the others in the meadow, the echo of the horses' hooves resounding across the wooden drawbridge was as loud as ocean waves crashing in a storm. Torchlight gleamed brilliantly off the sea of polished armor. The movement of the mass of helmeted heads launching in unison even looked like a silver blue wave advancing toward the shore. They washed out to join their companions in the grassy meadow beyond the castle. Already, at the farthest point of the island, could be seen torches and warriors on horseback. As far as the eye could see were men on horseback lit by torches. It was an awesome sight.

As the party in which Ysabelle and Gray were traveling began their trip through the gate to the outside, they heard the hoofbeats of an oncoming rider moving swiftly past them. Ysabelle turned in the direction of the rider just in time to see Adam, hair flying, eyes wide, an enormous smile plastered on his face, fly past them to the front of the procession. He was half-dressed, busily tucking in his blouse with one hand while he held his reins with the other. Ysabelle couldn't keep the smile from her lips as she watched him pass by them hurriedly, though she was careful not to let him see her expression.

"What are ye smiling about?" Gray tilted his head and studied her closely.

She instantly made her face impassive. "Nothing you would be interested in, husband. Just a bit of something your brother had need of my assistance with. You'll be happy to know I was infinitely helpful and secured his undying devotion for the duration of my life."

Gray sighed deeply as his eyes searched her expression. "What malicious plot did ye assist that infantile rogue in?"

"Malicious plot? Your beloved wife?" Ysabelle did her best to feign innocence. "Milord, I have no knowledge of any plot. I simply assisted your brother with a problem he was having difficulty with. One that I was uniquely qualified to handle."

"And when, exactly, did ye have the time to be of assistance to him, my – what did ye call yerself? – beloved wife? I was of the opinion that ye had been constantly in my most stimulating company for the last several days." He arched an eyebrow in anticipation of her answer, waiting for the half-truth that was sure to come.

She smiled coyly at him. "Well, husband, after you fell into such a deep slumber last night," she grinned, "your beloved wife was awakened by a knocking at our chamber door. You were snoring loudly–"

"I do not snore."

She shrugged her shoulders delicately and continued, "You were snoring loudly, so I slipped out of your grasp and answered at the door. In truth, I was more than a trifle surprised that such a fearsome warrior as yourself did not wake at the intrusion, but I consoled myself with the certainty that a band of robbers would have waked you eventually while they were pillaging, but it was of no consequence at the time, as I was in no danger. At the door was Alane, in need of assistance."

"In no danger indeed! It's painfully obvious that ye are not well acquainted with my brother." A thought occurred to him. "Ye did not go with him in yer nightclothes!" Gray's pinched face was taking on a red tint as he forced himself to rein in his fiery jealousy. His chest tightened painfully at the thought of his rogue brother viewing his wife in her nightdress.

She laughed at the wild emotion he was attempting to conceal. "Nay, husband. I put on my day gown, then went to attend his need. I was back within your loving arms within half the marking of an hour. I am sorry to say that I was not even missed." She pursed her lips in a pout and lifted her chin defiantly, waiting for the inquisition.

Gray studied her for a moment, his lips quirked in half amusement, half irritation – she did love to bait him – then turned his attention to his stallion in order to calm himself. He petted the horse's flank as he answered, more to the horse than to his wife, "I'm certain ye were a fascinatin' accomplice. I envy my brother his company when I was still abed with none."

"Don't be cross with me, Gray. I had a much better time with you and, I assure you, was eager to return to your side and your bed." She reached out and stroked the side of his face with her fingertips, effectively sidetracking his thoughts and dispelling his irritation.

He curtly nodded his assent, again annoyed that with one small touch she could affect him so profoundly. He shifted his eyes forward to record Adam's progress.

The younger man reined in at the front of the queue beside Alane, who trailed directly behind Katharine and just in front of Garen. Alane clapped him on the back and said something inaudible to everyone else, but that made Adam laugh uproariously. Even at this distance, the company could see that his head was thrown back in mirth.

Alane grasped both of Adam's hands and shook them warmly. "So ye made it out of the bonds, did ye, brother?" He slapped Adam's back hard enough to throw him forward on his saddle.

Adam could hardly contain his laughter as he nodded. "I did, but I must admit that it was difficult. I almost missed our departure. How you ever tied me to the bed without waking me is beyond my imagination."

Alane grinned mischievously. "I enlisted the aide of one skilled in such doings."

Adam cocked his head to the side as a slow smile spread across his face. "Ysabelle?"

He nodded. "She was more than happy to be of assistance to me. I was certain her laughter would wake ye from the hallway when she had finished. I had to clap my hand over her mouth to silence her, and even then she almost shook my teeth out of my head with her convulsing."

Adam grinned. "I can see why she ignored me as I rode by, though to tell the truth, I was a bit too engrossed with reaching you to pay much attention to her."

He nodded, grinning. "Aye. Though I have no doubt she enjoyed the spectacle of ye ridin' by breathless and half-dressed. She has a bent sense of humor, ye know."

"I know. I spent enough time with her to be the brunt of it more than once. Poor Gray will have his hands full once she warms up to him."

"By the looks of things, I would have to say the girl looked fairly warm when I woke her last night." He chuckled. "Though if I were in possession of such a prize, I would be certain not to sleep so soundly. Ye never know when someone might come steal yer prize away."

Adam turned to study Alane, "You would never...."

"Nay, I wouldn't. But I'd be lyin' if I said I hadn't thought about it."

"You are a true rogue. No wonder Gray is vexed with you most of the time."

Alane's lips twisted in a mischievous grin. "So sad. He's not really vexed with me, ye know. It's just that he was so bored he needed me to provide a diversion to entertain him. He's not happy unless he has someone to boss around that won't listen. Now, I'm quite grieved to say, I've been replaced. Although it's a relief to know that she will vex him far more than I ever could, as wives will, and when she bears him children ... I daresay he will be the happiest man on the earth – for no one will listen to him then. Ye'd best put yer cloak on, Adam, or ye'll be chilled through by the time we reach the ship." Alane spurred his horse into a gallop as he sprinted to catch up with Katharine. Adam dug his heels into his horse's sides in an effort to keep apace.

Katharine turned as they reached her. "Well, Adam. It was nice of you to join us." She grinned knowingly.

Adam inclined his head. "It's entirely my pleasure, Mother. You should be thankful that I was able to join you at all. I was ... a little ... well, tied up."

She nodded, hiding her grin. No doubt Alane was behind this. "I never had a doubt. If you weren't resourceful, you would never have found your way here to begin with. Tuck in the back of your shirt, son. It looks as though you're wearing a gown instead of breeches."

"That's next week, if he continues to sleep so soundly," Alane interjected with a laugh.

When they approached the place where the trail narrowed and they had to go single file down the rocky path to the ship, a line formed as the warriors slowly made their way down the treacherous terrain. As each torch bearer in their turn reined in aboard the ship, his torch was extinguished, his horse goaded down the ramp to the hold, and his gear stowed. A good many warriors had disappeared down the hidden trail before it was Katharine's, Alane's, and Adam's turn. Adam silently prayed that his horse was familiar enough with the trail so that he wouldn't have to swim in the frigid water below. He had enjoyed more than his fill of icy water after the fertilizer incident. His prayer was rewarded, however, when his horse led him safely up the gangplank and onto the deck of the first waiting ship. The other two sat waiting their turn, yard out from the first. Adam heaved a sigh of relief when he was finally on his own two feet once again with his gear stowed in a trunk below.

As the ship slowly filled and finally pulled in the gangplank, he searched the passengers for Ysabelle and Gray, but didn't see them.

He found his brother. "Alane, have you seen Gray or Ysabelle?"

"Nay, brother. They will most certainly be aboard the next ship. Gray's commander of the second unit. If mother were ever to step down, he would assume command, but for now, he simply commands the second unit of the warriors when we go into battle. He rather annoys me, or at least, his lack of ambition annoys me. Instead of bein' in command, he waits for my mother's direction and does what he's told, even though he's an astonishin' leader in his own right. His own troops will attest to that. If I were a jealous man, I would wish for his abilities. But I much prefer to be a riotous pain in the arse for 'im. It suits me own abilities in a far better capacity. And, of course, it entertains everyone else involved."

"You really enjoy being a problem for him?"

He nodded, grinning from ear to ear. "In the past, it's what I've always lived for. That and botherin' good old king Edward. Different motivations, of course. I infuriate my dear brother out of adoration and jealousy. I infuriate Edward out of disgust – pure and simple. The French court loves me. They're always up for a good intrigue and any plot against their enemy, and who better than me to give it to them? However, I've grown bored with these somewhat divertin' entertainments. I've decided upon a new devise. I believe, dear brother, that ye shall be my next project. I surmise that ye should be allowed to learn the value of havin' a brother." Alane cocked an eyebrow. "What think ye of that?"

Before he answered the blatant challenge, he licked his lips and gave his brother the full weight of his most competitive stare. "I'd wager you have your work cut out for you, brother. But by all means, feel free to give it a go, Alane." Adam put his hands upon his hips and gave his friend a what-do-you-think-about-that look.

Alane rose to the challenge. "I believe I shall. Ye may be in desperate need of a diversion. Aye," he nodded, "I believe ye are. And as yer brother, tis my duty to see that yer needs are met. Since my lands essentially take care of themselves, and with Edward's own flesh wantin' to wed me and my big brother Gray, my place at court is fairly secure. I can see no other course open to me but to teach ye the value of havin' flesh and blood to lend their wisdom and experience to yer new life's choices. Is there anything ye require as of this moment, Adam?"

He chuckled. "No. But if I think of anything, I'll be sure to inform you first."

"Ah, I'm forever in yer debt." Alane bowed low, almost kissing his horse's neck.

Adam mirrored his brother's low bow. "As am I. Shall we proceed?"

"Aye."

The clank of the anchor winch being cranked by four mighty-looking men caused both brothers to turn their heads toward the stern. Alane grinned. "Ah. A captive audience. Poor brother. Tis a pity ye could not have been born to another mother. Yer life might have been less fraught with hardship."

"If I have need of assistance concerning you or your 'hardships', I have only to turn to my other newfound brother and his very capable wife. I am certain the three of us could handle you quite admirably."

Alane grimaced and gave a mock shudder. "I would prefer that ye refrain. There are no tubs available here for us to bathe in – though I suppose we could jump in the icy sea…."

Adam laughed. "How about we simply suspend all roguish behavior on this leg of the journey?"

The other man sighed woefully, then agreed. "Aye. Tis the only logical solution. Pity. I'll have to tend to my duties aboard to take my mind off this sad state of affairs. Helm," he raised his voice to a shout, "plot a course for England. I'll fetch my sextant in a moment to help check yer course." Alane turned on his heel and disappeared into the companionway just to their left.

Adam stood staring stupidly, just looking around the deck. In a moment, he caught sight of Garen hanging in the rigging, in turn looking through his glass at the murky darkness, then turning it toward the other two ships to watch the remainder of the men boarding.

"May I come up?" Adam shouted. Garen nodded his assent, and Adam began nimbly climbing the intricately knotted ropes. As he reached the commander, he was rewarded with a broad smile and a compliment.

"If I didn't know better, I would think ye'd been climbin' riggin's from when ye were a wee one. Ye did a fine job."

"I can tie a decent knot, as well, and know a fair amount about sailing," Adam boasted.

"Then make yerself useful and repair that bit of disarray up there." He pointed to a fraying bit of rope at almost the top of the central mast. It wasn't a problem for the ship, but Garen was curious to see what kind of a job the boy would do. Adam nodded and began climbing. He always preferred activity to inactivity. He deftly repaired the unraveled sections of rope, then climbed back down to his shipmate.

"A fair job, I daresay. It seems ye're good for more than just constructin' barn roofs, boy. With a wee bit o' trainin', ye might be a decent mate." It was the best compliment he could muster. Adam was appropriately pleased. "Whatever I can do."

"Aye." Garen handed him the glass. "Keep yer eye to this. Make sure the other two ships get properly loaded and there are no lights out to sea. It's hard enough to keep this place a secret. If ye see anythin', give us a shout. I'll be up before ye can blink." And he was gone.

Adam dutifully watched the open sea and the progress of the ships in turn. After the second ship had been fully loaded, including the huge figure of Gray and the comparatively tiny figure of Ysabelle, at Gray's command it hoisted anchor and pulled away from the natural dock, allowing the final ship to anchor and begin boarding. Percy assumed command of the final ship, Lance at his side as first mate to lend his experience, seeing to the stowing of gear and horses and making sure all the warriors under his command were present and accounted for. When all were aboard and all their gear loaded, Percy signaled for his own ship to hoist anchor and follow in the wake of the first two ships. Soon all three had hoisted sail and were underway.

Father Corey shouldered his heavy pack with a low grunt, said good-bye to his meager surroundings, and left out the door of the small rectory. The new priest was firmly installed, all of Ethan's bones had healed well, and he was ready for his journey to London. Through his many contacts at the palace and the monastery, he had learned of Ysabelle's capture by the Gentleman Pirate, and of Randall's being lost at sea. That information gave him the needed time to heal and prepare to see his queen. He didn't relish giving her his information. She had such a tender heart, she would no doubt cry, and he hated to see a woman cry.

He located the direction of the old North Road, said a short prayer for safety in his travels, and set out.

At last the blasted ship was fully repaired. To Randall it had seemed like an eternity. In order to set sail as soon as possible, only Abyrnathy and his own crew, as well as the first officers of the three abandoned crews, boarded the newly christened *Survivor* and hoisted anchor. The three captains voluntarily remained behind in order to manage their men and keep the island orderly until help eventually arrived. Anxious to reach home, although no more anxious than all of the other men, Abyrnathy's crew rejoiced that they were finally setting sail for their own shore. Randall was relieved to be chosen, knowing that Abyrnathy was less than hospitable to his presence. With great haste, he gathered his belongings and boarded the dinghy that would take him aboard the ship. He couldn't keep the smile from his lips as his feet touched the newly hewn deck – solid as a rock.

"Plot a course for Dunwich, Phillippe," Abyrnathy called to the helmsman.

"Aye, sir," was the instant reply. Phillippe, usually morose, was actually almost sprightly in his demeanor, thrilled to be finally heading for home. It seemed like a decade since he had seen Marguerite and their bairn, Elspeth. The babe would no doubt have doubled in size in the months he had been gone.

"Take in the starboard and make it fast!"

"Aye, sir!"

"Keep lively, men! We're heading for home!" A rousing cheer went up from the crew as they all tended to their stations and pulled out from the small cove protected from the weather by the head of the island.

Randall stood by the railing, facing the bow, yearning for a small glimpse of home. It wouldn't be much longer, and he could almost feel the soft, feather mattress of his own enormous mahogany bed. Impatiently he began the pacing that would take him miles around the small deck of the ship. He had learned so much, especially from that priggish weasel Alistair. If he were to be believed, one of the king's favored and trusted barons was the Gentleman Pirate. The prissy, self-righteous cod swore that they had been compatriots in the favor of the king, making sure there was plenty of gold and arms aboard the ships. Randall was more than eager to point his finger at Alistair as well. He well knew the king's distaste for the man and was more than willing to assist Edward in ridding himself of the bothersome leach. But in order to take care of this situation as quickly and cleanly as possible, he had been forced to allow the man to accompany him home.

The tale of the turncoat baron would be an entertaining story to relate to his majesty. Making him believe it, now, that was a different proposition altogether. After all, the king's own niece had her eye on the traitorous baron. And Edward had grown so soft as of late. God help them all if the tears of a sniveling niece could make the crown ignore a traitor. Of course, there were other ways to rid the crown of him.–

Randall smiled as he anticipated the look on his liege lord's face when he broke the solemn news to him. It had been a profitable trip after all. Yes, he thought as he mentally licked his lips in anticipation of the kill, it had been quite profitable after all

The three ships landed under cover of night. The warriors, picking their way carefully in the dark, disembarked from the vessels – each unit going in its own direction in accordance with the strategy Lance had designed. Katharine, Gray, Ysabelle, Alane, and Adam, along with a small contingent of soldiers, made camp less than a mile from the mooring. Gray and Katharine shared a feeling of unease about their audience with Edward, and none of the small party slept at all well.

Morning broke cold and clear, the sun dazzling and the air so crisp you could cut it with a knife. By the time the bright light roused Ysabelle from her sound sleep, Gray, Adam, and Alane had all of the horses saddled and all of their gear stowed for travel.

Gray approached Ysabelle's sleepy form. "Wake, my wee precious sleepy one. Penrith is two days' hard ride from here, and we must away."

She sat up and rubbed her eyes. "Penrith?"

"The village my castle will overlook when it's finally completed. Here's some bread and cheese. Eat it, love. Twill be a long ride before we break for food again." He held out a small piece of cloth, containing bread and cheese, to his wife. Then he turned to help finish breaking camp.

Ysabelle ate heartily. Adam finished tying his blankets on the back of his saddle, then wandered over to talk to her.

"It seems we haven't had much time to talk to each other lately. I have to admit I've missed you." His boyish grin cheered her as he wrapped his arm around her companionably. Gray noticed the affectionate gesture and his wife's response. He had to brace himself against the instantaneous wave of jealousy that tore through him. They were friends, that was all. So why did he want to break his brother's arm just for touching her?

Ysabelle leaned against Adam's arm, put her head on his shoulder, and sighed. "You speak the truth. I've missed you as well. Did you receive what you expected in the reception your mother gave you?" She looked at him from beneath slanted lashes, not wanting to scrutinize him too carefully. She had not been there for him. She had been too busy with her own selfish concerns to trouble herself with her dear friend's heart being laid bare before what could have been the biggest rejection of his life. Her cheeks heated as the shame washed over her.

"All that I desired and more. I never expected to be relieved of my status of only child. Even though I knew it was a probability, the knowledge never really made itself a part of me."

"Yes, all that is true. But did your mother ... receive you ... kindly?" It was hard to get the words out of her mouth, when they were so intimately tied to the secret desires of her own soul.

Hearing the uncertainty in her voice, he tried to comfort her with the truth. He squeezed her shoulders. "She did, Ysabelle. I should never have doubted. She wanted me, loved me all the time that I was missing from her life. Needed me. Felt a hole in her heart where I was missing." He could not contain his smile. Only God would have put together such a perfect homecoming for him – except for his brother Alane's antics anyway. Yet even those warmed him. He was important enough to play practical jokes on. Alane had made it clear he had affection for his newfound kin. What more could a brother want?

Her words came out haltingly. "Do you think it's that way ... often with lost children and their ... mothers?" It was so hard to ask, so hard to be so vulnerable to him, but of all people he would understand. He was a lost child in his own right. Not Gray – with his adoring mother and intrigue casting brother and loyal men who would lay down their lives for him.

"We both know that sometimes it doesn't work that way." He reached down with his hand and tilted her face up so she would look him in the eye. "But I truly believe, without a doubt, that most of the time mothers love their babies passionately and that only desperate circumstances separate the two."

She felt the tears threatening. "Do you truly believe that? Do not deceive me, I prefer the uncomfortable truth to a honey-soaked lie."

He nodded. "Aye, lassie, I do."

Only with the greatest control could Gray keep from interrupting the intimate conversation. The tears in her eyes unnerved him totally, and he prayed she was not confiding some unforgivable sin that he had unknowingly committed, or how unhappy she was. But he cared enough to allow her this moment. It was the best he could do for her.

Ysabelle shook her head and wiped the moisture out of her eyes with her fingertips. She had made peace with it, at least for now. "Then we'd best get to our horses. Gray says we've a long, hard ride to get to his estate."

Adam simply smiled and nodded. With a final squeeze of her shoulders, he rose to his feet and sauntered off in the direction of his mount.

She stood to her feet, shook out her skirts, and tightened the cord at her throat that held her cloak on her shoulders. Hastily she folded the blankets she had shared with Gray, mentally thanking him for not interrupting her while she talked with Adam. She had seen the look on his face, he had looked almost was though he was being tortured. Carrying their blankets under her arm, she approached her husband and placed her hand on his arm. Gray looked down into her eyes, searching for some clue as to how she was feeling. She was decided on something, it was obvious from the set of her jaw and the settled look in her eyes.

"Shall we go now, Gray?"

He couldn't help but smile at the way his name sounded on her lips. "Aye, we shall." He lifted her onto her mare and mounted his stallion in one fluid motion just as Katharine called out that they were leaving. Ysabelle kept her mount close to Gray's, so close they were almost touching. The pace was grueling, but she never flagged. It would be a long journey, she knew, but she was in the company of the only family she had ever known, and Ysabelle felt a contentment like none she had ever known before.

Penrith was almost as beautiful as Ellshope. Of course, Gray was quick to explain, his own holdings, which he affectionately called by the name Thistlebloom, were vast. The castle itself was under construction and had been since the early spring of last year. If all went well, it would be completed by fall. From a distance, it looked as though the structure was already completed. It wasn't until they were much closer that Ysabelle could see the men working on the wall.

"Why – it looks like Ellshope! You've made it a replica of your home. Tis beautiful to look upon."

He nodded. "Aye, lass. I have done. Ellshope will always be my first home, and I could never be satisfied anywhere else. Besides, I could never stomach the English way of building a fortress of wood. There is no defense of such a place. Wood burns too readily."

"I can agree with you there. Stone is ever so much more stalwart. But Thistlebloom? Gray, it's such an odd name. Whatever does it mean?" Ysabelle stared at the construction of the immense palatial castle before her, unable to take her eyes off of it. This magnificent place was to be her home.

He chuckled in response. "I suppose it is a bit odd. But have ye ever noticed that some of the most beautiful things in nature come with their price firmly attached?"

First she nodded her head yes, then she looked at him oddly and shook her head no. Confusion played across her knitted brow.

Gray laughed again. "Take the rose, for instance. It's one of nature's masterpieces, yet each rose's fragility is protected by sharp thorns." He reached out and caressed the side of her cheek with his knuckles. "Like ye lass, ye're fragile, yet a man could impale himself a thousand times over tryin' to forge his way through the thorns ye've erected around ye to protect yerself. I'm overly grateful to have any blood left in my skin after the scathing battle ye put me through."

She huffed in indignation as he continued thoughtfully, "Have ye ever seen a thistle, Ysabelle? Surely, ye must have."

She nodded.

"Their flowers are such a beautiful, vivid purple color – quite regal really – but a thistle can give a man a nasty pain and sometimes even cause him to be ill."

She looked at him, incredulous. "And you named your estate after a flower that can hurt a man or make him sick? You are a daft man indeed."

He raised his eyebrows at her, then his face softened into a warm smile. "There are many who would agree with ye – though none brave enough to say so to my face. Even so, even with all its faults, I find the thistle's bloom the most beautiful of all flowers. I myself have found that nothin' worthwhile comes without a price. But if a man is willin' to pay that price, he is forever pleased he did."

Ysabelle couldn't explain exactly why, but she was beginning to feel extremely warm and contented. Without thinking, she took Gray's hand. He smiled to himself. He loved it when she touched him, and each day she seemed to reach out to him more and more often. Under the watchful eye of Kennady, his second in command, the erection of his home was coming along quickly and efficiently. He had a new wife to install in it when it was completed, and she was beautiful both inside and outside. Even better, she appeared to have at least the beginnings of affection for him. Aye, this would be a good year.

She bit down on her lip self-consciously. "Will Mr. Desmond be here already?"

He studied her face intently. "Nay, lassie. He'll be set out to open my small home there for the coming spring. It's a bit early for it, aye, but I thought you might adjust a wee bit easier if he was out of the way while you settled in. Do ye mind?"

She smiled at him. "No. Thank you. I ... um ... appreciate your thoughtfulness."

He nodded. Gray, anxious to see the progress that had been made in his absence, dropped Ysabelle's hand and spurred his horse into a gallop and called to Ysabelle over his shoulder. "We'll be able to sleep in a few of the chambers, although we'll have to sleep on our blankets – as the castle has not been furnished yet."

Not wanting to be alone just yet, she spurred her mare after him. When she caught up with him, he was evidently conferring with the man he had left in charge in his absence. A large man, every bit as tall as Gray, but without the thick muscular build, he had a long, white scar that ran from the corner of his right eye and the length of his high cheekbone to his ear. Obviously a wound that should have taken his sight, Ysabelle considered how lucky he was to have his life as well as his sight. Gray called him Kennady.

They conferred for a short moment more before Gray turned to Ysabelle and offered her a tour of his estate. She readily agreed. He showed her forests and a beautiful lake fed by a cool, fast-running brook. The winter sun shining brightly off the lake almost made her feel warm despite the chill of the air. This was a lovely place. They rode through the valley where field upon field was being grazed by cattle or lying fallow, waiting for the spring planting.

Despite the biting cold air, many of Gray's vassals were out of doors. Some were removing stones from the fallow fields and building a low wall around a large area of pastureland. Two women were washing clothing in a shallow, slow-moving bend in the lovely clear brook that intersected the far-reaching pasturelands. The water had to be icy, Ysabelle thought, grateful that it wasn't her hands that kept dipping into the frigid water. The pasture grasses were a light brown in color from their winter sleep, but this would be a sight to behold come spring. She could already see the rioting colors of the wild flowers as they fought for place with the bright green grasses. Sighing at the thought, she turned her head in the other direction.

Five youngish boys, no more than ten harvests, were playing a game of skill involving throwing rocks at broken bits of crude pottery sitting atop the finished portion of the low fence being built by their elders. With just a dusting of snow in small patches here and there, they couldn't make enough ammunition for a snow fight. When a stray rock hit one of the older men, he took to his heels, shouting and waving his arms he ran the diddling boys off. The imps romped just out of the man's handhold, laughing and shrieking until they reached the safety of their mother's protection. She watched them, remembering the children from her own small village and how they loved to devil the men when they could wriggle out of their work. It was never their intent, that, but trouble came about anyway. She wondered what chores awaited the errant boys when they reached their homes and smiled.

Oddly enough to Ysabelle's mind, whenever the baron was spotted by any of his vassals, they waved and smiled and called out hearty greetings to him as though they were glad to see him. In the village where she had grown up, all but the hardiest ran for cover when the baron was about surveying his lands.

"It seems your vassals and serfs have affection for you," Ysabelle observed.

"Aye, they do. Though I'm not certain as to why. I do try to be fair with my vassals. I use my soldiers instead of the peasants to build the fortress. It helps in strengthenin' their bodies, after all. That way, my men build their endurance and fortitude while the men and women from the village can tend their fields and not suffer from lack of food. I take only a small percentage in taxation, only what I must, of their yield, but I've no control over the taxes they must pay or what they must yield to the king. Of course it's naught when compared to what I have to give up from my coffers. I don't ask more of them than they can comfortably give. When they come upon hard times, I do try not to increase their load. In return for fairness, they give me their loyalty, and in some cases their affection."

A wiry, balding farmer was tending a beautiful crop of rich green winter wheat nearby that made the surrounding meadow seem brown by comparison. He hastily put down his digging tool and rushed forward to greet his baron. He grabbed his hat from the top of his head and bowed deeply.

"Good day to you, Baron. It's good to have you back with us. Will you be stayin' long this time, milord?"

"Nay, Spurlock. We'll be headin' towards London tomorrow mornin'. How's yer sweet wee Madelyne doin'? Is she in better health than when I was last in residence here?"

"Aye, milord. She's up and about again, nearly runnin' her mum daft. She never sleeps, and I'm afraid she has a temperament to match her fiery hair."

"Don't ye fret over that, Spurlock. Tis the wee lassies like that who make the most interestin' women. I have great affection for the wee heathens myself." He winked at Ysabelle, enjoying her blush as understanding slowly dawned that he was talking about her.

Ysabelle realized her mouth was hanging open and immediately snapped it shut. She could hardly believe what she was hearing. Not only did Gray know the names of his peasants, he knew whether or not their families were well and inquired after them.

The Baron of Penrith motioned his vassal forward. "Come, Spurlock, meet yer new mistress. I've taken a wife. Meet my beautiful baroness, Ysabelle Duncan."

Spurlock immediately dropped to one knee and bent his head while placing his hat over his heart in the most solemn of gestures. "Milady, you have my eternal devotion and loyalty. May God bless you with a long and happy life with our good baron here."

When he looked up, he was gifted with a beautiful smile from his new mistress. He could tell by the misty look that had come over her that she was very pleased by his dutiful offering of fealty.

"And many thanks to you, kind sir. May you be blessed with plenty to eat and a warm home."

The farmer nodded happily, tugged his forelock, and slapped his hat back on his head as he went back to digging weeds at the edge of his field, a large grin on his face. She was a fine woman, their new mistress. A fine, fine woman.

Ysabelle turned to Gray. "The baron who ruled over us in … well, where I grew up, he taxed us more than a fourth of our yield. We could hardly live on what was left to us."

"My vassals pay less than a tenth of their yield, although I make concessions for those who are in dire situations. The fields are lookin' as though they might be well ready for the spring plantin'."

"It's no wonder why you're held in such high esteem by your people. I've never heard the like. With each new thing I learn of you, I find I regard you with more respect … and affection."

He clutched at his heart mockingly. "Do ye mean to say that ye didn't immediately respect the pirate with whom ye first became acquainted? I will no doubt have to tend to my broken heart because of yer ill use of my good nature!"

"I haven't actually seen evidence of your good nature, but in all fairness to you, milord, I will most certainly be on the lookout for it." She laughed out loud, snorting. The inelegant sound caused a fit of the giggles, which produced another snort.

"Well now, that's a ladylike sound if I'd ever be hearin' one," he teased.

"And no gentleman would ever notice," she shot back.

"True, but I never claimed to be a gentleman, now, did I, lass? In point of fact, I am certain that I offered ye assurances to the contrary when we met."

"No. You didn't. Tis a good thing as well, for I would hate for you to endanger your immortal soul for lying." She grinned up at him boldly as he rubbed his chin, feigning deep thought.

"It would seem that I have endangered my immortal soul for many more grievous sins – tying up young ladies, pilferin' the belongin's of a tyrant king, forcin' a poor wretched wench to wed me…. Aye, it seems as though I've a wagonload of repentin' to do. Perchance my poor wife could put in a good word for me with the Almighty?"

Ysabelle lifted her chin rebelliously and spurred her horse into a canter. "I'm not sure there are enough words to rid you of the black stains on your soul, husband!" she tossed over her shoulder as she flew in the direction of the unfinished castle wall. By the time she had cleared it and was riding through the upper bailey, Gray had caught up to her, thundering down upon her, his stallion wild with the excitement of the chase. Gray effortlessly lifted her from her horse and pulled her onto his lap, kissing her passionately without so much as a break in his stride. Ysabelle's mare followed along obediently as her master led the way to the recently completed stables, squeezing his wife tightly about the waist.

"I see ye have completed the stables, and I noticed that there were well-built stone barracks in the lower bailey. I was curious as to why those are finished, yet the castle remains incomplete."

Gray dismounted. He reached up for Ysabelle and pulled her down beside him. "Well, lass, it certainly wouldn't be equitable for my soldiers to be cold and unsheltered while they labored to build a grand home for me, would it now? And where would any of us be without well-cared for horses?"

"I also noticed that many of the village homes had been freshly repaired."

"Before I came here, this town was constantly at the mercy of border raiders. They lost much of their livestock and food to them, not to speak of the damage the raiders did to their homes and their men. More than one dirt farmer lost his life to overzealous thieves."

She arched her brows. "So you had your soldiers repair their homes before you tended to your own?"

He nodded. "Of course. It is my sworn duty to protect the people who give me their oath of fealty. My feelin's for Edward have nothin' whatever to do with my responsibility to these people. Any duty conveyed upon me is mine, no matter who gave it to me, even that crown-wearin' tub of entrails." He worked the leather girt free and removed the saddle from his stallion. He slapped its flank and it went skittering into its stall, where fresh hay and oats had been set out in preparation for the baron's return. When Gray turned his attention to the mare's girt, Ysabelle waylaid him by placing her hand on the back of his neck. He froze. She slid her hand around to the side of his face, then placed her other hand on his other cheek.

She leaned up on tiptoes and gently kissed his lips. "You're a good man,

Gray Duncan. And I'm a fortunate woman to have been kidnapped and forced to wed you. Although, I'm certain milord received a much fairer bargain than my humble self was privy to. Such a stubborn, arrogant man you are! Tis amazing I haven't caused you physical harm." The gleam in her eyes belied her somber expression.

He almost came undone. She had spoken the words he had longed to hear. Not words of love, exactly, but words of acknowledgment, and a gratefulness to be married to him, even if it was masked behind her saucy tongue. He knew her well enough to know she hid her emotions behind that defense. It was enough for him, though. No, more than enough. At least for now. He pulled the mare's saddle off and sent her to her stall in one quick motion. He picked up both saddles, one in each hand, and carried them to the back of the stables and hung them in their customary places, then slowly and deliberately walked back to where his precious new wife was standing, looking at him quizzically.

He had not answered her. Panic jumped into her throat. Had she said too much? Had she become too vulnerable? She would have fainted, but it was something a weak little chit would do, and heavens, she hated to be seen as weak! She held her composure, but the devil if she wouldn't have disappeared into the ground if she'd been able.

Gray stopped directly in front of her, and when he spoke, she could hear the catch in his voice. He didn't dare touch her for fear he would lose his tenuous grasp on his emotions and take her in front of God and countrymen. "Ysabelle, ye please me. So much ye please me." He broke into a wide grin, devilment flooding his expression. "And it's high time ye came to yer senses and realized what a gift ye have in me. I'm not only a fortunate man, but possessed of great intellect and wisdom to have had the foresight to kidnap ye and force ye to marry me. It simply demonstrates anew my uncommonly good judgment."

Rolling her eyes, Ysabelle turned and started at a brisk walk to the stable door. "It's certain, milord. What a wonder I didn't consider that."

He caught up with her in a few long strides, slipping his arm about her waist and matching her stride easily. "Well now, it was only because the depth of yer emotions for me addled yer thinkin'. Tis a common problem among the women of my acquaintance." He grinned mischievously.

She turned and gaped up at him, appalled at what he had just said, trying to decide whether to curb her anger or just give him a good slap. She decided on the slap.

He caught her hand midair, and pulled her close and kissed her. "I was making a jest, my wee fiend."

She gave him her most ferocious glare. "Perchance you should refrain in the future. I didn't find you the least bit amusing."

"Aye, lass, in the future I'll consult the court jester before I make an attempt at amusing ye. Please accept my apologies for my most cruel and callous behavior." He bowed mockingly.

She nodded gravely, fighting the smile that threatened to plant itself on her face. It was very difficult to stay angry with him, despite the fact that it was not the least bit difficult to become angry with him. He took her hand in his, and wordlessly they walked to the men's barracks where their evening meal awaited them. Gray grinned to himself. She was such a transparent thing. Jealousy. Aye, God was favoring him today.

"Might I have a moment of your time, milord?"

Gray glanced up from his fireside conversation with Kennady, surprised to see his wife before him. She hadn't so much as looked at him all evening. It had been her embarrassment at the revelation of her emotions, he knew, but he hadn't expected her to get over it so quickly. Standing to his feet, he excused himself from the conversation and gave his full attention to her.

"Aye, love? Ye wanted somethin' from me of this evenin'?" He studied her intently, searching for an answer to her presence.

She blushed from his full attention on her face. "Well, not precisely this evening, but later in our residence here at your home."

"Our home," he corrected.

"Well, yes, I suppose. Our home." Stalling, she gave her bottom lip her full attention as she gave it a vigorous chewing.

"And?" he prompted her impatiently.

She looked up, surprised. "And what?"

"You have a mind like a flea," he observed dryly. "You wished to speak to me of somethin'?"

Ysabelle blanched, then, gathering her courage and voice, spoke aloud her wish. "May I have a garden of my own?" Her hands knit together in terror as she wound them around and around each other tensely. "Not a large one, mind you. Just a small one, wherever it would suit you and wouldn't be in the way."

He stared at her, unbelieving. "Truly, is this favor all that you ask of me, my love?"

Her head hung down against her chest, she was mortified that she had even asked. "It is."

Reaching out with his hand to lift her chin so that her eyes met his own, he kissed her sweetly. "Freely I give you this small request, and any other you may issue, lass."

Ysabelle smiled brilliantly at him, her shoulders rising slightly from the weight that had been lifted from her. She would be able to provide for herself, for the first time in her life – at least as far as vegetables and herbs were concerned, that is.

"If you'll come with me to the lower bailey as soon as the sun rises in the morning, I will show you the various portions of land that will be made available to you, love." He bowed courteously, kissing the hand which he still held in his own.

She beamed. "Done. I shall be with you at cock's crow." Turning to leave, she stopped and faced her Gray. "Thank you, husband."

Grinning devilishly, he grabbed her and pulled her toward him in front of all of his men. She blushed. "I fervently await the moment," he whispered. Then he kissed her soundly and sent her on her way.

When he seated himself in front of the fire once more, Kennady appraised him brazenly, one eyebrow lifted in question.

"And you found her ... where?"

"She was a sea sprite, caught by a mortal."

Kennady looked at the baron dubiously, his nature was not ordinarily in the least fanciful. Whatever had come over him, Kennady fervently hoped it wasn't catching. Of course, the woman was beautiful, but it was foolish for a man to allow himself to become so sotted with any woman.

SIXTEEN

Home!

England's shores were within sight and Randall could fairly feel his heart jumping out of his chest! Within one day's time, he would be standing before Edward, telling his extraordinary tale of betrayal, deception, and intrigue. Not your usual throne room bedtime story, the story of the turncoat baron would no doubt be told for the next several hundred years. Randall smiled.

Alistair watched from the mast he was tied to, and grimaced at his captor's shark-like grin. The thought of his name and the recognition bringing in the Gentleman Pirate would afford him would make him a man even history would not forget. Never mind all of the clandestine operations he had undertaken in the name of his king that no one would ever know about. Now his name would go down in history. He stroked his bearded chin absently. This thing would be the first thing he would change. The slovenly growth itched all the time. Why any man would prefer to wear a beard was a mystery.

He drew himself up with pride, accepting in his mind the accolades he knew were coming. He would be a hero – a man people told their grandchildren about – not a man people feared, a name that caused people to shiver and cross themselves. Not that he was a vain man – no, of course not. He didn't really care for the recognition, it was only important to serve his king. Even so, he began spinning the tale in his mind, even as he planned his speech to the king. Tomorrow would be a good day.

Less than a full hour later the boat was at its dock, men chomping at the bit to disembark, the town's sailing men on the dock waiting in droves to discover what had happened to all of the sailors aboard. Randall almost injured two other men in his impatience to get off the ship. Alistair in tow, Randall almost sprinted down the gangplank. No one would get him on the ocean again for a good, long time. He briefly fought the urge to bend and kiss his homeland's shores, but was not given to the dramatic and therefore restrained himself. There would be plenty of time to enjoy the comforts of home – after all, he would be in England a very long time if he had any say in the matter, which he usually did. Of course, Edward would certainly understand why he would not want to take any ocean voyages in the near future. He was a reasonable man. The fetid, fishy smell of the wharf, the noise of the carriage, the soothing rhythm of the horse's hooves – thank God above, it was good to be home.

He had barely installed Alistair in his small room – shackled to the heavy bedstead, of course – and settled himself by the fire in the closest tavern with a huge, dripping, mug of ale when he heard the latest gossip circulating around the wharf. The king was planning to wed his dear niece Elaina to a favored baron. If rumor were to be believed, the unsuspecting baron was completely unaware of his liege lord's plans, although it was certain that any baron would be only too pleased to do any favor for his king, especially if the favor were to ally the baron with his sovereign by marriage.

Snow had begun to fall heavily outside the front window of the tavern. Randall drew a huge gulp of the bitter ale into his mouth, then held it there while he considered. If the weather continued on like this, he would surely have to wait several days before he would be able to travel. No matter, he would be in a soft warm bed, a fireplace only feet away from him. It would give him longer to plot his course as well, and if his beliefs were accurate, he would need all the time he could get.

Randall knew only too well what a soft spot Edward had for Elaina, and the whole of the court knew that Elaina had an unabashed liking for the Baron of Penrith. The round-eyed, simpering fool made such obvious overtures to him it was almost painful to watch. To the man's credit was his seemingly infinite patience – he had spurned her kindly each time. So kindly, in fact, that the senseless chit was too obtuse to understand. She took his mildly stated rejections as encouragements. Not that any of those simpering women needed any encouragements where the handsome giant was concerned, Randall thought coldly, so far past jealousy in his mind that the mere thought of Gray could make his blood boil.

As he reached for another drought of ale, his hand trembled with fury. His own desired lady Sara had been so besotted with the baron that she had sought an annulment from the earl she was married to in order to gain Penrith's favor. He ignored her, of course, and she was turned down by the church in her request. Randall remembered the look on her face whenever Baron Gray came into court – the ungrateful witch nearly swooned. So many times over the course of the last year he had sent her gifts and softly written words, but she hadn't even looked his way. No, she was determined to snare Gray, and would look at no one else. But he had enjoyed the last smile at her expense. After he had finally given her up – *I bent down on one knee and the bitch laughed in my face!* – a few well-placed words in the king's ear and she was sent packing from the royal court. The hag had wept loudly all the way out of London. The memory brought another evil smile to his mouth, and he licked his lips happily as he took another huge gulp of ale.

Randall could only assume that this ingrate of a baron was without a doubt the baron he was preparing for ruin. The very thought lightened his black mood. He rose from his chair by the fire and ventured to the window. There was already a heavy accumulation of the white stuff, and as huge as the flakes were coupled with the speed of their descent, he knew it would be several days before he would be able to set out for London.

If he could only have left on this evening, he could reach court before the king did anything foolish. Of course, if he left this evening, he would be sentencing himself, his prisoner, and his horse to a slow, painful death in the plummeting temperatures outside. Randall shook his head in frustration, he couldn't even see the shops across the street. There would be no leaving this night. He crossed back to his chair, sat down heavily, and shouted to the barman for another mug of ale and be quick about it. As he finished the last dregs of the mug in front of him, he sighed wearily. If only nature were a person, he would be able to make her pay for delaying his journey. Thinking these thoughts, he put his feet up on the chair opposite him and laid his head back with his eyes closed to wait for his mug of ale.

An escort of at least fifty armed men waited on horseback for their small party just outside London. Gray and Katharine eyed each other meaningfully, both preparing themselves for anything. Ysabelle instinctively nosed her horse closer to Gray's, while Adam reined in to bring up the rear. Both put their free hand on their daggers, hoping they would not have to use them. Katharine notched an arrow to her bow and sighted it on the captain of the group. He raised his hands, palms up and open, in answer, showing in gesture that the soldiers meant no harm.

As soon as the bright tunics were spotted, Percy fell behind the group and made himself invisible in a small stand of trees. He would follow them in and gauge the situation, then meet with Lance and Garen. Together the three would devise a plan to extract their leaders from whatever fate awaited them.

Gray goaded his horse into a full gallop, reining in only when he drew alongside the senior officer of the escort.

"What meaning is this? Why are soldiers awaiting our party?" Gray rested his hand on the hilt of his sword while he waited for the man's answer.

The officer blanched, visibly pulling himself under control before he could utter the words in his throat. "I am Sinclair, a captain in His Majesty's guard. I and my soldiers are merely an escort for one of the king's most favored barons. We are ordered to escort you to the palace, where a celebration is being planned in milord's honor. His Most Royal Majesty wishes to speak to milord personally first, however."

Gray eyed him skeptically. "Is that so?"

The poor man almost tripped over his tongue, so fervently did he wish to appease the enormous, obviously angry baron before him. "A-aye, milord. You, sir, and your entire party are most graciously welcomed to the palace and will be lavishly attended after your long journey."

For a moment, no one spoke, and by the time Gray decided upon a course of action, the rest of his small party was reining in behind him, waiting to hear the outcome.

He dropped his hand from the hilt of his sword, but he did not smile. "We shall allow ye your escort, but I am eager to speak to His Majesty the King as soon as would be appropriate."

Sinclair nodded curtly. "It shall be done." The escort spread out and engulfed the small party, leading them through the heart of the city and out the other side to the palace grounds.

Finally! It's taken enough of my precious time to get here!

Randall turned to look at his charge. Alistair was bound tightly to the pommel of his saddle. He looked so silly, simpering like a child over the gag in his mouth, that Randall had to use extreme discipline not to laugh. The man had talked himself blue begging for mercy before he received a gag in his mouth, and now he was crying like a small child. Randall felt the revulsion rising in him.

Act like a man, you ferret!

Of course, the simp would have to be a man to act like one.

As he spurred his horse on, Randall felt his saddle tug just slightly as the reins of Alistair's mount pulled taut. In less than three hours' time, he would be comfortably installed in one of the palace bedchambers, a plump and lovely chambermaid washing his back. Then he would dress in his best, and put a halt to this jest of a wedding His Majesty was planning. He grinned viciously as he considered the scandal his remarkable revelation would cause. Yes, it was going to be a very fine day, indeed.

Not stopping at the stable, the small group was led directly to the front steps of the palace, where they dismounted and were shown directly to the guest wing. Gray paid particular attention to the outside of the palace, as he was almost certain he would be making a hasty retreat with his family. He memorized the position of every exterior window and every tree sturdy enough to climb down upon. He was grateful that his mother was in such commanding shape for a woman her age, he wouldn't have any need to worry for her safety. She could best five of the palace guards when she was ill. He remembered the battle Ysabelle had put him through on the king's ship as well and grinned, thinking she would be proficient enough to hold her own through this ordeal as well. She did look a wee bit green, however, but he put that off to the long journey they had been on.

Ysabelle caught his gaze upon her and smiled warmly in return. *Travel must not agree with me.* If it hadn't been for the robust health of all of her companions, she would have sworn she had eaten something tainted. The leg of the journey from Thistlebloom on to London had been horrid. She had felt simply vile each morning, and then again as the evening wound down. Each time they stopped so the women could have a moment of privacy, she would find herself behind a tree retching. Although Ysabelle was too ill to notice, Katharine looked on speculatively, and by the time the party reached the outskirts of London, she looked like a cat who had just snagged a sparrow. Had Gray not been caring for their horses in the meantime, he would have wondered about her long absences, but as they had only been married for two months, he decided it was her usual behavior.

As the armed soldiers escorted them through the gates of the grand castle, Katharine eased back to ride behind Ysabelle since Gray had taken over the lead. "You seem to be a trifle ill, daughter." She stated it as fact, hoping the girl would agree and confide her difficulties in her.

Ysabelle complied. "Tis the truth. I have felt poorly at least a portion of every day since we left Thistlebloom. Might you know what ails me? I understand you versed in the ways of healing."

Katharine nodded, careful to hide her smile from the girl. She leaned in closely to Ysabelle and whispered so that the others could not hear, "How long has it been since you've had your monthly?"

Her face drained of all color, then turned as bright as crimson, before she could force her answer out. "It was almost three weeks before the wedding, milady. I haven't suffered it since. You don't imagine...." Her eyes grew round, then her mouth dropped open as Katharine nodded her head vigorously. She unconsciously began wringing her hands.

"I do. I shall keep your secret, but you must tell your husband soon."

"A babe? But will my husband be pleased?" Ysabelle's stomach was beginning to tie itself into knots anew.

"Aye, he will be pleased." Katharine winked at her, then resumed her position at the head of the queue right behind her oldest son.

Ysabelle locked her knees tight around her saddle, praying she did not become faint, this would be a rather inopportune time to fall off her horse. She focused on the vista in front of her in order to calm her mind. Could it be true? Would she be granted this gift of such a good man? Even if he decided he had made a bad bargain, she would have his babe. The warmth that flowed over her was almost her undoing, and she puzzled at her reaction to the possibility of bearing Gray's babe.

As the detail of the grand palace became evident, Ysabelle caught her breath in the back of her throat. Adam made a similarly strangled sound behind her. Katharine turned to look. Adam held up his hand in a stalling gesture, then indicated in gestures that he would explain later. The group dismounted and took a moment to stretch their cramped legs while they awaited their escort into the palace itself.

An unseasonably warm day, the many courtiers taking air in the gardens and strolling about the grounds looked on curiously as the party was escorted inside. Women whispered behind their ornate fans while men looked on stoically, making quiet wagers as to whether or not the king would have his way over the formidable baron.

As the Duncan party followed behind the servants through the white flagstone corridors, each was shown to a lavishly appointed room, where their belongings were quickly deposited. Ysabelle was the first to be shown to her quarters. Much to the servant's objections, Gray stepped inside with her. The meek, stoop-shouldered man showing the way began to object, but was silenced by a heavy glare cast in his direction by Gray's stormy eyes.

"Milord, His Majesty has another chamber appointed for your grace in preparation for–"

"I will stay here. Transfer my belongings to this apartment at once, sir."

For a moment, the servant could not find his voice. Gray stepped closer, towering over the man, terrifying him into submission. He nodded briskly in agreement with the enormous man's commands, although as he scuttled back through the dimly lit passageway, he could be heard muttering and whining to himself, "It will never do ... oh, no, twill never do. The audacity! It's simply not done! His Majesty will most certainly have a fit!"

Gray shut the door before the servant was out of sight and grinned at the nervous servant's departure. Grabbing his wife around her waist, he pushed her backward through the room until she had no choice but to sit down on the massive canopied bed. She became tangled in the gold brocade draperies for a moment, then surfaced laughing breathlessly.

He hoisted her up into the middle of the bed. "It seems as though we've created quite a stir, my love."

Ysabelle nodded, crawling off the bed to stand in front of him. She smoothed the wrinkles from her skirts. "It does make me wonder for what purpose you were summoned, husband. It would seem that my presence here is not a happy one."

"Do ye have yer dagger, wife?" A shadow crossed his brow for less than a moment.

"Nay. It wasn't in my belongings when they were brought to the chamber."

He pulled his own from his belt. "Then ye shall wear mine. Keep it hidden, but don't hesitate to use it if ye are threatened in any way." She nodded her agreement as he tucked the weapon in the folds of her gown. He secured it to a ribbon attached to the belt that hung around the tilt of her hips, making sure that it could not be seen from the outside. He nodded his satisfaction, then picked her up and unceremoniously dropped her back in the center of the bed..

He pushed her backward onto the sea of pillows, wrapped his arms around her waist and pulled her close. He whispered into her hair, "It's happy for me. And who else in this benighted country matters to ye, my love? Stay by my side and ye'll be safe."

"No one else matters, husband, you know that. And every time I have been by your side, husband, I will remind you that I have ended up in the most difficult of situations. Perhaps it is being by your side that causes me to still find myself afraid...." Her expression become grave as she lifted her face to his and whispered, "Can the king force you to annul your marriage to me?" The agony in her voice was heart wrenching. Aye she loved him, even if she didn't know it yet.

Gray nuzzled her upturned face. "Only God Himself could force me to do anythin', and even then I would spend a great deal of time decidin' upon how much I cared for my immortal soul! I'm not certain I would make the proper decision, if I had to choose between ye, my love, and immortality."

Her eyes were huge as she covered his mouth tightly with her palm. "You speak blasphemy. No man feels such a way for his wife!"

He squeezed her tightly to him. "Nay, woman. I do."

"You don't!" A hint of a smile was beginning to curve her lips.

Gray's eyes danced with silver as he pulled her even tighter to him, so that she was pressed so closely their bodies were almost one. "Ye have doubt of it?" His grin was devilish. "I could show ye...."

"Nay, I do not," she managed between giggles.

He released her after a hard kiss. "Tis good that ye have such an affinity for clear thinkin'. Although I must admit I'm a trifle disappointed. I would've enjoyed convincin' ye of–"

280

Ysabelle started as a loud knock sounded at the door. "Before you are called to go to the king, I have something I must tell you."

She looked so grave Gray stopped cold and waited.

Ysabelle said nothing as another knock, this time much louder than the first, came very close to rattling the door on its hinges.

Gray looked as though he had all the time in the world. He crossed his arms over his chest in a relaxed stance and called out, "A moment of privacy, pray. I will open to ye in a matter of moments." He cocked his eyebrow at his wife and waited.

She cleared her throat, attempted to speak, and succeeded in uttering a small squeak. Gray kept the grin from his face as she again cleared her throat. "I have need to tell you about something important that has been brought to my attention."

"And have ye finally decided to give me yer words of love?" It was obvious from her face the issue was grave, so he was careful to keep the worry out of his voice.

She rolled her eyes. "Have you no other thought? I am … I mean we are … or rather you have … oh, the devil with it – I'm carrying!"

He looked perplexed. "Carrying what?"

"Your sword! Heavens! Have you no sense? I'm carrying your child, you daft man!"

Not for the first time since he had met Ysabelle, his discipline deserted him. Gray's mouth dropped open, he first smiled, then laughed, then grabbed up his wife, spun her around, and gave her an embrace that should have crushed bone. She would certainly have bruises tomorrow, but she couldn't keep the smile from her face. He held her tightly to him and rubbed his chin on the top of her head, grinning like a madman. "Are ye certain of this, love?"

"Nay, but your mother is, and I trust her word."

"Aye. Tis the proper thing to do." Carefully laying her back against the bed pillows, his hand went to her belly and rubbed it gently. "The other proper thing for ye to do, wife, is rest."

She nodded, fully intending to rise as soon as he had left the room, which it seemed he had no intention of doing. He bent his head to hers and kissed her thoroughly.

"The door," she reminded him. He was slow to release her.

"Oh, yes." He turned with a mischievous grin and pulled the bar free.

Gray quickly composed himself and called, "Enter!"

A smallish man with hunched shoulders and a wildly tousled shock of silver hair came through the heavy wooden door. He took in the scene instantly, his eyes raking over the beautiful woman on the bed, the unattached baron disheveled beside it. Would these nobles never tire of their wicked behavior? He made a vain attempt to keep the revulsion from his face as he began his speech. His stately manner was only surpassed by his pompous, blasé way of speaking.

"His Majesty the King wishes an audience with you, milord. His Majesty shall see you as soon as you have put this on." He held out a golden tunic with the baron's coat of arms sewn into it in the most beautiful crimson thread.

"What say ye, man? What is the meaning of this? I have never been asked to change my attire before for an audience with the king." Gray raked the man with his granite gaze, placing his hands on his hips and bracing his legs apart in defiance of such a ridiculous order.

The man was rattled. No one had ever presented him with defiance before.

Gray turned and winked at Ysabelle. Her face was as red as fire. Heavens, she was such a delight when she was embarrassed. When Gray turned his attention back to the hunched-over man, he was careful not to allow any trace of any emotion cross his passive face. "Aye," he said simply, and he followed the man out into the corridor.

Immediately after the door closed, Ysabelle jumped off of the bad and moved to the fireplace across the opposite wall. The logs were ablaze, and the warmth was delicious, for she suddenly found herself cold. First she tried sitting in one of the two enormous chairs that flanked the huge stone fireplace, but could not seem to get comfortable. She tried the other large chair next, with the same result. There was a tiny sewing rocker next to the bed, hardly big enough for her own spare frame, and she spent a moment in that chair as well, but it was no good. She walked to the door and cracked it so she could look out into the corridor. It was empty. If she only knew where the rest of the family was, she would go to speak to Alane or Adam, even Katharine would be able to provide her with comfort. The hall remained empty, so she quietly shut the heavy door.

Ysabelle began pacing the floor, unconsciously twisting her hands into all manner of strange unions and chanting out loud, "Oh God, please … oh God, please … oh God, please.…"

A knock sounded at the chamber door. Adam removed the heavy wooden bar from the inside, and pulled the huge door inward, allowing his mother and brother entrance. They embraced briefly, both relieved to find the other still intact, then laughed at their behavior.

"Come in, both of you. Have a seat by the fire."

Katharine smiled and did as he suggested. Alane nodded but remained standing. Adam took the seat opposite her and settled himself. Her large, clear eyes, they were blue today, addressed him. "Why did you look so surprised when we approached the palace? You looked as though you'd seen a ghost."

"Not a ghost, a ruin. I toured the last remnants of this place when I was in England ... um, before–"

"I see." Her eyes sparkled as she looked at him. "Have you been comfortable here, Adam?"

He grinned, "Plenty. It's weird, though. Definitely twilight zone for me." Alane tried to follow his brother's words, but they made no sense to him. "You have news, I can see it in your eyes."

Katharine nodded. "It's true, Alane has been ... shall we say prowling about and discovered that Gray is in quite a bit of trouble."

"Only Gray?"

A smile broadened on her face as she nodded, sharing a meaningful look with Alane.

"Why him?" Adam's confusion was etched across his brow.

"It would appear that Gray is about to be married," Alane answered, grinning ear to ear.

"But why ... how ... what about Ysabelle?" He leapt to his feet as his voice raised to a shout. He unconsciously placed his hand on the hilt of his sword as he eyed his brother viciously. How dare he laugh at this horrible situation!

Alane stepped forward and placed his hands gently on Adam's shoulders. "Calm yourself, brother, we have a plan. I may be a ruffian, but I would never allow harm to come to that delicate wee flower. Now, are ye ready to calm yer barbaric feelins and use yer head? With only four of us against the entire palace guard, I fear we'll need what wee bit o' help a codfish like ye could give us."

Adam breathed deeply, then let it out slowly through pursed lips. "So tell me about this plan."

The servant didn't even knock. Simmons simply entered, began gathering Ysabelle's things, and ignored her questions.

"What are you about?" she demanded. "You have no business here.... Those are my things!" She reached for a gown that he was efficiently stuffing into a bag. He snatched it away with a cold glare.

"You will be leaving, you worthless guttersnipe. We will have none of your whoring on the baron's wedding night!" The look in his eyes turned her very insides to ice.

"His wedding night? But he is–"

"Nothing to you from this moment forward! He is marrying the king's niece as we speak, and you are relieved of your … illicit duties!"

She opened her mouth to protest. Simmons glared viciously at her and left the room with her belongings before she could utter a word. Ysabelle started towards the bed, she had to lie down. She would wait for Gray. Gray would straighten out this misunderstanding. Tears rolling freely down her cheeks, she had just settled herself on the lush pillows when a soldier entered quickly into the chamber and ordered her out.

"I will not go! I am Baron Duncan's wife and it is my right to stay with him!" She tried desperately to give her voice strength, but Simmons' harsh words had left her shaken.

"Get out, whore!" He hauled her to her feet.

She flinched as if slapped. It could have been Nana Inez standing in front of her – the look of disgust, the sneer in his voice.

You're the child of a whore, and no better than a whore yourself! It's all you're good for, and all you'll ever be!

"I am NOT a whore, you pompous goat!" The anguished cry ripped from her chest, almost doubling her over. The soldier grabbed her roughly by the arm and dragged her out of the chamber, down a long dark corridor, and out the servants' entrance to the kitchens. She had not the strength to struggle, all she had hoped for was being stolen from her.

Her bags had been thrown all over the ground, her gowns scattered in the dirt and kitchen refuse. Sobbing, Ysabelle bent and picked up her clothing. She should have known better. No matter what vows he had made, Gray had turned her into nothing more than a camp follower. No doubt he was eager to gain the lands and moneys which would be his with this marriage to royalty.

But the child? What of our child? He would never abandon his child!

Her mind knew it was true, but her heart, convinced long ago of the treachery of man, would not believe.

That which I have always feared has finally come to pass. I have become a whore.

She began to sob as she stuffed the last of her scattered belongings into the leather bag and tied her cloak haphazardly about her neck.

If he wants a royal wife, then by God, he can have one!

Her thoughts held no power, there was no conviction in them.

She squared her shoulders, gripped her bag tightly, and walked away from the palace.

Thank you for the gowns, you lying rake! At least now I will have the proper wardrobe with which to begin my life without you.

She wiped her tears with her fingertips and told herself this was a new beginning, the real one – so why did it feel like the end?

Entering the throne room, Gray was surprised to see the courtiers fully assembled for the king's 'private audience' with him. The giant, high-ceilinged room had been ornamented in grand fashion, with twelve-foot candle pillars lining the gallery and lighting up the dais. In the front of the room, almost seated on the dais, Gray spotted Katharine, Alane, and Adam. Why were they here? And why had no one thought to bring Ysabelle? He would have to address this slight to his mother at a later time.

Alane was wearing his typical devil-may-care grin, and there was a sparkle in Katharine's eyes as well. The only one of them who didn't appear to be enjoying this bit of mystery was Adam. He looked completely ill at ease. When Gray sought out his eyes, Adam glared at Alane and Katharine and nodded his head at his brother. His great frustration was evident. What the devil was going on?

Edward was in an uncharacteristically jovial mood when he called the young baron forward toward the dais to speak to him. The queen looked uncharacteristically disgruntled as her husband addressed the young noble.

"Aah yes, Baron Gray Duncan of Penrith! I am pleased to see you have finally graced us with your presence. It took you quite a lot of time to get here, did it not, son? Well now, no matter. I'm pleased to see your family in attendance as well. As you well know, I am a very direct man, as you have a reputation for being yourself, and I am prepared to get directly to the business at hand," he chuckled. "Or rather the pleasure at hand."

Gray controlled the burst of irritation he felt at the levity the king was having at his obvious expense.

The Bruce would never behave in such a way.

Gray knew this from his own experience with Scotland's reigning monarch. Whenever the two were compared, Gray found Edward to be equal to the scum that accumulated on the barrels of drinking water at sea. His morals alone....

Get on with it, ye fool!

"I see by the look on your face I have piqued your curiosity, Baron! Oh yes, I can see that I have! Come closer, dear boy, and I will tell you of our rather indelicate proposition then, and put your curiosity to rest." Edward crooked his finger, signaling Gray to move closer.

Phillippa looked on angrily. Here was yet another life that would be ruined by the inane custom of marrying for title, wealth, and land. At this very moment, she altogether despised her husband. The honeymoon period after Isabella's death had only lasted a matter of months. Then her husband had returned to his lecherous liaisons with any courtier who would indulge his perverse tastes. In the privacy of her chambers she referred to him as the "royal ache in the backside."

He climbed the stairs slowly. As he approached the monarch, he was rewarded with the king's foul breath, heavily laced with ale, pluming into his face. The queen leaned in as well, straining to hear the quiet conversation.

"As I am sure you are well aware, I have a niece who favors you greatly, young man, and since you have shown her no favor whatsoever, I have decided to step in on her behalf. It has been my great pleasure to help her acquire her chosen man, if it is possible. And I am certain that we can come to terms, and quickly at that. I am prepared to sweeten the pot, as it were. Along with my darling niece's hand in marriage, I have decided to give you a dukedom, extensive lands, and enough gold to buy a small kingdom. Ah-ah, none of your protests, young man. It is high time you marry. Why shouldn't the lucky lady be my niece? I am not a man given to fancy, however. I'm well aware that many of our courtiers find you charming and handsome, and that you are considered quite a match. My niece understands that she is not a beautiful woman and will take no offense to discreet dalliances on your behalf, as long as you provide her with heirs and are willing to play the doting husband in public. We are cunning, you and I. And I am certain you will find this match to your liking – if not at this moment, then after a time. Cheer up, boy – can there be anything better for a man in your position?"

Gray's mouth hung open. For the second time in his life, he was completely speechless. A movement from the corner of his eye caught his attention. He turned in time to see the bishop take his place in front of the crowd. The king was planning to have the wedding now!

Gray pulled himself together, but only with great difficulty. He stepped back and studied the slightly sotted monarch for a moment, noting the way he listed upon his throne and leaned his head upon his hand, hoping there was no time like the present to disclose his marital status. Phillippa's face echoed her intrigue with the entire situation. Her lack of excitement about the impending nuptials was evident, adding to the baron's confusion and feeling of peril. Looking back to Edward, Gray weighed his decision carefully. Drunkenness always rendered Edward more than slightly comical, which meant it was unlikely Gray would lose his head for his confession. Although it was the man's niece he was about to reject, albeit with a sound reason – perhaps he would lose his head after all.

He cleared his throat. God help him, he had come all this way, done so many things, only to lose his head over an ugly woman. "My liege. I am honored that you would consider me for such a noble woman as your lovely niece–"

The musicians began their chorus – it was such beautiful music. "I will not accept no, Gray. You will grow to love her – it's certain. Now buck up."

Gray would not be deterred. He had to shout to be heard over the music. "I sincerely desire that I could do what you have asked of me. But Your Majesty, I must confess to you, Sire," he took a deep breath and prepared himself to deliver the disclosure.

Edward leaned close enough to almost intoxicate Gray with his breath. He waggled his eyebrows up and down and whispered, as though the two were a part of some great conspiracy, "Well, what is it, boy?" he shouted, almost falling off his throne.

Gray began to speak, but nothing came out. The musicians stopped playing, for his intended bride had reached the end of the runner and now stood only feet behind him. Unaware of her presence, he cleared his throat again, and in a voice far bolder than he felt – proclaimed, "You see, Your Majesty, I have been married these last three months. Not only that, but God has seen fit to favor my union. My young wife has discovered that she is with child."

Chaos took over the throne room. The young bride, looking terribly white and distressed despite being dressed in her finest, uttered a shrill scream and fainted dead away. The bishop sat down hard on the step and began fanning himself with his prayer book. The king shouted his denial of what he had just been told and stood to his feet just as the queen was gaining hers, and the two monarchs bumped heads, knocking the queen into a sound sleep and the king back upon his royal behind.

The king registered shock on his face, then tried to compose himself as best as his drunken state would allow. He cleared his throat and clapped his hands for silence. "Now? You're married now? And a child even? Now? After all these years of ignoring the women of this court? What the devil possessed you to do such a thing, Baron?"

Gray could not hold back the smile that spread across his face. "A young woman named Ysabelle possessed me. She ensnared my heart, and I haven't been myself since."

Edward nodded, a stricken look on his slack face. It took him several minutes to fine his voice. "So I see. Many a courtier has set her cap for you in the past and not even received a nod in her direction for her troubles. This woman must be extraordinary. Have you been bewitched?"

Gray shook his head. "I have not! My wife is good and most faithful to the church," he answered vehemently.

"Her name."

"Your Majesty?"

"I would have her name!" Edward demanded.

"She is called Ysabelle."

"Ysabelle?" The king looked vaguely uncomfortable. "Her title?"

"The Baroness of Penrith," he answered, knowing his elusiveness would rile the king, but incensed by the notion that title meant more than a person's character – as was evidenced by at least half the courtiers present. Had he been paying attention, he would have seen Phillippa sit up straighter and lean into the conversation. Her eyes narrowed on the unbowed man in front of her while her mind whirled. *Could it be the girl?*

"Baron. Seek you to anger your king?"

Gray shook his head. "Nay, Highness. My wife has no title."

The king nodded. "Land? Wealth?"

Gray simply shook his head. Her majesty nodded in unison with him, a slight smile curling at the edge of her lips.

"Was it a marriage of affection then?" Every one present waited to hear the baron's answer. What he had done was unheard of, even ridiculous. He could have doubled both his lands and added to his already-overflowing coffers by making the proper and expected choice.

"Affection, my liege? Nay. I love her." Several gasps were heard and the ladies who had quieted themselves began to wail anew. The queen's smile broadened. *It had to be.*

"What does this young siren look like? Truly, she must be as beautiful as Venus herself." Phillippa looked at her husband oddly, it was such a strange question for him to ask. Who cared what the girl looked like? Unless he had the same suspicions as she. They both leaned forward to hear the answer.

Gray looked perplexed, but answered the strange question. "She is quite beautiful. She has long dark hair that has red fire woven through it, flashing green eyes, and a temper that belies her gentle nature. In truth, when I first met her she tried to use a sword on me." He heard the women gasp their outrage at what they would consider her vile conduct. He had not done her any favors in admitting that fact in this public place. He turned to glare at the nobles behind him. "Ysabelle is courageous. She is most intelligent. And more than all else, she is my choice, my wife, and she is bearing my child."

"I see. Well whatever this young woman has, there is no doubt it is exceptional. I must meet her. Yes, that is just the thing." He took the time to knit his brows together, not an easy task when one's face is numb, and leaned down toward this mysterious young man who had the resolve to tell his king no. "Is she with you here? Now?" Edward watched as his niece was carried off to her chamber under the watch of her weeping mother and frowned deeply.

Gray knew by his king's expression that he should tread lightly. "Aye, Your Majesty, she is that. She is yet awaiting me in my chamber. I would be honored to present her to you whenever you so wish, Your Highness." Gray bowed to hide the laugh that threatened him. His brother Alane would have called this a red letter day if he had been the one to cause such difficulty in anyone's life. The whispers among the courtiers may as well have been shouts, so loud were they.

Alane himself was mirroring Gray's movements, although sporting a full and raucous laugh, in the row beside his mother. Attempting to cover his unseemly behavior, the brother erupted into a coughing fit that sounded suspiciously – at least to anyone who knew him – like great peals of laughter.

Gray was so relieved that he wasn't yet being led away to a scaffold for piracy he could have shouted for joy. His family's intrigues had not been discovered, the king simply wished to force him to wed his ugly niece. Internally sighing with relief, he couldn't wait to tell Ysabelle of this. They would share a hearty laugh together.

Edward scratched his chin, gave a brief but meaningful look at his wife, then straightened himself in his gilded chair. "I wish to meet this young siren who has managed somehow to soften the hardest heart from among my young nobles and thrown my court into total disarray. Bring this woman to me. I wish to meet her now. Then I will decide whether we shall petition for an annulment for you, Baron."

Gray bowed. "As you wish, my liege. It shall be done. I will tell you now, my liege, that there will be no annulment. She is mine and will remain that way." He turned on his heel, hoping fervently that the king's attitude wouldn't harden against him or transform to his detriment in the minutes he was away.

From the doorway behind the king came a cough. Edward turned to see Randall, his prisoner in tow, entering the throne room. He stood to his feet in pleased surprise. It was about time that something good happened on this horrid day.

"Randall!" the king shouted as he waited to greet his friend. "You have missed all of the happenings of this morning! A pity, I believe you would have enjoyed them."

Randall approached the dais, his charge in tow, and bowed low to his king. When he lifted his head, his eyes were sparkling with enjoyment. "I am afraid, Your Majesty, that whatever happened here on this very morning will have rather less meaning to you when you hear of my own most shocking news."

Edward frowned, perplexed. "You speak in riddles, friend, and I am in no mood to decipher them. What of this news?"

"I have uncovered the true identity of the Gentleman Pirate, my lord." His smile was broad, he was enjoying this, his moment of truth.

He hurried to the apartment where his precious wife was stowed, said a brief prayer that the king would find her as enchanting as he did, and threw open the door. The room was empty. Ysabelle was gone, along with her things. Panic began to build in Gray, his chest tightening, his throat closing up. The roar that escaped him was primal – the sound of an animal in acute pain. He drew his sword and started out the door of his chamber. He ran headlong into Alane and Adam.

"She's gone! What's happened to her? Where's she gone?"Gray was shaking Alane like a rag doll, no small feat as Alane was even larger than he.

Alane and Adam looked confused. Adam spoke first. "Ysabelle? She's gone?"

Instead of answering, Gray moaned loudly. "We must find her!"

Alane, feeling his brother's suffering, took charge. "Ye go to the king, perhaps he had her moved to another chamber, he was expecting ye to be married to his niece this afternoon. Adam and I will begin searching for her." The agony wracking his brother's face spurred him to action. He grabbed Gray by the shoulders and embraced him tightly. "We WILL find her, brother!" Alane slapped Gray's back and took off at a run, Adam quickly on his heels.

It took Gray less than a second to change directions and head for the throne room. He strode into the middle of a storm.

"Seize him!" the king shouted as guards surrounded the huge baron on all sides. Instinctively he drew his sword and felled three of the guards in the blink of an eye. He was turning to a fourth, murder in his eyes, when the king's bellow reached him.

"STAY YOUR HAND, BARON, OR THIS MOMENT WILL BE YOUR LAST!"

Gray froze. He turned to the king, agony stealing his voice from him. "My wife is gone!" It sounded more like a croak. Tears threatened. Only by summoning every ounce of discipline he possessed was he able to keep his

290

emotions in check.

The king stood. "She is what?"

His sword dropped. Defeat coursed through him. Without her, there was no reason to continue breathing. "Gone." Shoulders slumped, his eyes begged his ruler for help.

SEVENTEEN

Edward had seen that look on a man's face before, just once. He had glimpsed it in his own eyes in the looking glass just after his Isabella had died. The bond was forged. "Bring the baron to me!"

The guards half-carried, half-dragged the Baron of Penrith before the throne. "Serious charges have been leveled at you by my most trusted advisor, Randall. We will talk of those in a moment. Now, what news have you of your wife?"

Gray passed a hand over his face. "She is gone from my apartments. Her belongings are gone as well. There is no trace of her." For the slightest of moments he wanted to weep like a woman, but instead he mustered his considerable strength and began to turn his grief into action. His thoughts were hauntingly similar to his wife's. There was no time for anything as indulgent as self-pity. He drew himself up to his full height and faced his king head on. His voice was strong. "She would never have left of her own accord. There is some plan afoot that I must know of."

Edward nodded. "Summon the servants for the west wing of apartments. I will know what has happened to this young lady." Servants went scurrying in very direction. He turned his attention back to Gray. "And now to you. Randall has accused you of being the Gentleman Pirate." Gray's face registered his surprise.

"What have you to say for yourself, Baron Duncan?" He leaned forward to hear the answer. He hoped to hear a denial. He truly liked the man.

Gray faced him proudly, rage igniting in his gray eyes. His voice was soft, and even more threatening for its quietness. "I will not lie to you, my liege. I cannot tell you who the Gentleman Pirate is, but I can tell you that I am not, in all honesty, him." The anger masking his face was intimidating. A lesser man would be quaking in his tunic. A muscle in his cheek twitched, emphasizing the hard, strong jaw that outlined the hardness of his mouth. He was terrifying to behold in this state – it was all too clear why he had such a fearsome reputation.

A shout of outrage issued from Alistair. "I saw you there! I saw you there! It was you! Traitor! TRAITOR!" Alistair was dragged from the room by the guards who had taken over as his captors. Randall's look was smug, satisfied that he had done enough damage to do the baron in, no matter what the outcome.

"You understand, of course, that because of the faith I have in my advisor and dear friend, I will have to hear more on this matter, Baron." His gaze shifted to Randall. "I will need evidence, much evidence. And until it is settled to my satisfaction, both you, Baron, and Alistair will remain under house arrest."

"But my wife...."

"She shall still be found, but not by you. Unless it is your desire to bias the situation you are currently in against you?"

His heart sank. He could not search for Ysabelle. "I understand, Your Majesty."

The guards led him back to his chamber. Two remained outside the door to guard him, while inside he began plotting his escape so that he could find his beloved wife. By heaven, childbirth might take her away from him, but he'd be damned for all eternity if he'd allow some high-handed servant to throw his wife and unborn child into the cold and not go to find her. He threw on his heavy cloak and began to tear the sheets from the bed. He quickly made a rope of them, and, after checking the ground below his window for any stray soldiers, began his descent.

Mere feet from the ground, Gray felt the cold, hard steel of a sword thrust into his back. It did not draw blood, but the intent of the guard was obvious.

"That'll be plenty far enough, Lord Duncan. Out for a bit of a walk, are you? You'll be returning to your chamber in the same way you left it, and I'll remain and keep watch to see that yo arrive safely."

Gray chanced a look at the ground below him and whispered his favorite expletive when he saw the fifteen men, swords drawn and ready for a fight, standing below him. On his best day, he could battle ten of them, but with his mind so distracted over his missing wife, he could not trust himself with a challenge that prodigious. He nodded his understanding, and wordlessly began his ascent back to the window he had just vacated.

Once inside, he prayed to his Maker to keep his young wife safe. It was the only thing he could think to do, and God help him, he couldn't stop the torturous thoughts whirring through his mind.

Please God, bring her back to me safe! Don't take from me another!

The servants assembled in front of their king, trembling and shaking in fear. Someone had stolen away the baron's wife. If she was found harmed, the responsible party would be put to death. Simmons was terrified. Not only had he thrown her out, he had called the woman, a baroness of all things, a whore! He thought he might die of shame, if the terror of being confronted by the king did not cause his heart to burst within his chest first.

He took a deep breath, squared his shoulders, and stepped forward before the king had even the time to ask a question. "Your Majesty, I am the guilty party. There is no excuse for my behavior. I threw the poor woman out. I had no evil intent. I thought she was his leman. I simply wished to rid the baron of his … shall we say … unhappy friendship … before His Grace wed Your Majesty's niece. I had no idea that the two were wed. The baron has never before been inclined to marry and I thought.… I beg your forgiveness, Your Majesty, although I know my sin is unforgivable." He bowed low, fully expecting a sword to lop him off at the neck.

The king rubbed his chin and studied his faithful servant quietly. "You will be taken to the gaol until I have decided on what to do with you. I will take your faithful service into consideration."

"You are most gracious, Your Highness." Simmons walked without complaint to the waiting palace guard and meekly followed him out of the room.

Edward turned to the four palace guards who remained at their post by the entry. "Find her."

They bowed their heads in agreement. "Immediately, Highness." They turned in unison and left the throne room. The king turned back to the matter at hand.

"Randall? Well, get on with it, I do not like to be kept waiting!" Edward shouted the last, his nerves shot after the last half hour's pandemonium.

"Forgive me, your Highness." He paused for effect. "The Gentleman Pirate is none other than Gray Duncan, the Baron of Penrith!" All over the room was heard the sharp intake of breath, along with a few shouts and moans – the loudest moan issuing from the king himself. Several female courtiers erupted into a loud series of wails.

"Have you proof of this? You are walking on dangerous ground, my friend."

"I do, Your Majesty. I am certain you remember your courtier and nephew, Alistair?"

Edward nodded, anger sobering him considerably. "I hold little faith in any of his words, Randall."

"Of course, my lord. However, it is what he witnessed, not what he can say, that is the damning proof for the baron. He was aboard the treasure and arms ship, the *Laney*, when it was captured by the Gentleman Pirate. Although the pirates wore masks to hide their identity, there are few that fit the description of their leader but your own Baron of Penrith. That, coupled with the traitorous activities of the baron's father when he was alive, are the evidence against him. Alistair heard his voice also, Your Majesty, and knows the baron well. He is certain of his identification."

The king remained quiet for a long while, stroking his chin and studying the two men kneeling in front of him. Finally, he addressed the court, purposely keeping his eyes off of both Randall and Alistair. "Nobles, you have heard the charges made against the Baron of Penrith. They are extremely severe. I shall hold court on this matter in two days' time, and will listen to all things relevant to this matter."

With a wave of his hand, Edward signaled to the court physician – busy patting the hand of the queen and fussing over her – to remove Her Highness to her apartments. He rubbed his hand over his face, fatigue seeping into his expression. He lifted his head to see his page down and to his right, holding a full pitcher of ale and looking like he desperately wanted to down the entire thing. Waving him over, the king drained the outstretched cup, then another, and another. It occurred to him that he was very thirsty indeed, and by the time he took his leave to go to his apartments, the entire pitcher of ale was gone.

A man draped in the brown robes of the church turned quickly and left the entrance of the throne room to scurry down the hall. As he approached the queen's apartments, he pulled back the brown hood which covered his head and whispered something to the guard who stood in front of Her Majesty's apartments. The man stepped aside and allowed him entrance.

He found Phillippa lying prone on her bed while the court physician fanned her and patted her hand, a nettled look on her face. She kept protesting that she had fully recovered herself, but the physician was too distressed to listen to her.

The priest bowed low to Phillippa, and she waved him over to her bedside. She excused the doctor and her attendants. All but the physician exited, but he was quick to follow when the queen raised her voice to him. He scuttled past the priest, giving him an evil glare on his way by. The man in the brown cassock didn't even gratify him with a nod.

The priest bowed again to his queen, kissing her hand. When he raised his eyes to look into her countenance, there was an unreadable gleam in her eye.

"Your Majesty? What thing do you know? I can see in your face you harbor a secret. I have come to bring you news, though it appears you would have news for me as well."

She pulled him to his feet, grasping both his hands tightly in her own.

"She is here!" she whispered coarsely. "The girl, Ysabelle! At least she was. She has slipped away from us because of the haughtiness of that grasping cur Simmons. Somehow she had managed to come here, and she is married to the Baron of Penrith!"

"How could this be? I was coming to the palace in order to tell Your Majesty that the girl had been taken by the Gentleman Pirate!"

The queen nodded to Father Corey. She had been told. It also occurred to her that her information, in the light of what Randall had to say, could well have been true. She smiled over that private rebellion on Gray's part. Every day she liked him more, a flaw she would have to work on. "So I had heard. No matter. She was truly here. And once you find her again she will be safe. No harm will come to her with that man as her husband. Don't you see? Once she has been returned to her husband, we may rest easy. Your task, father – it is almost finished." Her smile could light up a room. Ethan had no idea what could persuade the king to philander on such an extraordinary woman.

Ethan tried to wrap his mind around the information that had been given him. The thought that kept ringing through his mind was both ridiculous and compelling. "Is this the Scotsman who holds a barony on the border of England?"

"Why, of course. Where else would Penrith be, Holiness?" She nodded. "His esteemed brother also holds land and title. They have been most helpful to His Majesty's causes. Did I also tell you that our mutual friend is with child?" She smiled again over the possibility that the baron might be the notorious pirate. "Why, pray tell, holiness, do you ask?" Her gaze narrowed on his face, watchful for any emotion that might give him away, but he had been at this game far too long.

Father Corey bowed his head in humility. "Your Majesty, please forgive my forward tongue, but these vassals have come to the king's court for what purpose?"

"His Majesty and I had intended to wed the baron to our niece, who has fancied him for ever so long. However, seeing as the baron is already wed, and to someone who I have sworn myself to protect for my lifelong, I can hardly justify any action that would harm either of their persons."

He nodded. "I understand. And does His Majesty also believe the identity of the young woman?"

The queen grinned broadly, stifling a chuckle. "Judging by the speed with which the color left his cheeks, I would assume so." Her eyebrows lifted as her grin spread across her face. "Yes, I would say that he also believes she may be his daughter."

Ethan smiled. He would not have to persuade anyone of anything.

Ysabelle would be safe. If he found her quickly. Randall would be thwarted, for Phillippa would have her way. A frown overtook his face. "Did you say that the girl is with child?"

"I did. What think you?"

He truly couldn't articulate all of the emotions swirling through him. He wished so desperately to be able to protect her better than he had Katharine, yet despite what he had taught her, she was now missing, carrying the child of a man notorious for his lack of interest in women. The baron had proclaimed his love for her in the middle of every courtier. Did he lie? Was he good to her?

Her Majesty interrupted his reverie. "Twill be a lot of trouble for the baron's family, however. We summoned his brother and his mother as well. To attend the wedding, of course. You should have seen his brother. He's a rake, that one. He could barely contain his mirth at his brother's inconvenience. Or perhaps it was the inconvenience of his monarchs that gave him such levity."

Ethan's eyes brightened at something that had stuck in his mind and now forced its way forward. "Did her Majesty mean to say that the baron's mother, Lady Katharine Duncan of Ellshope, is in attendance at this very place?"

Her eyes narrowed shrewdly. *Such a strange response.* "Do you know the lady, Father?"

He sighed. "I did. Once. A very long time ago."

She grinned knowingly. "Shall I reintroduce you?"

Father Corey blanched. "N-no," he protested. "I must find the girl. And I'm certain the dear lady would not remember my humble self. It has been a great many years since the time of our meeting, and I have grown ever so much older since that time."

Phillippa held her smile in check as she rubbed her chin thoughtfully. "Hmmm. Yes. I'm quite certain of it. There is no doubt I must have you both to sup with me in my apartments this very week. The lady Katharine has a reputation for being an extraordinary woman. I think I would like to meet her. Did you know, Father, that she was intended for my husband's grandfather? Of course you know that. The union never came about. Of course, I'm certain you knew that as well." She watched his face unsettle and change with each word she uttered.

Father Corey contained himself. "I do recall hearing of such a thing," he said, attempting to keep his voice steady, "but I must away. The girl–"

"I believe you were in the employ of the king's bishop at that time, were you not?" she ignored him. Five minutes would make hardly any difference in his search, and the king's personal guard were no doubt already searching London for her.

Shock registered on his face. "I'm certain I don't know what Her Majesty is referring to."

"Oh, but you do. I believe you went by the name of Ethan at that time, did you not, Father Corey?" She smiled coyly at him as she gave him a knowing look from underneath her lashes. "Do you think I am foolish enough to take any man into my employ without knowing everything about him? Certainly not. I am the queen of England, you understand. There is very little about you that I don't know." She cocked her head to the side and studied him as he squirmed uncomfortably under her gaze. "And yes, I do believe I shall insist on your joining me for the nooning meal on the Lord's day. You should have found our Ysabelle by then. What think you?" She smiled at the pained look on his face – there was a story there, she was certain of it. "Now, be off, and be quick about finding the girl. Her husband was beside himself with worry, and that devil Randall has returned from his journey. No doubt my husband shall send that monster after her, and if he were to find her first ... there would be no hope for her."

He bowed his head, panic flooding through him while excitement battled for its own place. *Katharine! I shall see Katharine! But first I must find my little Ysabelle. God preserve her and her child until she can be found, and may she remember all I taught her.* The streets of London were so dangerous, and she was such a pretty, defenseless, young thing. Keeping his head bowed, he backed out of the queen's apartments, leaving her with a quiet, "Your wish is my command, my queen."

The alleyway was dark, but God save her, it wasn't deserted. Two men were coming toward her, their leers evident even from this distance. Ysabelle yanked her dagger free and held it tightly, hidden deeply in the folds of her gown.

"Well, look what we gots here, Idan. Looks to be a princess or some such. Looks to be down on 'er luck as well, the poor thing."

"Aye, Wilkin. But now she's met us, she can be about our business and make us a bit o' gold.. Look at that face, the waves in that dark 'air- practically floats about 'er it does!"

The one called Wilkin had gotten close enough to touch her, and he reached out and grabbed hold of her hair. Wrapping it around his fist, he roughly yanked her head back and started feathering kisses on the exposed part of Ysabelle's neck. The one called Idan laughed and grabbed Ysabelle from behind.

Terrified, she waited until Idan was plastered to her to use her dirk, needing to be sure the blade would find its mark. He rubbed his groin up against her backside, laughing and shouting crude remarks about her body. He licked the side of her face, making her grimace in revulsion. He turned his attention from her for long enough to suggest to his accomplice where they should take their bonny prisoner. As soon as his hold released slightly, she used her fist to jam the blade of her weapon high up on his thigh. She twisted the blade, then yanked it out, whiplashing it into the soft belly of her other attacker. He moaned and let go of her, falling to his knees. Idan was on his back on the ground, thrashing about and screaming like a pig being slaughtered.

From the end of the alleyway came a primal bellow. Sweet heavens, there was another one, and he had seen what she had done. She met the bellow with a scream of her own, not of fear, but of rage. *They have no right! I am not common property to be done with as they wish!*

Ysabelle took to her heels, trying to outrun the latest addition to the abominable pair, pausing only at the end of the alley to lose the meager contents of her stomach. Her stomach empty, she still heaved until her muscles screamed in agony. Her newest assailant had stopped to aid his fellows, but they were making more noise now than even before. Not daring to look over her shoulder, she held on to the bricked corner of the building by the street, digging her fingers into the rough bricking to help maintain the tiny amount of composure she had left. It was silent now behind her in the alley, and terror of the unknown that lurked behind the quiet enveloped her. She could only pray the horrible men had gone away. But there was nothing she could do for herself now, she could not make her feet move, nor her legs and hands stop shaking.

Tears rained down on the dirt beneath her feet. She looked at them oddly, she had been unaware that she was crying. Shock deadening her nerves, she never heard the approach of the third ruffian. All of a sudden there were strong hands encircling her waist. She opened her mouth to scream, but a hand clamped over her mouth.

"Shh, Ysabelle, I'll not hurt you."

She straightened up so fast she bumped the chin of her savior. He grunted in reaction. The voice was familiar, but her nerves were too frayed to allow her to place it. Ysabelle turned to see the face of her beloved Father Corey. Dumbfounded, she stared at him, mouth hanging open. Gently, he took her chin in his hand and closed her mouth. He kissed her forehead.

"I've been looking for you since your unfortunate exile from the palace. Her Majesty the Queen sent me to find you. I was afraid I was too late when

I saw you in the hands of those ruffians. Your husband is beside himself with worry. Let us get you back to him, shall we?"

She tried to speak, but couldn't find her voice. Instead she dropped her head upon the shoulder of his soft brown robe and sobbed. It took a good ten minutes for her to gain control of the wild emotions coursing through her. When she finally quit her sobs and gave way to the hiccuping that always followed that kind of release, her old friend's robe was wet through.

"It was my fault, Ysabelle. I was supposed to protect you, but when you were captured by the Gentleman Pirate, I at least thought you safe from the king's man Randall. I cannot tell you why your future is cared about by your king and queen, but you have a sharp mind and can draw your own conclusions. Do you understand?"

She nodded, then shook her head. "You said my husband was worried about me? Is he still my husband then? Did he not wed the king's niece?"

Ethan gave her a gentle smile. "Nay, child. He spoke most forcefully, and eloquently, to the king of his undying devotion to you. Our king wants to meet with you, as does our queen. Come with me, and I will make all things right for you."

"I had always suspected that you were more than you said. Is that why you came to our village then? To protect me?"

He nodded.

"Then you are not a true man of the cloth? Are you not in fear for your immortal soul for this deception?"

Chuckling, he gave her shoulders a gentle squeeze and turned her so that she could walk beside him. "Truly, I am a man of the cloth. I have been in the service of the church since I was a small child." His face clouded over for the briefest of seconds. "I was sent to your village to watch over you. If I had been able, I would have taken you from that evil woman and raised you myself, but that would have caused problems for both of us, child. Since I was unable to protect you in that way, I thought to protect you by giving you an exceptional education."

"It was a good plan, Father. Your teachings have served me well. It was in many ways thanks to you and those teachings that I am alive at this very moment. You taught me to use a blade."

"I am glad of that. I would not be able to live with the guilt if...." He couldn't finish.

"Then I will be more than happy to dispatch you as soon as I have done my duty to my king," a voice boomed from behind them. The pair turned quickly. Carefully keeping her face neutral, Ysabelle faced the tall man proudly. Father Corey squeezed her hand in warning, but faced Randall without a hint of fear. He had learned a long time ago not to fear those things that damaged the body, only the soul was important.

"And what, pray tell, would your duty to your king be, milord?" Ysabelle asked boldly, quelling the quaver that threatened her.

A malicious, toothy grin slowly settled on his features as he turned his face to address his prey. The smile did not reach his eyes. "Why, my pretty toilsome dove, to send you to be with your Maker. And after you, your dear friend will make the same journey. How are your ribs, Father?"

Ethan didn't respond. He kept a wary watch on Randall's hands. "It was my understanding that you were ordered to take care of the girl, not kill her."

"My first loyalty is to my king, and his interests are best served by her death. Even if he doesn't understand that."

Ysabelle was lost. "How could my death mean anything to the king? I'm not a person of any consequence."

Randall's eyes narrowed. "Tis very true. Your mother, the king's chambermaid, was of no consequence either. Yet he seemed unable to rid himself of his love for her. When you were born and given to me to see to your care, I placed you with that shrew Inez fully expecting her to kill you eventually. I was quite displeased to know you had survived for so long. And no thanks to you, you old fool."

She could not fathom what he was telling her. "You placed me with...." Her head was spinning. "I am the king's daughter?" She shook her head, attempting to clear it of the confusion that threatened to overwhelm her.

"Not for long. I supposed it only just for me to explain to you why you must die, dove. And because the king was my friend, I will allow you a moment to prepare your soul before I kill you. Tis a pity your husband is not here. I would enjoy watching the torment your death would cause him. He is quite taken with you, for some reason. Father, I assume you are ready?"

Ethan nodded his head humbly, his hands hidden beneath his vestments as he gripped the two daggers he carried with him in both fists. Ysabelle gathered her strength and courage about her like a cloak. She would not go quietly, like a lamb led to the slaughter.

Randall spoke again, as he grasped Ethan's lower arms in a vice-like grip, exposing the two daggers the old priest clung to. "Do not think to fool me, Holiness. I saw the mess you made of those two gentlemen in the alleyway. A trifle out of the ordinary for a man of the cloth, wouldn't you say? Give them to me."

"I will give them to you when I am a cold, lifeless corpse."

"Precisely." Randall jerked on Ethan's arms, fully expecting to disarm him, but was taken aback instead by the older man's surprising strength. This was not the man he had beaten nearly to death nearly four months ago. This man was as strong as a bear. He could not have been wrong! He was sure of it. He frowned as he considered that the priest might have pretended far graver injuries than he had actually sustained. But he had no time to wonder, he had to concentrate on the old man.

"To hell with you, old man!" he grunted as he began to overpower the priest.

"You first, you devil!"

Watching the struggle, Ysabelle slowly worked her way around the pair until she was behind Randall. She was honor bound to help her friend. He had saved her life, now it was her turn. Randall was winning their contest of strength. Of course, he was at least ten years younger and much larger than the priest, but the older man was putting up a valiant struggle. She waited until Randall's concentration was fully on Ethan, then plunged her dirk deep between his shoulder blades.

"You first," she whispered, tears flowing down her cheeks.

Randall's head snapped up, neck arching in agony, his hands reaching in vain for the hilt of the dagger that was embedded in his back. Blood poured from the gaping wound, soaking Randall's cloak and adding to the bloodstains on Ysabelle's gown. Between the two men she had stabbed and Randall, her skirts were almost completely soaked with the deep red color of blood. He dropped to his knees, his face masked with pain, as he made one last attempt to unseat the blade of the knife. His eyes met Ysabelle's, and in them she saw only shock that he would be bested by a mere slip of a wench. Pitching forward onto his face, Randall made a gurgling gasping noise, then breathed his last shuddering breath.

Backing up, unable to stomach the horror of what she had done, Ysabelle turned from the grisly scene and screamed – a gut wrenching, terrifying sound. Father Corey immediately moved to comfort her, whispering soothing nonsense words as he drew her into his arms and stroked her hair. He was her protector, yet she had saved him. It was a sorry state of affairs, and he mourned in his heart the innocence she had just lost.

Again she soaked the front of his robe as she spent the very last energy she had left. She cried enough tears to turn a desert fertile, and the priest wondered at her in amazement. A short time later, Ethan guided a dazed, silent Ysabelle back to the palace and placed her lovingly into the arms of her grateful husband.

Hearing the commotion and shouts, Gray bounded from his chair by the fire to his feet and threw his chamber door open. The guards would not allow him egress, but when he saw the rumpled form of his wife being carried towards him, he used his formidable size against them and easily overpowered them. The others that had been lining the hall sucked in their breath at his gargantuan strength, and decided not to challenge him as he rushed to the side of his wife.

For a moment, he simply stared at the man holding his Ysabelle. He could not risk looking at her face, it would be his undoing. His rage and anguished worry had pushed him to the breaking point as it was, and any sign of violence done to his beloved would push him past the point of no return. She was covered with blood, but she was breathing. Was the man holding her friend or foe?

Gray's eyes pierced the shields Ethan had worked so long to construct over his own thoughts. The priest felt as though the young baron could read his mind and retreated from the discomfort that thought released in him.

"Thank you," Gray said simply as he gently took his wife from the embrace of the priest. He gingerly lifted her into his arms and carried her down the last stretch of corridor and into their chamber. Gently he placed her in the center of the bed and covered her with the soft blankets. Not a word was spoken over the sorry state of her gown, or the dazed look on her face. Cooing to her like he would a baby, he welcomed her back and assured her that all would be well. She was asleep within seconds.

Turning back to the priest hovering in the doorway, Gray raised his eyebrows as the robed man summoned him over. "She has been through an ordeal...." he began as he explained all that Ysabelle had been through since he had caught up with her.

Gray listened, his face impassive, until Ethan conveyed the conversation that Randall had engaged in right before the two men had struggled. Although his expression didn't change, a vein on Gray's temple began to bulge and a muscle in his jaw twitched, reflecting the fury in his eyes. The rage there chilled the priest, although he instinctively knew that fury would never be released upon sweet Ysabelle. This baron loved her with more than his words, and Ethan could have asked for no better for her. He could rest easy.

Seeing the concern in the older man's eyes, Gray softened towards him, trying to relax himself, but to no avail. After finishing his tale, he bowed to the young lord and turned to leave.

"Father Corey," Gray demanded his attention, even though his command had been whisper soft. The priest turned. "If you are the man who cared for my wife during her growing-up years," he paused a moment, waiting while Ethan nodded that indeed he was, "then I would have you know that my wife speaks of you with kindness and great affection. I would also have you know that you have," his voice broke, but he regained control quickly, "my eternal gratitude. You have returned to me a treasure worth more than all I possess. I thank you."

"You are most welcome, Baron. I love the girl."

"As do I."

"Which is why I am comfortable to leave her in your care. She loves you as well."

Gray nodded that he had heard, but did not comment on the priest's profession. Father Corey turned his back on his former charge and her husband and made his way down the hallway to seek an audience with the queen and again relate his unusual tale. And then perhaps he would get to see Katharine....

EIGHTEEN

It wasn't until noon the next day when Ysabelle finally opened her eyes. Sitting in front of the fire, head hanging in his hands, was Gray. When she spoke his name, his head came up as swift as a wolf, his eyes taking in every detail of the woman in front of him.

"Ye are safe now, Ysabelle. But are ye well?" His voice was hoarse with concern.

"Haven't you slept, husband?" She took in the haggard appearance of his face, the lines of fatigue around his mouth. She sat up slowly, praying the nausea from the child she was carrying would not get the better of her on this occasion. She so desperately needed to touch him, take the comfort he offered her and give her own in return.

He didn't answer her. "Are ye well?" He crossed the chamber is three powerful strides to stand by the bed. "Is the child ... our child...." He couldn't finish. His eyes grew wet as he awaited her answer.

Smiling, she covered her belly protectively with her hand. "All is well, love. I and the child are nearly recovered."

He sat down by her and cupped her face in his large hands, studying her eyes for the truth. "Ye have been through a trying ordeal, my sweet. I worry for ye."

She sighed, shaking her head at him. "It was not my ordeal that was almost my undoing, although I never wish to think about the life I took with my own hands again. I pray God forgive me. Although I must confess, I have been through more difficulties in the short time since I have met you, than in all of my other years combined. Twould seem that relating to you is unhealthy for me. But in excess of that, the most discontented feeling I have had was believing that you would wed the king's niece for all that she could give you and abandon me. It almost caused me to pray for death. And that, Baron Duncan, is inexcusable." She shook her head, remembering the desolation that she felt when she was informed of his impending marriage and gave her thoughtless husband a fierce scowl to show her displeasure.

He pulled her to him lovingly, the grin on his face tiger-bright. "Please forgive me my inconsiderate behavior. Does this mean, then, that ye have changed yer mind, my love? Ye would now prefer death to being separated from me? In truth, twas not so long ago ye would have preferred death to being in my presence." Stroking her hair, he awaited her agreement. She would finally give him the words he so desperately needed to hear.

Ysabelle started to deny that truth, but was too weary to keep up her useless defenses any longer. She sighed. "Tis the truth. But when I thought you lost to me, I felt so truly alone, abandoned...."

"Desolate?" he supplied, his grin broadening.

Rolling her eyes, she found her first laugh in three days. "Aye. I felt desolate. Although I am most uncertain whether or not being in your presence might not bring about that very thing – my death, I mean. You do have a talent for getting me in difficult circumstances."

"Nay, wife. It is yer lack of faith in me that causes yer suffering. Had ye believed in me, ye would have waited in the king's garden for me to come and straighten out the misunderstanding."

"Perhaps. But while I was lost, it came to me that I.... It would seem I have true feeling for...." She inhaled deeply, preparing for the difficult admission. "Gray, I think that I love you."

He let his breath out explosively. "I think ye do as well, and it's high time ye admitted it to both of us." He squeezed her to him, kissing the top of her head, her temple, the bridge of her nose.

"Oh, Gray! I thought never to see you again. Oh, my love! I'm so glad you returned to me." She grasped his waist and squeezed him with all of her might.

"I've returned to ye? I was believin' it was ye that was returnin' to me." He couldn't help but smile at her rather backward emotional outburst. "But now that ye have professed yer love for yer husband, and from the look on yer face it would seem to have been a painful confession, ye have single-handedly taken away all the fun I was to have in convincin' ye of yer true feelings. Since ye were so thoughtless, I will now have to find my fun in another fashion. I believe I'll begin my quest for pleasure as soon as possible."

His hands moved to the fastenings of her gown, and he had it off of her shoulders in less than a second. She giggled and tried to pull away from him, but he captured his wife in a searing kiss instead. The kiss turned hot, a rousing reminder to them both of their separation, and by the time Gray pulled away from her to regain his wits, both husband and wife were trembling with desire.

Sighing sadly, he looked her up and down in an overstated fashion. His eyes lingered on her waist, and she turned the color of fire. "Much to my personal vexation, however, the king wishes to meet with ye, wife. And since I have had a long discussion with Father Corey, I now understand why. Put on yer ivory gown, the lovely one with the blue embroidery that looks so splendid upon ye, and do it with haste, or I will have to help ye finish the task, and that will take far too much time."

"I think not, I have been away a full day from you, and it would seem to me you're lacking your usual control," she goaded him playfully.

Feigning anger, he reached for her, but she dodged his grasp and slipped away from his large hands. "Shall I violate ye before ye meet yer father, lass?" He looked ready to pounce.

Ysabelle froze. "Then you know…."

"That Edward is yer father? I do. I find it amusing that he sought to wed me to his niece and wed me to his daughter instead." He chuckled and brushed his lips over his wife's. "Now be quick about yer task. I have want to throw ye back upon the bed and–"

"Perhaps I should throw you on the bed instead." Ysabelle blushed over her boldness, but she didn't back down from her boast. "I find I wish to love my husband." She slowly approached him, swinging her hips and smiling seductively. Standing directly in front of him, she walked her fingers up his broad chest and gave him her best sultry look.

Surprise, then pleasure washed over his harsh features. "Then, my sweet wife, ye shouldn't have slept the day away." He squeezed her again and nuzzled her face with his whiskers.

"You'll leave a burn on my face if you don't stop this teasing."

"Mayhaps ye should put on yer gown then?"

Jumping out of his reach and moving quickly to where he had placed her bag, Ysabelle wasted no time in putting on the gown. She took a moment to tie her hair with a matching blue ribbon, causing her dark curls to cascade down her back in lovely waves. Pinching her cheeks, she turned in a circle in front of Gray, waiting for his approval. As always, he would have liked to gaze upon her for hours, but there was no time for such an extravagance. He wished fervently for a moment to explain the circumstance to his mother. Of course there was no time. Thank God his gentle wife wasn't being nearly as difficult as the day on which they wed, when Lance had to drag her down the aisle. It was obvious, though, that she was reticent to meet the king.

"Ye're beautiful, lass. Ye look lovely as well." She blushed pink over his compliment. "Don't be afraid, I won't let anyone harm ye."

"I won't be afraid if you won't."

His smile vanished. "And what, lass, am I supposed to be afraid of? I am never afraid!" His voice took on a harsh edge.

Her smile was luminous as tossed her head and laughed. "Loving me. I will take care of you, my love. I will be the warrior at your back."

Relaxing his stance, his grinned devilishly. "Aye, ye will, and after the tale Father Corey told me, I could have no better protector."

"Tis time you came to your senses," she decided with a nod.

A loud knock sounded on the chamber door. Simmons, hat in hand, humbly entered the chamber and knelt. The first words out of his mouth were a plea for forgiveness from the Baron of Penrith and his wife, whom he had so sorely abused.

Gray's ire was instantly rekindled at the sight of the man who had caused him such worry, and he thought to knock the man into a sound sleep, but Ysabelle stayed his hand. She reached out and touched the kneeling man's head in a gesture of forgiveness. He didn't dare look up, but when she took his hand and helped him to his feet, he again begged her forgiveness and swore he would make amends for his abominable behavior.

Before Ysabelle could answer Simmons, Gray stepped forward and scowled at the hunched-over man fiercely. His icy glare could have turned the servant to stone. The bent man shivered beneath the hostile weight of it. "See that ye do. And if ye are ever unkind or anything but gracious to the baroness again, ye shall not live to see yer next harvest."

Simmons nodded, groveling before the enormous man's fury. "Aye, milord. It will be my greatest honor to serve such a gentle lady and see to her every need personally."

"It is only because of her gentle nature that ye are alive at this moment, and ye had best see to her care."

Nodding forcefully, Simmons then cleared his throat and spoke up timidly. "Milord? The king wishes audience with you over the charges brought against you."

"I am ready. See to it that my mother, brothers, and wife are safely installed in their chambers, Simmons. And give my mother a message for me. Tell her that the time has come."

"I will see to it, my lord. All will be as you have commanded." Simmons left the room backward, genuflecting all the way out into the corridor. He then turned on his heel and ran.

"Ye will remain here, wife. I shall return to ye in all possible haste." Before she could protest, he was gone.

"I'll not sit and wait to be thrown out again." She started out the door, only to be intercepted by Simmons. "You'll not change your attitude toward me simply because my husband is not here to protect me. I will not go meekly again." With that, she pulled her dagger, which she had finally found

308

in her baggage and secured to her belt when she dressed, and brandished it in the servant's face.

He blanched. "No, miss, you misconstrue my intentions. My apologies were true. I sorely regret my mistreatment of you, milady. And I have every intention of making my abhorrent conduct up to you. Tis why I've come. I have become privy to certain information which, I believe, might assist your husband in his defense. But you will have to come with me right this instant."

She eyed him suspiciously. "Not to the kitchens?"

"Nay, milady, to the throne room to speak for your mate."

"If I see you have deceived me, I will be every bit as ruthless as I have heard others tell me my husband is. Do you fully understand me?"

"Aye, milady. But we must hurry." He grabbed her hand and began tugging her out the door.

Ysabelle pulled back with all her strength. "Why would you do this for the baron, when he was not gentle with you concerning me?"

Simmons stopped. "I have told you, gentle lady."

"You have not told me enough for me to trust you in this." She crossed her arms over her chest and challenged him with her eyes.

He sighed. "The man who brings the charges against your husband, Alistair, was in charge of the punishment of my sweet daughter when she was a maid here in the palace. She did not adequately clean his chamber, or at least that was his excuse for what he did to her. He had her lashed, forty he had given, he did. Her back was a bloody mess. He wouldn't even allow her mother and I to care for her after the punishment was meted out. Said it would be too good for the likes of her. The wounds, they turned septic. We were allowed to see her right before she passed on from her young life. She swore he had done her so because she wouldn't give him her virtue. The bastard thought to hide the truth from us, but she was still wearing the bruises from where he forced himself on her." Exhausted from the emotion of his speech, Simmons shoulders sagged in defeat.

Having compassion on the old man, Ysabelle took his arm and pulled him toward the door. "Then we should go with all haste to release my husband from this devil." She smiled graciously at him, and he managed to return one of his own.

Katharine opened her chamber door to the pounding of Alane's fist. "Tis time, Mother. I have sent the signal to Percy and Lance, and they will be here within the hour. Gray is speaking for himself to the king, and one of the servants told me that Randall is dead. The only witness left against him is that vile cur Alistair. I have plans for that deceitful vermin."

"I have to say that you are dependable when the matter is urgent. Is Adam prepared?"

"He is."

"Then we should go." He threw open the heavy door and waited for Katharine to exit. Following her, he was ill-prepared for the soldiers that waylaid him. It took six to subdue him, and that only after a sword was pointed at his already constrained mother's throat. "I shall be peaceful. Stay your hand."

The sword dropped from Katharine's throat, just as the hilt of a sword crashed down upon Alane's head, knocking him into sleep. The guards couldn't carry the enormous man, so they dragged him instead. When Katharine and Alane were brought to the throne room, bound and surrounded by guards, Edward leapt to his feet, his face mottling with anger.

"Who has ordered this foul deed done to invited guests in my palace?! I will have the name of the presumptuous roué."

Alistair, who until this time had been standing at the side of the dais awaiting his turn to speak, blanched as he turned to his lord. "Your Highness, twas my doing. I beg pardon of you. I was only assisting His Majesty in apprehending the crew of the Gentleman Pirate," he squeaked.

Edward vented his wrath on the prissy, preening little man. "Have I suddenly been deposed and you crowned monarch of England? Has the worm turned in your favor? Or are you simply wishing for the words you speak in front of me to be your last? What have you to say for yourself? Speak up!"

Alistair was fairly quaking by the end of the king's tirade, and what pasty color he had possessed at the beginning of the king's angry speech was completely gone by the end of it. "Mercy!" was all he could screech out, his voice climbing a full octave.

"Unhand the Lady Katharine and the baron. I will wait until I have heard the facts before I choose to have anyone taken into custody." He gave Alistair a meaningful look. "Am I understood?"

"Aye, my king," he sputtered.

Edward leveled his gaze on the two captives. "Are you prepared to be witnesses in this matter?"

Katharine stepped forward and dropped into a curtsy, the anger on her face hidden by her bowed head. "We are, Your Majesty."

Edward seated himself comfortably in the richly appointed throne. "Step forward, Lady Katharine Duncan. I have long wished to meet a woman of your reputation." The lecherous look on his face was too plain to be ignored. Katharine felt as though spiders were crawling all over her.

At that moment, the queen, trailed by Father Corey, entered the hall.

Seeing the way her husband looked at the lovely woman in front of him, Phillippa's face hardened, and she composed herself for the battle she faced. She would save the baron, if only to right the wrong her husband had done to his own flesh and blood, family should never be discarded. That was a lesson her own father should have been taught before he had wed her to this lustful, libidinous monarch, who had no affection for her.

She approached the dais, stopping to take Katharine's hand and offer her a whispered word of encouragement. The women instantly recognized in each other their mutual distaste for Edward, and smiled warmly at each other in acknowledgment of their kinship.

"I will do my best to save your son, Lady Katharine," she whispered.

She smiled cryptically and responded, "As will I, but I thank you for your assistance, Your Majesty." Inclining her head to Her Highness, Katharine backed away from the dais to stand by Alane, who was awake and fighting mad.

"I will now hear the evidence on both sides of this charge. Alistair, I will allow you to begin."

Alistair, now in control of his fear and certain he would gain the king's favor, stepped forward. "I was, as you know, Your Majesty, on His Highness' treasure and arms ship, the *Laney*, when it was boarded and plundered by the Gentleman Pirate. The crew, as well as myself, were bound and crowded on the deck to await whatever cruelty the vermin chose to mete out."

The king's eyebrows arched at that, as the Gentleman Pirate was the only known pirate to allow the crew of a captured ship to retain their lives.

Coward.

"When all of the pirates were above deck, I witnessed Baron Duncan, whom I have more than a passing acquaintance with, commanding the crew of the pirate ship *Vengeance*. He was their leader. I can attest to that fact." He nodded with certainty, a smug grim praying about his lips as he glared at the baron opposite him.

"Was this man, that you claim to be the Baron Duncan, wearing a mask at the time? Did you see his face?" the king inquired.

"Yes, Your Majesty, he was wearing a mask. However, there are few that rival the baron's size and bearing, and the deep red color of the hair was the same, as was the deep tenor of the pirate's voice."

The kind nodded. "I see. Have you any words to give in your defense, Baron Duncan?"

"I do."

"Proceed."

"I can tell you without marking a slight stain on my soul that Sir Alistair's assumption concerning the identity of the Gentleman Pirate is false. I am not that personage, and I can swear to that fact on the grave of my beloved father – God rest his weary soul."

Edward nodded again. "A moving speech, from a trusted vassal. Are there any witnesses to this assertion you have made?"

"I am a witness!" It was Katharine's voice that answered the monarch.

A murmur of fear rippled through the attending throng. A woman dared speak without introduction or permission in the king's court? Scandalous!

Appreciating the woman's renowned boldness, Edward smiled and waved her forward. "Lady Katharine, as Duncan's mother, I would expect no less than for you to testify in his behalf. Please continue."

She nodded. "My son has never been, nor will he ever be, the Gentleman Pirate. He has not the skill, the patience, nor the stomach for such an endeavor." Although her words were an insult, the gentle lady was smiling. Gray's scowl was as intense as his mother's smile was satisfied.

Ah, yes, she lives up to her legendary reputation!

Edward used the crook of her finger to urge her forward. "Gentle lady. Do you realize you insult your son?"

She stepped forward without hesitation – head held high and proud – again startling the gathering of courtiers.

"Nay. I do not!" she answered brazenly. "I am simply attesting to the fact that *if* my son were a pirate, I can assure His Majesty that Gray would not allow the crew to live, or bother to keep his identity hidden." She ignored the gasp of the crowd. "He is a proud man, you see, Your Majesty. He would proclaim his identity to all and challenge them to catch him! Which, of course, they would not."

She smiled knowingly as she had just related their differing opinions on pirating, remembering their heated discussions on how the deed should be done. "In addition, Highness, Lord Duncan would not be so foolish as to leave any witnesses to his vile acts alive to testify against him later, especially if he were acting traitorously to the king whom he served." She nodded decisively as though she had explained everything.

Edward could not help himself. Like a puppet with no control of his own body, as she nodded he nodded in agreement with her. He could not draw his eyes from her lovely figure, even at her advanced years, and he couldn't help but wonder what pleasures awaited him beneath such a lady's skirts.

Edward cleared his throat. "Are there any more witnesses to your defense, Baron Duncan?"

"Aye. My brother will attest to my innocence of this charge as well."

Edward motioned the even larger baron forward, listened to his vehement defense of his brother's integrity as well, and dismissed him to his chamber. "Are there any more witnesses who will testify on your behalf, Gray?"

A new woman's voice again shattered the pregnant silence. "Aye, Your Majesty. If you would be kind enough to listen, I would speak."

Gray kept his face from showing the shock that washed over him at the sound of his young wife's voice. He had ordered her to remain in their chambers. He would have a word with her when they were in private later and instruct her on her duties as his obedient wife. He heard a scuffling noise behind him and turned just in time to see two of the king's personal guards roughly grabbing hold of Ysabelle's arms.

Before either man had time to blink, he was upon them. Gray snagged one shocked soldier by the throat and threw him the length of the hall, then turned his fury on the other. He had the terror-stricken man flat on his back with his booted foot planted firmly on his chest before the man had time to yell. The muscle in his cheek twitched repeatedly in his fury.

"Apologize to the lady." His voice was all the more terrible because of its quiet tone and lack of emotion.

"A thousand pardons, milady," the panicked man squeaked out.

"Will ye be mishandling any gentlewomen in the near future, cretin?"

"N-no, milord," he stammered out.

Ysabelle favored him with a sympathetic smile as the man regained his feet. He bowed to her and rushed back to his place in front of the courtiers.

"Are you quite finished, Baron?" Edward bellowed from the dais.

"I am, Majesty. But I will not tolerate for my wife to be so unkindly used."

Edward's face reddened. "You will not tolerate?! Child, come forward so that I might see you better." He motioned her with the crook of his finger.

Ysabelle looked at Gray, he nodded. Receiving his permission, she started to approach the dais. A thought occurred to her, and she turned back to him. He leaned in to hear her.

"If on the morrow we are still drawing breath, I'm going to make you pay for being so thoughtless as to get caught and cause me such distress. It was most ungentlemanly, milord," she whispered.

He grinned, "Ye forget, lass. I never claimed to be a gentleman."

"Aye. I'll have to remember that in the future. That is, if you're fortunate enough to have one." She turned and moved away from him towards the king.

As the young woman came nearer, the color drained from Edward's face, and a quiet noise escaped his throat. She was the exact picture of Isabella.

Intentionally controlling his reaction to the familiarity of the face of the young girl who presented herself in front of him, Edward motioned the girl closer.

He nodded graciously to her and smiled. "And who might you be, young lady?"

"I am the Baroness Duncan, Your Majesty, Lord Gray's wife, and I was aboard the treasure ship *Laney* when it was boarded and taken as well." She waited for that information to sink in, watched the remaining color drain from the king's countenance, then proceeded boldly.

"I also was taken captive by the Gentleman Pirate, although I was later allowed my freedom. I can tell you, Your Majesty, without reservation and in all honesty, that my husband, Baron Duncan, is not the Gentleman Pirate."

Edward seemed momentarily at a loss for words. It wasn't her testimony that robbed him of speech, but seeing this girl, so close to him after so many years, and hoping against hope she was who he suspected her of being.

When he recovered himself, he asked, "And your name, my child?"

She was close enough to him to hear the hitch in his voice. She purposely ignored the sympathy evoked by the sound. Squaring her shoulders, she found her strength.

"I am Ysabelle Duncan, Your Majesty.'

Ysabelle, her name is Ysabelle!

"And from which family is your parentage, Ysabelle?"

Taking a deep breath, she steeled her nerve. "I do not know my family name, Sire, as I believed that I was an orphan until only a few months ago. No longer without family, thanks to my good husband, existence is no better for me now, though, Highness, as I now understand that I was discarded by my father as a mere infant. A woman who did not know or love me was paid to be my caretaker. Although I stand before you with the title of baroness, in truth I have no title except that which my husband has given to me through marriage. I have no lands, no wealth, no favors to ask, no compelling reason for a monarch to listen to me. I have nothing to gain, save the freedom of the man who loves me, and whom I love above all others. I beg your mercy for his life, and if justice be served – as I am assured that it will be – you, Majesty, will find him innocent. In addition, and I beg your indulgence, Highness, if there is truly any justice to be served here, my lord, the Lord Alistair has many things to account for to his liege lord."

Gray smiled for the first time since he had entered into this battle for his life. Ysabelle was his stroke of luck – a winning creature. Pride overcame him as he watched her boldly address a lifetime of fears – head held high, back straight as an arrow, bearing regal. Warmth spread through him as he admired this woman, his wife.

Intrigued, the king leaned toward her in an unconscious attempt to close the distance between them. His voice was soft, almost tender, when he addressed her.

"I see. And what are these crimes of Alistair that you speak of, child?"

Ysabelle did her best to ignore the emotion she thought she heard in her father's voice. He didn't know who she was. This privileged king couldn't possibly imagine that this terrified girl standing before him trying to keep her knees from knocking together might be his daughter. It was not possible for him to know, and even if he did, he would have no feeling for her. His desire for her as his daughter had already been amply demonstrated. He had ruthlessly discarded her life like so much rubbish.

She drew a deep breath and continued. "The man before you, the one you call a faithful vassal, beat an innocent girl to death simply because she would not yield to his lustful desires willingly. The poor girl was a servant in your household, Sire. In addition, she was the daughter of a faithful servant to the crown. If that is not sin enough to blacken his soul, I'm certain there are many here who...."

Holding up his hand, Edward stopped her recitation. "Whose child are you speaking of, Baroness?"

She bowed her head and curtsied. "Your faithful servant, Simmons, Highness."

"Simmons? He was the very man who ousted you from this palace, child, and caused you and your husband great distress, was he not? And yet you defend his daughter to me?"

She nodded earnestly. "I do, Your Highness. Much has occurred since that time. And what happened to me was an honest, albeit unkind, mistake. Simmons has been a good and faithful servant to you, my lord, and he has made his heartfelt amends to me."

Dumbfounded, the king could do nothing but nod his understanding. Her defense of her abuser was so moving, so different from the vengeful nature he so often witnessed around him. Her noble principles radiated throughout the room like rays of the sun. Silence reigned among the men and women who usually had so many things to say.

The entire court centered their attention on this bold young woman who dared speak in this manner to the king of England. Every cultured eye in the grand hall examined this young enchantress who stood in front of them, so strong and unafraid.

She had done what so many beauties had failed attempting – she had snared the Baron of Penrith. Curiosity and jealousy battled for place as the women sought out weakness in Ysabelle Duncan. Had she been less good or less beautiful, the envious noblewomen desperately searching for imperfections would have pecked her to pieces, but even in their spiteful rage, none could find fault with her.

Gentlemen smiled broadly, gentlewomen frowned deeply and whispered indecent things in their jealousy, but the most magnified reaction in the room was that of the king. His eyes, large and round, sought any other mark to look upon even as his gaze was drawn over and over again to the face of his daughter.

"I must consider all that has been related to me on this matter. You may step back to your husband's side, good Baroness."

For a moment Edward was silent. Then his head dropped into his hands. After several minutes he finally straightened up on his throne – eyes reddened, face slack – and slowly beckoned the young woman up the steps of the dais.

Phillippa, quiet and ever watchful, kept herself stately and composed, but a light smile played about her lips and her eyes danced radiantly.

Finally, after all these years, she has come home. Ysabelle is the child! It's her!

The king studied Ysabelle closely. He could hardly believe his eyes. *How like my Isabella!*

Edward could not accept the similarity between this young woman and the love of his life. The likeness was astonishing! She could be none other than the daughter he had abandoned. Guilt overwhelmed the monarch at the same time the picture of this young woman married to the Baron of Penrith confused and called to him.

It cannot be her! It must not be her. Dear God, forgive me for what I have done to my own flesh. My daughter stands before me and without a word accuses me.

Gray stepped forward, emboldened once again by the enormous pride he felt in his wife. "I proudly present to you, Highness, my wife, Ysabelle."

She stepped forward, gave a low, graceful curtsy, raised her face to the monarch, and smiled beatifically.

The king flinched visibly. His reaction confused her and her smile faltered ever so slightly. She intentionally reinforced the curve of her lips and gazed boldly at Edward.

"It is a great pleasure to meet you, Your Majesty," her voice was low and husky, the epitome of her mother's sensuous articulation. "I have waited long years to meet you."

He had no choice but to notice. The pain engulfing him was unbearable.

Ysabelle's eyes were the exact green shade of her mother's.

The queen noticed easily her husband's distress and considered leaving him to founder, but had no desire to cause the young woman any more discomfort than was necessary. She broke the awkward silence by extending her hand to the young woman and graciously welcoming her to court.

"It is such a pleasure to know you, dear woman. Welcome, and I pray that you may be comfortable during your stay here."

Ysabelle embraced the queen's hand gently with both of her own and bowed low. She was all that Gray could have hoped for. Her grace, her dignity.... But Phillippa's reaction confused him. Was it possible that she knew the identity of his young wife as well? No, it couldn't be. No woman would be so gracious to a bastard child of a lecherous husband.

Edward looked as though he has suddenly grown quite old, while Phillippa seemed inordinately pleased – as though she had won some amazing prize.

From the back of the room came the sound of a throat clearing loudly, to which the queen looked up sharply, nodded her head, and excused herself. Neither Ysabelle or Gray turned their heads away from the king's scrutiny to look toward the interruption. The baron's eyes remained fixed on his wife's face, determined to take her from the hall if she began to falter.

"All parties involved in this matter are confined to quarters. Ysabelle, Baroness of Penrith, I would have a private conference with you in my apartments." Edward issued his command.

NINETEEN

Gray struggled to maintain his control. He kept his face purposely calm, yet his mind whirled. The king would never cause physical harm to his own child, the wife of one of his favored barons, would he? Certainly not. But could he destroy her heart? Aye, with but a word. But was Ysabelle so frail as to be undone by his rejection? That remained to be seen. Gray had two options, wait to see what happened, or thrust his dirk into the king's heart.

Discretion is the better part of valor, son.

Yes, Father.

He would wait. But he would wait outside the king's chamber door. If she so much as sniffled, he would finish the job his father began so many years ago.

Ysabelle looked at her husband, waiting for his nod. After the briefest of hesitations he gave his assent. Edward was pleased by the loyalty she already displayed towards her husband. It would be a sound marriage. She curtsied low and followed her king, surrounded by his escort, to the outer corridor that led to his personal apartments. Gray allowed the soldiers to usher him to his chamber, planning to wait until there were fewer to put his plan into action. He behaved as though he had not a care in the world, they would be less likely to be ready for him that way.

Catching the eye of Alane, he passed a wordless message. Alane nodded, then turned to his mother, also under guard, and relayed the silent missive. Katharine blinked twice in answer and allowed herself to be led to her chamber peaceably. It wouldn't be long now.

The knock on the door made her jump. It was not the coded knock one of her children would have given, yet there was no reason for her to be summoned before the king since she had already given her testimony in her son's behalf.

She removed the heavy bar and opened the solid door a crack. "What business have you here?" She didn't bother with courtly manners. This was, after all, the court of Edward, where his courtiers possessed few worthwhile manners and even less convicting morals.

"Lady Katharine, Her Majesty the Queen Phillippa has requested your presence in her chambers. There is much Her Majesty wishes to discuss with you."

Katharine opened the door wide and smiled at the woman who summoned her. "I would be delighted to visit with Her Majesty."

In her opinion, there was little that couldn't be solved with an honest and open woman-to-woman chat, and Katharine had heard tell that Phillippa was a woman who embodied uncommon clarity of thinking.

Smoothing her hair, Katharine followed the serving lady down the corridor and through many ornate hallways until they were standing in front of the double doors. Taking a deep breath, Katharine stepped through the doorway. Directly in front of her was a sitting area, with a small table that was laid with all manner of delicacies – roast pheasant, swan, berry tarts, hot black breads covered with melted cheeses, and the finest wine. There were three beautifully crafted crimson and gilt chairs in front of the fireplace, making a cloistered, intimate arena for conversation. She waited patiently while the queen entered from her private apartments, smiling in a self-satisfied manner that immediately made Katharine suspicious.

She dropped into a perfect curtsy. "Your Majesty?"

Philippa smiled radiantly. "Lady Katharine. I have heard so many glorious tales about you that I am not certain whether to embrace you as my sister or bow before you."

Katharine laughed. "I assure you, an embrace is far more appropriate than anything else. We are both wise enough women, Highness, to know that no person is as grand as the tales told about them."

"Most true. You needn't be so uncomfortable. Please, sit down. Our other guest will be here momentarily."

Out of habit, Katharine took the chair that faced the door. It was always best to see any who entered or exited a room. At least that way she had time to defend herself against any enemies. A flaw of character, that, but she had learned a long time ago the caution was a necessity.

"Our other guest?" Katharine asked.

Phillippa smiled mischievously, "Oh yes. I have found an old friend of yours, someone who has known you these many years, and has found it a privilege to count you his friend."

Eyebrows arching in curiosity, Katharine eyed the queen suspiciously.

A quiet knock was heard at the door. Surprisingly enough, Phillippa herself stood and answered the knock, allowing a man garbed in the brown cassock of the church entrance. He kept his head bowed, his face hidden, until the queen called him by name.

"Father Corey, it is most kind of you to join my new friend and me for our midday meal. I would like to introduce – no, that would be wrong, since you already know her – I would like to reacquaint Your Holiness with your old friend, Katharine Duncan of the mysterious and much searched-for Ellshope. My lady?" Obviously enjoying the discomfort of her two prisoners immensely, Her Majesty took both of their hands and placed them together in a warm embrace.

If Ethan could not find a way to breathe, and soon, no doubt his heart would leap out of his chest completely. He hadn't touched her in so very long, and even then, the touch he remembered most vividly was the one that knocked him off of his horse. She had been a wild one in those days, that one had. *Holy Father, let my voice work without squeaking! I have not felt this way in oh, so many years!*

Clearing her throat, Phillippa nudged them just a bit. "Would you not like to greet such an old friend, Father?"

Katharine kept trying to peek at the man's face under his hood, but he seemed determined to remain hidden. The man in front of her drew a long, deep breath and brought his head up to look at her. He was very familiar, indeed. *His eyes were so kind. ...*

She started to speak, "Please forgive my short memory, Father, but although you do seem familiar to me–" As realization dawned, Katharine's eyes flew wide as her mouth dropped open. "Ethan?" He nodded. "Ethan!" With no regard for the formality of court, Katharine wrapped her old friend in a fierce embrace.

Phillippa watched from a pace back, thoroughly enjoying the show. If her confessor blushed any redder, he might well set her apartments on fire. *He loves her!* It was amazing, really, for her to think of the man in any way but as a virginal member of the church. For the first time, she saw him as he must have been as a young man, in love with the woman he was embracing now, giving her up to another man without even declaring his feelings.

Ethan had no intention of ending the closeness until he saw the understanding expression on Her Majesty's face. She knew, and he could not risk allowing Katharine to gain that knowledge as well. "Katharine! It is so joyous to see you again. You are just as lovely as you were when Duncan stole you away from me in the forest so many years ago."

"Now that sounds like a fascinating story, please be kind enough to relate it to me," Phillippa did not so much state as order.

Ethan began the story of Katharine's capture by the evil bishop, his own transport of her, and how she used the leg of a wooden stool to knock him senseless before running like a deer into the forest. All three of them laughed at his amusing retelling, and when Katharine picked up the tale of her overbearing captor, Garrett Duncan, and how she clubbed him on his head as well, the three had to stop talking just to control themselves.

The queen wiped her eyes. "Oh, my! I was sure I liked you greatly, Lady Katharine. Any woman who uses a club on a man has my lifelong respect. I would have you show me the way of it for any time when I find my husband … well, indisposed."

"I would be delighted," Katharine answered with a wink. "Many a man's disposition is much improved by finding himself facedown in the dirt. Present company excluded, of course, old friend."

Ethan laughed again. "I would have to agree. I have always been most humble and agreeable."

"Be careful, Father, you'll end up doing a full day's fast as penance if you aren't cautious," Her Majesty said laughingly.

"You speak the truth, Highness, although I have held my tongue for so long I am certain God will negotiate. He did create humor as well as humility. They begin the same for a reason, both are excellent in the eyes of our Lord. A merry heart doeth good like a medicine."

"Perhaps now I shall be excused from tomorrow morning's mass, Father, since I have already had two sermons today?"

"Aye, my queen. And you, Katharine, have you need of a confessor on Ellshope, or is old Father Kelvin still seeing to your souls?"

"He is. Although he grows deaf and irritable, at least his penances are light, for he can hear no confessions. I find it quite satisfactory. Especially when it is so difficult for me to obey all of the many dictates of the church."

Ethan laughed softly and nodded his head. "Still? I had thought time would have mellowed you, my girl."

"Either your eyes are going bad, or you are sorely in need of a new definition for the word 'girl'. Where have you been, these many years?"

Smiling at Phillippa, the priest's eyes became misty. "I was caring for a small parish in the country, and a sweet young girl who lived there."

"Always softhearted for the damsel in distress, aren't you, Father?" Katharine's eyes were warm as she studied him.

"It is my lot in life. But this girl was very special. I believe she is someone you know."

"Really? And who might this mysterious young woman be?" Her eyebrows arched, waiting.

"None other than your son's wife, Ysabelle."

The coincidence was staggering. "Truly?"

He nodded. "And every day of my happy acquaintance with her I was reminded of you, dear lady. She had a wild, spirited quality, and a tongue that

321

could carve a man to pieces if she had a mind."

Smiling broadly, Katharine recalled Gray's words to that effect. "Gray, my son, has already been carved, I believe. Her audacious behavior captured him from the very first moment. She took a sword to him."

Ethan chuckled. "That would be my fault, you see. I taught her swordplay. I also taught her to ride, read, write, think, and speak her mind. She'll be a fitting opponent for your son, I'm certain. She may even better him, if he's not careful."

She laughed. "I have no doubt of her abilities, but just as Garrett tamed me, Gray will tame her. He'll not break her spirit, just channel her abilities a bit. They will be a sound match."

The three spent the afternoon chatting and enjoying each other's company, until it was time for them to adjourn. Sadly, Ethan and Katharine bid their farewells to each other and embraced a final time. As they took their leave of the queen's apartments, Father Corey stopped for just a moment and started to turn. *I can ask her....*

Her long, dark, gray-streaked hair flowed down her straight back as she strolled down the hall with the same gentle graceful walk he remembered from years before. He was entranced. By the time he finally found his voice, she had turned the corner and was gone.

Edward didn't look at her even once, which was somehow comforting. If he had examined her too closely or showed any compassion toward her, she would have worried that her emotions would play her false, but thankfully he hadn't even glanced her way.

When they finally reached the double door leading to the monarch's chambers, the liveried servant opened the doorway wide and gestured for the small party to enter. Edward glared at his escort, and they obeyed his silent command to remain outside without comment. They were used to his proclivities. Though, in truth, he had never before taken another man's wife.

She was most certainly a beautiful woman, but with difficulty the king's men admitted to themselves their disappointment in their monarch. Furtive glances toward each other was a testimony to the guard's distaste. Until now he had only corrupted women who were deserving of his attentions, not young virginal women who had no knowledge of the way court worked. And it was no small matter that she was the Baron of Penrith's wife. The man was a terror, and had the reputation for being merciless in war. And the king would no doubt begin one if he wasn't careful. Didn't Edward realize that Duncan commanded an army almost equal in size, but certainly better trained, than the king's own? As an ally, he was a powerful and effective asset. As an enemy – the king was planning his own demise.

The latch clicked into place, the lock caught, holding the door fast.

Edward turned to look at Ysabelle. She nearly fainted.

Dear God, don't let him hurt Gray. And don't let me betray him in word or deed. Please!

Slowly she slipped her fist inside the folds of her dress and gripped the handle of her dirk. The cold steel against her sweaty palm reassured her greatly.

She took a deep breath. "I would have you know that my first loyalty lies with my husband in every way, Your Majesty, and I will do all that is in my power to sway your...."

He waved his hand dismissively at her. "No, no, my dear girl. You misunderstand my intentions. I have no interests in discussing the baron. I simply wish to ask you a few questions as to your upbringing."

Her eyebrows shot upward. "My upbringing, Highness?" She tightened her hold on the weapon. A sweat broke out on her forehead. *Dear God, I don't want to know any longer.*

"Of course, my dear. I am only interested in your background."

Though she tried, she couldn't read any intent in his expression. Ysabelle sighed. "Then I am certain to be of great disappointment to you, Your Highness. I have very little knowledge of my parents. As I told you, Sire, they abandoned me as an infant, or perhaps I should say discarded me. I was raised by an evil woman hired to care for me, who never divulged the identity of my parents." She sucked in her breath, hoping the king would not vent his frustration upon her. Though in truth she did not care, she wanted only to bite and scratch and screech at him for making her feel so insignificant all of her life. What right had he to throw away a child?

He looked old and tired as he waved his hand at her and sighed. "No, no, my dear. I am not expecting a performance from you. I simply wish to know what you know about your life."

She breathed out heavily, not sure whether or not she was yet ready for this confrontation. Her father was obviously fishing for information, and she decided on the spot to give him the glaring, unkind truth, since it was he who exposed her to such undeserved meanness in the first place. God help her, she was terrified. It was worse than when she was waiting in the hold of the king's ship and Gray was about to find her. At least in that situation, the pirate would have to decide whether or not to behead her. The king could so easily have her head for his dinner entertainment and not even bloody his hands.

How did I get here? What does he want from me?

Ysabelle sucked her bottom lip into her mouth and gave it a thorough chewing. The pain helped her keep her emotions in check.

Edward planted his hands on his hips. "Well, girl? Are you going to tell me who you are?"

She swallowed hard. "Your Majesty. I will tell you what I know – all that my hired mother told me of my past."

"You knew the woman who cared for you was hired?"

"Yes, Your Majesty. Nana Inez told me. She told me many things I had no wish to know." His face hardened, panicking poor Ysabelle. "Your Majesty cannot blame the poor woman," she rushed out. "She is not to blame, she was picked according to her lack of skills by the man Randall."

"Randall?" His eyebrows shot up. "How did you come by this information, Ysabelle?"

"He told me himself, when he came after me in the streets of London. He was planning to end my life, Sire, and felt it only just that he should tell me why."

The king's voice dropped to a low growl. "And just what did he tell you? I will know."

Quickly weighing her options, Ysabelle decided there was nothing left for her to do but tell the truth. "I will tell you, Sire. But before I do, I wish for you to know that I am with child, and any action taken against me will stain your soul with the sin against an innocent as well."

He looked furious, so she quickly rushed on. "The man Randall told me that he had been given me as an infant to place in a home, but that because of his loyalty to his master, he believed it would be in his employer's best interests if I were to have an unfortunate mishap. With this end in mind, he chose Inez, believing her to be so without skill that the woman would eventually kill me. She did not do so, although she visited more pain and cruelty on me as a child than any should be forced to endure." Ysabelle had gone from fear to fury in her recitation. She no longer cared whether the monarch was angry with her.

"And would you know the whereabouts of my man at this time?" His voice was curiously flat, devoid of emotion.

"I would, Sire, but I am loath to tell you."

"I wish to know."

She dropped her eyes to the his feet. "He is dead, Highness." She was proud of herself, she didn't think her voice quavered at all.

He could barely understand her, her voice shook so badly. "And who, may I ask, killed him?" He fully expected to hear Gray's name, so therefore when she gave him his answer, he could not contain the shock that nearly bowled him over.

"I did, Majesty." She could not take her attention from the ornate shoes of the king.

He sounded incredulous, but she could not bring herself to look up at his face. "And just how did you accomplish this amazing feat, Ysabelle?" He willed her to look at him. She was not in an accommodating mood.

She sighed heavily and put her hands to her face. "I thrust my dagger in his back to protect a friend he was going to kill."

"His name."

"Father Corey, Sire."

Would there be no end to the surprises on this day? "The queen's confessor?"

"I would not know, Sire. I know only that he was sent to look after me as a child, and he was the only kindness I ever knew. I am aware that Lord Randall was your advisor, but I do not regret my action. I would choose to save the life of a good man with no influence over the life of an evil man with vast influence without a qualm. I cannot apologize for my act."

"Ysabelle, look at me." With great difficulty, she raised her eyes to his face. "I will not punish you for this thing. You were defending yourself from an evil man. Perhaps my loyalty was misplaced."

She about fell over. "Sire?"

"Please continue with our first topic. We will return to this in a moment. Tell me of this woman."

"Her name was Inez. I called her Nana. She was weak and unkind, there is no doubt of that. But I was a more difficult child than any woman would wish for as a daughter. I was unruly and strong-willed, worthy of the hate she bore me. Please, sir, I was already a young woman when she told me. It was my own fault. I had provoked her beyond her ability to forgive."

"In what way did you provoke the woman who took care of you, Ysabelle?" Compassion laced the king's voice. Ysabelle kept her guard against him, compassion had been used as a tool against her in the past.

She lowered her eyes in shame. "I dropped our meal in the fire. It was a rabbit, all that we had. It took me all day to catch it. After all that work, I ruined our dinner. She became angry and threw me out. She told me it was only just, that I deserved the punishment."

"And did you believe her?"

She shook her head guiltily. "Although I know it is a sin that may stain my soul, I did not."

Edward sighed heavily, his guilt making him feel as though he carried a blacksmith's anvil about his neck. "Then you are wise as well as beautiful.

Poor child. Would you, Ysabelle, throw your own child out into the streets for such an offense?"

Although she was certain of his censure, she lifted her chin and answered honestly and vehemently, eyes blazing out at him from under her thick lashes. "I would never expect a child to make my supper for me, especially a small child. So no matter what judgment you might pass on me, or what evil you might think of me, Highness, no. I would not abandon a child because of something she did, or didn't do. If a child cannot trust those whom God gave her to care for her, there is no trust left in the world."

He swiped a hand across his brow, sadness shrinking his features, making him look worn and haggard. "Neither would I, child, neither would I. Or at least I once thought I was above such behavior."

"One would hope their monarch had such character," she mused.

He continued as though he hadn't heard her. "And when you were lost on the streets of London, did my man also tell you who his employer was?" He held her gaze with his own, willing her to be truthful, his eyes misty.

Whispering her reply, her voice was so soft the king had to lean close to hear her. "He did." The tears that had been threatening finally spilled over her lashes and down her cheeks. Once they began, she could not stop them from falling. Her control now completely departed, weeping overwhelmed her.

"I thought as much." The tenderness in his voice was her undoing. Ysabelle began to sob, and Edward pulled his daughter into his arms for the first and last time he would ever hold her. He allowed her to vent her years of pent-up rejection and desolation. Guilt tore at him like a wild animal – evoking a feeling unlike anything he had ever experienced. Could there be any more painful remorse?

When the tears finally gave way to hiccuping, Ysabelle finally found her voice. Still leaning into the king's chest, she whispered the question she had longed to have the answer to since she found her true origin. "Why did you toss me away, Father? Could you not love the child of a chambermaid? I was of your blood as well. I would have loved you as my mother did."

It took a moment for Edward to find his voice. "I loved your mother in a way I have never loved before or since, the love of a child who would be king against the will of his heart. She was all I had ever wanted, my Isabella was. You were named for her, child. And when you were born, as she lay dying, she made me promise to care for you. For that moment, I could not even look upon you. Even though she had been ill, in my selfish mind you had stolen from me the only woman I had ever loved."

"But a child cannot bear the guilt in such an occurrence...." she protested.

As he stroked her hair, Ysabelle could feel him nodding his agreement. "Tis true, but I was too grief-stricken, too heartbroken, to think clearly. And with your pink, precious face, your dark, fuzzy hair, you already had the look of her, it was clear even at that early time. I thought that to look upon you daily would only cause me greater pain. So I sent you away. It was a sinful, selfish thing to do. But even in that, I had promised your mother I would see to your care. And my intentions had truly been only for your best. I would send you someplace where you would be well cared for, educated. I had a dowry in waiting for when you had need, so that you could make a good marriage to someone who would care for you, but would keep you far away from my eyes. I did want the best for you, but I placed my trust in the wrong man. Look at me, daughter." She raised her tear-stained face to his.

"With all the sorrow in my soul, I apologize for all the pain and suffering my inattention, nay, my woeful neglect, caused you, child. I would never cause you pain intentionally. Please forgive me for allowing you to be so sorely abused, and for not claiming you as my daughter." He was quiet for a moment, considering, then continued, "Although, you realize that even though I may claim you in private, in public you are simply the wife of my baron."

"I understand, Sire."

"Father."

New sobs erupted from the core of her very being as she attempted to say the word. He waited patiently for her to regain control of her weeping.

Sniffling, she finally urged the word to her lips. "Father."

"Thank you. For your time, my child. For your honesty and understanding. For your forgiveness at the wrong done to you. And more than anything else, thank you for restoring my daughter to me. I am most grateful. You may return to your husband now. However, don't go far. There is still the issue of the charges that have been leveled at your husband that must be attended to."

Making her best curtsy, Ysabelle honored Edward with a warm smile. "Thank you, Your Majesty. I am greatly thankful of your generosity."

"Before you leave, will you tell me a truth?"

"I always speak the truth, Majesty."

"Did you lie to protect your husband? Is he the Gentleman Pirate?"

A smile quirked her lips. "In truth, I would probably lie, cheat, and steal for him. But I was not lying. I was aboard the ship, and he is not the Gentleman Pirate."

His eyes narrowed on her face. "Can you name the man, then?"

She said, with complete truthfulness, her eyes full of sincerity, "I can

327

name no man."

He sighed. She spoke the truth. In a way, he was relieved. He nodded his good-bye. Edward watched after her, a pained look on his face.

"God forgive me for what I have done," he whispered. As his head fell heavily into his bejeweled hands, he dropped the first bitter tears he had wept since the passing of his Isabella. He then wished, for the first time in his life, that he could turn back time and change his past.

The door was flung open, banging against the stone wall and nearly jumping off its hinges. Gray, Alane, Adam, and Katharine leapt to their feet, drawing their swords as one and staring at the deranged-looking woman who leapt into the room wild-eyed. Ysabell ran through the now open door and slammed it again behind her. She tried to pick up the huge heavy bar to place across the brackets of the door, but it was far too heavy. Gray came up behind her without a word and effortlessly helped her lift it into place. Once the bar was secure, Ysabelle turned and threw herself into Gray's arms, sobbing. He soothed her by holding her tightly and stroking her hair. He whispered nonsense words of comfort to her, slowly she regained her composure.

When her sobs ebbed away to loud hiccuping, she finally pulled back to look at him. His tunic soaked through, she touched the wet spot with her fingertips, ashamed at her lack of restraint.

"Please forgive me my outburst, I know I must appear completely crazed to you all!" she whispered into his chest. She could not see the silent nods of denial on the part of her audience.

Gray backed up a step, so she could no longer hide in his tunic, and lifted her chin with the crook of his finger. "Are ye well, my love? Did that foul Edward tread upon yer delicate heart? Tell me what made ye weep, sweetheart, and I will set all to rights." He searched her face.

Four sets of ears waited to hear even a hint of treachery, looking for any excuse to kill the monarch. The men surrounded the palace wall, waiting for the signal from their leader. Word had been given to the king of his peril, and the monarch was even now deciding whether or not to make war upon the waiting forces of the Baron Duncan.

She shook her head. "No, it wasn't anything like that. He was in no way improper or unkind to me." She dropped her voice to a whisper and choked the painful words to her lips. "He knows, husband, he knows. He even apologized to me for my abandonment and asked me to call him," she wrenched out the final word, "Father."

Gray let his breath go explosively. He hadn't even realized he was holding it. She was pleased at his protective reaction, and instinctively snuggled close to the safety he afforded her. In his arms, her pain ebbed from her like the tide going out. He held her tightly.

From behind her there was a small cough. For the first time realizing she had an audience, Ysabelle looked around her, the entire family was convened in her chamber. Their faces set mutinously, she could almost feel the disappointment flowing out from the small group. There would be no battle today. Her eyes grew large.

"Am I correct in assuming you are preparing for battle?" She didn't wait for anyone to answer. "I won't have it! I have only just discovered how much I care for my husband and helped snatch him from the grip of the hangman's noose. I will not lose him now to a battle that need not be fought when I can keep him alive and make him miserable myself!" In her mind's eye she saw her new family lying on the exquisite marble floors in pools of their own blood, and a chill ran through her. It was hard to make light when all she wanted to do was weep like a baby.

"I'm uncertain as to whether the whole of the king's army heard ye. Could ye possibly raise yer voice a wee bit louder?" Alane asked that impertinent question. She frowned fiercely at him, he frowned in return, but his mock anger gave way to a mischievous smile.

Adam grinned himself and joined in. "She does take the surprise out of the attack, doesn't she, brother?"

"Aye. And she's a high-handed wee bully as well. Did ye hear how she tried to boss us about? Should we give in to our pretty little dictator? After all, she has had a trying day."

Katharine answered that question, her voice gentle, but steel in her eyes. "For now, we shall make my young daughter content. Don't take offense, Ysabelle, our men were prepared to rescue you, if need be. However, we were saved that duty by your safe return. I shall call Wylie out of his perch now. He was faithfully watching you while you were in the presence of the king. But, Ysabelle, make no mistake, I will not call our armies off until I am certain of my son's release. I will not stand by and wait for his death. Twould be a sin, that. If he is to die, he shall do it in battle, as a warrior should, not at the hand of a detestable, presumptuous king." She touched Ysabelle's shoulder gently to soften the harshness of her rebuke.

Ysabelle straightened away from her husband's chest and smiled up at him. "Then I think that you shall have no need for your warriors."

"And how do ye reckon that, my sweet wife?"

"In my dealings with the king, right before I quitted his apartments, he asked me if I spoke the truth concerning you, husband. I swore on my own integrity that you were not the Gentleman Pirate. Then he nodded and asked me if I could name the man who claimed that title."

"And yer answer, love?" Gray questioned her.

Her smile was triumphant. "I told him I could name no man." Her entire audience burst into laughter.

"She's a clever one, that!" Alane sputtered through his laughter. "I've always said so."

"Aye," Adam agreed. "She is a cunning wee wench, she is." He loved their language!

"And ever truthful, don't forget that flaw in her character," Katharine reminded them. "'Tis the reason I find her so appealing. I've always enjoyed shocking those around me with the truth as well. It seems so unsettling for so many."

"Her truthfulness isn't why I find my wife so fetching. And if ye would all be so kind as to take yer leave, I shall discuss my reasons with her in privacy." A devilish grin lit Gray's face as Ysabelle blushed red as fire. His family excused themselves at a rapid pace.

Ysabelle's face felt like it was on fire. "You are the devil, to embarrass me in that fashion!"

"If ye think I'm a devil for embarrassin' ye, wait until I put my hands on—"

A loud knock interrupted his lecherous declaration. He sighed forcefully enough to move the fur covering on the window.

"Blast! I f we don't leave this vile place soon, I shall die from frustration!" He gave his wife a brief squeeze before shouting in a less than hospitable manner. "Enter!"

The scowl on his face was fierce, and Simmons cowered before him. "A thousand pardons, milord, but the king has sent for the baron and his wife."

"Be at ease, Simmons. I'm no longer angry with ye. We shall come at once. Please have our belongin's made ready to depart from here with all possible haste."

"As you wish, milord." The servant bowed after giving the baroness a grateful smile and scurried away to attend to the baron's command.

Taking her hand, he kissed her quickly. "Shall we get this over with, love?"

She nodded and followed him into the corridor, completely confident of the outcome. They would be leaving here soon – together. It would be a good day. And if he didn't take her into his arms soon and show her again how much he loved her, she would die from her own sense of frustration. Not that she would ever admit it to him, the man was far too arrogant already. If he were to know how much she wished to be one with him once more, he would become unbearable. Smiling at the thought of his all-too-arrogant expression, Ysabelle looked up at her handsome husband's profile and marked it in her mind. It would be her anchor in those inevitable times when she wished to take her dagger to him. She would remember his strength, his gentle love of her, his kindness, and his impossible sense of humor that made her so willing to strangle the man in his sleep.

All the courtiers were assembled to hear the verdict of their king. There was so much whispering in the hall that the small disturbances combined together to make quite a commotion. As soon as the baron and his wife stepped through the huge double doors, the hall fell silent in anticipation.

Edward was already stationed on his gilt and scarlet throne. He waited patiently, Phillippa sitting by his side and almost looking enraptured. Alistair was present, standing as proudly as a peacock with tail feathers aplume. His usual priggish self-righteousness, his constant and favorite companion, a satisfied smile lit his thin-lipped face.

Gray and Ysabelle approached the dais hand in hand. Despite his bravado, the touch of Ysabelle against his warm palm calmed his rapidly beating heart. She would be an anchor for him in this time of storm, a harbor for him unlike any he had ever known. But tomorrow she would no doubt make him daft. Grinning at the though, he bowed his head to Edward, hoping he could hide his less-than-deferential expression.

"Are you prepared for my judgment in this matter?" he addressed both parties.

"We are, Your Majesty," Gray answered, the deliberate formality back in his voice, eradicating his faint Scot accent.

"I am, Highness," Alistair agreed as well, looking smug, assured of his victory.

"Then listen all, listen well. I decree that the charges against the Baron of Penrith are false in their entirety and that he is free to go."

Alistair screeched his protest, "No! I won't allow it! It cannot come about this way! I am right, and that man," he pointed at Gray, "is the most vile traitor to the crown!"

Edward's next words were ordered in a roar, so he could be heard over his nephew's outraged bellowing. "BE SILENT! Alistair, nephew, you, however, have been charged with the murder of a loyal servant to the crown. You are not judge or jury in my palace, nor will I brook your interference in any matter pertaining to any one in my employ! I am having you taken into custody until the matter can be seen to. If you are deemed guilty in this matter, nephew, you shall be forthwith stripped of all title, lands, and wealth.

You shall be left to make your own way, in any fashion you are capable of. I have no doubt that if this is to come to pass, you shall have an extremely grueling go of it. Guards, take the prisoner to the gaol until he can be dealt with."

Gray watched his vile former associate led off to irons with great satisfaction. He had been a truly detestable man. There was no honor in him, and the crime he was being accused of was long overdue. Never did it enter the baron's mind that he also was guilty of the crime he was accused of. He was only guilty of finishing what his father had begun – no more, no less.

"As for you, Baron, I have taken a great liking to your new wife. You are hereby ordered to treat her with the utmost kindness and to love her with all your heart. What say you to that, man?" The challenge was there, but it sustained no bite.

"As you wish, Sire." Gray didn't even bother to contain the euphoric smile he wore. He turned his wife with his hand splayed on the small of her back and prepared to take his leave with her.

"And you, Baroness," Edward stopped their retreat.

"Sire?"

"You shall make certain that your husband continues to wear his smile. I had never seen it before this visit. I wasn't even certain that the man possessed teeth." The king's jest elicited a loud burst of laughter from the gallery, and the tension was broken. The room gave a collective sigh.

"Let me assure you that he does, Sire," Ysabelle laughed as well. "I've seen them at least twice myself." She beamed up at her husband, whose smile was just as wide as her own, and the two took their leave.

They didn't go towards their chamber, but instead left through the front entrance and met Alane, Adam, and Katharine at the stables. Mounted, with all their baggage secured, the three waited patiently for the last of their party. As the family rode out of the castle gates and over the drawbridge, Ysabelle was shocked to see several hundred warriors surrounding the exterior castle walls. There were so many of them their horses stood flank to flank with no space in between them. They were all wearing the Duncan colors, mounted and ready to do battle.

The expectant hush was broken when Katharine raised her hand, then closed her fist triumphantly. A loud cheer split the air as every armored warrior answered their leader's signal.

TWENTY

They had won the battle without even lifting a dagger. Gray was free. Katharine let go with a fierce primal cry while goading her mount into a gallop. Gray, Ysabelle, Alane, and Adam followed her fast-paced lead, her faithful warriors spreading out like a fan and surrounding them. To the outside eye, it looked as though a huge army was advancing upon some unsuspecting foe – an awesome sight to Ysabelle's mind. The mass of soldiers moved as one, following their leader in victory toward the south.

Garen approached Katharine, the question in written his eyes. "Where are we going, milady?"

She smiled, her eyes reflecting the sadness of her mother's heart as she answered. "To the south, my friend. Tis time for my newfound son to go home." Her eyes searched Adam's. He nodded his agreement with the unhappy truth. "He has been with us more than a full five months, and it is time for him to go home. Mayhaps he will visit us another time."

"I would be more than honored to do so, Mother. As long as my passport to your … island … still remains intact, you can be sure I will return."

She nodded. "I understand." Katharine turned in her saddle. "I will require only the first contingent of men to ride with us to our destination. The rest of you may return home to your wives and children – not to mention your warm beds and the comforts they offer. Enjoy a hearty portion of savory mutton stew for the rest of our weary souls."

A loud cheer was her reward. The men saluted her as one, a bowed head and a closed fist over their armored hearts. God love her, they would be with their women in less than a month's time. The soldiers' smiles were broad as all but the fifty required as escort turned their mounts toward home.

Garen was sad to see them go, a wee bit jealous as well, but as he had no woman of his own, there was no real loss to him. The angels knew how much he did miss his warm straw mattress and the quilt his mother had made him as a child. It was a sentimental thing for a man his age and station to hold on to, he knew, but a warrior's life knew few comforts, and until God blessed him with a soft, gentle wife, his quilt was the one comfort he was certain to cling to. He nodded curtly to his contingent of men, and they hastily surrounded Lady Katharine and her grown children.

Alane took the lead, as he had no wife to protect, and great was his pride in his new position.

With great difficulty he resisted the childish urge to turn to his brothers and stick out his tongue.

Ah, life is good.

They set an easy pace. Katharine was in no hurry to lose Adam again, and Adam wasn't eager to return home either. But his father would think he was dead, and he needed to let him know he was okay. If all went well, he would be able to return another time. He was sad to go, but he had done what he set about doing – he had found his mother. Better than that, he had been assured that he was loved, wanted, and always welcome in her life. It was a little sad that she had no interest anymore in his world, but after spending time here, he understood. But he had a life to live there, family. And now he had family here as well.

"What's the sour look on yer face, brother?" Alane rudely interrupted his thoughts.

"I was thinking about what it would be like to have to live with you forever, brother. The thought nearly made me physically ill."

"It would be a sad life for you, I admit, but with Ysabelle to tend to my duties with Gray, I have no one else to lavish my attentions upon. Surely ye understand, Adam. One must do what one can for family, no matter how noxious they may be, which must surely be why I feel drawn to ye. I apologize, brother, for my candor, but it's of the utmost importance that ye know how important I am to yer well-bein'."

Adam laughed. "Well put. I don't think I could have thought of something so ridiculous so quickly."

"It's a gift. Not everyone has my amazin' abilities."

"We have many so gifted in my time. They're called politicians. They have a reputation for being full of … well, cow dung."

This time it was Alane's turn to laugh. "Then perhaps I should have been born with brown eyes rather than the handsome green ones I possess. I believe they are the exact same shade as yer own. It must be difficult for ye, but I rather think it keeps ye humble."

"And is there anything on this bonny island that would keep you humble?" he asked with a grin.

"I'm fairly sure there isn't. And if there is, I haven't come across it as yet. I'm sure to keep lookin', though, so that if I'm unfortunate enough to discover such a thing, I can give it a wide berth in the future."

"Alane, are you going to spend the next week tiring out our ears? I'm certain Adam has better things to do than spar all day with you," Katharine called from behind the two.

He feigned shock. "But Mother, could there be such a thing that would overshadow the joy I surely bring to all in our party?"

She rolled her eyes. "I'm certain there isn't, but I would like to have some last moments with my son before he leaves me. Might you be able to fit that in between your clever observations on life?"

"I will surely try, but it will be a trial. Only my deep respect for ye as my mother will allow me to put myself to such a grueling test of character."

"I thank you for your effort. Now, go tell Garen we're being followed. I've seen flashes of the sun on steel through the trees. Have three scouts find out by whom." They had strung out their small party over the course of a quarter mile while they traveled, Garen taking the rear to guard their backs.

His manner was immediately serious. "Aye." And he was gone.

As the path sloped up, the relaxed travelers naturally spread out into single file, following the narrow path that would take them through the small pass between the hills they were traversing. Looking up at the thick trees closing in on them, Katharine couldn't help but notice what a good place this would be for an ambush. Numbers and skill would be on her side, yes, but not if they were picked off one by one. She put the index finger of both hands between her lips and let out a shrill whistle. Instantly every man in the party was on his guard.

Gray moved up in front of Ysabelle, and he was soon directly behind Katharine, his wife's horse immediately behind his own. He took a moment to be grateful she was a skilled rider. That was at least one worry he did not have to congest his mind with. All eyes searched the pass as the group began their move through it.

Katharine's eyes scanned the trees and the ground cover, watching carefully for movement, or any glint of sun on steel. Gray moved through the pass next, Ysabelle close behind, as something caught his eye. He raised a closed fist, signaling his men, just as and enormous tree limb came crashing down towards them. Shoving Ysabelle violently from her mount, he leapt from his own with a shout of warning to his mother.

She turned in time to see a huge crush of boulders cascading down from some sort of trap suspended in the tall trees, filling the path completely and making it impassable. The horse she rode, spooked by the noise and the tremor in the earth, reared up and came near to throwing her. Holding on for dear life with her knees, Katharine worked to get the animal under control. Just as she began to calm him, Katharine was knocked clean off her horse by an attack from behind.

Gray gained his feet and glanced quickly at Ysabelle to make sure she was sound, and seeing that she was only a bit dazed, he rushed to help his mother. He was almost to her when a yelp from behind him stopped him in his tracks. The clearing was surrounded by thirteen filthy, frightening, unwashed men brandishing curved swords. They had been lying in wait for them, no doubt thinking to rob them, for these outcasts had no other function in life. Instead of gleaming, their swords were crusted with dried blood – obviously left over from their successful encounters with passersby.

The men were already working at clearing the pass, but they would get there far too late to be of any assistance. Gray looked about him carefully, taking in the entire situation. On each side of the clearing, a woman he loved was being held at knife point by one of the filthy heathen. While Ysabelle should have looked scared, he was shocked to see that she wore an expression identical to the one Katharine wore. She was furious. He smiled at her reaction, unnerving the man holding her with his filthy dagger at her throat just a bit. Turning to his mother, he caught her wink and drew his sword and his dirk, turning in a circle to glare a challenge equally to all their would-be captors.

Ysabelle was astonished at the metamorphosis in her husband. The look on his face was vicious, feral. Gone was the loving husband, the tender lover. In his place stood a man who only vaguely resembled that other self. Standing before her now was a vicious warrior, a savage barbarian bent on destruction. She had never seen this man before. He was even different in aspect from the businesslike pirate she had first met. That man had been set on a task, bent to a business undertaking, no matter that it was illicit. The dark look on Gray's face now made her shiver, and she was sure these foolish bandits were wondering whether they should reconsider their conquest and retreat. They chose bravado instead.

The leader puffed himself up and addressed Gray. "We'll be takin' yer gold, yer food, and yer women. Now give over."

Gray's voice was quiet when he answered, but the force behind it was chilling. "If ye leave now, ye'll go with yer skins intact. If not, ye'll meetin' yer Maker with much haste." His eyes flashed.

"Ye think too much of yer large frame, man. It's the big ones hit the ground hardest. And I'll be takin' yer pretty woman to me own bed before I kill her."

"Ye'll be dead in the span of three minutes."

Katharine silently, slowly drew her own weapon. She was careful not to shift her shoulders even a hairsbreadth, lest it alert her filthy captor to her movement. Ysabelle did the same. The girl waited, knowing she should watch Katharine for some sort of signal. She nervously chewed her lip, not knowing what it would be or when it would come. She knew the older lady well enough, though, and her husband too, for that matter, to know that these men had picked the wrong party to waylay. Had the man holding her not smelled so much like a decaying compost heap, she might have almost felt sorry for him. As it was, she thought she might relish using her dagger on him, if just to get away from the stench.

Capturing the girl's eyes, Katharine waited for Gray to settle the matter. They would attack him, she knew, thinking he would be immobilized by his fear for the women. It took less than a second. Three men attacked at once, two from behind and one from in front. Even though Gray towered above them, they thought their numbers would easily subdue him. With lightning reflexes, he slashed the first comer almost through to his backbone with his sword, leaving him in a writhing heap on the ground. Without even turning around, Gray crossed his arms over his waist, causing the men behind him to run themselves through on his sword and dagger. The dirk pulled free easily, but he had to release the sword and turn to pull it out of the bandit's side, causing two more of the filthy beggars to feel safe enough to rush him. At the last moment, seeing his blade would take more time to free than he had, as it was imbedded in a tree behind his vanquished foe, Gray ducked and tripped the rushing men with his massive outstretched arms. Grabbing them by their filthy shirt backs, he then ran them both, hollering like babies, headfirst into the broad tree his sword was still buried in. He pulled his blade free and turned to challenge the rest of the infidels.

Undaunted, their leader gave a fierce cry, and the remaining five rushed Gray at the same time. Katharine saw it was time to intervene. She shouted Ysabelle's name, calling her attention from the violence being done to and by her husband. Ysabelle focused on her mother-in-law's face, nodded her understanding, and simultaneously both women slipped their daggers under their arms and thrust them into the chests of the men holding them captive while attentively watching the unfolding fight.

Shouting their surprise, the two men holding the women crumpled to the ground in agony, one after the other. Katharine grabbed her captor's filthy sword, as hers was still strapped to her saddle. Ysabelle did the same.

Without thought for themselves of their safety, they turned to throw themselves into the fray just as Gray was using the last of his still standing attackers as a projectile, throwing him directly into the broad trunk of a nearby accommodating tree. There was the sickening sound of bone crunching, and the man dropped, unmoving, to the soft grass. Ysabelle looked at her husband, stunned. It was only a few seconds more before the soldiers broke through the rock barricade to get to their leader.

They looked around in satisfaction, but no surprise, at the scene before them. Some had the gall to laugh out loud. Ysabelle rushed to her husband, tearing a strip of white cotton from her chemise and using it to stem the flow of blood from his lip and his forehead, no doubt the leftovers of one of the few blows that landed on him. Enjoying her ministrations, he leaned down and kissed her with the good side of his mouth.

"Are you well, husband?"

"Aye, now that you are safe. Now that was a wee bit o' sport, wasna it?" His labored breathing belied his cavalier attitude.

From behind them came Alane's voice, "It sure took ye long enough to defeat this motley crew, brother. I could have done the same in half the time." Alane was grinning ear to ear, unable to contain his pride in his brother.

"Then by all means, next time ye're the first through the pass."

Gray cuffed him affectionately on the shoulder before turning to fetch the horses. They hadn't gone far, and were grazing just below the clearing. Mounting, Gray and Katharine looked at each other, allowing the relief to flow silently between them. It could have been so much worse. The highwaymen often traveled in groups of fifty or more, and though usually untrained, their desperation and hunger lent them an edge that could be, and often was, quite lethal.

The last of the boulders were finally moved from the trail, and the party moved ahead on their journey. Coming down the far side of the hill, a large grassy pastureland stretched before them. An artist's pallette of wild flowers peeking through the sparse remnants of snow evidenced the coming of spring. The air had warmed considerably since they had all left Ellshope as well, and the change was more than welcome. The newly green grass was a welcome change from the cold hard ground they had been sleeping on, allowing the tired soldiers a small amount of cushion. Although still quite chill in the dead of night, the softness of the ground combined with the inevitable lifting of the spirit in springtime gave an air of joviality to the men.

Only Katharine was pensive. In a few short days they would reach the Salisbury plain and Adam would walk out of her life again, possibly forever.

In their blankets that evening, Gray and Ysabelle talked softly together as they lay intertwined.

"Where is it we're going, Gray?" A thought occurred to her and panic flashed in her eyes. "You're not taking me back to my village, are you?"

He pulled her tighter. "Nay, lass. Don't trouble yer head. We're takin' my brother Adam back where he belongs, we are."

"And where exactly would that be? Will we be travelin' across the ocean?"

"Nay, wife. We willna be goin' that far. Ye'd likely not believe me if I told ye where we were goin'. It's a farfetched tale even to the most untamed imagination."

She leaned up on her elbow to look into his face, her curiosity piqued. "And you will be happy to tell me everything you know, and I'll be the judge of your sanity. Take heart, husband, I've only seen you raving mad on one occasion, so experience is on your side of the story."

He smiled indulgently, took a deep breath, and launched into the story as he knew it. "When my mother was twenty-six years old, she lived in another place, or rather, another time...."

Several hours later, Ysabelle lay down to sleep, amazed at what she had heard from the lips of her very own husband – a man who rarely laughed, and almost never jested. If what he had told her was true, the world was a most wondrous place, and she was about to witness an event that would color her entire way of thinking for the rest of her life.

The small party came to a halt in a meadow north of the Salisbury plain. They were far enough away that they could not see the rock formation, but close enough that they could reach it quickly at a brisk pace. Adam, Alane, Katharine, Gray, Ysabelle, and Lance had broken off from the rest of the soldiers to finish this short journey on their own.

In truth, Katharine was certain that she could not safely bend her men's understanding of reality without endangering all she, and they, knew of their world, and she was unwilling to risk their existence. Time travel was something that would get you put away in the most advanced circles of thinking, here it could get them all burned as witches – or worse. And in her time here she had seen tortures and deaths so much worse, not anything she wished to witness, or experience, firsthand again.

So the small family traveled in company the last two days' ride. Spring was ebbing into summer, trees had budded out into their green coats of leaves, wildflowers decorated the countryside, and winter cloaks were now held in reserve for cool nights around the campfire or otherwise carried tied to their owners saddles.

Alane, the only one of the group besides Ysabelle who had ever learned to cook anything worth eating, was skinning rabbits his mother and brothers had snagged with their arrows. While he prepared the meat, Ysabelle dropped several handfuls of savory herbs into the pot of boiling water that sat on the flat iron plate propped over the fire. She stirred the stew with a wooden spoon as he dropped the meat into the steaming pot. A lovely aroma settled over their small camp.

Adam and Gray unsaddled and hobbled the horses, while Katharine went uphill to scout the area for any threat. She had climbed a tree for a better look, precipitating an endless round of comments from Alane concerning women's curiosity. He kept Ysabelle laughing constantly, for when he was through with his observations of his mother, he started on his brothers, for the first time having a new audience with which to regale with his tales of their childhood together.

Without warning, Gray chucked a large stick at his brother's head, missing it narrowly. "Enough of your lies, Alane. Ysabelle, don't believe a thing that liar has to say about me or anyone else."

Alane feigned shock, his hand flying to his chest in mock horror. "What say you, brother? Me, lie about those whom I hold dearest? What heresy is this? I must report you to the church for your astonishing disrespect of your family!"

"I dinna have to miss your head, shall I take better aim with the next stick, rogue?"

"Nay, brother, that willna be necessary. I'm certain I can remember many other stories to enthrall your dear wife with. A thousand pardons."

"You only get one. Now concentrate on our supper before I skin you and throw you into the pot. I don't relish explaining to Mother why I was forced to be your death. Although I'm certain she would understand completely."

"Aye, tis true. A sad statement on a mother's love." He turned to Ysabelle. "Well, now, sister, shall I show you how to make oatcakes to eat with our stew?"

She nodded, grappling with the laughter that threatened to erupt from her, and assisted Alane in his cooking of the tasteless, but filling, cakes.

The rest of the evening passed without incident. Blankets were laid, warm bodies slept. Alane kept watch.

In the middle of the night, Adam, who couldn't sleep, approached his brother for what he was sure was one of their last conversations.

"Can I ask you a question, Alane?"

For once grave, Alane answered without a smile. "Aye."

"Why do you not seek to be a leader of men, as is your station?"

"Tis a question I've been asked afore, but never have had the occasion to answer. I was always able to deflect it with my wit. But for you, brother, because our time is short, I will tell ye. My brother, a great leader of men, doesna need the help. I am, with my own men, considered an efficient, if

340

amiable, leader. I am a good commander, but not a great one. So I choose to entertain, when greater men are about."

Remaining silent, Adam waited for his brother to collect his thoughts and finish.

"Dinna think me unkind, I love my brother, and give him my deepest respect. But of what use can I be, when he can do so much without my help? He's a good man, and would always include me. But I canna tolerate charity – even from a well-intentioned brother. But I have yet to find my own way, except that I seem to be able to discover the secrets that many are loath to tell others. I think they believe me harmless. And though that mistaken judgment furthers the cause of Scotland, tis hard for me no to take offense at that estimation of my character. No matter that I jest to my own self, the things I say are not true. I am a good and worthy leader. I care for the people on my lands."

Adam nodded. "I am most certain that you do. I have seen nothing in you to invite reproach, brother. You have a good heart and a fine mind. Attributes that I have discovered are few and far between in both your time and mine. I respect you as a brother and a friend."

"Thank you for that, aye. Ye have been a good friend to me. I am proud to call ye brother."

"As am I. I'll miss you."

"Nay, ye won't, I'll be sure of it. Ye'll think of me every day."

Adam gave a mock shudder. "I hate to hazard a guess at what you mean by that."

An enigmatic smile spread across Alane's face. "Ye shall see in time. I wouldna let you wait for long to discover my roguish plot." At last Alane's eyes resumed their mischievous gleam as he winked at his brother. "Tis part of my charm."

Laughing, Adam retired to his blankets, still sleepless, still grieving the loss of his new family.

TWENTY-ONE

The sky was not even beginning to lighten when Adam woke Katharine.

"I just wanted to tell you how much having this time with you has meant to me."

"And me. You'll never know what you gave me by coming here."

"Thank you, mother. I have loved you, longed for you, my entire life. To finally have you as my own, to finally know you as my mother – you can't imagine what that means."

"Aye, I can. To have you back again, to know I didn't lose you, you have fulfilled every dream I ever had. You have turned out so wonderfully, so smart and handsome. Your father did a good job. You owe him your thanks."

"You can come back with me if you want...."

"No. I can't. My live is here. In some strange way it was always here. I just didn't know it. Please forgive me, but I don't belong in your world. My place is here. I have a grandbaby coming."

He shook his head sadly, "I understand, I really do, Mom. We were made for a different time. But unlike you, I have many ties to bind me to the time I'm in. Although, perhaps I can come back...."

"If ever you can, please do. I love you desperately and want to see how your life turns out."

He leaned toward her and wrapped his arms around her, "Thank you … for filling the gaps, for loving me, for being alive, for giving me a family. I am eternally grateful. And I will love you, and my brothers, and even the sister I didn't get to meet, forever. You will always be my family. And if it is possible, I will return. Maybe with a wife and a baby in tow."

"It would have to be a terminally believing wife...."

"They're out there. I know they are. Just trust in me. I'll see you again."

"I guess I'll have to. Okay. I believe you will. I … I'll always love you, Adam."

"And I'll always love you, Mom."

"Then there's little more either one of us can say that will matter."

"True. We're adults. And we've said so much."

She nodded. "We did have the advantage of knowing the date which we must separate from each other."

"And that's something very few really ever know. And I'm grateful for the time we had. I wish it could have been longer."

Sighing deeply, Katharine nodded her head sadly. "I'll just hold, for now, the hope that one day you will return. But even if you don't, it will have to be enough. Let's wake the others. It is time."

With few minutes remaining, they woke Gray and Ysabelle. Alane was already busy saddling the horses, readying them for the short ride to the stones. Each one rolled his blankets, gathered his belongings, and mounted their horse.

Gray nosed up beside Adam. "I'll miss ye, brother. Ye're a fine man, ye are, and I'll always remember ye fondly."

"I'm glad I got the chance to meet you, Gray. Take care of Mother, she'll feel this loss greatly."

Gray nodded. "Aye, I daresay ye're right. Tis a shame ye can't remain with us forever. We'll all be missin' ye. Tis a sad thing to lose yer kin." Moisture gathered in his eyes, and he roughly embraced Adam.

"I'll miss you too, Gray. Take care of yourself, and your lovely wife there."

"Aye. I will at that."

Together the small party set off over the hillock that separated them from the stone formation. As they crested the small rise, each of them sucked in their breath. In the gray morning pre-dawn, the place looked eery, spooky. In this moment the mysterious altar of stones was worthy of every ghastly tale ever told about it.

Adam was the first to ride toward it. Time was growing short, the sun would soon rise and he would have to go. As soon as he reached the stone circle, he went in search of the mark he had made to commemorate the stone he had used as a portal. On the first go round, he could not find it. By the time he made his second search, Ysabelle had reached the stones and was searching with him.

"Here it is!" she called from the other side of the circle. "This is the mark you made, is it not?"

He came over to look. "It is. Thank you. You'll have to stand back now, Ysabelle." He quickly hugged her, then walked her over to where the rest of his family was standing.

"It's time," he announced. Eyes welling with tears, Adam embraced first his mother, then his brothers, then his mother once again. He shook hands with Lance, then turned back to the stones. He positioned himself at the mouth of the horseshoe-shaped formation, then drew the leather pouch from his shirt, where it had been secured about his neck since he had come to this place. Pulling the drawstring open, he drew out the ring, carefully lined up the symbols and the stones, and held out his hands.

The horizon was brightening slowly, but it would be only a matter of seconds before the sun broke free and popped up over the horizon. Turning to smile encouragingly at his companions, Adam noticed that Alane had disappeared.

He'd better not screw this up!

The bright edge of the sun appeared, causing the stone of the ring to shine dazzlingly. It flashed, growing brighter and brighter with every millimeter the sun rose over the horizon, until Adam had to close his eyes against it, then it winked out.

"Good-bye! I love you all!" Adam called as he started towards the stone formation that would take him home. He didn't dare look behind him, he might not be able to leave. Squaring his shoulders, he stepped through the portal, feeling a huge and heavy weight on his shoulders. There was the feeling of spinning, then his stomach lurched, and then his feet smacked into something hard, that he knew to be grassy earth. But it was freezing cold, and wet with snow. The weight disappeared from his back.

Adam took several deep breaths, steadying himself from the dizzying trip. He opened his eyes on the world he had left. High chain link fence, small house to pay the entry pounds to look at the great Stonehenge, guard dogs looking at him curiously, Alane....

Alane!

"Alane! What in blazes are you doing here?"

Alane was flat on his back, staring around him in a daze. "In all my livin' life, I never suspected that it was true. Sweet heavens, I've never seen a metal wall – one ye can see through yet, and we left the springtime and are now in snow." He sat up. "Is it true then? Have I truly come through to another time? Your time? The future?"

Adam looked at him strangely. "Yes, Alane, you have. I have to hand it to you, brother, you've really outdone yourself this time, and you don't even realize what you've done. The thing is, you can't go back home for at least six months – til the next solstice. You'll have to stay with me."

Shaking his head slowly, Alane finally looked up, but instead of a frown, his customary grin was fastened haphazardly in place. "And what else have I to do but make sure ye have a good life, complete with the family ye'd rather leave behind ye? How else are ye to be certain to remember us? I'm to be ... shall we say ... a living memory to ye. And I'll be havin' a wee bit o' wild adventure and sport as well. What say you, Adam? Shall we have a bit of a frolic for a time?"

For a moment, his face was blank, trying to get his mind around the enormity of bringing his brother forward in time. Then Adam began to laugh, the rich sound of it growing until it was booming across the flat plain.

"Brother, ye've not gone mad on me now, have ye? Just this moment would not be the most fittin' time for that, wouldn't ye agree, now? I'll be needing' yer help in this place, aye and for certain, so buck up now and pull yerself together, man!" He looked the slightest bit worried, obviously troubled that Adam had completely lost his senses.

Pulling himself together, Adam reined his laughter in with difficulty. "Alane, my dear impulsive brother, you may have bitten off more than you can chew here. But there's no worrying about it now. We'll have to make the best of it, so get ready to see things you will take days to recover from the sight of."

From behind the two came a man's familiar voice. "Hullo, boy. I'd 'oped to see you 'ere this morning. And who is that you've got with you, there?"

Adam turned slightly to see, behind the chain link fence and peering intently at him, face lit up with a broad grin, the friendly troll face of his dear friend, Colin. Beside the little shopkeeper stood the tall, stately figure of Hugh, also grinning ear to ear and raising his perfectly manicured hand in friendly greeting.

Rising to his feet, Adam turned to help pull Alane to a standing position.

"Come on, Alane. It's time to meet the locals." Grabbing his brother by the arm, Adam dragged him over to the fence, then, showing him how to put his toes in the holes, scaled the chain link and dropped to the ground in front of Colin and Hugh, Alane right behind him.

Impulsively Adam embraced both Hugh and Colin, then stepped back a little, flushed from his show of emotion to these men whom he had only known for such a brief time. His behavior went unnoticed, however, so he turned slightly to the side and began introductions.

"Colin, Hugh – I would like you to meet my brother, Alane."

Gray, Katharine, Ysabelle, and Lance stood gaping at the empty opening of the stone doorway through which Adam and Alane had disappeared.

Lance was the first to speak. "Tis one thing to know strange things occur. Tis entirely another to watch them happen."

Gray swallowed hard. "Aye."

"Did you know Alane would follow Adam through the doorway, Katharine?" Ysabelle was looking at her mother-in-law suspiciously.

Katharine nodded. "I suspected as much. Such a foolish thing would be exactly the sort of temptation he would not be able to resist. He would see it as a grand adventure."

"Aye, that he would," Gray agreed. "And it will be, too, I have no doubt. Will he be comin' back again, do ye think, Mother?"

She nodded once as Lance asked the same question with his eyes. "He'll be back. I'm certain of it."

"As for going back, lads and lassies, the time has come for us all to return home. It has been nearly five months since many of us have seen our families, and I, for one, miss my wife and my bed. I'm more than certain the remaining men feel the same." Lance swung up into his saddle.

Gray lifted Ysabelle onto the back of his stallion, then swung up behind her, securing the reins of her mare to his saddle. "Twould be nice, aye, a bed. Dinna ye think so, wife?"

She blushed, embarrassed, but that didn't stop her from nodding her head vigorously. "It would. The ground is becoming quite uncomfortable as of late." She pressed her hand to her quickly rounding stomach, smiling and smoothing her skirts over the noticeable lump beneath them.

Gray reached around her with both hands and caressed her growing belly. "Tis high time I took proper care of my wife and bairn. I wish to treat ye as delicately as ye deserve, love."

"But we've still the ride ahead of us, Gray. You may treat her delicately in two weeks' time. Aye?" Katharine was the last to swing into the saddle, and she did so in one graceful, fluid movement.

"Aye, Mother. Now let us fetch the men. Tis high time we set our sights on Ellshope."

"Ellshope?" Ysabelle was confused. "Shouldn't we be traveling to Thistlebloom?"

"Ye've forgotten, lass, we've been banished for a time. But I had been thinkin' that twould be a good thing to birth our wee bairn with the help of my mother and Eloise on Ellshope. It would mean a great deal to all of us. What say ye, Ysabelle? Dinna ye think it should be a good thing to do?"

Leaning back against his chest, she sighed deeply, contentedly. "I could not think of a better place to bring our babe into the world. Whither thou goest, and all that entails."

"Ye're not vexed, then?"

"Nay, I'm delighted."

He nodded his approval, winked at his mother, and commanded, "For home!"

EPILOGUE

England, Present Day

Heathrow Airport was steadily buzzing as usual as Adam dragged a gaping Alane towards the concourse where their New York flight would depart from. He kept having to remind Alane that they had a plane to catch, as every few seconds the newcomer would stop to watch planes take off or land – eyes huge with wonder.

"And we'll be gettin' inside one of those ... planes ... and flyin' off into the air just like that?"

"Yup. That's what we're gonna do. You were the one wanting a grand adventure. And if this doesn't qualify, I don't know what does."

Alane swallowed through a huge lump of fear and excitement in his throat. "Aye. Tis the truth. It can't be worse than fallin' into the fertilizer, can it?"

Adam laughed heartily. "Nowhere near that bad. In fact, I think you'll like it."

They had to stop and give their boarding passes to the attendant at the gate, and Alane looked down the boarding ramp dubiously at the barely visible airplane door. His face was a just a little pale, but growing more so every second. Before he could cut and run, Adam firmly grabbed on to his upper arm and pulled him along the ramp. At the metal doorway, Alane paused ever so slightly, uttered a silent prayer, and crossed himself. Then he stepped into the plane.

Adam had used his remaining money to purchase first class seats, so there would be room for Alane's rather impressive frame, and he took advantage of the service to order his brother a good, stiff drink to steel his nerves. Flying could be nerve-racking for those who had grown up used to it, but for someone who had never even imagined such a thing could be.... He changed his mind and ordered Alane a double.

Without so much as a wince, Alane drained off the entire contents of the glass. A little color returned to his face as he took a deep breath and let it out through pursed lips. The flight attendants began their safety spiel as Alane fought with his seat belt. Reaching around his brother, Adam fastened the errant seatbelt ends together and smiled encouragingly into the tense face beside him.

Engines revving, the plane began its takeoff run, runway speeding along beside the windows. Alane stared breathlessly at the ground rushing by, but it wasn't until the nose of the plane tilted upward that his knuckles began gripping the armrest so hard that they turned a stark white.

"Are you going to be all right?" Adam looked worried.

Alane flashed a strained smile at his companion, his complexion taking on a greenish tint. "In all my livin' life, I never thought I'd really fly through the air. I pray me heart can stand the strain."

Adam smiled as his brother closed his eyes, his lips moving in silent prayer. He placed his hand over Alane's white-knuckled hand closest to him, and felt the man relax as the plane's deep ascent leveled out a bit.

Cracking one eye, Alane produced a mischievous smile, the sparkle alight in his eyes again. "Tis most surely a grand adventure, brother! I'll never forget it!"

"I didn't think you would. Wait til you see a little something we call a bikini!"

Ellshope

Gray sat in the corridor outside the small bedroom. His legs drawn up in front of him, arms resting upon them, head hanging down on his chest in what looked like sleep, but was truly the position in which he had been fervently praying for his wife and child over the past nine hours. The floor was freezing, reflecting the icy chill that held the countryside under a thick blanket of Christmas snow. Gray bolted upright from his seat on the stone floor of the hall. He had heard a wee babe's cries. They were hearty, healthy bellows that eased his heart considerably.

Dear God, please don't forget my Ysabelle....

The door opened upon the smiling face of Katharine.

Her smile spread to him, "Then they are well?"

She clasped her hands together and nodded, satisfied. "They are. All three of them."

He staggered back a bit. "All *three* of them?"

"Your wife and two sons are well and happy. A glorious Christmas gift to us all. You may see them now." She couldn't keep herself from embracing him, they had all waited so long for this day. Gray had finally found his happiness.

He bolted past her into the inner sanctum of the room. A fire burned brightly in the hearth. Eloise was busily tidying up the bed, before she took the dirty sheets down to be washed by the servants. She curtsied to Gray, then kissed him on the cheek and whispered, "God has blessed ye with fine bairns, son. And a fine wife besides. I'm happy for ye, truly."

He kissed her back. "My thanks to ye, Eloise. Tell our Alec, will ye?"

"Aye. Go kiss yer wife." She left the room and shut the door gently behind her.

Ysabelle's eyes were heavy as she watched the exchange. When Gray sat down by the side of the bed, he stroked the face of first one child, then the other. He watched them as they breathed evenly, eyes watchful, one greedily sucking on his fist. Gray pulled the fist out of the little wet mouth, pushed his finger into the tiny palm, and smiled contentedly as he little fist closed around his large finger. He told the other babe hello, then, leaning down to give his wife a kiss, took her hand, and whispered, "I love ye. I always will. Thank ye for the wee bairns. Though heaven knows if they're like their da, they'll be wee beasties afore many months pass."

She fought back the tears.

"What's wrong, love? Are ye weepin' for joy?"

"Nay, I'm sad for you. I'm sorry you had to wait until now to hold a babe of your own."

"Aye, but now I have a wife and two fine bairns to love. I canna tell ye I'm sad about that. I have what I've always wanted for my own, a family to care for. What more could a man ask for?"

Ysabelle was quiet for a moment, then she looked up at him and smiled. "A daughter?"

He reached down and gathered her into his arms. "Aye, and may she be just like her mother."

"Do you mind if I rest a bit first, love?"

He laughed quietly, so as not to startle the quiet twins. "Aye. Take all the time ye wish. I'll be here until death separates us, and that gives us many years of time, God willin'. Go to sleep now, my sweet Ysabelle. Ye'll be needin' yer strength when these wee soldiers get hungry."

Gray rose, kissed each baby first, then his precious wife, then quietly left the room. Ysabelle was fast asleep before the door even closed. He embraced Katharine, still standing in the hall.

"It's good to be home, Mother. It has been a grand adventure so far, has it not?"

"It has. And with two little boys to raise, I'm certain the wildest adventure is yet to come."

"I have no doubt of that. Mother?"

"Yes?"

"Thank you for bringin' my sons here safely."
"It was truly my pleasure. I love you, Gray."
"And I love you."
Aye, it was good to be home.

*

Printed in the United States
30449LVS00001B/376-378